HALFWAY TO TOMORROW

HALFWAY TO TOMORROW

RENÁ A. FINNEY

URBAN BOOKS

URBAN SOUL is published by

Urban Books
10 Brennan Place
Deer Park, NY 11729

Copyright © 2007 by Rená A. Finney

ISBN-13: 978-0-7394-8058-8

Printed in the United States of America

PROLOGUE

Swinging the back door open, Gwen quickly ran down the steps. If she hurried, she would be able to join her friends without having her little sister, Tiffany, tag along and invade on yet another afternoon of fun. Before Gwen could get to the end of the driveway, Tiffany, her worst nightmare, was yelling out her name.

"Gwenee, wait for me! I want to go! Can I go with you, pleeease?" Tiffany was standing on the steps getting ready to cry. She always knew how to be dramatic enough to get their parents' attention, and get Gwen in trouble in the process.

Stopping and turning around, Gwen yelled back, "No, Tiff. Now go back in the house and play with your dolls or watch television. I'll be back in a few minutes."

"No, you won't. You never want me to go with you. I won't be bad and I won't get in the way." Gwen walked back toward Tiff in an attempt to quiet her and convince her that she really didn't want to go after all. She noticed how Tiff's big, wide eyes were forming pools of tears. Her pigtails had begun to come undone at the ends because of all the jumping and playing she had already done. Tiff's white and blue Stride Rite tennis shoes were tied in double knots; she was still trying to twist her feet all the way into her shoes so she would be ready for their afternoon adventure.

"Tiff, you always go with me. You know that. Don't you think I want to spend time with my friends without you? Gosh, I don't ever have any time to myself." It was hard for Gwen to understand why she had been assigned the responsibility of caring for her baby sister. Their parents always made her feel that being old enough to watch after Tiffany was a reward, but Gwen saw it as a sentence for some bad deed that she had done and couldn't remember.

Gwen was twelve, and she felt she deserved to hang with girls her own age. Having her five-year-old sister with her all the time had gotten her picked on almost every single day. When she told her mom this, she received a long lecture on responsibility, and how family always comes first. Her mother added that the other girls were not going to grow up with the same good morals that she had, as if this were somehow rewarding.

"I'm going in the house and tell Mommy if you don't let me go. Then you're going to get in trouble and won't be able to go." Tiffany turned and started to go back into the house, yelling as she went.

Gwen sat on the steps and waited for her name to be called. She knew that playing with her best friend, Patrice, wouldn't happen now since her mother would insist she take Tiff, and she didn't want to take the "mouth" with her. Most of the time she never complained about having to carry Tiffany with her everywhere she went. But every now and then, she wanted to be able to go around the corner without her tagging along.

Sure enough, their mother came to the door and demanded that Gwen bring her butt into the house. "Why don't you want to take Tiffany with you?" Their mother stood in the pale blue and yellow kitchen with her hand on her hip.

The room was tidy with everything in its place. The smells

of cinnamon and vanilla filled the air and drifted through the open window over the sink. The apple pies and pound cakes their mother had been baking all morning for the church's building fund were cooling off on top of the counter. Forgetting her plight for a minute, Gwen hoped that at least one of the pies would be for their after-Sunday-dinner dessert. Gwen looked directly at her mother and tried hard not to blink. She knew that if she did, her mother would think she was trying to get smart and that it wasn't just a natural response.

"Mom, I get tired of carrying her everywhere with me. I don't ever have any time to be with Patrice. All the girls in the neighborhood laugh at me and call me names because Tiffany is always by my side. Patrice is the only one who understands and doesn't call me names or talk about me."

"I don't care what you say. Tiffany is your sister and you should always take care of her. Besides, I have to get Ms. Lucille to wash and press my hair and then go to the grocery store, so I was going to ask you to look after her while I'm gone."

"Why can't T.J. watch her for a change? He always gets to spend time with his friends and play ball all day and half the night. I'm the one who gets stuck with my pain-in-the-butt, nagging sister." Gwen threw her thin body down in a chair, folded her arms across her chest, and pouted. She realized this rebuttal could cause her mom to explode, but she risked expressing how unfair the whole situation was.

"Well, Ms. Grown. Since you want to complain about it, you can keep an eye on your sister today and every day for the next month." Gwen's mom turned to pick up her sweater that was thrown across the arm of the chair. "And just for the record, that won't conflict with anything that you'll be doing because you won't be able to leave the house for that entire period of time."

Tiffany stood against the refrigerator and played with the

magnet that Aunt Rose had given her sister as a souvenir when she returned from her trip to Atlantic City. She was clearly taking in all of this and was ready to snicker, but when she heard about the punishment that Gwen received, she looked sad. It wasn't until their mom had started the old blue Chevrolet Impala, backed out of the driveway, and gone well down the road that she dared to speak.

Toddling over, Tiffany stood in front of Gwen. "Gwenee, I'm sorry. I didn't mean for Mom to yell at you." Tiffany tried to pull Gwen's arms down so she could climb into her lap, the way she always did.

"No. Get away. You are such a troublemaker. Now I can't even leave this house for a month, all because you had to put on an act and get your way." Gwen jumped up, running through the house and up the steps to the bedroom she shared with Tiffany. It was her refuge—but at the same time it was a reminder that her life would never be free of her baby sister. She walked over to the window and looked out. She was so upset with her mom for not understanding her need for a little freedom. Sure, she loved Tiffany, but she didn't want to be confined to these four walls every time she wasn't willing to change her plans to include her little sister.

Gwen could hear slow steps coming up the staircase. When Tiffany got to their room, she peeped around the partially opened door and came in slowly. She went to her side of the room, to her bunk bed, and reached under the pillow. Gwen knew that she kept almost everything under that pillow and was very protective of her collected things and considered them sacred.

Tiffany pulled out a book and pencil and sat down on the bedspread covered with lavender, pink, and yellow hearts. Her head was down and her back was turned, so Gwen couldn't tell what she was doing. Concerned that she might hurt herself and cause even more trouble, Gwen walked over to her.

"Tiffany, what in the world are you doing?" She watched

as Tiffany hummed a nursery rhyme and wrote the only letters she knew how.

"I'm writing stuff," she answered, and kept her small fingers wrapped around the big, thick pencil.

"What kind of stuff?" Gwen sat beside her and observed her round little cheeks puffed out with effort under her wavy black hair.

"I'm keeping all my thoughts in this book. I saw Buffy do it on *Family Affairs,* she was keeping a book just like this and she wouldn't let Jody see what she wrote inside."

"A diary," Gwen answered nonchalantly.

"Yep. And no one is supposed to look at it." She tilted it a little, away from Gwen, to make her point.

"Girl, you can't even write one word. How are you going to write a diary?" Gwen chuckled, amazed that Tiff even remembered that particular episode.

Tiffany answered seriously, in a matter-of-fact voice, "I can't write words, but I can write my thoughts 'cause I know what I'm thinking."

"Do what you want." Gwen got up and went to stretch out across her bed. With her face dangling over the side of the bed, she stared at the beige and blue scattered rug that covered a portion of the hardwood floor. She attempted to figure out what she could do to keep her mind occupied while keeping an eye on Tiffany.

After a few minutes, Tiffany got down and climbed onto the end of Gwen's bed. "Gwenee, do you want to see my diary?"

"I thought you weren't supposed to share your diary with anyone," Gwen replied without moving or looking into Tiffany's wide eyes.

"I know, but you're my sister and I love you. You are the only person that I want to share my thoughts with. I won't ever not tell you things. You can always read my thoughts." She smiled a big wide smile and scooted close, handing Gwen the book.

Gwen began to feel bad for the things that she had said. "Tiffany, I love you and I get mad, but I will always take care of you. And right now I'd like to read your thoughts." Reaching over, Gwen pulled Tiffany down beside her and tickled her until she was screaming with laughter.

"Gwenee, you're my best friend. Am I yours?" Tiffany was pulling on Gwen's ear, something she did when she was sleepy, and Gwen nestled beside her sister waiting to see if the sandman would claim her exhausted body.

Gwen mused at Tiffany for a moment. Patrice was her best friend, but Tiffany was her best friend too, even though she was her little sister. "Tiff, you will always be my best friend. Come on and I'll bake you some chocolate chip cookies."

Tiffany was halfway down the stairs before Gwen could even move off the bed.

CHAPTER 1

The den, dining room, and kitchen were so crowded there was hardly enough room to add another body. Everyone was eating for a second or third time or resting up before consuming a second or third helping. It was mind-boggling how people used holidays as an excuse to pig out.

Gwen joined the crowd and ate far too much. She knew she should consider watching her weight, but at thirty-five, she had to admit that everything was still in the right place and in adequate proportions—or so she was told. *Well, wait a minute*, she thought; it had been some time since anyone had witnessed her disrobing. To be on the safe side, she decided she would hit the gym next week and work on ensuring that her "stuff" was still tight.

Family gatherings were used to highlight everyone's accomplishments, or lack thereof. Well, Gwendolyn Nicole James had accomplished a few things. After she graduated from college with a degree in communications, she worked a couple of jobs that were just not to her liking. She finally settled into an executive position at a public relations firm where she had worked for seven years now. She had recently sold her starter home and had relished the purchase of her dream home. Gwen spent at least a couple of hours in the front yard every weekend adding yet another flower. She had a little money in the bank and had for the past ten years invested some of her hard-earned money to prepare herself for retirement. She had known from the time she graduated from college that retirement would mean more than a gold-plated mantel clock and leftover cake to take home.

Gwen was also blessed to have good friends and a family who loved her. By her distant relatives' standards, her life wasn't half bad. But of course there was no Mr. Gwendolyn James. Most of the time she was all right with that, but at these events she secretly wished that she had an "old plug." That's what her grandfather used to call that male significant other in a woman's life. He would say that it was someone who could keep things in working order, both around the house and in the bedroom. She hadn't understood her grandfather back then, but now she had to agree with him. Having someone to handle her physical maintenance needs would be just great—someone to keep her bed warm at night.

According to the James and Williams clans, since Gwen was the oldest child of Claire and Thomas James, she should have been married years ago. The Williamses were the extended branches on her mother's side of the family tree. They felt that her brother, T.J., who was three years younger than Gwen, was living life according to their timetable because he beat her to the punch and got married right out of high school. Tiffany, the last of the James children, was seven years younger than Gwen and was the right age to marry, but even she still had time to meet Mr. Right, according to their know-it-all butts.

What did her kinfolk know anyway? They were dysfunctional themselves, products of dysfunctional parents, and had passed on the dysfunctional gene to their children. Gwen always thought that her extended family should spend more time trying to fix their immediate-family dramas instead of putting their two cents' worth in on other family members' affairs. Oh well, they would be going home soon.

Gwen sat in her father's favorite recliner. It had been positioned in the same corner for as long as she could remember. The blue color with its herringbone texture had begun to fade, and yet somehow the recliner had created an identity that mirrored the man who had enjoyed spending every evening in the same chair for the past three decades. This chair created a lullaby effect for him and rendered his body a restful sleep on countless occasions. It was no wonder that his first housewarming gifts to his children had been recliners. They each knew that their recliners were not really theirs but distinctive chairs that he could call his own when he came to visit.

Gwen glanced around the den. The James family had definitely outgrown the house that held so many of her childhood memories. She managed to block out all the noises that threatened to consume her private thoughts as she looked around. Gwen thought how interesting it was that she could remember events that had happened when she was just three, and still couldn't remember to pick up her laundry from the cleaner's. Yes, this house held a lot of memories, and she always felt safe and warm here. But the safety of the family house paled in comparison to the security she felt at this very moment, cuddled in her father's recliner. She smiled at the faint smell of Polo, his favorite cologne.

Trying to shake her melancholy mood, Gwen fought back tears . . . tears that she couldn't quite understand, especially since she wasn't sad or PMSing. It had been this way for a couple of months. She began to brace herself because she knew that these feelings were always followed by an outbreak of hives. The hives were her body's way of alerting her that something was about to happen that would have an adverse effect on her.

Of course she had gone to several allergists and taken numerous tests, and still no one could tell her why these red patches from hell surfaced all over her body at times. What she did know was that her outbreaks of hives caused her to slow down. Sometimes she had to shut down her entire life until the episode passed.

Determined to head off this trauma and not have it ruin her Thanksgiving, she got up and went in search of her purse so that she could take her medication. Just as she was searching the family room for her Coach bag, she noticed Tiffany sitting quietly beside their mother. It was stunning how much they were beginning to resemble each other. Tiffany and Claire James shared the same mahogany complexion, small lips, dimpled cheeks, dreamy brown eyes. Tiffany's hair was shiny black and framed her face in a shoulder-length bob.

The years had been kind to Claire James; her beauty had remained intact. Rather than showing the effects of aging, she had simply softened and matured to age sixty-five in a way that made her reflect a soft and sophisticated sparkle. The only real signs of her true age were her graying temples and the fact that her hair, which had once been heavy, was now thinning a little.

Gwendolyn James envied her mother's and sister's trademark beauty. Although many people told her that they all looked alike, it was hard for Gwen to see it. Her reflection mirrored their beauty, but her hair was dark brown, much shorter and often too soft to hold curls. For that reason she sported a short tapered cut that gave her a very chic and seductive appearance. The truth was, she was very similar in looks to the mother and daughter look-alikes who sat before her, but there were so many other reasons why she felt envious of the twosome. Today wasn't the day to think about all that baggage, though.

Finally, retrieving her purse, Gwen took a deep breath as she downed two pills and a glass of water. While she was in the kitchen, she decided to load the dishwasher and start cleaning the mess left by the clan. Gwen again noticed how distant Tiffany appeared. She decided to break her out of her trance. "So, Tiff, who loads the next set of dirty dishes?"

Tiffany replied dryly, barely looking up, "I'll do it."

Oh, heck no! Gwen knew for sure now that something was wrong with Tiffany. Tiffany James hated doing dishes. The first major appliance she purchased for her home was a dishwasher. Gwen was determined now to get to the bottom of what was ailing Tiffany.

Just then the kids all ran through the den, the kitchen, and out the back door, so there was no chance to question Tiffany at that moment. How the kids ran through that maze of family folk was beyond Gwen.

Thomas and the male members of the family were spread out in the living room watching the fifty-two-inch television that the kids had given him on his last birthday. The new generation of men who had just graduated to an age appropriate for watching the bowl games were as proud as peacocks.

This year's game was significant to T.J.'s twelve-year-old sons. For years, Baron and Darion had begged to be included in the all-male shenanigans, only to be told that they were too young.

The boys were identical twins born a mere eight minutes apart. Both boys were a blend of their mother and father in looks and mannerisms. Their heads were covered with black curly locks and the two had perfectly angled eyes and wide smiles that accented their slim jawlines.

Today was an honor above all honors. Thomas James inducted Baron and Darion; it was as if he were wrapped in a royal purple cape, held the royal trident, and stepped down off the bowl game throne just long enough to dub them knights of the bowl games. It was customary that the father of the inductees would walk them around the other royal family men and seat them in front of the tube to claim their royal kingdom. T.J. carried out the duty happily and basked in the afterglow, realizing that today his twelve-year-old twin sons had achieved special recognition. Baron and Darion sat in front of the big-screen television in complete awe, as if they had never before seen the technological wonder that was chatting play calls and encouraging the watchers to have a Bud on every other commercial.

Meanwhile, Claire and her sisters Georgia, and Rose had relocated to the kitchen table to feast on an array of desserts that had been prepared. The table was covered with sweet potato and pumpkin pies, peach cobbler, chocolate, coconut, and hummingbird cakes, and both rice and bread puddings. The spicy sweet smells were enough to add a couple of fattening pounds to anyone who even dared to take a quick sniff. Indulging in at least one of the delicacies would pack on even more.

Suddenly, the back door swung open. Patrice came bouncing in. "Hey, everybody! Happy freakin' Turkey Day! Where my girls at, Mommy James?"

Claire had to laugh. Patrice had always made a grand entrance, even as an outspoken and fast-growing little girl. But Claire James had fallen in love with her just the same and had come to view her ways as "uniquely Patrice."

She smiled. "Hey, Patrice. You always make such an entrance. Come here and give me a hug. You look beautiful." The two embraced.

Patrice leaned across the table and kissed Georgia and Rose on their cheek before commenting, "As usual, Mommy James, a girl has got to keep it tight. The men would expect nothing less."

Gwen walked over to her friend and they did their usual touch-fingertips, kiss-and-hug combination. "Hey there, Ms. Thing. What took your tired butt so long to get here?"

Patrice walked in step behind Gwen as they headed toward the den. Her mouth went on nonstop. Gwen's quiet demeanor and whispering voice were exactly opposite to Patrice's, and so their friendship had the perfect balance.

The years had changed both of them, but Patrice the

most. She still had the mouth, but now she was a tall, cocoa-brown sister with everything in the right place. Ever since high school, she looked just like a runway model ready to catch the world by storm. She sported a sassy tight black pantsuit with silver accessories. Her hair was pulled up in a twist and she glowed. Patrice Michelle Henderson had been Gwen's friend since grade school. Back then, she had been skinny with long pigtails and Coke-bottle glasses. Gwen loved her and wouldn't change a thing about her best friend.

Patrice answered, "Girl, you know I had to make my rounds before I could even think about eating. All my old, present, and prospective flames are in town, so I had to make several stops."

Gwen laughed as she listened to her friend. "Well, now that you've made your rounds, 'Dr. 'Trice Love,' I'm glad you're here."

As soon as they sat down in the den, Patrice began to entertain Gwen, Tiffany and some of their cousins, telling them about her latest challenges and those that had fallen prey to the legend that was Patrice Henderson. Gwen noticed that Tiffany only half listened, and was staring off as if looking for some distant, unknown place.

Gwen decided to seize the opportunity. Stepping across her cousin Jamel, she touched Tiffany on the shoulder. "Can I talk to you a minute?" Pulling her lightly by the arm, Gwen dragged her up the steps and didn't stop until their old bedroom door closed behind them.

Claire had redone the room years ago. The walls had been painted a soft lavender color. Contrasting comforters covered the twin beds, and matching draperies completed the look. Even though the appearance was different, the room felt the same. Gwen sat on the bed and Tiffany sat down beside her, so close that their legs were touching.

Tiffany spoke slowly. "Gwen, I really miss you. Maybe I moved too far away."

Gwen looked at her and replied, "Girl, you are tripping

too hard. You had a fit until everyone agreed with your move to Atlanta. Mind you, the eastern shore of Virginia isn't right around the corner from Georgia, but the distance really isn't all that bad. Besides, you got photos out the yin-yang, and you take more every time you come home as if T.J.'s homely looks are ever going to change." Both of them always kidded T.J. about his looks, when in fact he was a tall, dark, and handsome wonder with dimples to die for, thick full lips, and curly lashes that covered a perfect set of dark brown and almond-shaped eyes.

Tiffany attempted to smile. "I know, but sometimes I wish I could see you every day. Seriously, Gwenee, I miss you so much."

Hearing the name Tiffany hadn't used for so many years got Gwen's attention. Suddenly, she noticed that tears were filling Tiff's eyes. She reached out for her hand and sighed before she spoke. "What's wrong? I didn't say anything to you, but I've been breaking out for a month and I immediately knew something was wrong. I just didn't know you were the reason. Tiff, I've been feeling your emotions as long as I can remember, so spill it. You know you can tell me anything. I love you and I know that something is out of sync."

Tiffany got up and looked through the window at the kids playing in the backyard. "I don't know where to start or how to tell you this. The last couple of visits I've made home, I came with the intention of telling you. I also tried to tell you when you came to Atlanta in July for your birthday. The time was never right."

Gwen walked over to her and their eyes locked. The usual sparkle and thirst for life weren't visible in Tiffany's eyes. They were filled instead with an element of something that Gwen couldn't identify.

Tiffany continued. "I could never find the words to tell you that I—"

Just then, Patrice opened the door without knocking.

"You hoes tryin' to leave a sista out? You know we blood. You decide to have a heart-to-heart and not include the third Musketeer." She hardly took a breath as she went on. "If one of you has gotten some and didn't call to give me a play-by-play, I'm going to be hot."

Tiffany tried to brighten up. "Patrice, you know that you're my girl. It's nothing that I want to burden you with now. I just need some love."

Patrice looked cautiously at Gwen as if questioning what had just gone down. Gwen didn't respond; instead, she yielded to Tiffany's wish and moved to hold her. Patrice spread out her arms and embraced Tiffany on the other side. The three of them stood in the center of the room, embracing and holding on, trying to fill Tiffany's near-empty supply of love.

Gwen could feel Tiffany's tears on her cheek as she held her tight. At that moment, she felt her face tighten and could feel the bumps about to surface. Yes, something was wrong. She could feel it.

CHAPTER 2

It was no use prolonging the evening. Tiffany hadn't returned any of her calls. What were answering machines for
anyway? Gwen couldn't understand why she hadn't called
her back. After all, Tiffany didn't have a steamy love life to
speak of, unless Tiff was holding out on her. She had sworn
off men more than two years ago in pursuit of peace, happiness, and holy living. Gwen had been listening to her mini-
sermons so often she thought about doing the spiritual thing
herself. It wasn't like any love interests were banging down
her door. Yep, she was going through a dry spell. The Sahara
Desert was probably a lot more moist than she was.

Bored out of her mind, she decided to call Patrice. Just
what she needed, someone to tell her what she should be doing
on a Saturday night. Despite the put-down that she knew she
would get, she turned over and reached for the cordless phone.
She thought for a moment about what a godsend this device
was, as she moved around freely without the restraints of a
phone cord. She caught a glimpse of her reflection in the
mirror and admired the Victoria's Secret midnight-blue silk
gown that clung perfectly to her curves. Gwen didn't know
why this evening she had bothered to shower, cover her body

in a seductive fragrance, and adorn this silky number. Maybe Vicky's secret was that a handsome *GQ* brother would walk out of her closet the minute she climbed into bed.

She quickly hit the speed dial, and after three rings it was answered. "Hey, what's up?" Gwen chimed into the phone.

Patrice was out of breath. "I was on top until you so rudely interrupted my flow. This had better be life threatening. If not, hang up and let me yell at you at a more suitable time." She paused. "Unless you want to live vicariously through me and get off on what I'm about to do."

Gwen had to smile to herself; Patrice would do exactly what she said unless she hung up. "No, thanks; call me." Gwen was hoping Patrice would talk her through this episode of boredom and help her make sense of this otherwise crazy world.

Now what? Patrice was on a freak expedition and she couldn't reach Tiffany. Rolling onto her back, she looked up at the ceiling and willed for her life to be different. No significant other was going to hold her and whisper sweet nothings in her ear. She didn't even have a dog or a goldfish. All was wrong in her world, and at this moment she couldn't make it right.

It was well after midnight and long after a dose of Rachelle Ferrell when Gwen finally drifted to sleep. Rachelle's music, although considered old school to some, always had a way of soothing her and reaching that part of her soul that needed a lubricating balm. It was as if she understood perfectly what Gwen was feeling. After Rachelle's lyrical interpretation of life, Gwen was always able to see her life more clearly.

Jazz was just one of the things Gwen had acquired a taste for while in college—that and a serious cocoa-brown specimen by the name of Marcus McGuire—but that was another story. She could recall spending many evenings at Humphrey's swaying to the beats that were created there until the wee hours of the morning. While everyone else in her circle of friends was crowding into the gym on campus getting all hot and sweaty, dancing to song after song, Gwen had spent her downtime at the jazz club not far from campus. On those evenings, she had been all too anxious to exchange her campus ID card for a glass of sparkling water with a slice of lime. Humphrey's was one place where she could be herself. Gwen imagined that she was back in time, enjoying an evening set to jazzy music that awakened her senses and gave her inner being the incentive to soar above the ordinary.

Just when she had fallen asleep, the phone rang. It had taken her so long to get to sleep, she couldn't believe she was being disturbed. Turning over slowly, she tried to convince her mind to wake up as she searched for the phone. When she pulled back the sheets, she noticed that in her desperation for a sleep partner, the phone had become a substitute and was now positioned between her legs. Had she been fully awake, she would have been very embarrassed.

"This better be good," Gwen said into the receiver, yawning.

"Gwen, this is your mother."

She sat up in bed and attempted to get herself together.

"Mom, are you okay?" Gwen glanced around the room, noticing it was still dark out. "What time is it? Is Dad all right?"

Claire started again. "Gwen, listen to me. It's Tiffany. She's in the hospital."

Gwen's mind went into fast-forward, her heart dropped, and her face suddenly felt incredibly hot. "What? When did this happen? Was there an accident? Who called you?" The words flew out of her mouth all at once.

"Gwen, you've got to settle down a minute and listen."

Suddenly her mother's words hit her like a ton of bricks.

"Tori, called and said that Tiffany has been in the hospital since Monday." Claire recalled how Tiffany and Tori had met at Virginia Union University and became the very best of friends. Both took pride in being from small towns and holding on to similar values and beliefs that many girls shed the minute they unpack their overloaded trunks. When Tiffany decided to move to Atlanta, it wasn't long before Tori landed a job there as well. "Obviously, she thought she'd be going home in a day or two, so she didn't want to worry us. But you know me; before I hung up that phone, I wanted to know what was wrong with my baby. The two of them are so close, going through college together and moving to Atlanta, I figured she'd know exactly what was going on."

Gwen thought, *All right, are you going to tell me before I jump through this phone?* She waited while her mother rambled on for another minute. Finally, she almost screamed, "Mom, what is wrong with Tiffany?"

Claire's voice dropped to a whisper. "Gwen, honey, did Tiffany say anything at all to you?"

Gwen was losing it. "About what, Mom? The times we talked, I could tell that something heavy was going on, but she wasn't ready to let me in, so I let it go."

Claire James took a deep breath and spoke slowly. "Tiffany has AIDS. She's in the hospital with pneumonia and some other complications."

Suddenly Gwen remembered all of the times Tiff had come home and wanted to talk. She also remembered the cards and letters from Tiffany that filled her mailbox almost daily. The phone calls in the middle of the night. The hives. It all made sense now. She had been feeling Tiffany, and her body had been alerting her that something was going bad. Gwen wanted to cry and scream until someone told her it wasn't true. Her sister couldn't be facing this god-awful disease.

Her body was covered in a cold sweat and she came around to hear her mom screaming her name. "I'm here, Mom. It's going to be all right. We've got to get to her. She needs us. I'll call the airline the minute I hang up and get us on the next flight." She hung up the phone without saying good-bye.

Gwen closed her eyes and wrapped her arms around her

legs tightly for what seemed like forever. Finally, she managed to get up and go into the bathroom. Without turning on the lights, she discarded her gown and stepped into the shower. Gwen attempted to reach for the water faucet but she just couldn't muster the energy or the coordination to turn on the water. She leaned her back against the cold tile on the wall. Her body slid down into the dry tub as she cried uncontrollably. Gwen thought that if she left the lights off, she wouldn't be able to discern the horrible truth she had just learned. She wanted it to all go away. She needed this all to just go away.

CHAPTER 3

Gwen got her mom, dad, and T.J. on a flight out of Norfolk International Airport at 9:00 a.m. and it arrived in Atlanta at 10:56 a.m. It seemed as if they had been in the air forever. She glanced over at her parents, who were sitting across the aisle. They both looked like they had aged five years in such a short time. It's funny how hours of stress can take a toll on your body.

T.J. reached over and squeezed Gwen's hand. They hadn't held hands since . . . well, never really. Their only show of affection had been insults, or maybe a slap upside the head. And now her brother's strong hand was wrapped around hers.

"Hey, are you all right? You haven't said a word since we took off. No one expects you to be a rock in all this. My shoulder is here. You know that, don't you?" T.J. could always read her mind.

"I know, T.J. I was just thinking that I should have made Tiff talk to me. You know, she wanted to tell me. I mean, she tried to tell me when she was home for Thanksgiving, but Patrice interrupted and I just let it go instead of insisting that she talk to me."

T.J. looked out of the plane window. He stared as if something were written in the clouds. Maybe there was a mystical answer for Gwen and even something to soothe the ache inside all of them.

He sighed heavily. "She may have wanted to tell you, but she wanted to do it in her own time, when she was ready. You're trying to deal with some guilt that really isn't yours to deal with. Lighten up."

"I can't, T.J., I should have known. I wonder how long she knew, and how she dealt with it without us. She must have been out of her mind with worry. How did she manage to sleep at night knowing that at any time she could get worse?" Gwen sighed briefly.

"T.J., she was living each day and not knowing if it could be her last. Every day, she knew she might leave me." Gwen knew she was being selfish, saying "me," but everyone knew how close Tiff and Gwen were. From the time that Tiffany could walk, she was Gwen's shadow, following her everywhere with a head full of pigtails and a constant, irritating smile. Tiff was her baby sister, and Gwen needed her as much as it went the other way around. So, why hadn't Tiff opened up and let her in? She couldn't have solved this or made it go away, but she could have helped her deal with it.

"Hey, fasten your seat beats. They just announced that we're getting ready to land." Claire turned to them and managed a faint smile.

The hustle and bustle of the airport made the next steps take forever. T.J. and Gwen went to the Hertz rental counter, while their parents went to claim their baggage. After an hour, T.J. pulled onto I-75. Emory Hospital should have been twenty minutes from the airport, but they arrived in ten. No one chastised him for driving like a crazy man. They all needed to get to Tiffany.

When they finally parked, Gwen got out and helped her

mom from the backseat. They walked in silence through the parking lot into the hospital and followed the signs to the intensive care unit. As soon as the elevator doors opened, they walked straight to the waiting area and noticed Tori sitting solemnly in a chair across the room.

Tori ran to them with puffy eyes and a strained look. "Hey, guys. I'm so glad you're here."

Claire hugged Tori. "How you holding up, baby? Have you gotten any rest?"

"I'm okay, Ma James. I'm just glad that you all are here with me now. I would have called sooner, but Tiffany didn't want me to." Her words became an undetectable murmur, and she started to cry. Tori was a beautiful woman. Her long brown hair cascaded over her shoulders, and she stood almost five eight in stocking feet. Her features were picture-perfect and her doelike eyes were always accented with eyeliner to make them look even more intriguing.

They all stood frozen in place. Tori's crying confirmed the reality of their impromptu visit. They waited for a few minutes, no one wanting to ask the question.

Gwen decided to break the silence. "Where is Tiff's room?"

Tori spoke in a whisper. "A-4. Through those doors at the end and to the right."

"I'll go in if it's all right with you all," Gwen said, and everyone nodded.

Gwen walked slowly through the heavy double doors and looked around before a nurse approached her. She mumbled her name and whom she was there to see. The nurse smiled and pointed toward a beige curtain. The intensive care unit was one large floor with each room separated only by a thin curtain. Gwen's legs felt like they were in quicksand, and her mind willed her to be some place else, anywhere but there. Gwen noticed a bright red sign that read CONTAMINATED BLOOD. She wanted to cry but couldn't, not at the moment.

On the other side was someone who needed her to be strong, and she was determined not to let Tiffany down.

Gwen peeped around the curtain and had to blink twice. Tiffany didn't look like her little sister. Tubes were everywhere, twisting around her head leading to various machines that were attached to her weak, fragile body. Under the starched white sheets, Gwen could see Tiff's chest moving slowly up and down. She was fighting to breathe despite the oxygen tube in her nose.

Gwen walked closer to the bed and touched her hand. "Tiffany. Open your eyes. It's me, Gwen." Gwen waited and rubbed her sister's hand softly. Finally, Tiff opened her eyes a little and slowly reached her hand up toward Gwen's face.

"Hey, Boo. I'm here. You're going to be fine." Gwen had to keep talking despite the lump in her throat that threatened to take over her speech. "Why didn't you tell me, sweetie? I would have been right by your side. We've always been so close; you know you could have told me. All this time, you carried this burden without me."

A tear started to run down Tiffany's face. Gwen reached out with her fingertip and wiped it away. Tiffany looked up into her eyes, and through swollen, dry lips, and the saliva that had gathered at the corners of her mouth, she whispered, "I'm sorry. I love you, Gwenee."

Before Gwen could respond, the nurse came in and said she needed to take Tiff's vitals and give her something for pain.

"I'll be back, Tiff. Don't worry. I'm here, and I'm not going anywhere."

Nothing in Gwen's life had prepared her for that moment. How could she let death steal her sister, and who in the hell had sentenced Tiff to this horrible state? She had so many questions and no answers. How could she make this better? There was no arm to put on the broken Barbie doll, no excuse to make up, and no all-night talk to have. This was a deadly disease and she just couldn't make it better.

Gwen returned to the waiting room stiff and silent with tears of anguish escaping from the swollen lids of her dark eyes. She walked past her family without looking into their questioning, pain-laden faces.

"Gwen, wait." T.J. spoke through the hoarseness in his throat. He couldn't stand the look on Gwen's face. She looked as if she would collapse under the weight of it all.

"Let her go, T.J." Thomas reached for his son and nodded toward the direction Gwen had gone. "She needs to be alone right now. Her heart is breaking, and as much as you love her, your words can't soften this blow."

When Gwen finally slowed down, she had absently stumbled to the entrance of the hospital. The only thing that forged through the pain was her need to get out of the building. The sanitary smell clung to the dense air and was squeezing her lungs. She wanted to slow down after she almost ran into an elderly woman in a wheelchair, but she forced her feet to move until she was on the other side of the revolving doors.

Her head was light, and she felt faint. The picture of Tiff's fragile body played over and over in her mind. Gwen sat down on the sidewalk a distance away from the busy entrance, and allowed her head to fall to her knees.

Gwen could hear her name being called, but couldn't lift her head. She had been sitting with it between her knees for so long that her entire upper body had gone numb, which echoed what was happening inside her body.

"Gwen, come on and get up. It's too cold for you to be setting out here. T.J. said you had run out and I spent the last past hour looking for you."

The voice finally registered in Gwen's dull senses. With great effort she lifted her head a little and looked into Patrice's face. "'Trice, I just can't understand. Why?" Before Gwen could say another word, Patrice had wrapped her arms around her tightly.

T.J. had called and woken Patrice up long before the sun had come up. He told her what was going on and asked her to meet them in Atlanta at Emory Hospital. Without giving it much thought, Patrice called the airline, packed a bag, made a couple of quick calls, and was on the next thing smokin'. Since she lived in Richmond, she mentally gauged her arrival time. Considering Gwen's hour-long drive to Norfollk Airport from their small eastern shore town and their flight travel time, she figured that she would arrive an hour after them. Patrice was more than a friend, she was family and she couldn't let them go through this ordeal alone.

The day after they arrived, Tiffany slipped into a coma. Gwen believed that the coma was Tiffany's way to block out the pain and sadness that she saw in their faces.

Claire, Tori, Patrice, and Gwen kept a constant watch over Tiffany. Thomas and T.J. returned home to take care of some business and would return the following weekend. Thomas James had never been much for handling stress or knowing what to say when someone was sick, especially one of his kids. He always felt that he should be in control and take care of them. Gwen could only imagine how helpless he felt.

Patrice was scheduled to attend a meeting in California with some important overseas investors. Although she made several pleas, her boss would not consider sending someone else in her place. She had laid all the groundwork and had been instrumental in tying up all the loose ends on this deal. Leaving Gwen behind to be swallowed up in grief was difficult and cut to the very core of her being. Patrice decided after a lengthy good-bye with Gwen that she would concentrate on getting the details finalized so she could return swiftly.

By the fourth day, Gwen managed to come out of the

shell that had consumed her ever since she had gotten off the plane. Walking to the window, she stood beside her mom and spoke softly. "Mom, why don't you and Tori go get some coffee and something to eat? I'll stay here in case she wakes up or the doctor comes in."

"Gwen, I'm all right, really. I just need to stay here with my baby and pray. The good Lord is the only one who can intervene, and I'm trusting him for a miracle." Tears that had been held back for too long began to fall lightly against her brown cheek. The one that always seemed so soft whenever Gwen touched it as a child. Now it was wet with tears.

Gwen turned and walked toward Tiffany, who was surrounded by medical equipment. Claire began to moan out loud. "He can't take my baby. He just can't take my baby. How am I supposed to live without her?"

Gwen reached for her mom and she fell helplessly into her arms, unable to hide her frustration any longer. Holding on tight, Gwen couldn't help but cry with her. She thought silently, *I don't want to lose my baby sister either, but I wonder if my mother even realizes that she has T.J. and me.*

Almost as if she sensed their desperation, Tori entered the room. after a quick restroom break, and moved toward them. She caressed Gwen's arm. "Come on, Ma James. Let's get something to eat."

Defeated, Claire allowed Tori to lead her out of the room.

Gwen sat down in the chair next to the hospital bed and tried to get herself together. As her face began to break out, she remembered that her medication was back at Tiffany's condo. She reached in her bag to find eyedrops, and noticed the slim-sized Bible that she always carried. Removing it from the bag, she held it tight to her chest and began to pray.

"Lord, if ever I needed you, it's now. Everything is wrong and Tiff is lying here with this disease that could take her life at any time. Ever since she was born, I always felt that I had to protect her. She always wanted me to fix everything, or at least promise her that things would be fine, even when deep down inside I was doubtful. Oh, God, there are so many unanswered questions and I don't know how to cope." A shiver went down her spine and she continued. "Why didn't she tell me? I could have spent more time with her. I could have done something." Hot tears fell onto the Bible, and she fought to stay composed so that she could finish her prayer. "Please, God, spare her. I don't know how she contracted this disease, but I know that she is a gentle, caring person who would never hurt anyone. Yet she is lying here fighting. I need her and I don't know what I'll do without her. Lord, that's my mommy's baby and she couldn't stand having to live without Tiffany. Please help us to endure this and strengthen us as a family."

When Gwen opened her eyes through the haze of tears, she reached for Tiffany's hand and whispered, "Amen." She felt that Tiffany had heard her prayer, and she was confident that the Almighty was listening too.

The following evening they all felt like battered soldiers. When a couple of Tiffany's church members volunteered to spend the night, the family reluctantly accepted so they could go home and get some rest.

They exchanged small talk during the fifteen-minute ride to the condo, talking about everything from the change in the weather to the new buildings that were being constructed nearby. Gwen said, "I can see why you two like this area so much. It's so alive and all the lights make it so beautiful at night."

"Yeah, the first time we came for a visit, we both agreed that this was the place for us," Tori answered.

Tori's BMW stopped in front of the driveway. "Ma James, we're here." Tori touched Claire's arm gingerly. She stretched and opened the car door.

They all got out and walked to the door. As soon as they entered, they kicked off their shoes in the foyer.

"I'm going to bed, and try to get some sleep." Claire kissed both of them on the forehead and turned to go upstairs.

Tori turned on the TV, flopped down on the beige leather sofa, and started to channel-surf. She finally stopped to watch the eleven o'clock news. Tori was a morning news anchor for one of Atlanta's television stations. Her face was so familiar around town that people would stop and ask her for recaps of the news stories that she had discussed. Men would just gawk at her, which irritated her more than it complimented her.

They only watched for a moment before Gwen couldn't stand it anymore.

"Why didn't you tell me?" The words were out before Gwen knew it. "Who gave you the right to keep something so serious from Tiffany's family?"

Caught off guard, Tori turned the volume down before speaking. "Look, Gwen, it wasn't my decision. You do not understand the depth of my friendship with Tiffany. For the record, you're not the only one hurting. I love her too, and I've had to live with this secret for one year. Not you, but me." She jumped up and walked over to the fireplace. Over the mantel was a photo that Tiffany and Tori had taken last Christmas. The two were looking their usual best.

"I'm sorry, Tori. I didn't mean to jump down your throat. I just haven't had a chance to digest any of this. I always thought that Tiff and I were close. But she chose not to tell me, and I just don't understand why." She sat in the side chair across from the fireplace. "I mean, there had to be times when she needed to make certain medical decisions. The thought of her doing all that alone hurts like crazy. I know she had you, but we are her family." Gwen began to cry out of anger and hurt. "I've always taken care of her and fixed

things when she needed me to. Now she's in the most difficult crisis of her life, and she decides not to share it with me."

There was still so much Gwen wanted to say. She wanted
to know about the man in Tiffany's life, and who could have
infected her with AIDS. Was it a fling, or was she in a serious relationship? But Gwen stopped before she could ask;
she had to admit to herself that she wasn't ready for the answers.

When Tori tried to speak, Gwen didn't have the energy to
listen. "Save it, Tori. I can't deal with this right now."

Tori spoke anyway. "Gwen, all you need to know is that
she was protecting you. She didn't want you to live the hell
she was living. Can you imagine waking up, not knowing
when it would get worse or when you wouldn't have the energy to even wash your face? Every time she wanted to tell
you, she would get sick just thinking about it. Can't you see
that? She knew you would want to fix this for her, and a big
part of her wanted you to. But she knew that as much as you
may have wanted to, you couldn't." Tori took the seat across
from Gwen. "And that's why she spared you and carried the
burden all alone. The only reason I found out was that she
forgot to hide her pill bottle when she was in a rush one
morning. I went into her room to borrow a pair of earrings
and saw the bottle on the bed. Of course, I was curious because she hadn't been herself and I was wondering what she
was taking. Can you imagine how I felt when I saw that the
prescription was for AZT? When I told her I was going to
call you all, she cried and begged me not to. I went against
her wishes this time and I'm glad I did. I just hope she for-
gives me."

Tori moved to kneel in front of Gwen. "Let it go, Gwen.
Your anger is a waste of time. Tiffany needs you right now.
I'm sure all of this is taking a toll on you, but you're the
strong one, so we all need you to keep us together. Come on
and get some rest."

"You go ahead. I'm going to have a little herbal tea to settle my nerves. Maybe it'll help get rid of these hives." Gwen touched the back of her neck with her right hand and rubbed the little lumps that were there. "Yeah. I could sure use a celestial moment."

They both struggled to laugh, but neither had fully recovered from the heavy conversation that had just gone down.

"No matter what, Gwen, please know that I love you like a sister. I would never intentionally hurt you or try to take your place with Tiffany. The two of you share a very special bond, not just because you are sisters, but also because you are friends. Don't ever doubt her love for you. It's always been there."

"Yeah. I hear you, and I love you too." Gwen looked over the island in the kitchen as she spoke the words. Tori turned and walked up the steps to her bedroom.

As she glanced around the kitchen, admiring the mauve and beige hues in the room, Gwen could feel Tiffany's presence. Smiling to herself, she spun around to fill the teakettle and place it on the range. While she waited for the water to get hot, she reminisced about the time Tiffany and Tori had moved into the condo.

She had driven down to help them get settled. Tiffany had taken great pleasure in decorating the kitchen alone, dubbing it her personal space since Tori could hardly boil an egg. Gwen had watched her make a fuss over the cabinets, wanting everything to be in its own little place. She had lined the shelves with every kind of spice you could name, placing them neatly side by side in alphabetical order. Tori and Gwen had teased Tiffany, calling her a "neat freak" for going through such measures just to put some spices in a cabinet. But that was her way; and now as Gwen reached up for the cabinet knob and opened it up to see neatly stocked shelves, she marveled at Tiffany's handiwork while removing the box of tea from the shelf.

After making a cup of cinnamon apple tea, Gwen walked over to the living room, opened the patio door, and walked out onto the balcony. Gazing out over the city, she stood in awe at its size and beauty. Closing her eyes for a moment, she could almost hear it speak. She had always loved the bright lights, the busy streets, and the lively sounds of a city. That was the kind of backdrop she desired for her comings and goings, a city that never slept.

Gwen spoke out loud. "Why did I even decide to live in the boonies?" Then she remembered how she had packed up and moved back home after graduating from Virginia Commonwealth University. Once she no longer had Marcus in her life, the city she always enjoyed lost its luster. The sounds of the night no longer soothed her to sleep. Instead, they stirred the loneliness and pain inside her. Moving had been her only solution. She had vowed to never return and resented not only the man for what he had become, but also the city that offered him a lifestyle that satisfied his loins like water to a thirsty man.

Dwelling in her yesterdays a while longer, Gwen remembered when she had first gone to college. After only a year, the city bug bit her. When she did visit home, mostly to see Tiffany, she could hardly stay through the duration of her planned visit. She laughed as she recalled the lyrics of the Crusaders' "Street Life." She would bounce through the door on her way back to Richmond, dancing and singing, "Street life, it's the only life I know." Her mom would shake her head realizing that her daughter would never be the same. And a country girl she could never be again. Gwendolyn Nicole James had found her home, and it was definitely not the country town she had grown up in. The city had become her lifeline and she was happy there.

It all seemed so ironic now. A city had been to blame for her first heartbreak, and now it would cause her second. She looked out over the city that she felt was responsible for the disease that was stealing Tiffany's life. Turning her back on the bright lights and noises, she knew she would never feel anything but resentment toward this city—any city would bring nothing but bad memories.

CHAPTER 4

Patrice had returned after her meeting and sworn that she would be a permanent fixture for as long as Gwen needed her. Seeing no need for Patrice to miss time from work when there was no change, Gwen finally talked her into going back to Richmond. Thomas and T.J. visited for a couple of days and returned home again to keep things together on that end. Tori did her daily programs at the station and spent the remainder of her day and evening at the hospital. Gwen and Claire continued to watch over Tiffany—well, them and the Jim Jones crew. The family had decided, after Gwen walked in one day to find them tampering with Tiff's tubes, that they'd never leave Tiff alone with them again.

Gwen and her mother were too exhausted to stay at the hospital another evening.

Tori had agreed to spend the night with Tiff since she was off the next day. In front of the television, Gwen was engulfed in an episode of *My Wife and Kids* when her mom peeped around the corner.

"Gwen, come and get something to eat. I made a little dinner."

The mention of food made her stomach growl. The stale

sandwiches that she picked up from the hospital cafeteria were a far cry from anything that included real meat, and after a bite or two they always ended up in the trash can. To make matters worse, she had drunk enough caffeine to last her a lifetime. She stood up and stretched; her jeans were so loose. She hadn't been eating regularly, so she knew she had lost some weight. Not to mention how she looked. The hives had become a constant now, covering not only her face but most of her body. Because of that, she hadn't put on any makeup and had little concern for what she looked like. "An old maiden" would probably describe her to a tee, inside and out.

"Oh, Mom, something smells good."

"I thought we could use a decent meal. Lord knows, I can't remember the last time we had one."

Gwen sat down to a plate of meat loaf, red-skinned potatoes, green beans, and corn bread. Her mom sat across from her and poured ice-cold lemonade into their glasses. After she blessed the food, they began to eat in silence. It was an awkward silence. Gwen looked over at her mom, who seemed distant and strained. "Mom, what are you thinking? Are you feeling okay? You probably should have them check your blood pressure tomorrow."

"Oh, I'm as well as I can be. I'm just so worried about Tiffany. She is so sick and she looks so weak."

"I know how you feel, Mom. I can't sleep or rest without waking up in a sweat or crying myself to sleep."

"Baby, prayer changes things. And right now, Tiffany needs all the prayers she can get. Now, let's try to eat so we can get a good night's rest. When I finish, I've got to call your father. You know he's not talking much. When I call him, he is just so darn quiet. He's always had such a quiet demeanor, and it's times like these when I hate that trait in him. I never know exactly what he's thinking."

"That's Daddy. He's never been one for a lot of words. But you, on the other hand . . ."

They both started to laugh. The sound of her laughter warmed Gwen's heart. Her mother always had a laugh that made you think that it filled her very soul.

Just then the phone rang. They both jumped and looked at each other. Gwen moved slowly to pick up the cordless phone that sat on the kitchen counter. "Hello." She closed her eyes tightly and waited for a reply.

"Hey, sis."

"Oh, hey, T.J."

"You sound a little off."

"It was just the phone. It startled me a little."

"I talked with Mom earlier, so I know there isn't any change. I just wanted to check on you and see how Mom is holding up."

"I'm okay, and Mom is hanging in there. I'm going to have them check her blood pressure tomorrow just to be on the safe side." Gwen leaned against the counter. T.J.'s likeness came into her mind. He was the spitting image of their dad. He and Kim had married fresh out of high school in a fairy-tale ceremony. No one thought they were old enough. They proved everyone wrong. Their marriage worked. Fifteen years and two kids later, things were good between them. They were as in love as they had been when he first brought her home during their high school days.

"Gwen, are you there?"

"Yes. I was just drifting."

"Well, big sis, I'll let you go. Kim and the boys send their love."

"Tell them I love and miss them all."

"Call me if you need me. If there's no change, I'll be up next weekend. I want to put the Christmas tree up and finish some shopping. I'm not in the mood, but I want the boys to enjoy Christmas despite all that is going on.

"Gosh. In the midst of all this, I forgot that Christmas is next week. I'm glad I bought Baron and Darion's gifts early. At least that's done. I'm sure everyone else feels like we do.

Besides, Christmas is for kids. Tiff is the only one who went all out during the Christmas season. Decorating the tree the day after Thanksgiving and acting like a little elf all the way up until Christmas Day."

T.J. chimed in, "You got that right. She would do Christmas up." They both got quiet.

"Well, Gwen, I'll call you tomorrow night. I love you. Kiss Mom and Tiffany for me."

"I sure will. And, T.J., I love you too."

By the time Gwen hung up the phone, her mom had finished the dishes and showered. She came into the kitchen wearing a pink-flowered duster. "Well, Gwen, I'm turning in. I want to get to the hospital early so Tori can come home and get some rest."

"You go ahead and get some rest. I'm going to watch a little television and then hit the sack myself."

Gwen went to the hall closet and grabbed a blanket from the top shelf. Returning to the sofa, she curled up under the blanket and flipped from channel to channel for the next hour. Loneliness filled the room like an invisible vapor . . .

Totally frustrated, she began to channel-surf again, finally stopping at the HBO station in time to catch *Boomerang*. She didn't have a relationship to dominate like Robin Givens, and her whole world was falling apart. Just when she thought she couldn't cry anymore, she did. Her body rocked in a frenzied, uncontrollable cry. She thought about an old proverb their grandma was notorious for saying when they were going through something difficult: "Baby, what don't kill you will make you strong." At this very moment, though, Tiffany's life was hanging by a thread, and this whole ordeal wasn't making Gwen any stronger. Or so she thought.

CHAPTER 5

Downtown Atlanta was brightly lit with Christmas decorations on every corner. The city was so alive it seemed to be waiting for Christmas to arrive. Gwen sat in the backseat looking out the window at the tall buildings and the hustle of the people who had chosen this city as their home. She wondered how many of them were honestly happy with their choice, and how many had just become complacent and were making the best of it. Life was funny that way. One minute you're living large, doing all the things you dreamed of, and the next you're just going through the motions. She guessed that common thread ran through everyone's lives regardless of where they decided to put up their teepees.

Shifting in her seat, she half listened to Boys II Men singing their version of "Silent Night" on the radio. Gwen had allowed Tori and Patrice to talk her into going out to dinner. They felt that she needed a reprieve from the hospital and constant thoughts of Tiffany's illness.

It was hard to believe that Christmas was only five days away. It seemed as though she had been in Atlanta forever, when in reality it had only been three weeks. T.J. would be leaving in the morning to get ready for the big holiday. He had been committed to helping his family deal with Tiffany's condition, and Kim had been very supportive and understanding of his need to be at Tiffany's bedside and help shoulder the impact that this trauma was having on all of them. However, she and the boys were missing him terribly. Gwen, on the other hand, had no one missing her.

Tori pulled her BMW into a parking garage and, after circling a few times, finally found a parking space. Tori, Gwen, Patrice and T.J. climbed out and walked toward the elevator that would take them to their destination. It opened to the busy underground district of Atlanta, a well-known hot spot of the city with an array of shops and restaurants.

Tori walked briskly toward Paschals Restaurant, her hair bouncing in the breeze. Although she was all bundled up, she still looked radiant.

From the doorway of the restaurant, they could see that the place was packed.

"Girlfriend, I hope the food and atmosphere are worth the wait," Patrice said as she scanned the area around the bar.

"It is. And even though there's a line, it always moves relatively quickly. Trust me on this. You won't be disappointed." Tori was smiling as if she was about to let them in on a big secret.

"Well, all righty, then. I think I'll go over to the bar, wet my whistle, and partake in a little conversation with some hopeless individual, who, after a few minutes in my presence, won't know what hit him. Ta-tah." Patrice did her usual twist over to the bar and sat on a stool next to a very attractive milk-chocolate guy. He was impeccably dressed. From what Gwen could see, he was already enjoying the sudden attention Patrice was paying him.

Patrice was gorgeous tonight. Her hair was pulled up into a French roll and tendrils framed her perfectly shaped face. These features did not elude her latest prey.

"James, party of four." Gwen eyed Patrice, who winked and continued to talk to Mr. Fine. The slender-built hostess greeted them with a smile. Her frame was very delicate, and she held a hint of innocence. The James party fell in step behind her as she swung her shoulder-length auburn braids and swayed her hips to some beat that played for her ears only.

They were seated beside a large waterfall fountain. The water gushed out over a ridge that reflected a hue of rainbow colors. As she placed menus on the table, the hostess told them that the special of the evening was blackened salmon with olive relish over rice pilaf, and a vegetable medley, and the dessert was chocolate mousse. "Can I take your drink orders, or would you like to wait for the other member of your party?"

"Oh, can we wait a moment to glance over the drink list? As for our other party, she'll probably be detained for a while."

"Does she ever stop?" Tori questioned. "I mean, she's been over there for almost thirty minutes and she don't know that guy from Adam."

"She's in her natural habitat. A place that has food, drink, and men."

Tori laughed along with Gwen and T.J. and began to glance over the menu.

"What she needs is a strong black man." T.J. spoke without taking his eyes off the menu that rested in front of him. As if feeling the daggers from their eyes, he looked up. "What? Why are you two looking at me like that?"

"'Cause! We want you to tell us, oh wise one, what are the qualities of such a specimen? And where should we hunt to find one?" Gwen spoke in a straightforward tone, telling T.J. that he had barked up the wrong tree and had no idea what he was in for.

Before he could speak, the server came. She was a strawberry-blond, blue-eyed girl who looked straight out of an episode of *Baywatch*.

"Hi! I'm Hope, and I'll be your server tonight. Can I get

you guys something to drink? And an appetizer?" She was speaking to everyone, but her eyes were fixed on T.J.

"I'll have a strawberry daiquiri," Gwen said.

"I'll have a Long Island iced tea," Tori added. "And some calamari rings."

"That sounds good. I'll have a Long Island iced tea too. And bring me some hot wings," T.J. mumbled without taking his eyes off the menu.

"I'll be right back with your drink orders."

"Tori, did you notice that?" Gwen said, glancing over at T.J.

"Girl, I didn't miss it. Ms. Thang couldn't take our drink orders while looking at Mr. Innocent over here."

"What are you guys talking about? She was just being pleasant. Gwen, if you're through exaggerating, I'm thinking of having a steak." His attempt to change the subject was weak but Gwen decided to let it go for the moment.

T.J. and Gwen exchanged small talk while Tori listened in thinking how Tiffany's presence would make the moment complete. Tori just hoped that getting out for dinner would lift everyone's spirits a little and allow them time to think about something other than hospitals, doctors, and daily medical updates.

Just then Hope came bouncing over. "Here you go, guys." She placed the drinks on the table, leaning in front of T.J. just a little longer than necessary. Her bustline spilled out of her tight white blouse.

"What can I get you?" she asked T.J.

"Ladies first." He pointed to Tori and Gwen.

Tori was visibly disturbed. "Thanks for helping us get noticed. I'll have the blackened salmon over the rice pilaf and the vegetable medley, and a side salad with house dressing."

Gwen stared at the menu. "Let's see. Everything looks great. Hmmm. Let me get your broiled stuffed flounder, baked potato, butter only, and a side salad with house dressing."

Eager to get back to T.J., Hope leaned forward again. "What about you, sir? What can I get for you?"

"Oh, well, I'll have the T-bone, medium well, with grilled onions and mushrooms, herbed mashed potatoes, and coleslaw. And can I get an extra roll?"

"For you, no problem." She took the menus, placed them under her arm, and walked away.

"That shot my last nerve," Tori blasted out. "She almost jumped on the table to get your attention, T.J. Now, while you were calm, the average black man would have been all teeth, trying to get the digits. Doesn't matter that she's as preppy and white as they come. She obviously has a case of jungle fever, and I can imagine that many a brother would have been willing to step to her." Rolling her eyes, she took a sip of her drink.

"I didn't really notice anything." He smiled. "Okay, she may have been a little forward, but as a strong black man I'm in control enough to ignore that. Just because someone tries to come on to you doesn't mean you have to succumb to the advances. My baby is in Virginia, and she is all the woman I'll ever need. Don't get me wrong, attention is great for the old ego, but I know my limitations."

Gwen had to speak up. "Boy, you know Kim would throw a fit if she saw some woman trying to get up on you. She would definitely redecorate the décor up in here."

T.J. drank a portion of the dark liquid. "True dat. My Kimee don't play."

They sat for a moment. Hope brought the appetizers, still looking at T.J. like she wanted to jump his bones. "Anything else right now?"

Gwen answered before Tori could bite Hope's head off. "No, thanks."

This was definitely one of Atlanta's hot spots. The place was packed with all shades of black people and even some white, which added a splash of color. Gwen could see how

Atlanta got the nickname "Hotlanta." It was sure 'nuff a place that one could get used to.

In the background, someone keyed up a jazzy tune and it started playing through the ceiling speakers. Gwen closed her eyes and bounced a little to the smooth sounds that flowed through the room. All that was missing that would make her evening complete was someone to whisper in her ear.

Tori spoke up. "See, I knew you would love this place. The music they play is enough to intoxicate you."

"It was a good choice, Tori." T.J. leaned back in his seat and ran a hand over his chin. "I could sure enough enjoy this kind of flow. Me and my boys could chill hard here."

"Speaking of boys, you were supposed to share the wisdom that you have acquired from what talk show?" Gwen chuckled while reaching for a hot wing. She began to feel her muscles relax and knew that the daiquiri was working its magic. She had always had a two-drink minimum; after that, she wasn't herself. Her body, fully aware of her limitations, was about to enter into a serious relaxation mode as she thought about ordering another drink.

"Here comes our food." T.J. grinned. "Before I lay some wisdom down, I need to bless my food and start on my meal."

Hope obviously thought T.J. was smiling at her. "I have your food right here, handsome. I believe you ordered the T-bone medium well." She began to place his entrée in front of him. "And here are your two rolls with extra butter. I hope you enjoy everything."

"Isn't that something you say to the entire party after everyone has been served?" Tori snapped.

"Oh, I'm sorry." She nervously placed everything on the table, attempted a weak smile, and walked away.

"That was just too sad," T.J. managed to mumble after shoving a mouthful of food in his mouth. "Tori, you didn't have to be so cold."

"Yes, I did. You didn't have to entertain her attempt to

flirt. She all but took her snug outfit off right here in front of you."

"All right. So much for a pleasant meal." T.J. put his fork down, removed the napkin from his lap, and wiped his mouth, all in one swift movement.

"Your attitude is all wrong, Tori. You sound like most of the black women out here today. It's as if you all expect a man to be a dog. You're waiting every moment for a tail to grow and the salivating to start. The sad thing about the whole situation is that men begin to think that since that's what you all expect, they might as well be the dogs you think they are."

Tori lashed back, "I'm only speaking the truth. And deep down you know it."

"Not all men are dogs, but they're all labeled K-9s before they even enter into the relationship. Brothers get so tired of you women ragging on them." T.J. leaned forward, picked up his fork, and put it back down again, his piercing eyes never leaving Tori's face. He started again, "I have a lot of friends, strong black, employed heterosexual brothas that are willing to step correctly to a woman. After a few dates, women expect them to break down. There's not a man that I know who doesn't want a fantasy-type relationship. They want to commit, they want to pamper a woman and be pampered, and oh yeah, they want to say the L-O-V-E word. But as soon as they do, the woman's defenses go up and they shut down, because they believe that a brother cannot be into a monogamous relationship. All men aren't controlled by their manhood, you know."

Just when Gwen thought he was done, he took a deep breath. "We try to love you black women and you don't want to be loved. Sooner or later a brother gets tired and gives up, and then he becomes the dog that you expected him to be in the beginning. The one that you created."

"T.J., that's enough. We get the point." Gwen finally spoke

up, not wanting this to turn any uglier than it already had. She hadn't expected this topic to open up a Pandora's box.

"There are good and bad brothers out there; you just need to weed through to get to the good ones. That's not to overlook the fact that a lot of women settle. Sometimes guys don't bring more to the relationship because you all don't demand more. You get what you give. Women put up with no-good, cheating men by choice. If you feel that you deserve candlelight dinners and roses, stop letting your man take you to McDonald's. Any guy, no matter how big his Johnson is, who comes up in your crib after ten p.m. isn't worth the time it takes to open the door. Squash all that trashing you're doing and look through a different pair of glasses. I'm telling you this as a brother, Gwen, and, Tori, I'm telling you as a friend. Now can I finish my dinner?"

"All right, T.J., I didn't know you could get that deep. And I definitely didn't know that your boys Paul, Shawn, and the rest of the gang were about something. I'll have to actually speak to them now instead of giving them the usual are-you-crazy stare."

Tori spoke up. "I'm not buying any of that. T.J., you know there are a larger percentage of dogs out there than decent men who are willing to commit. Men are dogs, they are programmed to be dogs, and they won't ever be anything but dogs. You're trying to tell me that there is a brother who can wine and dine me without expecting to be in my drawers twenty-four-seven. Please, that is just not the norm. Men are just so full of it. And I for one can't take the drama." Tori began to look as if she was talking to someone standing a distance away. Her bottom lip began to tremble and her eyes looked dazed. She lowered her voice. "It's just not worth all the drama. I can understand why so many women are turning to lesbian lovers. I applaud those women who are strong enough to admit that they can get more out of a relationship with a woman than they could ever get from some lying, trifling dog."

T.J. and Gwen both looked at Tori as if she had just started speaking Portuguese. Before they could respond, Patrice came over and sat beside Tori.

"What did I miss?" Patrice was all teeth.

"Besides dinner?" Gwen asked sarcastically.

"Oh, I had dinner with Derrick. And while I didn't get around to dessert, I think I'll be tasting that sweet before I leave town. If he's half as sweet as he looks, I'm in for a real treat, and I can't wait." Patrice licked her lips while glancing over the dessert menu. She didn't even notice the expression on their faces or the edginess and tension that circled the table.

T.J. and Gwen had just been suffocated by Tori's words, while Tori sat there like the words had left a bitter taste in her mouth.

"Who's down for some dessert?" Patrice looked up and immediately sensed the tension. Looking stunned, she raised her hands helplessly. "What did I say?"

It was nothing Patrice had said, but the statements that had left Tori's lips moments before. They were something that Gwen and T.J. had to think about.

CHAPTER 6

They arrived back at the condo after midnight. The new sleeping arrangements forced Gwen to deal with the silent fear she'd had since she got to Atlanta. She was going to have to sleep in Tiffany's room. During the time she had been there so far, she'd always managed to avoid being in Tiff's room for longer than a minute.

Now she sat on the end of Tiffany's bed taking in everything around her, inhaling the scent of Tiffany. The room's fragrance was a mixture of Estee Lauder's Gold and hints of vanilla that poured in from the bathroom. The room was beautiful, decorated in hues of blues, burgundy, and ivory. Gwen walked over to the entertainment center that was recessed into the right wall and turned on the CD player. While she flipped through the CD collection, she noticed that there was already a CD in the player ready to be keyed up. Reaching for the remote, she hit PLAY without checking to see what she was about to listen to. Suddenly, Eric Benet's sultry voice echoed through the spacious room. Gwen thought it unusual that Tiffany would be listening to Eric Benet since she always listened to Yolanda Adams, Kirk Franklin, or some of the other contemporary gospel artists.

As she listened, she felt a warm sensation run down her spine. It was an unusual feeling, leaving a weird chill throughout her body. She decided to lie down a moment before taking a shower. The evening had been a little more eventful than she thought it would be. The conversation would linger and play over and over again in her head, like a song that was out of beat. What was Tori trying to tell them? Was she just frustrated with the ratio of decent men to decent women? Gwen just couldn't be sure.

Still completely dressed, she slipped under the comforter and pulled it up to her neck. She could smell Tiffany all around her. Gwen attempted a smile that didn't register for her brain to alert her mouth. Tears made their way to her eyes and fell against her cheeks. She spoke a whisper in the darkness. "Tiff, how did we come to this? I don't understand how this could happen to you. I just need to make some sense of this."

Gwen suddenly realized that she had been listening to the same song over and over again. The CD was a single; Eric was singing about spending his life with someone. Her eyes jumped as if she had been hit out of nowhere with an unseen force. "There was someone, wasn't there, Tiff? You were in love, and knowing you, you never stopped loving him." Gwen reached for a pillow and held it tight. "Who was it?"

Gwen thought about the journal that Tiffany always kept. She knew exactly where to find it, but she was too mentally exhausted to get up and look through Tiffany's drawer for it. She would read it later and hope that it would shed some light on this whole ordeal.

Gwen could hardly open her eyes. She was a little dazed, and figured she must have dozed off. Reaching her fingers up to the inner corners of her eyes, she rubbed softly. When she opened her eyes, Tiffany was sitting next to her smiling.

"Girl, you always did sleep hard. I've been sitting here

looking at you slobber all over my pillow." Tiffany started to laugh.

"You're one to talk. I'm still trying to figure out what sawmill you worked for after school with all that snoring you did at night."

Tiffany playfully hit her with the small heart-shaped pillow that matched the comforter.

"Tiffany, I'm glad you're okay. I was worried about you. But I knew you would be just fine. I didn't even want to think about you leaving me."

"Gwenee, that's why I'm here." Tiffany helped Gwen sit up in the bed and took her hands into hers. "I'm going to have to leave you. It's time. My body is so weak, and I just can't fight this. I'm tired, Gwen."

"Come on, why are you talking like this? You've always been a fighter, and I've never known you to give up. It's just not in you." Gwen squeezed Tiffany's hands. "Ever since you were a child, you've been stubborn, never giving in to anything. You've got to fight like that now."

"Yeah, I know. But it's always been because you wouldn't let me give in. I just never wanted you to be disappointed. It was never really me who was strong. I was just blessed with a really strong sister who never let me give up. But, sweetie, it's my time now and because you, Mom, Dad, and T.J. are holding on so tight, I'm caught in the middle. You see, I can't go on because you all won't let me."

"What are you talking about? You can't want to leave us." Gwen moved her hand to Tiffany's cheek and turned her head toward hers.

"I'm caught between two worlds. Look. I'm prepared to go on. I'm not afraid of what's ahead of me. As much as I love you all, and God knows that I do, it's just time for me to rest. My body can't take all that it's going through. I'm just a shell lying there. The real me—the spiritual being—left that shell and is waiting to continue the journey."

Gwen looked down, not wanting Tiff to see her tear-stained face. "Tiffany, I can't let you go. I've always taken care of you, and this shouldn't be happening. You're too young. This is not the way you should go. Don't ask me to let you go. I can't, okay? I just can't."

Tiffany lifted Gwen's chin. " You have to. I'll be fine and I'm ready. I'm not scared. You know, heaven is a wonderful place and I've been preparing myself for this for a while now. I love you. Besides, you should know that I would never really leave you. A part of me will always be with you right there." She touched Gwen's chest right where her heart was pumping the blood that was now rushing quickly through her body. "They'll listen to you. Tell them to let me go. Gwen, my body can't withstand the battle. I've got to go on."

By now Gwen was crying uncontrollably and couldn't speak.

"Come here." Tiffany hugged her and smoothed her hair gently. "Please, Gwen, do this for me. Come on, say you will. I need to hear you say it."

Gwen held her tight and mumbled in her hair. "All right, Tiff." As soon as the words escaped from Gwen's lips, Tiffany stood up. She was adorned in white from head to toe. Her hair flowed down her back. Her face lit up with an angelic appeal, so different from the face that Gwen had looked upon during the past few weeks. This was her Tiffany, and she was at peace. Tiff blew her a kiss and turned to walk away. Gwen jumped up to reach out for her, but before she could get any closer, Tiffany disappeared.

Someone was banging on the door. "Gwen, baby, are you all right in there? I heard you screaming." Thomas came running through the door and lifted Gwen's head off the pillow. Her eyes were swollen from the tears, and she was trembling.

"Baby, are you okay? I told you to take it easy. You're

going to make yourself sick. Come now. Stop that there cryin'. Get yourself together. Everything is going to be all right. It might not seem like it right now, but it will."

Gwen fell into his arms. "No, it won't, Daddy. I've got to let her go."

It was barely daylight when they arrived at the hospital. It was so cold they could feel the chill down in their bones. Gwen had dressed in every warm piece of clothing she had in her suitcase, and even added Tiffany's down jacket, and still her teeth chattered as she got out of Tori's car. Patrice and Tori were exhausted from their late night and would be joining them later.

After the dream, Thomas and Gwen had talked for hours while she tried to shake the weird emotions she was feeling. The dream was more real than any she had ever had; she could remember everything about it. On top of that, her entire body was covered with hives.

Claire and Georgia were in the waiting room outside the ICU area. "Good morning, you all. We didn't think you all would be about so early." Mom got up slowly, her arthritis obviously causing her some pain. She stopped in front of her husband and kissed his cheek. "How'd you sleep, honey?"

"Oh, I'm okay, Claire. How your knees farin'?" A look of concern crossed his face as he bent down to rub through the fabric of her blue wool pants.

"Oh, I'm a tough old bird. A little pain ain't going to keep me down. I'm glad you all are here. Tiffany's doctors want to talk to us. The whole team of them. The nurse was calling the house to tell you all. They probably woke the girls up." Just as she got that out, Dr. Scott walked up to them.

"Good morning. I see the rest of the family is here, Mrs. James." Mom nodded. "Good. Well, if you all will follow me, we can go into the consultation room. Dr. Graham and Dr. Lewis are waiting for us."

As they followed Dr. Scott, Gwen's legs felt like they were moving through quicksand. The smell of ammonia and the pale beige walls closed in on her and she felt faint. T.J. noticed and quickly reached out for her.

"You okay? Come on now, you've got to hang in there for us." He held her arm and tried to steady her steps.

Gwen was suddenly so tired of being strong for everybody. Who was being strong for her? They reached a door that read, CONSULTATION ROOM, but it should have read, DOOR OF DOOM, because that's what it felt like they were entering.

Dr. Graham and Dr. Lewis stood up as they entered, and gave the family a hopeless smile. "Would any of you like some coffee?" Dr. Graham asked. They all declined.

"Can we just hear what you're fixin' to say?" Thomas could be a no-nonsense kind of man. He never had been one to avoid matters, good or bad. Today wouldn't be the day he'd start.

"Well, Mr. James, we need to make an important decision and we thought that this decision should be made by the family."

Dr. Scott continued, "We have the results of Tiffany's latest tests. Nothing has changed. In fact, she is growing worse. Despite all of our efforts, including the assistance with her breathing, the medicine that we started intravenously last week, and several other measures, Tiffany just isn't responding. The pneumonia is worse, and one of her lungs has shut down altogether. The other lung is taking a beating and starting to shut down as well."

Dr. Graham took over. "What Dr. Scott is trying to say, in a nutshell, is that Tiffany isn't breathing for herself; the machine is doing it all. I'm afraid we may be delaying the inevitable."

Mom jumped up as if a bolt of lightning had hit her. Her face was twisted in an agonizing glare. "What are you saying? That my baby is already dead? I won't listen to this crazy talk. She is still with us and you're going to keep that machine going." She began to scream. "Do you hear me? Keep it going!"

"Come on, Claire. Hear the doctors out." Thomas and T.J. were on either side of her, trying to get her to settle down and listen.

Gwen couldn't move. She could only hear Tiffany's words from last night echoing in her head loudly. If anyone else heard, they were not acknowledging it.

Dr. Lewis began to speak, sounding a little too feminine. "We know that this is a lot to absorb, but you had to have noticed that your constant vigilance over her hasn't caused her to respond to you in any way. We are basically shooting morphine in her every six hours to keep her comfortable. If it were not for the machine, Mrs. James, Tiffany would already have been gone. It's not going to get any easier for you all. In fact, it will only get harder. Not only is this taking a toll on her already-fragile body, it's very costly. We are going to leave you all to think about this. Take your time and let one of the nurses at the desk know when you're ready. They will page one of us."

Dr. Scott added, a little more sympathetically, "I wish there was something else we can do. But we've done everything. I'm so sorry." He continued to look at each of them, watching as the family started to unravel. It wasn't until Dr. Graham touched his arm that his head bowed in admitted defeat and he walked out of the room.

They all sat slumped over in their seats when the door closed, the noise sounding loud in the small room. Aunt Georgia, T.J., and Thomas were gathered around Claire, who was fussing and mumbling, "They just ain't going to stop that machine and let my baby die. As long as there is breath in her body, there is hope. Tell them that, Thomas! You go on out there and tell them that!"

Gwen was staring down at the gray and white squares of tile on the floor. Maybe if she stared long and hard enough they could all slip through the cracks to a world that was fair and that made perfect sense. A world where Tiffany would be well and they wouldn't be there having to make a life-and-death decision. Why was this man who held so many degrees asking them to play God? Didn't he know that their parents had only provided the physical act of conceiving her? The man up above was actually responsible for breathing life into her mortal body.

As if she heard some orchestra in the distance start up, Gwen tilted her head, trying to listen. Through the haze of the soft wind instruments she could hear Tiff talking to her. "Gwen, you have to tell them. I can't stay in between. You promised me. I've got to go. Tell them now."

Before the last word hit her ear she spoke out. "We have to let her go." All eyes were on her, questioning her outburst.

"What are you saying, Gwen?" Thomas was in front of her, lifting her face up so he could see if she had somehow lost her mind in the section of floor she had been looking at. Gwen attempted to stand up quickly, but her legs were like wet noodles and wouldn't obey. He reached over, grabbed hold of her arm, and held her tight.

"Mom, you raised us to believe in God for a miracle when we needed it the most. To have faith and trust him. Tiffany has laid there in that hospital bed for almost a month with no sign of progress, and right now the machine is breathing for her." Gwen reached out to her mother and continued. "Tiffany is caught between two worlds, and if God is ready for her, we can't hold her back. If it's not his will, then she will breathe on her own."

Claire pulled away hastily. "I can't believe you're saying

this." She turned her back. "She's too weak and fatigued to do anything on her own. Yes, I taught you all to have faith, but I think that right now we should let the doctors do all they can. I mean all that they can to help her."

"Mom." T.J. stood in front of her, stopping her from charging out of the room. "I believe the doctors are telling us that they have done everything they can. I don't want to see Tiffany lying there all hooked up if it means that she's no more than a vegetable. Come on. You can't want that either. Tiffany wouldn't want that."

"How do you know what Tiffany would want? She can't tell us." Claire was screaming at T.J. now. She couldn't believe that Gwen could even come up with such a crazy notion. Who was she to say that her Tiffany should be taken off the life support?

"Look, everybody, Tiffany doesn't want it." Gwen paused and continued slowly. "She wouldn't want to be kept here like this. We discussed it before. She said it would be like being caught in between two worlds. This is just too much. It's like torture." The inside of Gwen's mouth felt swollen. She tried to talk and felt as though she was choking. She started coughing, wheezing, and crying at the same time. Georgia came over, sat down, and rubbed Gwen's face with a lace handkerchief that smelled of peppermint and musk perfume.

Thomas spoke. "Claire, sweetheart. Gwen and T.J. are right. I don't know much about medicine or all these modern-day devices these fancy doctors use, but I do know that my baby girl is in there taking a beating. This damn disease is going through her body quicker than they can fight it. I watched her struggle, trying to breathe before this machine took over, and I couldn't bear to stay in the room. I watched her face change when the pain got bad. Even those large doses of medicine couldn't hide that pain. If I could take any of it away, God knows I would. I can't stand seeing her like this.

Baby, come here." Claire turned her face into his chest and began to cry harder. "It's in God's hands. We got to let him do what's right."

Thomas nodded to T.J. to go get the doctors, and Gwen walked over and allowed her dad to hold her while he held on to her mom.

Claire never bothered to look at Gwen or to comfort her in any way. She stood in her husband's arms and allowed her life to vanish into the floor.

Through all the hurt, tears, and emptiness, Gwen wished she could take Tiffany's place in this nightmare. As she watched her mother withdraw slowly into the confines of her pain and anger, she wondered if being in that bed instead of Tiffany would make it easier for her mom.

Gwen stood alone feeling the need for a private conversation with her baby sister. She held the single yellow rose tighter as the wind blew hard against her face. Yellow roses had always been their signature color for roses. Gwen thought they looked so delicate and fragile and Tiffany had always agreed.

Patrice stood by her car in the distance, waiting for Gwen to say good-bye. She understood, and yet didn't want to be too far away.

Gwen began to try to talk to Tiffany despite the lump in her throat. "Well, sweetie, I kept my promise. Mom will probably never forgive me, but you can continue your journey now. You are finally free. But you didn't tell me how I'm supposed to go on without you. How do I get past this? Tiffany, why? I've never understood why you didn't tell me. I could have done something. There's so much I don't understand. So many questions. Pastor said today that 'weeping endureth for a night, but joy cometh in the morning.' You're the religious one. Tell me, how can tomorrow be better than today?"

Gwen looked up hopelessly. "I wore blue today despite Mom advising me that black was the appropriate color. But you told me at Uncle Vernon's funeral that death is a celebration of life. So, Tiffany Tasha James, I'm thankful for your life and for your being my sister."

Gwen shifted the rose to her other hand and wiped at the tears that drifted down her cheeks. "I couldn't have picked a more giving and loving sister in all the world. I always thought I had to protect you, but you were the brave and strong one, enduring this illness for as long as you did. Sweetheart, you will always be my hero. I am going to miss taking care of you. T.J. has never enjoyed me fussing over him; you were always the opposite." Gwen hiccupped through the tears and tried to laugh. "Tiffany, please, please tell me. How do I go on?" She was on her knees now crying, holding on to the wet petals of the yellow rose. She had been holding it so tight that blood was beginning to trickle down her wrist. Gwen's nails had pushed the brier into her cold, wet palm.

Someone was touching her shoulders and pulling her to her feet. It had to be someone strong because it only took one swift pull.

"Not yet, please not yet. I can't leave her. She needs me." Gwen was crying harder than ever.

Gwen turned slowly and looked up into what she thought was T.J.'s face and found it was Marcus who held her tightly with tears in his eyes. This man she hadn't seen in years was sharing her pain, as if what they had once shared still stood. The funeral service had been packed, but Gwen did catch a glimpse of Marcus as she walked in with the family. She wasn't surprised because, despite the way their relationship had ended, she knew that he would want to be there for her and her family.

"It's okay, baby. I've gotcha."

Gwen turned once more and dropped the battered rose with traces of her blood on the petals on top of the white casket. She spoke again to Tiffany, her voice a faint painstaking whisper. "I love you, Tiff."

CHAPTER 7

Gwen had been driving for three hours. In the distance, she could see the tall buildings as she approached the downtown district. Reaching down, she changed the radio station to FM 99 and sang along with R. Kelly's "I Believe I Can Fly." What good timing for a deep song like that. She drove along and thought about the lyrics, trying to imagine what her life would unfold. She had just spent the past six months in a daze, not yet recovering from Tiffany's death and not wanting to.

Work had become just a place to go to spend a few hours a day. Her evenings were uneventful. She had grown tired of crowding in on T.J. and his family whenever she felt alone or needed to be around people whom she felt cared for her. Even though he and Kim were always so welcoming, she knew that they needed their space.

Her relationship with her mother had become so strained that being in the same room was awkward. No, her mother didn't come right out with it, but it was obvious that she felt that Gwen was somehow responsible for the choice that had been made. A choice that her mother had felt was untimely. If they had only listened to Claire and let the machine work a while longer, she wouldn't have stood in the dead of winter burying her baby girl. That day, with the coldness of it, would never lose its gripping hold on her heart and her spirit.

After some soul-searching, Gwen had decided to take a leave of absence from Westcott and Windsor Communications and go to Richmond, Virginia for a while. Patrice had begged her for months, and everyone felt that some time away would do her good. Not wanting to invade on Patrice's turf, Gwen made arrangements to stay at her girlfriend's house. Kyra needed someone to house sit and this arrangement was ideal.

Gwen and Patrice had met Kyra Simmons during their second semester. She moved into the dorm room next to them and the three hit it off instantly. Kyra was as bright and intelligent as the twosome. Captivating light brown eyes and high cheekbones settled on her gold-brown face. Kyra's academic preparation and hard work had paid off, and she had recently moved to New York for a one-year fellowship. The timing was perfect for Gwen's temporary move. It hadn't taken long for Kyra to convince Gwen that she would rather have her stay in her house than go through the trouble of finding someone interested in leasing it.

Coming out of her daze, Gwen found herself in the middle of downtown Richmond. It was well after the five o'clock rush, and still the streets were crowded. She reached down and dialed her cellular phone. After a few rings, a rich voice answered, "Hello, Patrice Henderson."

"Hey, stop trying to sound all professional. You know you probably got on a G-string under your business suit." Gwen laughed at her own comment.

"Hi to you too, Ms. Thang. And how did you know what I have on? I didn't see you in my bedroom this morning."

"Because I know you. You have this thing about being ready for anything."

"Yeah, well. I'm sure I've had more play than your cobweb-covered passion haven. If you don't use it soon, it will probably dry up and fall off."

"Thanks a lot. Tell me, why did I decide to spend my time off close by you and subject myself to your insults daily and in person?" Gwen was catching the sights that passed by on the sidewalks while she waited for the bumper-to-bumper traffic to move. She almost forgot how flamboyant city people could be.

"'Cause you love me." Patrice closed her electronic organizer after completing her last task of the day. "Now where are you?"

"Downtown. I thought that I would catch you before you left. I was going to drop my things off at Kyra's and meet you at your place so we can grab some dinner, unless you have plans already."

"I may be a little into myself, but I knew you would be here, and despite my two-way blowing up all day and my phone ringing endlessly, I didn't make any plans. I'm so excited. This is going to be like old times." Patrice had been at her desk all afternoon waiting for Gwen's call.

"Yeah, I know. Well, get out of there and go home. I'll be at your place around eight. Is that good?"

"Works for me. Gwen?"

"What?"

"I'm glad you're here." Patrice didn't want to get too emotional on the phone. She attempted to cut her comment short. "I've been worried about you."

"I know. I'll be fine. I just need to get my head together. You think we can go to Humphrey's after dinner? I haven't been there in—God, I can't even remember."

"Whatever. That jazz stuff puts me to sleep. But if that's what you want to do, I'll suffer through it. Keep in mind, though, if there are no good-lookin' brothers up in there, I'm outta there with quickness. As much as I love you, I don't care much for places that don't have at least five good-lookin' brothers to choose from."

"That's your problem. You always got to be getting your groove on. Can't we just go out, have a good evening, and enjoy the atmosphere? I mean, would it kill you if you didn't make a lust connection?"

"Okay, Ms. Saint. I keep forgetting those that do it keep it going and those that don't hate. Tonight, I'll forget about my sexual appetite and give you my undivided attention. Is that cool?"

"You'd do that just for me?" Gwen replied sarcastically.

"Yes, Gwendolyn James! Now hang up and leave me alone before I change my mind."

"Love you too. I'll see you later." Clicking off her cell phone, she dropped it down on the passenger seat and concentrated on the slow-moving traffic. Fifteen minutes later, she was driving through the gate of Valley Heights Estates. Gwen reached in her tote bag on the floor to grab the envelope with the house number, garage opener, keys, and the other important information that Kyra had sent her. Driving slow, she spotted the house, made a sharp left into the driveway, and clicked the garage open. Gwen had only been to visit Kyra one time since she moved into the house several months ago. The neighborhood seemed quiet, and the area was beautiful and ritzy. It was an upscale community, as reflected in its manicured lawns and hedges. Gwen had to grin. Her selection of neighborhood and housing would probably have been similar if she had remained in the city.

Turning the engine off and clicking the garage opener she got out and went to open the trunk. Gwen grabbed a couple of her suitcases and headed toward the door. As soon as she did, the alarm went off, scaring her. She jumped back, throwing everything on the floor. Darn! She forgot the alarm system. Running back to the car, she grabbed the envelope and retrieved the slip of paper with the alarm code on it. By the time she got back inside the house, the alarm was alerting the neighborhood that she was an intruder. After finding the light and three failed tries at disarming the alarm, she successfully turned off the noise. By that time the phone was ringing. *What next?* Gwen thought. She went into the living room, flipped on another light, and reached for the French phone.

Out of breath, she spoke into the phone. "Hello."

"Yes. This is Access Alarm and the alarm at this residence alerted us. Could you give us the access code and verification number, please?"

"Yeah, just wait a minute. I am staying here for a while. My girlfriend, Kyra Simmons, is the owner. She's away in New York and I just arrived in town. Hold on." Gwen put the phone down and backtracked to get the envelope. She noticed the cordless phone on the wall in the kitchen. After she picked it up, she reached for the envelope.

"Hello, I've got it here." Gwen recited the numbers like she was chanting a spell. Obviously it was just the spell she needed to cast out the evil alarm spirit because he quickly said, "Thanks" and, "Good night."

For the next hour, Gwen unpacked the car and carried everything upstairs to the bedroom. Since this would be her home away from home for a while she put her things away and began the task of acquainting herself with her new surroundings. Kyra's house was very glamorous with a contemporary flair. Everything was tastefully decorated, and artwork and sculptures were arranged throughout the house. There were two bedrooms upstairs with a separate bath for each one. The master suite had a bay window overlooking a lake, a large walk-in closet, and skylights. There was a large study next to the master bedroom. One wall was covered with a natural oak bookshelf, each with six shelves. Two beige side chairs sat across from the bookcase, and a large oak contemporary-style desk was positioned in the center of everything. The two large windows were treated with natural oak mini-blinds and burgundy scarf valances that coordinated with the oriental rug. Gwen walked to the bookshelf and scanned the shelves. The shelves were packed with every English higher academia text one could name. Kyra took her profession as a tenured faculty member at their alma mater seriously and gave of herself unselfishly to every student who enrolled in her classes.

At eight sharp she was entering the lobby of Patrice's condo. Buster was on duty and recognized her immediately. He was much more than the security guard for the building, Buster was like a grandfather to Patrice. He was a sweet old man, and was always in good spirits. He and his wife had become substitute relatives, and Patrice enjoyed every minute of it. She had told him that Gwen was coming, and his face lit up as soon as she came through the doors.

"Hey there, sunshine. How's life treating you?" Buster smiled and gave Gwen a big hug.

"I'm living, Mr. Buster. You keeping my girl straight?" Gwen chuckled and winked her eye at him.

"You know that's damn near impossible. That girl's slowest step is too fast for me. She needs you around to keep her out of trouble." Buster smiled and patted Gwen's shoulder.

"Well, Mr. Buster, I'll do what I can while I'm here. It's good seeing you, and tell your wife I'll be by to see her as soon as I get settled."

"I'll do that." He nodded and turned to greet some other tenants.

Gwen went up to the seventh floor, walked down the hall, and rang Patrice's doorbell. She could hear her coming toward the door screaming her name. Gwen was smiling so hard her cheeks were hurting. When Patrice finally swung the door open, Gwen could hardly say hello before Patrice had her in a bear hug as she screamed, "Oh, my Boo is here!"

Patrice finally let her go. They did their happy dance and began to sing in unison, "We gonna have a good time, a good time."

"Girl, you are too gone. There's got to be some medication available somewhere in Richmond for that sickness you got. I would hate to think of you living like this for the rest of your life." Gwen was laughing at their display of affection. To say they had missed each other would be a major understatement.

"Don't hate me because I'm perky, beautiful, and sexy." Patrice put her hands on her hips and threw her head back in a diva pose. "And besides, you are just as happy to see me as I am you. I can tell 'cause your dimples are deep enough to float a cruise ship." They hugged again and just looked at each other. It had been three months since they had seen each other because of their busy schedules. But despite Patrice's schedule, she called every single night. They would talk until the wee hours of the morning after her dates or on her rest evenings when it was just her, a pint of Häagen-Dazs, and Calgon.

"Let's go. I'm starved and you know how Friday night dinner crowds can be. Where are you taking me anyway?" Gwen rubbed her stomach. She hadn't eaten since she had gotten to town.

"We're heading to the West End, and we can cruise the main strip on the way to Humphrey's. Just leave the adventure and the driving to me." Patrice grinned wickedly. Gwen knew she was up to something, but asking her would be a waste of time, so she decided to just go with the flow.

They chitchatted about this and that while on the expressway and listened to a local radio station that was airing Michael Baisden's syndicated radio show "Love, Lust, and Lies." Patrice raced past cars and fussed at slow drivers until they hit their exit. They pulled into the parking lot of Skilligalee Restaurant. Gwen had forgotten all about this restaurant. It was one of her favorites, not only because of the good seafood, but also because Marcus had taken her there on their first date.

"All righty. Come on, ho. Let's go eat." Patrice was

putting on her lipstick and trying not to cast a glance in Gwen's direction.

"You know you wrong, don't you?" Gwen tried to look upset when, in fact, she wasn't.

"What, Gwen? You love seafood." She tried to sound all innocent.

"This was where Marcus and I went on our first date and on special occasions." Gwen felt a little sentimental when the words escaped through her lips.

"Oh, my bad. Sorry I didn't remember that. I mean, if I had, I would probably have decided on some place else. It's not like I would remember a detail like that. What was that, ten years ago? I brought you here because this place has the best seafood in town." She was speaking nonstop and never turned around to look at Gwen once as they entered the restaurant and were seated. "Besides, that shouldn't bother you; it's not like you still think about him. Whenever I mention his name, you change the subject."

Gwen finally interrupted. "Patrice, stop and breathe. You know your butt ain't slick, so stop the b.s., I'm not buying any of it. I'm going to enjoy my meal in spite of your pitiful effort to add memories of Marcus to our evening." Gwen smiled and opened the menu. When she looked up Patrice was staring at her. "What? I didn't dress to your liking? Is it my hair or makeup?" Gwen touched her hair and then opened her bag to get her small compact makeup bag.

"You look nice. Your hair is too cute and your face has a perfect glow. Not to mention that outfit. Girl, it is the bomb." She gave her a thumbs-up. "I think this rest period will do you good. There's nothing like smelling some smog-filled, overpopulated air to get you feeling as good as new."

"You're right, now let's order." Gwen was glad that she had decided on the midnight-blue pantsuit. Under the jacket she had decided to go against her norm and wear a black lace camisole. Minutes before she walked out the door, she had finally decided on white gold accessories and a pair of black Gucci sandals. She had taken the time to get a manicure and pedicure before she left home, so her nails and toes were looking cute. Gwen was pretty satisfied with her look tonight, and Patrice's compliment elevated her ego just a little bit more.

They feasted on appetizers, an array of seafood, and key lime pie for dessert while they talked about everything under the sun. Patrice wanted to reassure her her life would return to normal and the only way she would get over Tiffany's death was to talk about it. Patrice knew it would happen eventually, but now was not the right time.

As if reading Patrice's thoughts, Gwen couldn't help but think about the reason she was here. Tiffany's death was still so fresh in her mind that the pain just would not go away. She had not slept through the night once since Tiffany had been hospitalized, and she was beginning to think that the anxiety would never go away. Six months had done nothing to ease the edge of her sorrow. She had to admit it was good to relax and spend time with Patrice. She had really missed her. Gwen had heard the adage many times that laughter is good for the soul. She certainly hoped so, since she had been laughing so much for the past two hours that her sides were hurting. Maybe the time away would soothe her soul.

"Are you ready for the rest of your adventure, Ms. James?"

"I'm feeling so relaxed, I could sit here all night." Gwen stretched.

"You better come on before I change my mind." Patrice complained as she paid the check. "All these new clubs in the area with fine brothers hanging out the doors and you want me to carry you to Humphrey's. Imagine that!"

"Yes, and you already agreed, so give up the drama." Gwen reached over and pinched Patrice playfully on the arm.

"Ouch! That hurt! I don't like pain unless it's mixed with some pleasure. Speaking of pleasure, Andre's officially opens tonight. You want to check it out?" Patrice pouted her lip and looked over at her with a "please change your mind just for me" look.

"We can check Andre's out later. Tonight, we are going to be up in Humphrey's. I'm so excited. It's the place to be. You want me to drive?" Gwen was bubbling over.

"Heavens no. I'd like to prolong, I mean, drive slowly so we can enjoy the nightlife. This area has grown a lot."

They drove down the strip and turned onto Monument Boulevard. The old historical houses in the area were always so interesting. It was as if each house had its own story to tell. Gwen remembered driving through when she was in college, imagining what it was like when the houses were first built. After a few turns they pulled in front of Humphrey's. It hadn't changed, and Gwen could hear the music beckoning her to come in. She had waited so long and now she was moving slowly. She could sense a funny feeling overcome her. Dismissing it as nervous jitters, she got out of the car and waited on the sidewalk for Patrice.

"Come on, girl. Let's get inside. Can't you hear that alto sax calling me?" Gwen was looking at her smiling.

Putting her hand to her ear, Patrice replied, "No, I don't think it's you they are calling. I think they are trying to wake the dead over in the Monument Cemetery." She cracked up, laughing at her own joke, and could hardly straighten up.

Gwen tried not to laugh, but it was funny. "Ha, ha, very funny. Now come on."

Walking toward the club, she could see from the doorway that there was a crowd inside. People were packed in and more stood behind them waiting to get inside. Gwen glanced at the small portable marquee and grabbed Patrice's arm hard.

"Trice, Trice. Rachelle Ferrell is here tonight. I can't believe it. I bet we can't get a seat anywhere. You think they got any seats left? Huh?" Gwen was talking to Patrice and her eyes were scanning the crowded room for a couple of seats. When she turned, Patrice was talking to a tall, slender guy.

Gwen was getting pissed. She could miss her one and only chance to see Rachelle, and Patrice was busy conversing.

"Patrice, what are you doing?" Gwen asked, annoyed.

"Getting us two seats. Do you want to follow this guy or complain all night?"

They walked through the crowd toward the center table—the best seats in the house. Gwen couldn't believe their luck. This was an evening she wouldn't forget.

"How did you do this? What did you . . . No, I don't want to know." Gwen put up her hand.

"Then don't ask." Patrice was looking around. "I'm going to need a drink, preferably a double."

"Okay. I love you. You're my best bud."

She cut Gwen off. "Yada, yada, yada. Yeah, yeah, yeah. Of course I am at this particular moment. Your favorite club, your favorite singer. I could spit in your hand right now and you'd clean it off and say thank you."

A server came over, ready to take their drink orders. Patrice ordered an apple martini and Gwen decided to go light in case she had to drive. But after a quick review of the facts that there were several cab services available and that she was about to see Rachelle, she ordered the same.

Patrice's eyes widened. "Are we playing big girl tonight?" she chastised.

"I'm living, girlfriend. Just living." Just then the lights dimmed and the crowd started clapping. Gwen was joining them on the edge of her seat.

Rachelle came out and opened with a cut off her last CD, "Satisfied." Her new image was different, but Gwen loved her, so it didn't matter. She was grooving along with Rachelle and the crowd and was enjoying every moment of it. Despite her dislike for jazzy tunes, Patrice was soon bouncing along to the beat.

Gwen leaned over and yelled over the music, "What happened? I thought this was the valley of dry bones."

"Girl, I like some of her stuff and as of two drinks ago the martinis have taken over my body." They both laughed.

When Gwen focused back on the stage, Rachelle had slowed it down and was speaking to the crowd. "I hope you all have enjoyed my grooves tonight. Is everybody feeling me?" She spoke into the microphone.

The crowd responded with screams, yells, whistles, and claps.

"Yeah, I thought so. Well, I came through Richmond as a special favor to a friend of mine. I was en route to New York from Atlanta and received a call just this morning asking me to swing this way. And because of my love for this brother, I agreed. I see he got the word out and packed the house."

Again the crowd responded.

"He wanted me to drop by Humphrey's and do a set for one of my biggest fans. He asked that I do something special for her and let her know that she's special. So this closing song is just for her."

Gwen's stomach tightened again. She glanced over at Patrice, who looked away as she summoned a server for another drink. She turned back around and sat back to enjoy the last song.

"Is there a Gwen James in the crowd tonight? Come on. I hear you're my biggest fan."

Everyone looked around and so did Gwen until Patrice looked at her and said, "Fool, what's your name?"

Rachelle said again, "Gwen, are you here? Just wave your hand."

This had to be a joke. But Gwen finally raised her hand in the air and waved it. People cheered.

"It's nice to meet you, Gwen." Rachelle smiled.

Gwen decided she was going to kill Patrice. Obviously, she had planned this with one of her boyfriends. Gwen just blushed and smiled broadly. Everyone's eyes were fixed on her.

Rachelle continued. "Gwen, I guess you're wondering who invited me."

Gwen nodded.

"This wonderful, handsome man who happens to be a good friend and sometimes a nuisance. No, I'm just joking. He's a real good person, and I got nothing but love for him." She was pointing toward the door. As Gwen turned to follow the direction she was pointing in, Rachelle said, "Mr. Marcus McGuire, wave to Gwen and to this wonderful audience." Marcus stood at the door, was dressed in a beige five-button Armani blazer with matching slacks. A black silk crew neck fit snuggly underneath. His eyes danced and his skin radiated its usual sheen. Time had definitely played in his favor, and he was as good-looking as ever. His silky black wavy hair was looking good, with not a strand out of place. Even from this distance Gwen could tell that his outfit only accented what was already perfect.

Gwen couldn't close her mouth. Their eyes locked and she was completely caught up in the moment. She felt as though she was in the middle of a dream. The music started again and Rachelle began to send them further into their clone of memories with "Nothing Has Ever Felt Like This." Gwen was swept away. Marcus knew it was one of her favorite songs. Gwen couldn't move, couldn't think. She was being transported to another time and another place. She fought the urge to go to him, unable to even wipe the one lonely tear that had slipped out of the corner of her eye and was somehow connected to that closed, cemented portion of her heart. A soft touch on her shoulder got her attention. She turned and looked up into Marcus's smiling face.

"Surprise, baby. Do you think I can have the dance?"

Gwen obliged and reached for his offered hand. It was as soft as she'd remembered. She followed him to a section of the floor that appeared to be waiting for them. Turning around to face her, he pulled her close to him. The Issey

Miyake he was wearing immediately seduced her. Resting her head against his chest, she floated across the floor. They danced in silence, and soon she no longer saw the crowd, or Rachelle, or Will Downing's vocal twin onstage, but only felt the residue of a strong love that still existed and was alive at that very moment.

The applause started. She attempted to step back, but Marcus continued to hold her hand tightly while leading her back to the table. Patrice couldn't read her expression and only threw her hands up in helpless defense before Gwen could say a word.

"Gwen, don't blame Patrice. She was only helping me out. You're not mad, are you?" He bent down, and kissed her lightly on the cheek.

"No, I'm fine. Thanks for the surprise." Everything made sense: the restaurant choice, getting tickets for a packed house at the last minute, and the center table. Marcus had planned everything.

Just then, Rachelle came over and hugged Gwen. They all talked for a few minutes; then she handed Gwen an autographed copy of her CD and said good-bye. Marcus asked them to stay put as he walked Rachelle out to her waiting limo.

When he returned he was still smiling. Marcus said good night to the tall guy Patrice had been talking to and gave him an envelope. They did the brother-man hug, and he turned to them. "Come on, beautiful ladies, let me walk you outside."

They laughed and talked about old times for almost an hour, each of them remembering something that the others had almost forgotten. Suddenly, the conversation slowed down.

"Gwen, can I take you back across town, or maybe see you tomorrow for brunch or dinner? It doesn't matter. I would just like to spend some time with you and talk." Marcus spoke, hoping to receive a positive response.

Gwen looked down at the sidewalk then pensively at

Patrice hoping her friend would throw her a lifeline. "I'll ride back with Patrice and I don't think it's a good idea for us to see each other."

"Why?" He looked disappointed. "No, that's okay, don't answer that. I'm in town to help Andre with the club. So, if you change your mind, get in touch with me."

"Thanks, Marcus. But I won't be changing my mind." It took every ounce of strength she had to get into the car and leave him standing there.

After a minute Patrice started the engine and pulled away. They rode in silence for a while.

Patrice finally spoke. "Why did you turn Marcus down flat like that? He did all that just for you. You could have at least agreed to eat with the man. Damn it, Gwen! That was some cold shit. The past is the past. We were young then."

"Trice, I just lost Tiffany, and I lost Marcus once. Not to death, but I lost him just the same. I couldn't stand losing him again."

Patrice stopped as they approached a red light and she turned to look at Gwen. "How do you know that you would?" She reached over and took Gwen's hand.

"How do you know that I wouldn't?"

CHAPTER 8

Gwen spent all night turning and twisting. She could easily have blamed it on being in a strange environment, had she not struggled since Tiff's passing with nightmares and internal battles just to stay snuggled under the sheets till daybreak. She spent countless nights begging sleep to overtake her mortal body.

She finally threw her pillow to the floor in frustration and got up. The aromatherapy candle that she burned right before going to bed did nothing to help her sleep. But why should it? It never had before.

Reaching for her robe at the end of the bed, Gwen stumbled downstairs. She looked into the refrigerator and smiled. Kyra had stocked everything before she left. On the kitchen counter there was a note on lavender paper that she had overlooked when she arrived. Gwen picked it up and read:

Yes, I know you too well. I figured you would be rushing and would forget to go to the store to pick up simple things like bread, eggs, milk, ice cream, etc. So I ran to the grocery store before I left town. Do I love you or what? Gwen, I hope you will use this time to heal. I want you to be well. I know what you're thinking . . . I'm being a mother hen. If you need me, please call. I left all the numbers in the top right drawer of the desk in the study. Enjoy!

Kyra really was too much. But Gwen had to admit that she did know her. In the rush of the evening, she had never once thought about checking the refrigerator or going to the grocery store. Kyra had always played mom to all of them. She picked up after everyone when they all shared their first apartment off campus. When they were sick, she was the one to go the drugstore and pick up everything from Sucrets to chest rub.

Gwen leaned against the counter as she thought about how they were then and how they still continued to get along so well. Some things never changed. The lasting friendship between the gang was one of them. She viewed it as a special gift. She had met people who had become friends, and when distance or their perspective changed, the friendship suffered, reduced to nothing more than a brief hello if their paths crossed. There were no letters, cards, or phone calls. Gwen was not a betting woman, but she would have no problem putting up everything she had in her account to wager that they would never turn their backs on one another.

She made a mental note to call Kyra later and let her know how much she meant to her. She took a swallow of orange juice and smiled while imagining telling Kyra that despite enjoying the orange juice, she was still a mother hen and she would have made it to the grocery store eventually.

Walking into the living room, Gwen looked at the clock on the mantel. It was only five o'clock, but she didn't see any use in going back to bed. She knew that she wouldn't be able to sleep. If her sleep pattern didn't change soon, she would have to seriously think about going to see someone. The idea of airing her embedded hurt while lying stretched out in a horizontal position didn't thrill her, but she couldn't go on like this.

The last evening before leaving town she had dinner with T.J. He suggested that she make an appointment to talk with a psychiatrist. Denial and hurt had taken over and she lashed out at him. She knew he meant well; what bothered her was that she wanted to be "together" for him. What if he was having a hard time coping with Tiffany's death? Then he would need her shoulder. She just didn't want to appear like she was falling apart. On top of all that, she hadn't had a real conversation with her mom since the funeral. Life was really dealing her a terrible hand.

Turning back into the kitchen, she picked up the glass of juice she was drinking and headed to the solarium. As she curled up on the chaise lounge in an oversize T-shirt and robe, her eyes drank in the picture-perfect view. The sun-room faced the lake, and she noticed two breathtakingly beautiful swans that seemed to know that she was watching. They moved slowly back and forth as if they were putting on a show just for her.

Gwen uncurled her legs and put the glass down on the nearby table. She leaned back and reflected on the past evening and how special it made her feel. It was good to see Marcus again, and she had to admit that she was flattered by everything that had been arranged in her honor. There were feelings, strong feelings, that had remained. She had to admit, if only to herself, that those feelings scared her. Her past limited relationships—or lack thereof—proved to her that she was still holding on to the past, the good and the bad.

Attempting to force the thoughts out of her head, she continued looking out, noticing now that the morning was ushering in the sun like a proud bridegroom. Its stillness moved her and she couldn't turn away. It wasn't that she had never seen the sunrise before, but it was as if she was seeing it through different eyes. Life had changed and nothing had stayed the same. As desperately as she had wanted things to stay the same, they were changing so rapidly.

The sound of the phone made Gwen jump. Somewhere between the sunrise and reflecting, she had drifted off to sleep. She rushed into the living room and picked up the phone.

"Hello." Gwen sounded so dry, but didn't really care.

"Good morning, girly girl. How did you sleep?"

"Not so good. In fact, I've been up since five o'clock. I was in the solarium taking in the beautiful view of the lake. I guess I must have drifted off before you rang. What time is it?"

"Almost seven thirty. Listen. Jump into some shorts, a T-shirt, and sneakers. Oh yeah, and a cap. I'll be by in about fifteen minutes." Patrice was cheerful, considering it was still early.

"For what? I was going to relax the day away. Where are we going? And you know darn well it takes me a little longer than fifteen minutes to pull myself together." Gwen was whining.

"Stop your stuff! It's too early to listen to you whine. Just be ready." She hung up before Gwen could protest further.

Gwen finished her marathon dressing in the fifteen minutes that Patrice had allotted and decided to wait for her outside. Just as she closed the door behind her, she noticed a guy jogging into the cul-de-sac in navy blue shorts and a muscle shirt. She couldn't make out his appearance, but she could tell that he was well built. The lack of moisture in her mouth, alerting her that it was open, was telling her the same thing. Gwen tried to play it off when she saw that he was turning into the driveway.

"Good morning. You must be Gwendolyn James? Kyra mentioned that you would be moving in temporarily. I'm Kyra's next-door neighbor, Scott Elliott."

Scott extended his hand and flashed a smile that uncovered the prettiest set of pearly whites Gwen had ever seen.

His head was covered with what southern people would refer to as good hair; his complexion was butterscotch with a hint of caramel. On top of that, his cheeks and chin held the cutest dimples within their baby-smooth folds. Her ultimate weaknesses, good hair and dimples. She wanted to skip down the sidewalk and sing the Mr. Rogers theme, "It's a Wonderful Day in the Neighborhood," 'cause this neighbor was too wonderful.

"It's nice to meet you, Mr. Elliott." She smiled back and tried not to appear as nervous as she felt. She couldn't explain why she was nervous, but for some reason standing before this attractive man (who could very easily be a cover guy for an upscale magazine) had her nervous. Under all his sweat, she observed that Kyra's neighbor couldn't be over twenty-five years old. Maybe, he lived with his parents or was the companion of a well-to-do woman. Describing the residence next door as a "house" was a major understatement. A "mansion" would fit better. And from her quick observation, he was a bit young to acquire such wealth unless he was born into it. When his damp hand covered hers and squeezed slightly, she jumped as if an electrical current had shocked her.

"Oh, I'm sorry. My hands always get all hot and sticky when I jog." Scott looked down and rubbed his hands against his shorts.

"That's okay. Sweating is good."

He started laughing. "Is that so?"

"Well, that's what I read in some health magazine." She looked away. Of all the things to say, she would have to choose something that could be read in a seductive way. He had to have noticed that she was staring; the comment probably made her come across like some sex-craved hot mama.

"I guess I'll have to read more health magazines." He smiled again. "Well, Ms. James, I'm going to take a shower and join my mother for breakfast. I'll be seeing you around."

"Of course. Enjoy your breakfast." Gwen tilted her head to avoid the rays of the sun that were shining in her face.

"I know that you have some friends here, but I promised Kyra that I would check in on you periodically. If you need anything, just yell." He turned and jogged across the yard.

Gwen glanced at her watch. Just then Patrice came speeding into the driveway, blowing the horn. Gwen had been looking out for Patrice's convertible Mustang SVT; instead, she was leaning out the window of a sable-black Cadillac Escalade.

"Girl, what is this? You stomping with the big dogs these days?" Gwen was walking toward the passenger door.

"It's another one of my surprises. I've only had it a month and I'm loving it. It's big, but I'm getting used to it. I only drive it on weekends. When I take you to our morning appointment, you'll understand why I bought it." They hit the parkway and headed downtown.

Patrice was dressed in a pair of jean shorts and a navy blue T-shirt. There was a name scripted across the front; Gwen couldn't make it out. Patrice's hair was pulled up in a ponytail and she only had on a hint of lipstick.

Gwen decided on a black fitted T-shirt and a pair of jean shorts. She had gone through Kyra's things in the guest bedroom and found a white baseball cap with the VCU Ram emblem across the front. It sat on top of her short-cropped hair that she had opted to slick down after showering instead of the usual style she sported.

"Since when did you become a morning person?" Gwen glanced over at Patrice as she drove along happily.

"I've been a morning person for quite some time now. This project that I started over two years ago inspires me to do some things that I've never done before. When we get there, you'll understand a little more. By the way, how long you been waiting outside?"

"Oh, I was talking to Kyra's neighbor. I believe his name

is Scott." Gwen knew what his name was; she just didn't want Patrice to start up.

"What! The guy that lives next door? Girl, I've been trying to get a close peek at him for the longest."

"Well, I guess you can say I got an up-close and personal view. He introduced himself and told me to yell if I needed anything." Gwen tried to play it off by fumbling with the radio.

"I can think of a few things that I could use. But I bet you acted like Little Orphan Annie and didn't get the digits or a date. You probably didn't even get an invite for a Happy Meal." She busted out laughing.

"There you go. I'm here relaxing, not scouting. And besides, that boy is too young for either of us. I could smell breast milk on his breath."

"Dag, Gwen! You was that close? You should have just given him some tongue and made sure it was breast milk you were smelling and not Similac."

"Patrice, let me say this slow 'cause I know your mama dropped you on your head when you were a baby. I am not interested in getting into any one-on-one activity with no man. No matter what age. So, with that said, where we going?"

"Just sit back and ride. By the way, I was thinking that we could grab something to eat after our morning appointment," Patrice said while maneuvering through the interstate traffic.

"You know you don't have to entertain me. I realize you have things that you need to do. I'm no stranger to the area, and I don't want to intrude too much." Gwen was looking straight ahead knowing that she had hit a nerve.

"Look. I told you yesterday. I knew that you were coming, and if you don't mind, I would like to spend as much time with you as possible. Let me decide when to be tired of you. Unless, of course, there is another person other than Scott you'd rather see." Patrice grinned over at Gwen.

"Let's not go there. I will admit that I was flattered last

night, and I did think about Marcus after I got in; but let's just leave that conversation for later." Gwen looked out the window at the bow-tie-wearing guy crossing the street hustling to sell *The Final Call* magazine. The Muslims were so committed to their cause. It was barely 8:15 a.m. and right in the middle of traffic he was already pushing the magazines like there was no tomorrow.

"All right, Gwen. But we will talk about Marcus later. You two are both in town, and we all have the same friends, so avoiding him is not an option. And that's all I'm going to say about it. Besides, here we are."

They were pulling into the parking lot adjacent to a ball field. A group of teenage girls were standing in front of the building dressed in softball uniforms. Eyeing the color of the shirts, Gwen looked over at Patrice and noticed that her T-shirt was the same color. Patrice jumped out of the driver's seat and closed the door. Confused, Gwen got out, walked around, and stood beside her.

The girls gathered around Patrice, all talking at the same time. "Calm down, girls. I know I'm late, but we have half an hour before the other team arrives. I had to pick up my friend." She turned to Gwen. "Everybody, this is Ms. Gwen James. My very best buddy in the whole wide world." She gestured with her hands wide open to emphasize "wide."

Gwen rolled her eyes at Patrice; she could be so corny sometimes. "Hi. It's nice to meet you all." she smiled.

A light-skinned girl with microbraids walked up to her and extended a hand. She was obviously the spokesperson for the group.

"Hi. My name is Gina Webster. It's good to meet you. Ms. Patrice talks about you all the time. She's been so anxious for you to get here." She was beaming at Patrice.

"Oh, has she now?" Gwen was smiling too. "Well, this is certainly a surprise. But I'm sure I'll be seeing a lot of you all while I'm here visiting." She glanced at Patrice wondering why she didn't tell her that she was coaching a softball team. Patrice didn't know a thing about softball or any other sport. There had to be some man involved. She would just wait until he surfaced.

"Okay, girls. Let's go out on the field and warm up. Gina, get the equipment out and get everyone in their positions. I'll be right there. Kennedy, could you give Gina a hand?" A tall girl with long legs came toward them. "Sure. I don't mind."

Patrice finally turned toward Gwen and smiled. "What? Why are you looking at me like that?"

"'Trice. Did you forget to tell me anything on the way here this morning? Or better yet, during our many conversations did you forget to mention that you coach a sport that you know nothing about?" She playfully kicked Patrice's foot.

"Well, I should know something about it. I've been coaching softball and basketball for two years. When I'm not coaching the girls, I'm mentoring them. You know I'm every woman." She started to laugh.

"When did you become an expert? I didn't know this was something that interested you."

"Well, I decided one day when my boss approached me about everyone in executive and management positions doing community service work. When she passed me the list, I thought that I would pick something easy. So, I decided that mentoring a group of teenage inner-city girls once a week wouldn't take that much time. I mean, since I was once a girl myself." She smirked. "Well, after the first meeting with them, I was shocked. They were so smart-mouthed and sassy. They only talked about boys, sex, and getting their boyfriends to pay for hairdos and nails.

"The first month, I just wanted to give up. But I decided to stick it out. Besides, it was what my company required, and it would look good on my resume. Then it hit me one day as I was driving to a session. They reminded me of me.

And now I love working with them, and they seem to love me. So this is how I spend every Saturday and at least one or two evenings a week."

Gwen didn't know what to say. She could see a little sparkle in Patrice's eyes as she talked about the girls and what mentoring them meant to her. "I'm very proud of you, 'Trice." Gwen walked closer and hugged her.

"All right. Now, let's go get these girls ready for battle."

The game started. Gwen watched as Patrice yelled and screamed. She must have read a couple of how-to books, because the girls were leading by three. The excitement of the game eventually hit Gwen too; she found she was spending more time standing up cheering than sitting down. She was so excited that one of the parents asked her if she had a daughter playing. She responded, "No, but I have been taking care of the coach since she was in grade school."

The game ended with Gina hitting a home run. The players and the crowd went wild. Patrice was jumping up and down. Gwen couldn't remember the last time she had seen Patrice so excited about anything. She stood back and watched as Coach Henderson congratulated the other players and then hugged each of the girls who played for her team.

"I believe I owe you all a celebration pizza. What do you guys think?" Patrice was beaming with pride and clearly wanted to show her appreciation for their hard playing.

They responded in yells and screams.

"I'd prefer Red Lobster, but pizza will do," Gina stated sarcastically. She really did remind Gwen of Patrice. Obviously they had spent some time together. How else could she sound like her and act like her without being her seed?

"Mona, could you ask your mom if she could take a bunch of you in her minivan? I'll pile the rest of you in here." Patrice was gathering the equipment together.

"Gwen, you don't mind hanging out at Pizza Hut for a

while, do you? I did promise you a meal. And no one is there waiting to surprise you with jazz," she added mischievously.

"Of course I don't mind. I'd love to spend the afternoon with a bunch of teenagers whose hormones are probably raging and who will no doubt talk about boys the entire time."

"Sounds a lot like us in the early years, huh?"

"It sure does. Now let's go. I'm starved."

Gina ran up to Patrice and spoke hurriedly. "Ms. Patrice, my boyfriend is here, and he's going to take me for a ride. I'll see you guys at practice next week. Good game, Coach." Swinging her braids, she turned and walked toward a blue Range Rover with tinted windows.

"Gosh, the young fellows these days must be making some serious bank at McDonald's." Gwen was looking at the rims on the Range Rover that probably cost more than six months' worth of her car note.

"McDonald's doesn't pay the kind of money that Quincy is raking in. The boy is in deep with one of the neighborhood kingpins. In fact, I believe that the money he makes puts him up there as a kingpin himself. I worry about Gina. She's really into him. He treats her right, but I just don't like where his money comes from. She's with him twenty-four-seven, living the life, or so she thinks. I've been talking with her, but she's not hearing me."

"Well, you keep on talking. But if he is giving her things and exposing her to a life that she wouldn't know otherwise, you could be talking to deaf ears."

"I know. Come on, let's get some pizza. Just thinking about it makes me ill."

Gwen spent the rest of the afternoon with Patrice and the gang. They had a good time. Being around the young girls inspired Gwen in ways she didn't think possible. They showed a zest for life, asking her question after question. Everything from what she did for a living, to what she drove and whom she was dating. Gwen could see why Patrice had decided to volunteer. No matter how tough she tried to seem, she was just a loving person who had so much love to give. Gwen just hoped that she realized how very much she meant to the girls. They all listened to her as if she were Ghandi. It was wonderful to see that what she had to say was well worth their attention.

Patrice treated Gwen to a facial at a salon on the north side. They both walked out an hour later feeling relaxed and refreshed. After running a few errands, they returned to Kyra's house, deciding to order Chinese and settle in to enjoy their evening.

"'Trice, did I tell you that I had a long talk with Tori?" Gwen spoke while walking into the kitchen to get a bottle of wine out of the refrigerator.

"No, you didn't mention it. What did she have to say?" Patrice's forehead curled up in a puzzled look.

"Well, something had been bothering me for the longest. I tried to dismiss it, but for some reason it kept playing over and over in my head." Gwen opened the cabinet and pulled out two wineglasses, looked through the drawer for a corkscrew, grabbed the wine bottle, and joined Patrice on the living room floor. The patio door was open and a light breeze flowed through the room, mixing with the smell of jasmine.

"Spill it." Patrice poured both of them a glass of wine. Waiting for Gwen to talk, she removed her shoes and tucked her right leg under her butt.

"The night in Atlanta when we went out to dinner with T.J. and Tori, the three of us had a strange conversation." Gwen was staring straight at Patrice because she didn't want to miss her reaction. "T.J. and Tori got in a heated discussion about how men dog women, commitment, and some other things, when all of a sudden, Tori went off on T.J."

"I can relate. T.J. can be very irritating. I've gone off on him a time or two myself." Patrice grinned and sipped from her glass of wine.

"No, this was different. She exploded and turned as red as a beet. She ended her argument by saying that she understood why women turn to lesbian lovers. I mean, the way she said it sent chills down my spine." Gwen leaned over to pick up her glass, wanting to wash the taste of her statement out of her mouth.

"And you think she was trying to say what?"

"Well, at the time I thought she was trying to tell us that she was gay, bi, or some mess like that. So, I finally called her with the pretense of giving her my temporary address and phone number in case she needed to reach me." Gwen sat back further.

"And?" Patrice leaned forward.

"She cleared it all up. Tori said she had wanted to reassure me and T.J. that she was merely blowing off steam that night. On top of Tiffany's illness she discovered that her boyfriend had been playing her." Gwen paused, then continued. "Tori used that night to try to come to grips with the bomb that had just been dropped on her."

"Well, I'm glad you talked with her and I'm definitely glad she's straight." Patrice reached for the bottle of wine. "Girl that stuff is scary and I don't mind telling anyone that I'm all about getting my fix with a tool that is hard and long."

"I'm with you. It's been forever, but the only thing a sistah can do for me is point out a brotha." Gwen laughed with Patrice.

I know that's right." Patrice agreed with the comment just as the doorbell rang, announcing the arrival of dinner.

They turned the television to the Showtime channel and caught the movie *Love Jones,* talked, and drank wine until two o'clock in the morning. Patrice, feeling a little too light-headed to drive, crashed in the guest room. Gwen showered and went to bed. She couldn't believe how exhausted she was, and yet she knew she still wouldn't be able to sleep.

Gwen decided to go back downstairs and look around for a magazine. As she was getting out of bed, she glanced at the phone. Marcus had been on her mind all day. They were probably still at the club. Maybe she should have listened to Patrice and spent the evening at the club rather than sitting up drinking and watching television.

Just as she was walking down the steps, the phone rang. Any phone call after midnight had a way of unnerving her for obvious reasons. Walking into the living room, Gwen picked up the phone, not wanting it to wake up Patrice.

"Hello." She wrapped her hand around the phone, waiting for someone to respond.

"Gwen, I'm sorry. I know it's late, but you were on my mind." She could hear loud music and voices in the background.

"Marcus?" She knew who it was, but thought she would say his name out loud instead of having it echo in her mind.

"Yeah, it's me. I've been talking about you all evening to Andre and Vince, and I just couldn't take it any longer. I hope you're not upset that I called."

"No. How are the guys? And, of course, how's Richmond's newest hot spot, Andre's? The club's been blowing up all over the radio waves."

"Well, I guess Andre has one great promoter helping him out."

"Same old Marcus. You always did like to toot your own horn. I noticed the other night that your head is a little bigger than it used to be."

"I see you still got jokes and you still look good too, baby. You've picked up a few pounds, but from my observation they're all in the right place." Marcus could feel the bulge in his pants grow. Just thinking about Gwen was causing him to get excited. He had made love to her over and over and over again in his mind, and each time was better than the last. If she was half as good in reality as she was in his dreams, he was in for a real treat. They had dated for almost two years, and although they had shared the same bed and had many close calls, they had never made love.

Marcus recalled that one night after a frat party he had spent the night at Gwen's place. They had made out for hours until he was about to burst, but she would not allow him to penetrate her. He was so frustrated, but his love and respect for her only heightened. Gwen had always been his jewel, his special ruby, and the years that had gone by and the numerous women he had bedded hadn't changed that. No one was ever Gwen. Her body was perfect. He could remember how soft she was. He would lose himself in just fondling her. Her dreamy eyes, dimpled cheeks, and small delicate lips just enhanced her beauty. Marcus had traveled to many places, and he'd seen a lot of women, but Gwen had continued to be the most attractive woman he had ever known.

"Marcus, did you hear me?"

"I'm sorry, Gwen. I was in deep thought. What did you say?"

"I asked if Andre was around. I want to speak with him."

"He just went out for a few minutes. But I'll tell him to get with you tomorrow. Speaking of tomorrow. Gwen, would you please reconsider and have breakfast, brunch, dinner, or some type of meal with me? Even Jesus broke bread with the less fortunate." Laughter filled the phone line.

"You know it ain't right, using the Lord in your persuasion." Gwen was cracking up with him. "Call me around noon, and we will talk about it."

"What? Did you say you will consider it?" Marcus was smiling all over himself.

"Yes, I did. After all you went through Friday night, and

your pitiful effort of begging, I thought I would give you a break. Call me. Now, do you think I can go to bed?"

"Of course. Sweet dreams, baby." Marcus hung up the phone.

Gwen couldn't put the phone down. She just held it to her chest and closed her eyes. He had always ended their conversations late at night by wishing her sweet dreams. She really didn't like the feelings she was having, but she knew they wouldn't be going away any time soon. And what was the harm in having dinner? Putting the phone back in the cradle, she turned around and headed back upstairs forgetting all about the magazine. She rubbed her temple and wondered if she had just made a big mistake, but she figured she'd find out soon enough.

Marcus hadn't really changed that much, not unless you considered his being even more attractive than he had been back in the day. He was a pecan-tan wonder with black, wavy hair and a body that had no shame. His face was perfectly chiseled and his eyes were always so piercing. Yes, she had to admit it. Marcus McGuire had it going on. The problem back then was that everyone else on campus knew it too. His pledging a fraternity didn't help matters much. His popularity only grew. The same guy who used to have eyes only for her soon had girls at his beck and call, willing to do all of the things she wouldn't do.

Gwen snuggled under the sheets and tried to relax, but she couldn't slow the memories that came flooding forward. She remembered coming back early from Christmas break because she missed him terribly. He had decided to take a winter session course, and was staying in the apartment he shared with Andre since it was closer to the campus. Instead of calling, she decided to go straight to the apartment. Since all of them were close, Marcus had given her a key. Andre hadn't minded since she would always clean up, cook, and do their laundry. Major mistake—they had grown accustomed to her doing for them and wouldn't lift a finger to do for themselves.

Gwen recalled stopping in the hallway to look in the mirror at her reflection; she had wanted to make sure that everything was in place. Pleased at what she saw, she had continued down the hall and grabbed her keys to open the door. The minute she stepped inside, she could hear the soft sound of jazz and smiled because Marcus always studied with jazz in the background. The only other time he listened to jazz was when they were cuddled up. Gwen had thrown her bags and keys down on the counter and walked toward the bedroom. She had been so excited that she hadn't really stopped to listen for sounds.

Swinging the door open, she said, "Marcus, sweetheart, guess who drove three hours?" Before she could finish, her eyes took in the sight of Marcus in bed with one of his fraternity's sweethearts. Gwen tried to move from the spot she was standing in, but she couldn't. She wanted to yell, but no words would come out. Marcus was buck-naked with his head between this slut's legs.

Gwen would never forget the look on his face as he jumped up. A part of her wanted to believe that it was hurt, but the angry side just saw it as guilt. He reached for his pants and swore at the same time.

She ran toward the kitchen, grabbed her things, and hit the door. Marcus came running after her, begging her to stop. Of course, he said it was all a mistake, and he hadn't meant for it to happen.

For the next month, Marcus attempted to talk to Gwen via their friends. He would send roses, candy, stuffed animals, and leave letters everywhere. She would come in after class and just throw them all in the trash. The last straw was when he had his mother call and tell her how bad he felt and how much he loved her. His mother told Gwen how they, as women, should understand when their men sought the comfort of other women. Especially when they were respecting their one true love and waiting for the right moment. Gwen believed she called it "a man feeling his oats."

Forget that. She had been hurting bad and she hadn't wanted to hear anything about oats.

In retrospect, Gwen felt that part of it was her fault. She wanted to wait a while until they both knew that they were meant for each other. What was wrong with that? While she was holding on to the sacred triangle, Marcus had done a nosedive into someone else's haven. How could she ever forgive that?

Months went by, and Gwen wouldn't give Marcus the time of day. As a result, he turned into a real dog. She tried to pretend that he didn't exist, but she still cared so much. The more she ignored him, the more he continued his bedding frenzy. Finally, the end of the semester came. Marcus graduated and was accepted into a graduate school up north.

But he hadn't left before trying to talk with her one last time. She agreed to have dinner with him. Because of all the hurt, she had put up a brick wall, acting as if she was over him. When the evening ended and they got back to the apartment, he had come in. They sat in silence for almost an hour. When he tried to kiss her, all of the pain she tried desperately to lock away came forward; all she saw was that horrible night and the horrible dreaded feeling that absorbed her. Suddenly, she couldn't stand to look at him, and asked him to leave.

Gwen cried for weeks after that. She had never loved before, and she decided right then and there that she would never love anyone else the way she loved Marcus. What was supposed to have felt so right and so good felt like hell, and Gwen never wanted to experience it again.

Now Marcus was asking her to open a door that she had vowed never to open again. How could she just pretend that the past hadn't happened, or that the pain she felt then wasn't still very real now?

Who was she kidding? The one main question she found

herself asking now was, why was she still in love with Marcus? Gwen decided to turn off the lamp and try to think about what she had done. That was one conversation she wish she hadn't entertained. But love and having an itch after the midnight hour can make you do crazy things. Go figure.

CHAPTER 9

At twelve o'clock sharp the phone rang. Gwen had just finished having a late breakfast with Patrice and declined the offer to go to her church's evening service. Gwen hadn't set foot in a church since the funeral. It wasn't that she no longer believed in or knew the importance of worshipping; she just had a lot of unanswered questions, and she really didn't think that God would pick today to answer any of those questions.

Putting the last dish in the dishwasher, she picked up the cordless phone on the first ring. "Hello." She knew that it had to be Marcus.

"Hi there, beautiful. How are you feeling?"

"Oh, hi, Marcus. How's it going?" She made an honest attempt to not sound too excited to hear from him.

"Fine, now that I'm talking to you. I have the most perfect afternoon planned. I was thinking about picking you up around three o'clock."

"You know, maybe we could do it some other time. I've been here since Friday evening, and I haven't had a chance to unpack."

"Don't even try it. You already agreed, and I'm not taking no for an answer. You forgot that I know you too well. You unpacked the minute you got in town. You can't stand seeing things untidy, and the idea of living out of a suitcase would cause your little lips to tighten all up." He was teasing her now. "But if you really haven't unpacked, I will be more than glad to come over and give you a hand with your sexy underwear. All you have to do is ask."

"I don't need your help with my unmentionables," Gwen snapped. "You know what? I'm hanging up now and I will see you at three. By the way, what should I wear? Oops. On second thought, don't answer that. I'm not so sure I can handle your answer. I'll see you at three." Gwen hung up the phone before he could say another word. Mr. McGuire had once again gotten under her skin.

Gwen thought she must be out of her mind. She wasn't emotionally ready to deal with Marcus. A part of her was excited to be spending the afternoon with him, but the other part was like a scared deer caught in headlights. She had to think of something.

Picking up the phone again, Gwen dialed like she was calling to claim a radio show prize.

After a few rings a deep groggy voice answered, "Yeah."

"Andre. What's up, Boo? I know I woke you up, but I need your help."

"Gwen? Girl, what's going on? I ain't seen you in a minute," Andre Rogers's rich, deep bass voice replied. His voice was one that could romance, soothe, and make women fall all over him. It suited him well and emphasized his good looks and appeal to a tee.

"Is that your way of saying you miss me?"

"No doubt. Anyone else interrupting my sleep would have gotten the dial tone by now. I was planning on calling you later." Andre yawned into the phone.

"Well, how would you like to spend the afternoon with

me? I was thinking that you could pick me up around three o'clock. It's been a while since we did the bonding thing. And besides, I miss hanging out with my big brother." She knew that using the big brother card would get to him.

"I got to be at the club by eight o'clock, and I was hoping to rest until then. But if you want to hang out, how can I refuse my little sis? See you in a couple of hours."

"Thanks, Andre. It will really make my day. See you in a bit."

Hanging up, Gwen felt a little guilty. She knew the gang had all decided before her arrival that they would be a part of her healing process. She just hoped he would understand and not walk out and leave her on her own with Marcus.

Three o'clock came much too swiftly. Gwen was finishing her hair and putting last-minute touches on the hint of makeup she applied. Who was it that said less is more? Oh well. That was the approach for this afternoon's outing. Since she wasn't sure what they would do, she opted to wear an olive-green embellished halter dress with a multi-tiered hem and silver beaded, metallic Nine West sandals. She completed her outfit with simple diamond stud earrings. Slipping her slim wrist into her watch, she was set. Gwen took another look in the full-length mirror and mumbled, "Not too shabby, Gwen, old girl."

The outfit was working, emphasizing all her curves. Turning away from the mirror, she glanced at the clock: 2:35. She wondered whom she would deal with first. Before she had time to think about it, the doorbell rang.

Gwen was beginning to regret what she had done. She shouldn't have called Andre. She was a grown woman and should be able to be around Marcus without the threat of the past coming back to finish her off. Gwen decided she would just tell Andre about her insecurities and go it alone. Reaching for the door, she took a deep breath to keep from hyperventilating. Both Marcus and Andre stood in the doorway.

"Marcus! Andre!" She tried to sound shocked. "Come in here, Andre, and give me a hug. It's been forever." Gwen stood on her tiptoes to hug Andre and still could hardly reach his chest.

"Shorty, you looking good. And the hairstyle is working." Andre playfully ran his fingers through Gwen's hair.

"Thanks, Boo. God, it's so good to see you."

Marcus interrupted. "Hello. Remember me? I rang the doorbell." He moved in between Andre and Gwen and bent down to kiss her cheek. She hesitantly leaned her head over to allow him access. "Andre was telling me that he came over to spend the afternoon with you. Which couldn't be because you and I have a date."

"Gwen, you got some 'splainin' to do." Andre imitated Ricky Ricardo. Both he and Marcus crossed their arms across their chests and eyed her, waiting for a good response.

"Can you blame a girl for wanting to spend time with two of the most attractive men in town?" She smiled innocently.

Andre stroked his goatee and smiled devilishly. "'Tis true, but ya still wrong. I'm going to hit the bathroom." He disappeared through the living room.

Marcus moved farther into the foyer. "Gwen, if you were afraid to be alone with me, I wish you would have just told me. Andre is my boy, but it was still embarrassing as hell to find out that you arranged a date with both of us for fear that you would have to spend time with me one on one. I know that I hurt you, but that was a long time ago. I'm not that same person. That Marcus was young and naive, and had a lot to learn about life and love." He moved closer and lifted her chin up to look into his eyes. He wasn't sure what he would see, but he knew he had to try to make her understand that he had changed. "The one thing that the old Marcus learned was what it feels like to lose someone you really love, and have that person not trust you again. Can we just spend this afternoon and evening together and try to put the past behind us? At least for today?" His eyes pleaded.

"All right, Marcus. Just for today. Let's not even discuss what was and what can be. Let's just get through today. Now, go tell Andre that he can come out of the bathroom. I can't believe that you two still play the old bathroom trick. As soon as one of you gets into a conversation, the other pretends that he has to go to the bathroom." Gwen started to laugh and playfully pointed a finger at him. "Yeah, you busted. I know you two planned the potty run. You'll still get to spend time with me as agreed, but it will be a threesome." She started walking toward the living room to get her purse, and turned and spoke. "Consider Andre our chaperone." Gwen felt a bolt of confidence. She had won this minibattle, but winning the war was something she still wasn't up for. Still, she felt good at having served up a plan that Marcus didn't shoot down. She continued to walk without giving him a chance to object.

After they drove for some time, Marcus pulled his Lincoln Navigator in front of a brick rancher in a quiet neighborhood that she recognized immediately. She was so excited; although she talked to Marcus' mom occasionally, she hadn't seen her since the funeral.

"Well, Ms. Gwen, here we are, Sha-Mom's Restaurant. If I recall correctly, this was one of your favorite places to eat." He reached over the armrest and ran his finger along the inside of her arm.

She attempted to ignore the tremor that went through her arm and down through her body. It was only a touch, and it really shouldn't have affected her, but she found herself silently counting down from a hundred, trying to calm her nerves.

"When I told Mom you were in town, I thought I would be surprising her, but it seems that some other people already called and informed her."

They both turned around and looked at Andre, who was looking out the back window whistling. "What? Why you all looking at me? By the time I called Mama Bea, Kyra, Vince, and Patrice had already called."

"Yeah, I bet. If it weren't for the fact that Mama Bea has the best chicken and dumplings around, I'd be all over you. But right now, my stomach is growling."

"Girl, I'm behind you. Nobody can put a hurtin' on some chicken and dumplings like Mama Bea, and you know there's got to be some turnip greens in there too." They all jumped out of the truck and raced to the front door. Andre, of course, was the first to make it, cutting Marcus off halfway up the sidewalk. Gwen's heels prevented her from gaining on them, so she made it to the door after they were already inside.

She remembered the first time she met Marcus's mother. Not as his girlfriend, but as one of the posse. Mama Bea, as she asked them to call her, would cook for all of them at least once a month. They would all crowd into the McGuire home and pig out, laugh, and talk half the night away.

Mama Bea was a beautiful lady then, and hardly looked like the mother of two sons. She was tall and regal with a golden brown complexion like Marcus and hair well past her shoulders. Marcus told Gwen that his father met his mother when she was singing for a small band in New York. After that first night of being introduced by a friend of his, his father made it a point to be off work and cleaned up by the time the nightclub opened. He made sure that he got a front row seat so he could sit back and watch her sing her heart out. After a couple of weeks, her singing took on a new meaning, and it was no longer just empty words she crooned, but lyrics directed straight at the man who sat in front of her. He captured much more than her attention; he captured her heart. Zach McGuire accomplished his goal and Beatrice Watts traded in her singing life for a slower-paced one. She became a wife and homemaker and a year after they were married, a mother.

After Marcus' father died, during his last year of high school, Beatrice went to work as a seamstress at a nearby boutique to take care of her sons. She insisted on sending Marcus to college as the older of the two, and she vowed that somehow, Vince would follow in Marcus' footsteps. That vow was kept, with both boys graduating and earning MBAs as well. They made their mother proud, and she was sure that even from the grave her husband was emulating her praise.

Beatrice McGuire became Gwen's mother away from home while she was in college and would offer her advice, a shoulder, and take care of her when Kyra's remedies failed. Her house became Gwen's refuge when she needed to get away from everything and everybody. In fact, Mama Bea was the first person to tell Gwen that Marcus was attracted to her. Since he hadn't treated her any differently than he had treated Patrice or Kyra, she hadn't wanted to believe it.

But one evening, Marcus went by Gwen's room and asked her to take a walk with him to the grocery store. She had been studying all evening, so she was more than ready for a break.

The campus was situated in the heart of the city, but almost everything was within walking distance. All the streets surrounding the campus were historical ones with cobblestone sidewalks. They joked and kidded each other all the way down Grace Street. When they got to the parking lot of the grocery store, Marcus said he couldn't remember what he wanted and would go back the next day. They continued to walk for another hour or so, enjoying the ease of their conversation and the warmth of the spring evening. On the way back, they stopped for ice cream. Although she really didn't want any, Marcus convinced her to share a double-dip cone of butter pecan. Gwen got some ice cream on her nose and he reached over to wipe it off. His hand lingered and their eyes locked. They couldn't ignore the immediate chemistry that flowed between them. Gwen's eyes widened with an unfamiliar curiosity, and she couldn't turn away. Suddenly, she didn't see one of her sidekicks, but saw an attractive man for whom, somewhere between her first and second semesters, she managed to have deep feelings. Gwen wasn't sure when it had happened, but she knew at that exact moment things would never be the same between them. Marcus had tilted her chin up, caressed her cheek, and held it so gently, she was only aware of the slight movement of his hand. Gwen closed her eyes and waited patiently, and it happened. Marcus kissed her.

When she had finally floated back to her room, instead of searching for Patrice and Kyra, Gwen ran to the pay phone in the hall and called Mama Bea. Gwen told her all about meeting her prince. After a half hour of how it had happened and what he was like, Mama Bea finally asked Gwen his name. She remembered smiling and saying, "Mr. Marcus Phillip McGuire."

The older woman, who had lived long enough to know the signs of true love blossoming, burst out with a hearty laugh. "Thank you, Jesus! I thought you two would never get it together."

Now Gwen stood in the doorway years later, hugging Mama Bea tightly, remembering old times, and trying hard to keep locked the door that held all that was Marcus.

"Gwen, baby, are you okay over there? You've been so quiet since dinner." Mama Bea was busying herself, putting away the leftovers.

They had feasted on chicken and dumplings, pineapple-glazed honey ham, baked macaroni and cheese, potato salad, turnip greens, homemade rolls, and Mama Bea's famous peach cobbler covered with vanilla bean ice cream. Gwen stood finishing the last of the dishes, staring out the window at Marcus and Andre playing basketball in the backyard under the garage lights. They were yelling and screaming and, of course, trying to get the best of each other. Gwen couldn't really tell who was winning, but she could tell that they were having a good time. It really reminded her of old times and launched her further into the depths of the yester-days she tried so hard to forget.

"Gwen, dear, have you been listening to me?" Mama Bea came and stood next to Gwen.

"Huh? Oh, I'm sorry, Mama Bea. I guess I was deep in thought. What were you saying?" She tried to manage a faint grin to cover up the disturbed feelings she was having.

"I was asking you if you enjoyed dinner. I wasn't sure I'd done such a good job with the greens; they tasted a little salty."

"Mama Bea, the greens were great as usual. You have always been your own worst critic. Your cooking always puts a smile on everyone's face, and a couple of pounds around the middle."

"Girl, I know you said you gained some weight, but you could still use a couple of extra pounds. Not that it would make you look any more beautiful. You've always been such a pretty girl."

"Come on now, Mama Bea. You're going to make my head bigger than it already is, and Marcus jokes about me having a big enough head already." She slowed down after the last couple of words. When was the last time she cared about what Marcus thought of her? Gwen was losing it. It must be the atmosphere, or maybe Mama Bea's cooking was having an effect on her. A bad one at that.

"Well, you know how Marcus always likes to tease. That boy will never outgrow that. Come on in the living room and talk to me. Tell me all about that job of yours at that public relations firm. What's the name of it again?"

She was leading the way to the living room, and Gwen followed behind, ready for the conversation that she knew was coming.

"It's Westcott and Windsor. And I love it. I've been with

them for the past five years, so I feel pretty good about what I'm doing for them. And they seem to be pleased with the long list of clients that I've added for the company. I just never thought I would get paid for my gift of gab." They both started laughing.

"You've always been able to express yourself, that's for sure. But I think that's always been a positive attribute. And you're a people person, so it's no wonder that you've gained a lot of clients for them. Despite all that, I think now is a good time for you to rest. You've been pushing yourself too much, and your body can only take so much. I know you miss Tiffany, baby, but she wouldn't want you to abuse yourself the way you've been doing. The only thing that's going to ease your pain is time. I've been praying for that to happen, and I know it will. You just got to believe that."

"I know, Mama Bea, but I can't tell you how much I miss her. I mean, I still can't sleep through the night or function during the day without thinking about her. And it's not just a passing thought. It consumes my entire being. I have Dad, T.J., and Kim at home, but I was beginning to feel like I was draining them and forgetting that they experienced the same loss that I had." She could feel her throat tighten.

"I know you mentioned that your mother has turned her back on you." Mama Bea centered a lamp on the side table. "That has got to be tough."

"We exchange greetings and small talk but that's about it. She hasn't forgiven me, and I don't believe that she ever will. After we cleaned out Tiffany's condo, she packed everything up and moved most of Tiffany's things into our old room at home. I mean, she didn't ask if there was anything that I wanted to keep, and she won't even let me into the room. I went in there shortly after the funeral to look through Tiffany's things and to find the journal that Tiff kept, and she stormed into the room in a rage. She stood there and told me I had no right to go through her things. I asked about the journal and she screamed at me, telling me that she hadn't seen it. My mother looked at me that day as if I was the reason that Tiffany was gone. I will never ever forget the look in her eyes. It was as if she could rip me apart; as if she really wished it was me instead of Tiffany." Gwen knew that she had to stop before she threw herself further into the well of depression.

She hadn't told anyone before about the conversation she had with her mom that day, or that she believed her mom had taken the journal and didn't want to share any of its contents with her. Gwen wanted to pretend it didn't happen, but now, sitting here in a warm and familiar setting and knowing that the lady sitting next to her loved her very much, allowed her to let down her guard. She could be real with Mama Bea. She didn't have to worry about carrying the pain of that day any longer. Somehow, she believed that Mama Bea would help her to carry it.

God. She didn't want to cry, but the minute Mama Bea wrapped her arms around her, she couldn't help but let the tears flow, if only for a little while. Mama Bea smelled so familiar and so much like the seasons that had always touched their very special relationship. For the first time since the funeral, Gwen felt that she could just let the pain and the bitterness cease and leave her body.

"Baby, you've got to realize that your mom doesn't hate you or wish that you were the one that died. She's handling your sister's death the only way that she knows how, and that is to blame somebody. You know we've talked about this on the phone. You didn't make the decision to stop that machine; you were only letting them know that Tiff was already gone, and that having her between two worlds was not what she would have wanted. And despite what your mom thinks, if your sister were going to speak through anyone, it would have been you. In time, your mom will come around. But for right now, whether she comes around or not is not your battle. Your battle is to recover from some of the pain that you are enduring. Sweetheart, you have got to heal. You're in the right place, and I'm going to pray to the good Lord for guidance. I'll do all that I can to help you. Look at me." She reached her gentle, firm hand up and rubbed Gwen's forehead and touched the tip of her nose. "We going to get you all better, and then you're going to go on with the rest of your life the way that your sister would have wanted you to. Now go in that bathroom and wash your pretty face before the boys come in and Marcus starts asking a lot of questions and tries to rescue you from all this grief. As much as I would like to see him do that, I don't think that you want him to do the rescuing."

While Gwen stood before the mirror in the bathroom attempting to get herself together, she could hear the boys coming in, yelling and screaming like they were ten years old again. She could hear Andre telling Marcus that he cheated and that he wanted a rematch the next day. Of course, Marcus was up for the challenge. Gwen came into the kitchen just as they were stuffing their faces with more peach cobbler.

"We were wondering if there was any peach cobbler left. It didn't hit me until the last few minutes of our playing that we left you in here alone with the dessert." Marcus was joking with her as usual.

"Well, smart butt, I have to watch my figure. I got to keep my stuff tight." As soon as she said these words, she knew he would make a comeback.

"And how tight would tight be?" Marcus was cracking up, and Andre was joining in.

"You two are hopeless. Finish eating so that you can take me back to Kyra's. 'Trice should be looking for me by now. She was warned that if I wasn't in by nine o'clock, she should call Richmond's finest because you would no doubt have done something foul."

"Baby, my thoughts, and what I would like to do, could in no way be considered foul. Trust me." Marcus turned and allowed Andre to give him a high five.

"You know that you are sick. And besides, your dreaming

doesn't really bother me. You know what they say, one man's dream is another man's reality." And with that, she disappeared into the hallway in search of Mama Bea so that she could say good night.

CHAPTER 10

After an hour of joking around with the guys and dealing with Marcus' pleas to stay, she was finally alone. Andre had to get to the club and Marcus decided to join him rather than stay some place where he wasn't wanted. It wasn't that Gwen didn't want him around; she would have enjoyed snuggling up with him on the sofa, continuing to talk about how much each of them had changed, and at the same time how they were still the same. She just wasn't ready, and she was driving herself too crazy wondering if she should be over what happened. Wouldn't it be a cruel joke if after all this time she was given another chance with Marcus? To somehow pick up where the good part of their relationship back then left off and live the happily ever after that she always dreamed of? What if this was the time to bury all that hurt and move on?

If all that were true, then why were the incident and all the negative feelings that surrounded it, still stirring around in her head, screaming louder than the encore performances of the good times that she and Marcus once shared?

Gwen walked upstairs after turning on the television, hoping that the noise would entertain her and keep her company until Patrice came. As much as she wanted to think and sort out her feelings, right now she didn't want to be alone. Stripping down to her underwear, she hung up her dress on the closet door and turned to sit at the vanity table. Gwen looked at her face and studied the small lines that were under her eyes. Were they always that noticeable? Or maybe it was just that the little MAC she wore was starting to wear off. Who was she kidding? She knew they were from her lack of rest and her poor eating habits. Even Mama Bea scolded her for pushing her food around on her plate.

She rested her head on the vanity table and felt the coolness of the glass surface against her warm face. She wanted so badly to heal the hurt. For the first time since Tiff's illness, she admitted to herself what she had to do. Included in all the other information that Kyra left was a name of a close friend who had an office in Henrico County. In the morning, she would call and make an appointment.

Getting up, Gwen slipped on a pair of boxer shorts and a matching crop tank top. She removed all traces of makeup and applied some Vaseline under her eyes. On the way back downstairs, she turned to check the time. It was almost ten thirty. She wondered where Patrice was and smiled when some possibilities of her location registered in her mind. Girlfriend was more than likely up to her old tricks and had forgotten all about their plans to meet back here.

The television was tuned to the Oxygen channel, but Gwen decided to get some fresh air instead. It was so humid outside that she knew it would rain at any time. Opening the French doors to the patio, she walked out into the night and took a seat on the swing that was positioned a short distance from the patio, within view of the small lake. It was a quiet night and Gwen just wanted to enjoy the stillness. Looking around at all the neighboring houses, she noticed that most of the lights were still on. She guessed they didn't believe in the "early to bed, early to rise" philosophy. Very few city people did. Just as she settled back a little more and started thinking about Marcus, she heard a rustle in the hedges and jumped up.

As she moved closer to the patio door, she saw Scott making his way over to where she was standing.

"Gwen, I'm sorry. Did I scare you?"

It was dark, but she could still make out the curves of his chest under the shirt, and could definitely smell his wonderful scent mixed in with whatever that cologne was that he was wearing. "I just didn't see you coming. All I heard was a noise from the hedge." Gwen tried to still her heart that was beating wildly. She didn't want to tell him, but he had just scared her to death. Her wobbly legs could attest to that.

"I didn't mean to scare you. I was standing by my window and noticed that you were sitting out here."

"You mean to tell me that you can see the patio from your window?" Gwen grimaced.

"Yep, I sure can. Does that bother you?"

"Well, yes and no. From now on, I will think twice before I entertain anything that could become a show for curious eyes."

"If it helps, I'm not usually nosy. I just happened to look out the window tonight. Most of the time I never look out that particular window."

"I see." Gwen looked up at the sky with a frown. "Gosh, it's going to downpour any minute now."

"Oh, I didn't hear that on the news earlier, and I don't think the newspaper forecasted rain."

"You know, my grandmother always used to tell me that she could smell the rain coming. And for a while, I used to think it was the craziest thing I ever heard. She could also predict snow, thunderstorms, droughts, and hot weather. You name it, Grams could predict it."

"Was she often right?" Scott looked at her, seeming amazed by her storytelling. He noticed how the tone of her voice softened and the way her eyes sparkled as she talked about her grandmother, whom he could tell meant a lot to her.

"Let's just say my grandmother could have gotten a job at one of the local stations. She was always right on the money."

Scott wanted to ask her more about her family, but he knew that she had recently lost her sister and he was sure that it was still very painful. Kyra told him a lot, but he felt a pressing need to listen to her narrate her own story.

They stood talking for a few minutes. All of a sudden, a shower of rain began to fall.

"Well, I see that your grams was not the only one who could predict the weather. It seems you were blessed with that gift as well. Having a weatherperson right next door could come in handy. I'll make sure that I tuck that bit of information away for future reference." They both laughed lightly.

"I better get in out of this rain. It was nice talking to you again, Scott." Gwen turned and opened the door.

"Gwen, if you're not sleepy, I would enjoy continuing our conversation inside. I mean, unless you'd rather be alone."

She turned around slowly and faced him as he continued.

"I picked up a couple of videos from Blockbuster's and was planning to kick back watching them with a bowl of popcorn and soda. Of course, it probably wouldn't be your idea of an exciting evening, but it would sure beat being alone listening to the rain."

"I was expecting someone, but it looks like they aren't going to make it." She glanced at her watch. If Patrice hadn't made it over by now, she was sure that she had gotten detained. "So sure, I'd like to have some company." Gwen struggled to cover up the nervousness that she felt inside. She still hadn't figured out why he made her so nervous. But she was feeling the same butterflies she had felt days before. She continued casually, "You go get the movies and I'll supply the popcorn and soda."

"Great. I'll be right back." Scott turned and ran across the yard toward his house. Gwen's eyes followed his departure. She noticed that not only was he running, his feet were doing a skip thing along the way. She blinked a couple of times to make sure that she was seeing what she was seeing. She said to herself, "That just adds to my theory." Scott had to be as young as he looked. She hadn't seen anyone skip since . . . she thought for a moment. Well, she couldn't remember when. What luck? She was about to spend an evening of movies, popcorn, and soda with an attractive, sexy guy who probably got carded when he went to the corner store to buy beer.

Shaking her head, she turned the handle of the door and walked into the dimly lit room. Gwen decided to leave the lighting as it was since they were going to be watching movies. She thought about going upstairs to change before he came over, but decided that her attire was appropriate for an evening in front of the tube. She would have much rather enjoyed a chilled glass of white wine, but since Scott wanted soda pop, she would oblige.

Pulling out a bag of Pop Secret popcorn with butter, she tossed it into the microwave, hit the popcorn feature, and turned around to search through the cabinets for a plastic bowl. Gwen grabbed a couple of bottles of Sprite from the refrigerator. Just as she was about to take the popcorn out, Scott came in mumbling something about listening to some music while they watched the movies.

Gwen came into the living room loaded with enough snacks to keep them from having to get up and return to the kitchen to replenish the supply. She had added chocolate-coated peanuts (one of her favorites) and party mix just in case. Speaking as she unloaded everything on the coffee table, she asked, "What were you saying?"

"Oh, I was just saying that I brought over a couple of CDs and thought that we could sort of listen to them while we're watching the movie." He was standing on the other side of the coffee table, beaming as if they were getting ready for a road trip.

"Sure, I don't mind. Do you always listen to music while

you watch movies?" She knitted her brows together in a puzzled way, and waited for a reply.

"Almost all the time. Isn't that how it's done?"

"Whatever turns you on." Her answer caused him to smirk. Much like their first conversation, her choice of words could be perceived as having a couple of different interpretations. Gwen made a mental note to work on that.

"Here, why don't you put this in, and I'll throw this on?" Scott turned around and headed toward the stereo system that was situated against the wall near the fireplace. Gwen stood in place and watched his muscled form walk away. He looked like a Greek god. He was wearing a pair of black shorts that showed off his muscled calves and was still wearing the white muscle T-shirt she had noticed earlier. Getting a closer look in the light of the room, Gwen could see that the shirt had a University of Virginia logo on the front of it. His hair was glistening from the rain and curled up even more than the first day she saw him.

Soon, soft music was coming through the surround-sound speakers. Scott noticed that she hadn't put the DVD in or taken her eyes off him since he turned to put some music on. He smiled. "Well, Ms. Gwen, how about we put the DVD in? We can move the coffee table over and sit on the floor." It was a statement, but she still couldn't summon her body to move or her hand to unleash the video as he attempted to help her out.

"Oh, sure. Here you go." She felt a little silly. She was as nervous as if this was a date, but it clearly was nothing like that. Gwen had to chalk it up to being out of practice with the male species. It had been over a year since she really spent time with any man she remotely felt attracted to, and despite her reminding herself that this guy was just someone being nice to her out of a promise to her friend, her imagination seemed to be running away. She sat down on the floor, reached over to the coffee table, poured a little of the soda in a glass, and took a sip, hoping to cool herself down.

Scott sat down next to her, reaching across her lap to get the popcorn and grab a soda. He began to speak. "So, have you been keeping busy since you arrived?"

"Yes. In fact, I planned to stay in today, but a couple of my friends decided that I should spend the day out instead of getting settled."

"Well, I know you didn't come here to spend all of your time inside. And if you plan on hanging with some of the friends that I have seen coming in and out of here to hang with Kyra, you can forget about relaxing. And besides, she's told me a little about all of you. So I know about all the partying that you guys do when everyone comes to town to hang out." He reached into the bowl, took out another handful of popcorn, and stuffed it into his face.

"Kyra has been bending your ear with stories of our sordid past, huh?" She was so busy listening and talking to Scott that she hadn't noticed the video much, but she was straining to listen to the tunes coming from the speakers.

"Tell me, what did Mother Kyra have to say? Did she tell you that she was the mother hen and was always trying to keep the rest of us in check?" She grinned at the thought of Kyra trying her damnedest to steer them in the right direction. This was an impossible task, especially with Patrice. She knew no control and wasn't about to let anybody tell her to slow down or be careful. Living dangerously was her middle name.

"I can't disclose my information just like that. Besides, I may be in the middle of some serious research, and if I told you what I knew, then you may change your MO, and then I'd have to start all over again."

Busying herself with opening the box of chocolate peanuts, Gwen replied, "Whatever." His comment unnerved her a little. Why would he be interested in knowing anything about her? She could feel his eyes on her, but she didn't even bother to look up.

She pulled the remote control off the table and turned the volume up a little, needing to take her focus off what he had said. They spent the next two hours laughing at *The Best Man,* which was outdated but one they both considered a classic. They matched the characters with friends that each of them had in their lives. She had to admit that she was enjoying Scott's company. They were sitting now shoulder to shoulder, talking as if they'd known each other longer than the two-day passage of time that had gone by.

Soon, the credits for the movie were rolling across the screen. Scott made a bathroom run, and Gwen went over to change the DVD. She wasn't an action flick person, but she was game.

Feeling comfortable around Scott, Gwen yelled down the hallway, "Come on now, time's up. You could have flooded a river by now. Don't tell me you're not ready for part two of our evening."

"Girl, I'm more than ready. Hit the play button. I'm in there." Just as he yelled back, the bathroom door swung open and he came back into the living room, tugging at the waist of his shorts.

Gwen was laughing. "Boy, you are such a trip. Kyra never told me she had such a crazy neighbor."

"If she told you, you'd probably be staying someplace else, and you would never have had the opportunity to hang out with me. A major loss for you, I might add."

"I do believe that you are a little conceited. Is that what I'm picking up?"

"Of course not. I just know that I'm a fun-loving kind of guy and one that you would benefit from getting to know." They were joking around, but the comment Scott made was sincere. He pouted his lips. "But you know, if you don't want to get to know me, then hey, just say the word and I'm outta here with a quickness."

"Boy, sit your butt down so we can watch the movie." She

playfully hit him on the arm. For a couple of seconds he stared at her with a very intense glance. She could feel the heat from his eyes.

Pretending she didn't see it, she passed him the bag of party mix. "Here." Halfway through the movie as she was deep into the plot, suddenly she heard a beeping noise. She turned to Scott as he peeped down at his pager that was tucked in the waist of his shorts.

"Gwen, I'm sorry. I've got to go. I hate to leave, but I need to take care of this." He stood up and stretched.

"Sure, not a problem. It's getting late anyway, and I really should be going to bed. But hey, I appreciated the company." She was trying not to display the disappointment she was feeling.

"Maybe we can pick up where we left off tomorrow evening. I can always take the DVD back on Tuesday."

"Don't worry about that." She had already removed it from the player and placed the other in the case. She didn't turn around until she finished the task. "Here you go. And thanks for hanging out with me. You are a riot."

Scott was standing there as if he didn't know what to say. He felt a certain edge to her comment and wanted to believe it was because she didn't want their evening to end. Finally he spoke. "Well, I'm off. Make sure you lock the door behind me and turn on the alarm. If you don't mind, I'll come by to check on you tomorrow."

"I'll be just fine. You just go and handle your business."

With that she watched Scott turn and walk out the door. She tried hard to masquerade her disappointment, not really wanting their evening to end. Could she be that starved for company or was it just attractive male company that she was starving for?

As Scott was walking in the rain across the yard, he couldn't believe the timing. He was enjoying being around Gwen and was amazed that she accepted his pitiful attempt at using movies as an excuse to be in her company. She was so beautiful and he had thought of little else since the first day he met her. He never really believed in love at first sight, but he had to admit that he was more than attracted to Ms. Gwen James. She was everything that Kyra said she was and more. The most important fact in the forefront of his mind was that Gwen was single and very much available.

His love life had come to a abrupt halt since he gained his new position of pediatrician at the Children's Hospital. Since he was the new kid on the block, all of his time had been spent working the hours that the other pediatricians didn't want. And it seemed that he was almost always the doctor on call. Some of the physicians who had been there only a short time before Scott arrived assured him that it would get better. They told him it was their way of testing the newest staff physicians to make sure that they were as committed as they should be to the profession. Scott was also sure that the other physicians resented him because he came to the Children's Hospital highly recommended. On top of that, he looked a lot younger than his thirty-two years. Many who hadn't been made privy to his personnel file assumed that he was barely twenty-one, and he never took the time to correct their assumptions.

Scott had worked hard and sacrificed a lot, finishing his medical degree at the top of his class and whizzing through his residency. He spent four years practicing at the University of Virginia Hospital and felt that he shouldn't have to prove anything to the pediatric group, but since he wanted to remain close by his mother, he decided that his current position would have to do for now. He had five other offers from top-notch medical facilities, but they all required him to be hours away from the place he considered home. He also couldn't bring himself to leave behind many of his neighborhood friends who hadn't been as fortunate to get an education as he had been.

He always promised himself that he would return after college and try to help them improve their situations. What

had separated him from Todd, Mike, and Kip was a supportive mother who was always willing to move heaven and earth
to give him every opportunity possible in life. His friends
didn't have that and he was committed to providing the en-
couragement that they needed just to survive without living
a life of hustling. At his urging, they had gotten decent jobs,
and all three were enrolled in college part-time.

   As Scott walked into his kitchen, he picked up the phone.
He was already thinking of other excuses that he could use
to spend more time with Gwen until he got up enough
courage to share his real intentions. After a few rings, someone picked up. "Yeah, this is Dr. Elliott. Did someone page
me?"

CHAPTER 11

Patrice stood in the elevator of the Main Street Building checking out her silhouette in the mirrored walls. Still dressed in her Sunday best, she knew she looked good. The burnt-orange Tahiri suit was fitting in all the right places. The bronze three-inch Vera Wang sandals she had chosen set off the outfit. She decided to wear her hair down for a change, tucking it neatly behind her ears so she could show off her diamond-studded hoops. Even the elderly deacon passing the collection plate almost dropped his dentures. If she hadn't been in a church setting, she would have shown him a little more thigh and really given him something to look at.

Despite all of the things that Patrice indulged in, she always took the time to worship every Sunday at Gilead Full Gospel Baptist Church. She'd been a faithful member for the past ten years. She loved the minister and had become friends with many of the older congregation members. Not many of the younger women, married or single, befriended her. She understood why. The married ones never really took to her since many of their husbands fell all over her, and she knew that the younger women were simply "hating" her. That was fine; she wasn't there for them. Her only motive was to get her Jesus on.

She wished that Gwen would have changed her mind and gone to church with her, but she knew that she was dealing with a lot of hostility. She needed to let it release its hold on her. Being a friend meant knowing when to still your tongue and when not to overstep your boundaries. Patrice knew that a still tongue would be the only solution in this particular scenario.

It was well after 7:30 p.m. when the evening service finally let out. She took the time to kiss many of the older women she had come to love and who treated her like a daughter. They would bring her home-cooked meals and baked goodies, and almost everyone would introduce her to a son, grandson, nephew, or cousin. None of the matchmaking amounted to much, but she was content with loving herself. Inviting someone into her selfish world always caused more trouble than it was worth. Patrice was stopped by Pastor Randall, who smiled warmly as he shook her hand.

"Sister Henderson, it's so good to see your bright smiling face this evening."

Patrice smiled wider. If it was her smiling face he was glad to see, why was he peeping at her breasts like they were his next sermon notes? Pastor Randall was a forty-something heavyset man who could stand to lose a good fifty pounds. But he could preach the church into a frenzy, and his personality was befitting that of a minister. Sure, his eyes roamed a little but you know what they say about preachers and fried chicken is true. Find a preacher who loves fried chicken, and you can bet his love for a woman is equal to his hunger for the bird. At least that's what Patrice's grandfather used to say.

After exchanging holy hugs and pleasantries, Patrice decided to drive downtown to have dinner and wait for Gwen to return from her outing with Marcus and Andre. Gwen left her a detailed message about how she tricked Andre into going out with them. She couldn't wait to get the details.

Knowing Marcus, he probably sweet-talked her into leaving Andre behind. That, or used his tact to make her feel guilty for not trusting him.

Gwen was trying to put up all her defenses, but she was no match for the love she still felt for Marcus. Patrice felt that eventually she would give in. At least she hoped so. She knew that Gwen had been hurt. She spent so many evenings holding her hand and crying along with her; however, she had also spent just as many evenings listening to Marcus' apologies and confessions of how much he loved Gwen. They were all young then; there had been so many lessons for all of them to learn on their way to adulthood. Dooming him to a life sentence of hatred was, in Patrice's eyes, a little too harsh. Maybe tonight she would have another opportunity to voice her opinion. But right now, her plans were to get some dinner.

The Top of the Tower Restaurant was located on the seventeenth floor of the Main Street Building and was situated in such an ideal location that most of the downtown area could be seen from up here. It had such a pictorial view. The host recognized Patrice instantly and beamed at her. "Ms. Henderson, how are you this evening?"

"Just fine, Sam." Patrice smiled her usual Colgate smile at him.

"Will you be dining alone, or will you be expecting someone?"

"Not tonight. I'm all alone and want to enjoy a quiet dinner, take in the view up here, and relax a little."

"Oh, I understand that. How about your usual table by the window?"

"That would be great." Patrice followed him, passing by a couple holding hands as if they were planning the next forty years together. Passing by another table, she noticed two white gentlemen who were either gay or just very fond of each other because they were almost sitting in the same chair. Shaking her head, she slowed as she approached a gentleman sitting with his back to her. Since she made a habit of observing people, specifically men, from all angles, she knew she had seen the back view of this gentleman before.

"Here you go, Ms. Henderson, your favorite section. Can I bring you a drink before your waitress comes?"

"Yeah, how about a glass of Chardonnay?" It was Sunday, but Patrice needed a little something to help her relax.

She picked up the menu and began scanning its laminated pages. She could feel someone watching her and looked up to notice that the gentleman she passed was looking right at her. She smiled, noticing how fine he was and giving herself mental props for recognizing him. She just couldn't figure out where she had seen him before. He looked very distinguished, with brown-tinted glasses, a small gold hoop in his left ear, a Brooks Brothers suit, and sporting a Rolex watch. Watching men was a sport for Patrice, and since it was such, she took it very seriously. As she attempted to take another glance while he continued eating, she didn't notice a ring. That didn't mean anything; she just always made it a habit to check. The only ring she noticed seemed to be a Masonic or fraternity ring on his pinky—she couldn't really tell which from this distance. What Patrice could tell was that the brother was very fine and looked very employed.

Her drink arrived and she was embarrassed that she had done little more than glance across the room at the beautiful specimen before her.

"Let's see. I'll have a Caesar salad and chicken Alfredo." Patrice passed the menu to the server and picked up her wineglass. Not sure if he was looking, she licked her lips very slowly.

Busying herself with straightening her skirt, not wanting to act like she noticed or cared that he was watching her, she looked his way. He nodded a hello and she responded with a smile. Damn, he looked good; it had to be a sin to work a Brooks Brothers suit the way he was working that one. What she wouldn't give to be his tailor.

He had finished eating and was ordering another drink. She knew that he was prolonging things and was just waiting for her to say something or make the first move. Well, not tonight. She would just put on a show.

When her food finally arrived, she ate slowly and savored every morsel. She acted as if she were making love to her food, closing her eyes and repeatedly opening her mouth seductively. She knew she was being bad, but he was enjoying the show and could barely keep still. Patrice knew that crossing her legs and giving him a view of one of her greatest features was just icing on the cake. By the time she finished dinner, he asked the server to bring him her check. She was just going to go over and thank him, but, what the hell. She was horny and she could use a little something about now.

Patrice caught his attention, winked her eye, and whispered slow enough for him to read her lips, "Watch this."

She raised her skirt up slightly and uncrossed her legs. Never taking her eyes off him, she lifted up her hips a little and reached under her skirt, caressing her legs up to her thighs as she continued the journey. He never took his eyes off the show. She noticed that he put both hands in his lap, covering up what was no doubt trying to get out. Patrice opened her mouth a little while she pulled off her thong slowly. Slipping it down, she bent down and removed it over her shoes. Since no one was seated near them, she was giving him a private show. When she finally finished the task, she reached for her bag, left a tip, and held her bright orange silk thong in her hand. His eyes were still focused on her. He couldn't even blink. Walking over to him, she stopped, bent down close to him, and handed him her thong. With a devilish smile, Patrice whispered, "Here, I wanted to give you a little something to thank you for dinner."

"It was my pleasure. Thank you for the show and for this." He looked down at his moist hand holding her thong. "Is this mine to keep?"

"Let's discuss that later. My car is outside and I have nothing to do for the next couple of hours."

Patrice waltzed to the elevator and the distinguished gentleman eagerly walked behind her in unison. She asked if he lived alone. After he answered yes, she suggested that they go to his place. She didn't really like taking guys to her place, never knowing when they would get booty-whipped and the whole thing would turn into a fatal attraction.

Walking through the revolving doors, they were greeted with a gush of heat. The weather report earlier hadn't said anything about rain or a storm, yet it felt like something would fall from the sky soon. The show Patrice had given her present company had caused her body temperature to rise to a level that shouted, "Here I am, take me!"

She followed him to a new complex not far from the downtown district. Parking her car, she waited until he got out of his Mercedes and opened her door. Taking her hand, he grinned. "You know what they say about women who drive sports cars." He motioned to her midnight-blue Mustang SVT.

"What do they say about our breed?"

"That they like fast things."

He walked leisurely beside Patrice and she noticed how tall and sexy he was. "That's a matter of opinion. I just know what I like, and if I like it, I see no reason why I can't have it."

By the time she finished that statement, he was unlocking the door to his apartment. When he turned on a light, she immediately noticed that it was tastefully decorated. It was masculine, of course, but it was very upscale. Coming out of his jacket, he threw it over a chair in the corner.

"Don't you think you should at least know my name and get a few other facts? Just in case I've changed my appearance a little but you remember hearing my name on *America's Most Wanted?*" He laughed.

"I don't make it a habit of picking up men." Patrice thought, *Well, I do when they are as attractive as you are, but you don't have to know that.* "As for you being on *America's Most Wanted,* nope, I don't think I've seen you there." Patrice had finally figured out, on the short drive over, where she had seen this man before. He worked for Rutgers Investment Corporation as a financial analyst. His company happened to be in the Donovan Building on Eighth Street, the same building that she worked in. The investment-banking world in the city was small. After she figured out who he was, everything else came rushing to mind.

"You see, I recognized you from the Donovan Building on Eighth Street. You work as a financial analyst for Rutgers Investment Corporation. Your name is Bryan Chambers and you have made quite a name for yourself in the investment-banking circle. Stop me when I'm hot."

"I'm very flattered. Especially since I know that you're the diva of our competition: America Investments. I believe the name is Ms. Patrice Henderson. Otherwise known as 'No Holds Barred Henderson.' Yeah, baby, your reputation is all that."

They both laughed. Here she thought she was scoping him out, but he had reversed it and scoped her out.

"Well, Mr. Chambers, since I'm here, how about dessert? And do remember that I don't mix business with pleasure. So if and when I run into you, I will swear I never saw you before in my life."

"You are a hard-core sister. Will you still respect me in the morning?"

"Baby, if I do this right, it won't take until morning. What you will feel is the aftershocks of some very good loving." She stood up and walked over to him, reaching for his hand.

"Wait a minute; I'm definitely all for the aftershocks. But I'd like to make this an evening that you won't forget." Bryan walked over to the entertainment center and fumbled with it for a few minutes. After a few seconds, Frankie Beverly and Maze filled the room. Turning around, he lit a couple of candles over the fireplace, turned down the lights, and left the room.

Patrice was standing in the middle of the floor trying to regain control over the situation. She had a thing about dominating, and here he was setting the mood. Wasn't he the type who just wanted to get some and forget all about the ambiance? What the heck was going on with this romantic stuff?

He returned with a bottle of wine and two glasses. "Come on and sit down with me. I would like to have a drink before I have my dessert."

She obeyed. She could use a drink, 'cause this mood-setting was just not working for her. All she wanted was to get laid. Nothing more, nothing less. From her earlier observations in their office building, she knew that he had slightly bowed legs and a bulge that she couldn't help noticing now. She assumed that he was packing some heavy artillery. Now that she was on the verge of finding out what was behind door number one, he was teasing her with the prize.

Placing the glass in her hand, he spoke softly. "What should we drink to?"

Patrice wanted to say, "Getting laid." But instead she acted like a lady and replied, "New friendship."

"Sounds good to me." Raising the wineglass to his lips, he took a sip. "I'm sorry, Patrice. I didn't even ask you if you like Frankie Beverly and Maze. I have some other music if you would prefer something different."

"Oh no. I'm a Frankie fan." She sipped her wine and tried to concentrate on something other than the obvious.

Bryan took off his glasses and put a hand on her thigh. "Patrice, would you like to dance with me? I know that you only gave me a couple of hours of your time, but I would really like to make the best of it."

"Sure." Standing up, she followed him over to an open space in front of the fireplace. He pulled her closely to his body. She inhaled his fragrance deeply and slowly released her breath. It had been a while since she'd been with anyone she found this attractive and she could feel the heat between her legs ignite like a furnace. They swayed in silence. He breathed into her hair and held on as if she was going someplace. Frankie was singing "Reason," and Patrice was trying to stay focused on her real purpose for following this man into his territory. When the song ended, he lifted her head up toward his, and looked deep into her eyes. The depth of his stare made her quiver as he slowly and deliberately kissed her so softly, it seemed he thought she was a china doll that would break.

"You know, I've been watching you for a while." He started to speak. "But I heard so many horror stories from the guys in the building. They all told me you wouldn't give anyone the time of day and you had chewed many of them out for approaching you. Imagine my surprise when you came into the restaurant tonight. I decided I was going to say something to you even if you cursed me out. I felt as if I jumped a ribbon-winning hurdle when you accepted my paying for your meal. I've got to admit that the show blew me away. I've never had anyone seduce me in that way, much less in a restaurant." They both laughed. "So tell me, how often do you go around taking off your drawers in public places?" He looked serious.

"Are you saying you didn't like it?" She tried to look ashamed.

"Oh no, on the contrary, baby, I enjoyed every moment."

"I just wanted to have some fun with you. Now of course, I want to have sex with you. I don't believe in playing the shy, inexperienced type. Like I said, if I see something I want, I normally go after it." She paused. "Tonight, I want you."

"What about tomorrow?" He looked at her as if she was a mystery that he needed to figure out before the clock struck midnight.

"Honestly, I don't do tomorrows. I just live for today. Can you handle that?"

"Not really, but I can try to change your mind."

"I must warn you, once my mind is made up, I don't change it. "

Closing the distance between them again, he took Patrice in his arms and mumbled, "Let me at least try."

This time his tongue traced her full lips and finally entered her waiting mouth. The kiss deepened and she could taste the bittersweet essence of wine. He began caressing her back, sliding his hands down to her butt, and resting them there. In a matter of minutes her jacket and shoes were off. He was on his knees before her, massaging her thighs. Raising her skirt slowly, he licked his lips as he took in the sight of her. He started tonguing her ruby belly-button ring. She threw her head back and a lustful moan escaped her lips. Mistake number one: Never verbally let a man know he's doing something right. A moan is a sign of defeat.

But at that moment she couldn't help herself. Her legs were trembling and she felt like she was going to fall over. She was gripping the top of his head and trying to steady herself at the same time. Before Patrice could recover from his obsession with her belly button ring, he parted her legs a little and continued to satisfy his sexual hunger. He was a skilled brother and she was going to have to make a note of it just in case she decided to include him in her little blue book under freestyle. As she was fighting for control, he stopped and reached for her hand and started sucking on her index finger. Patrice kept her eyes closed.

Just when she thought he had forgotten about her clit, he went back at it, this time rubbing it softly with his fingers while he looked up at her. Yeah, hell yeah. She was moaning. Her body jerked. He put his face down there and drove her over the edge. Patrice came hard and tried desperately to regain her composure.

Bryan took Patrice by the hand and together they walked to the bedroom. Bryan placed Patrice on the large bed and leaned toward the nightstand to light another candle before sitting down beside her.

"Are you all right? We don't have to go any further." She could see his face radiated by the candlelight, and the look of sincerity reflected there. His eyes were like a drowning force that was pulling her deeper in, the more she looked into them. There had to be some solution to what she was feeling here. This was her, Patrice Henderson. She never lost control. *Never!*

"No. I want you." She stood in front of him, taking off the remainder of her clothes and removing his shirt. He slipped out of his socks and pants and stood in front of her while he removed his fitted briefs. Finally she looked down and there in front of her was a sight she couldn't believe. Never in her days had she seen such a well-built and chiseled man, and now she stood looking at his manhood that was in the ready position and lacking not one inch from being the perfect size.

Patrice hadn't had that much wine, so she realized Bryan must be the intoxicating feeling that came on her all of a sudden, and Frankie crooning in the background wasn't helping matters. Bryan began to nibble sensually on her breasts, taking one in each hand and rotating them simultaneously. He was still holding one of her breasts as he pulled her down beside him again. Patrice's head went back, finally hitting the pillow. He looked down at her smiling and placed light kisses all over her face before settling in on her lips. "You are so beautiful."

She couldn't speak, so she only smiled.

"Can I make love to you now?" He was the perfect gentleman. She nodded. So, he reached over into the drawer of his nightstand and took out a couple of condoms.

Oh, it was on now. Knowing that this was not going to be a one-round kind of evening, she gained the courage to take over.

Before he could put the condom on, she leaned over him and began to rub his manhood until he was gasping for air. Kissing down the length of his chest, she took the head of it into her mouth and started sucking on it. She began a rotation that was getting a reaction close to a standing ovation. He was pulling her hair and calling out her name. She wanted to stop and say, "Who's the woman?" but she refrained. Just as she felt him pulsating, she reached for a condom and, while still kissing him, she slipped it on and climbed on top, easing her body onto him little by little until she had all of him inside her.

Patrice started to ride him and created a rhythm that would satisfy the ache in the pit of her being. He caressed both of her breasts and rubbed her butt cheeks while he gave her more and more. Before she could quicken the pace, he looked up and asked her to open her eyes. Rule number two: Don't look them in the eyes while they make love to you. Eye contact connects to the heartstrings. Avoid it at all cost.

But she couldn't help it. She slowly opened her eyes and continued rocking back and forth. She made love to him as he talked to her with his eyes. No, this was not just a sex expedition; Bryan was making love to her. His eyes were telling her just how good she was making him feel. He leaned up and sucked her nipples until they got so hard, she thought they would fall off. Unable to keep her eyes open any longer, she closed them and bit her bottom lip. He was so good and she didn't want it to end. Just then their rhythm picked up, Bryan placed his hands on her waist, and thrust himself farther up in her. He was holding her so tight, she couldn't move if she had wanted to. She could feel their bodies merging and becoming one as the volcano inside both of them was getting ready to erupt. She looked down and at the exact moment she climaxed, she watched his face change as the wave rode over him too, pulling him in deep. Both their mouths were open, but no sounds came out. It was as if they were giving each other the opportunity to enjoy the moment. She collapsed into his arms and trembled while he massaged her moistened back and rubbed his fingers through her hair that was now covering her face and part of his.

Somewhere between the third round and midnight, she fell asleep.

Patrice awoke to raindrops hitting the windowpane. Not sure of her surroundings, she looked around and took in the sight of Bryan lying there beside her. The dark sheet only covered his midsection and he still had one arm across her back.

It felt good. Too good. She knew she had to get out of there. Slipping out of the bed, she picked up the few clothes she had left beside the bed and went into the living room in search of the rest. She didn't want to turn on any lights, so it took a few minutes for her eyes to adjust to the darkness. All the candles had burned down to a low ember.

Slipping into her clothes and shoes, Patrice ran her fingers through her hair. Grabbing her purse, she zipped it open and got out a pen and piece of paper. She scribbled a quick note. *Thank you for dessert*. Placing it on the coffee table, she tiptoed to the door and let herself out. Once safely on the other side, she sighed with relief.

That was a little too close for comfort. He wasn't the love 'em and leave 'em type, and that's the only type she dealt with. In another time and another place she would want a Bryan. But that's simply not how she got down.

CHAPTER 12

"Patrice Henderson," a weathered voice answered. It was good that Patrice identified herself because Gwen wouldn't have been able to pick up on her voice.

"'Trice?" Gwen asked as if she needed to confirm the identity of the masked answerer.

"Yeah, what's up?" Patrice replied coldly.

"Should I hang up and call back when my girlfriend arrives?" Gwen was half serious.

"No. This is me in all my glory. I'm just having a rotten morning and it's not even ten o'clock yet." Patrice's lack of sleep and remembrance of the evening were taking a toll on her. She sipped from the burgundy America Investments signature mug filled with hazelnut coffee and placed it back on the cup warmer.

"What happened last night? I got in about eight o'clock and waited up to hear from you. I called a couple of times and left messages. Are you tired of me already?" Gwen tried to turn it into a joke.

"Girl, stop your drama. No, I'm not. I had every intention of coming over after I finished having dinner, but I got caught up." Patrice crossed her legs, weakening as she thought about how she'd been caught up.

"What's his name and what kind of bait did he use that would keep you from making your usual escape? Unless, of course, you didn't want to get away."

"Perry Mason, what did you have for breakfast? All up in my Kool-Aid and not bothering to ask me the flavor. I should be asking you about your date with Marcus. Or was it Andre?" Patrice searched her desk for the minutes of last week's meeting, knowing that in thirty minutes she would be heading to the conference room with the other members of the executive team for their usual Monday morning drill.

"Now, who's up in whose business?" Gwen shot back.

"Are you going to give me a quick play-by-play? If not, then I'm going to prepare for this meeting in ten minutes or less and call you back. Hey, you want to meet me for lunch?"

"I can. I've got a few things planned for the afternoon, so I guess I can leave a little early and come downtown. Let's see. I hate the food in your building. Do you want to go to the place in the Main Street Building? What's it called?" Gwen quizzed her, not recalling the name of the restaurant.

"Top of the Tower. I went there for dinner last night, and I think the place needs to cool off a little. Gwen, I was very bad."

"What in the world did you do this time? I can't turn my back on you for one second."

"That's a story that will require you to have at least two drinks in you before you'll see the humor in it. Just meet me at Bennigan's on West Broad. I've got an afternoon meeting in that area, so meet me around one o'clock. Will that work out?"

"It'll work. I'm a woman of leisure and don't have an agenda that can't be altered. See ya when I see ya." With that, Gwen hung up and wondered what Patrice had done at the restaurant that would require her to drink the maximum two drinks. That's all it took to render her silly.

Jumping off the sofa, she went into the kitchen to finish her toast and juice. Climbing up on the stool, she gazed intently out the window. It looked a little cloudy, so she thought she should carry an umbrella just in case it decided to downpour before she returned home. Gwen wanted to wander around the city with no real destination, see what she remembered and what she had forgotten. She buttered her toast and took a bite. Before Patrice called, she had been set to have lunch at the little sandwich shop across from the campus. It was cheap back then, and they always had the best chicken salad sandwich around. After all these years, it was probably a donut shop or had been converted to some other establishment. She would just have to check it out another day.

Glancing at the phone, Gwen decided to call home and pray that someone other than her mother would answer. She had talked with T.J. and asked him to let their parents know that she made the trip safely and was settling in. After they fussed about why she didn't want to call herself, he finally agreed to give them the message.

After the fourth ring, she was all ready to leave a message when the receiver was picked up. "Hello." Claire James's high-pitched voice came through the phone.

"Hi, Mom. This is Gwen."

"I think I know your voice by now, Gwendolyn," she replied sarcastically.

"Of course you do. How are you and Dad doing? Did T.J. call you last week and let you know that I made it here safely?" Gwen moved from the stool and stood over the slick marble countertop for more support. It was as if something was sucking the life out of her.

"Yes, he did. Said you were getting all settled and were planning to spend some time with your friends. Your dad just went to Long's to get some things for a couple of repairs he's doing to the house. And I believe he said he would go by your place to make sure everything was all right." She stopped and waited for Gwen to say something.

"Well, just thank him for me. I mean for checking on the house. And let him know that I'm fine and that I'll call him later in the week." Her mother's blunt replies had her stumbling over her words as if English was not her native tongue.

"I'll do that." Before Gwen could say anything else, her mother hung up. She stared at the cradle of the cordless phone wanting to believe it had gone dead, instead of having to realize that her mother had just hung up without saying good-bye or that she loved her. Gwen wanted to sit there and try to figure out why she was treating her this way. She wanted to convince herself that her mother really did love her. But the fact of the matter was, she was beginning to feel that the love she always believed her mother had for her had now dwindled to nothing.

The brief, cold exchange of words had disturbed Gwen, and she wished she had never made the call. Rinsing out the juice glass, she was more than ready to replace this excruciating feeling. Lunch with Patrice was exactly what she needed. How bad could it be, having two drinks in the middle of the day? Whatever she felt after the two drinks would only assist in numbing her emotionally.

Gwen adjusted her Fendi sunglasses and waited for the traffic light to signal the ongoing traffic to stop. She had not allowed herself enough time to get all the way to the west end of town. She looked at the digital clock on the dashboard that was now reading 12:55. She had a thing for always being on time and was annoyed to realize that it would probably take her another ten minutes to get there. Knowing Patrice as she did, she knew that Patrice wouldn't be on time if her life depended on it, so she relaxed. Gwen rested back into the leather driver's seat of her Acura and hummed along with Erykah Badu.

Pulling into a parking space in front of Bennigan's, she noticed that Patrice was already parking her SUV a couple of rows over. Turning off the air and the ignition, Gwen reached over and picked up her bag from the passenger seat. She got out and clicked the car alarm. The weather report couldn't have been more off. It wasn't the forecasted eighty degrees, but more like ninety-eight degrees. She had slipped into a pair of jean capris and an island-blue fitted sleeveless wrap blouse. A pair of two-inch-heel indigo thongs had her looking casually sharp. Since it was so humid, she applied only a hint of lipstick and eye color and a little extra moisturizer. She wasn't sure if the makeup was aggravating her outbreaks of hives, and until she could get another opinion, she decided against it unless an occasion warranted her to take the chance.

"You really are a lady of leisure. I can't believe we are arriving at the same time. You're usually already seated and ready to fuss at me for making my fashionably late entrance." Patrice walked toward Gwen and wrapped an arm around her shoulder.

"Missed me, did you?" Gwen teased.

"How did you guess?" Patrice gave her the sad puppy dog look.

"That big bear hug may have given you away. Come on and let's get inside before I roast."

The air greeted them as soon as they entered the lobby of the restaurant. The sound of conversations, glasses clicking, and music joined in to welcome them. After a brief wait, they were seated near the front.

Patrice was looking good as usual. She was sporting a royal-blue short-sleeve jacket and matching slacks. Her hair was swept up in a twist, and she had accented everything perfectly with a gold choker and gold spiral-design button earrings. She was wearing her usual tennis and rope bracelets.

"So tell me all about your evening with Marcus and/or

Andre. Did it go as you expected, or did Marcus blow up and drag you off by your ankles as punishment for setting them up?" She was all ready to burst out laughing at her own scenario.

"Sorry to disappoint you, girly girl, but there was no ankle-pulling last night. I spent a lovely evening with both Marcus and Andre." Gwen took a sip of the water that the hostess had just placed on the table along with the menus after a brief announcement that their server, Natalie, would be with them shortly. "We went to Mama Bea's for dinner, so I was not only safe, but well fed."

"You mean to tell me that Marcus didn't say anything about the setup? And Andre didn't echo Marcus' appeal? You knew you were dealing with two of the Three Stooges. Marcus is Moe, not only the mouthpiece of the threesome, but the one that does all the thinking."

"Well, it seems that Marcus will go to any length to spend time with me. Even if it means sharing me with another party. He objected at first but I pretty much told him that either Andre chaperoned, or I wasn't going." Gwen looked over the menu and tried to decide what she was going to have. Since she was still dealing with some leftover raw emotions from her earlier conversation with her mother, she wasn't in the mood for food, and couldn't imagine anything going down over the lump that was still rising in her throat.

"Marcus is not the same old Marcus. You know he wants to get back in your graces, and I think he's not going to ease up until you at least listen to everything he has to say." Patrice stated what she felt was well overdue.

Gwen replied with a hard stare.

"But that's just my opinion. And by the look on your face, I can tell that you couldn't care less about my opinion." Patrice picked up her menu and placed it in front of her face.

"You know I care about your opinion. But where Marcus is concerned, I have to go with what I feel. And while I'm having to acknowledge that I have a lot of emotions that I haven't thrown away, I also have a lot of bad memories that are right there alongside the good stuff."

Sensing a need to change the conversation, Patrice spoke up. "What time did you get back from dinner?"

"Around eight o'clock, I think. But then I watched movies and clowned around till almost two o'clock."

"And who, pray tell, did you spend prime-time booty hours with?" Natalie came over with pad in hand ready to take their orders, but Patrice dismissed her with an eye-and-hand gesture requesting a little more time. She immediately smiled. She noticed that the two friends were in the upright and forward girlfriend position, and she obviously understood the body language.

"I just happened to be sitting out on the patio unwinding, and Scott saw me from his window and came over. He wasn't doing anything, and I assumed that you were tied up, so he offered me an evening of movies, popcorn, and soda. I accepted. Nothing to it, end of discussion." Gwen closed her menu, finally deciding on a simple chef salad and iced tea.

"Oh, it's that cut-and-dry, huh? You spend some downtime with a serious-looking brotha like Scott and you hold back information from your best buddy. Well, that's just peachy."

Patrice tried to seem upset, but Gwen knew that she just wanted her to share the entire evening with her from the time Scott walked in until the time he walked out.

"Patrice, I thought we were meeting so you could tell me what you did at the Top of the Tower last night that would require a cooling-off period. Dag, girl, would it just happen to be the same length of time that people have to wait when they purchase a firearm?" Holding up her hands, Gwen shook her head. "Knowing you, it could be almost anything. Before you start, just tell me one thing."

"What's that?" Patrice answered her in a singsong, high-pitched voice.

"Can you frequent the restaurant again or have you been barred?"

"Sure, I can go back. The performance I put on was for an audience of one. Come on, let's get Natalie's attention, and I'll tell you just what I did. And take out a notepad. You may want to try this because it was truly off the hook." Patrice looked at Gwen, totally serious now. "You know, Gwen, every now and then I even surprise myself."

Gwen leaned her head back against the booth and readied herself for yet another episode in the life and times of Patrice Henderson. She would be taking some mental notes because knowing her, it was rated way beyond X.

Their orders were in, and now Gwen looked at her with a sheepish grin. "Come on with the goods. You know you are dying inside to tell me just how bad you were."

"Well, I went to dinner last night with the intention of relaxing and enjoying a meal alone while I waited for you, but I ended up spending the evening with Bryan Chambers, a financial wizard who works for Rutgers, our competition."

"Patrice, tell me you didn't sleep with him. I know you like to live life on the edge, but your living life so dangerously bothers me." Gwen tried not to go off on the judging trip, because Patrice was her best friend and she never judged her or tried to make her feel bad about the way she rolled. But ever since she had lost Tiffany, she had become much more sensitive about casual sex.

"Don't go there with me, Gwen. Yes, I slept with him, but I did use protection if that makes you feel better. You know that using a condom is a rule for me. I will only allow kitty to take a walk out if my partner is sporting a raincoat." Patrice took a drink of her lemonade and avoided eye contact.

"There has to be more to it than that. From what you're saying you slept with him and that's a pretty normal evening for you. Wait a minute. Did you do it in the restaurant?" Gwen looked at her, stunned, not sure she wanted to know the answer to her question.

"No, although that is a fantasy." Patrice burst out laughing. "Gwen, I'm just joking, please don't have a heart attack on me. For a grown woman, you have lived such a sheltered and boring life. But unlike you, I don't judge."

"Patrice, I wasn't trying to judge you. You know why I feel the way I do. Go on with your story and I promise I won't say anything else."

"You know I don't believe that. But anyway, before we left the restaurant, I decided to put on a little show. I mean, from the time I sat down at the table until they brought my food, he was all down my throat. He had finished his meal and yet he sat there nursing a drink, watching me. I recognized him, but it took me a while to put the face to the place and that type of thing. But since he was so taken with the sight of me, I thought I might play with him a little."

"'Trice, what did you do to the poor guy?" Gwen was on the edge of her seat waiting to hear the rest of the story.

"Well, after I finished eating, he asked for my check. And since you are always on me about appreciating what people do for me, I whispered 'watch this,' and slowly came out of my thong. Then I walked over to his table and gave it to him."

"You did what? Girl, you are insane. And don't try to use my urging you to appreciate people as an excuse to take your drawers off in a public place and give them away." If Gwen had been a lighter complexion, she would have turned beet red. She couldn't believe Patrice's latest caper.

"Come on, Gwen. You have to admit that it was very original, and considering that it earned me about two hundred freak points, I can't let you make me feel guilty about it. But then we get to his place and he's nothing like I expected him to be. Don't get me wrong. He's attractive, sexy, and very appealing, but the one thing I didn't count on was for him to be so sensitive. All I wanted was a toss in the hay and here he was lighting candles, playing Frankie Beverly, and holding me like I was some fragile ornament he was planning on keeping."

The server brought out their food and kindly asked if they wanted anything else. When they replied negatively, she turned and walked away. Gwen poured the light dressing over the chef salad, bowed her head briefly to give thanks, and began to dig in. Patrice put a little ketchup on her fries, cut her grilled chicken sandwich in half, and did the same.

"So you stumbled upon someone who has real feelings, and he isn't just out there to love 'em and leave 'em. What woman in her right mind wouldn't mind spending the evening with that type? Sure, you set the stage and you made it obvious that you only wanted one thing, but it seems to me that he may want a little more out of it."

"I know, Gwen. And that's what's bothering me. I don't have time for emotions. I never have, and I'm not going to get all giddy at this point in my life. After about the third round, he wanted to hold me and talk about my hopes, dreams, and aspirations, and all I wanted to do was catch some snooze for a few minutes so I could get up and go home."

"You know we are so close, but, 'Trice, I can't ever remember you suffering from a heartbreak that would render you so hard-core. Why is it that you don't want a relationship where caring and sharing are the norm?"

Patrice picked the green cloth napkin up from her lap and wiped her mouth. She looked at Gwen very seriously. "I wasn't raised in that type of environment."

"What are you talking about?" Gwen looked at her, completely astonished and confused. Patrice had never talked about her family life much when they were kids, and what little conversation they had about home life ceased altogether when they started college. Patrice's visits home were always short and never really included an overnight stay. She would stay a few hours and then spend the night at Gwen's house or with her Aunt Virgie. Gwen never thought about it much, but now as she was sitting across from Patrice, every question that she should have asked long ago came rushing to the forefront of her mind.

"Gwen, do you remember our first semester at VCU?"

"Yeah, most of it. What specifically are you talking about?" She remained focused on Patrice's every word.

"Well, you do remember that we were in most of the same classes and I would share your books because the money my mom was sending me would never get to me or by the time it did, I would have to walk three miles to the post office just to get the twenty-dollar money order cashed." Gwen nodded her head, not sure where Patrice was going with this.

"Unlike your parents, my mom didn't see any reason for me to go to college. And even though I got excellent grades and teachers were always sending notes home letting her know that with the right amount of support, I could really make something of myself, she never encouraged me to pursue college. Then when it came time for me to take the SATs, I earned the second highest score in our county. I remember running all the way home and busting through the door, telling her all about it. Her only reply was that I would never make it, that I should put all that out of my mind and go ahead and start thinking seriously about how I could make some money to bring into the household and help her take care of my younger brother and sister."

Gwen couldn't believe what she was hearing. Patrice had never shared any of this with her. And now she sat there pushing her food around on her plate as if she could see all those years ago in the bottom of it.

"If it wasn't for my Aunt Virgie, I don't know how I would even have been able to salvage a little hope and go ahead with my plans to attend Virginia Commonwealth with you. On the day that we left, I was sitting on the porch with my few bags packed, anxiously waiting to go away. My mom came out, and instead of us having that mother and daughter talk that I'm sure you had with Mama James, she just said that she would be there waiting for me when I fell on my face. She continued telling me that my thinking I could make it was a joke and that my fast butt would be back with my tail tucked between my legs." Patrice turned to glance out the window and then back at Gwen.

"She never understood. I was always the loudest, most outspoken girl in the neighborhood because I just wanted to be noticed and feel important. All my life, I lived in a house where everything I did paled in comparison to what my younger brother and sister did. If we had a loaf of bread that only had two pieces and the heel, I was the one who got the heel. I recall having to stay home from school because she only had enough money to wash Keith and Shelby's clothes. So I took all that pent-up frustration and hurt and tried to be the one that everybody noticed and liked. And the more liked I became, the easier it was to go home at the end of the day and pretend that everything I suffered was not that bad, because on the outside I had people who loved and cared for me. Every piece of school clothing I got came from my Aunt Virgie. She was my lifeline. She even begged my mother to let me stay with her so she could provide for me, but Mom flatly refused—not because she loved me so much, but because then she wouldn't be able to make me feel like less of a human being from across town."

Natalie showed up and interrupted her. "Would you ladies like anything else?"

"I'll have some more tea, and you can bring another glass of lemonade for my girlfriend here." Gwen attempted a weak smile, knowing Patrice would need something to wet her mouth after this very bitter, hurtful story she was disclosing.

Unable to wait for her to leave, Patrice picked up again. "That first semester, I always told you that my money hadn't gotten to me, or that my mom was bringing it when she came to visit . . . when none of that was true. I would call home and tell her how expensive things were and how I really needed my books to keep up in class, and she would tell me about the things that Keith and Shelby needed. I had already taken so much from Aunt Virgie, I couldn't call and ask her for more. So, that first year I just winged it. You were always so generous and often just gave me things. I felt like an extension of you. You never asked if I had money or if I could afford this or that; you just automatically paid for two of everything."

"I never thought about it before, but you're right. It just seemed right, and to this day I never realized that I did that." Gwen reached for Patrice's hand and squeezed it tightly, encouraging her to continue.

"I was so embarrassed, but I could never tell you even though you were my best friend and like a sister. I just knew that I had to finish college for me, and prove my mother wrong. There was no way in hell I was going back home and allow my mom to gloat. She always took my being friendly with guys as me being easy, but I never slept with one single person in high school. I just wanted to be popular and wanted to have people attracted to me. The only way I thought I could do that was be the loud, fun-loving person that I was. And it really worked."

The drinks were brought out and the check placed on the table. The server said she would be back later to check on them.

"That first summer, I decided to take a summer course that was being paid for by the program I was in, and you went back home. I was really sad because I would be alone, but you wanted desperately to spend the summer with Tiffany and I wanted to be anyplace but home."

Gwen spoke up. "I remember that summer so clearly. I spent most of the money I earned from my summer job paying the phone bill I ran up talking with you every day."

Patrice nodded in remembrance with a hint of a smile. "Yeah, I remember all those calls." She picked up again slowly. "My adviser for the summer program, Ben Giles, spent so much time with me, and I started knocking on his door almost every day. He offered me a job grading papers and doing some library research for him. Since I didn't have any money and was considering going to the nearby McDonald's to get a job, I jumped at the chance. After a couple of weeks, we were spending more and more time in the office and he would order food almost every evening. Since the dining hall had limited hours during the summer session, I was all too appreciative of his kind gesture." Patrice swallowed hard.

"Then one afternoon, he called me to his office. I stopped doing my laundry and ran right over. He had received a letter from the financial aid office saying that one of my scholarships was being cut, and I wouldn't have enough money to cover the summer session. I was devastated; I sat in the chair across from his desk and cried. Before I knew it, I had told him about my mother not wanting me to go to school, and that going back home was not an option. I told him that I would sell blood or whatever else before I went back home."

Gwen looked at her with deep concern and wondered why this was the first time she was hearing all of this.

"He comforted me and told me to go home and he would sleep on it and come up with something. That night I hardly slept; and as if she was sitting up high on her broom taking in the whole situation, my mother called. When I went to the hall phone to take her call, she let me know that Aunt Virgie was planning on coming to see me in a couple of weeks and that she had declined her offer to come along because she knew I would no doubt have to return home in a while." Patrice frowned, deeply overwhelmed by the grief of her agonizing story.

"I can't believe your mom did that to you." Gwen attempted to control her temper. Even though it happened so long ago, she was still in a rage that her best friend had gone through the whole ordeal.

"She believed that my luck was running out and that I couldn't pretend to be the perfect college student any longer. She said she had already called my cousin Jerome and they were hiring at the factory where he worked as foreman of one of the line crews. It wasn't until later that I found out that she wasn't hovering over me, but she had gotten a letter explaining the cut in one of my scholarships. I was so upset. I ran to my room, got some change off my dresser, and ran back to the phone to call Professor Giles. I could hardly talk because I was crying uncontrollably. He asked me to meet him in front of my dormitory in thirty minutes and we would talk and try to work through all that was going on.

"I dressed quickly and was outside when he pulled up. I was still shaking, and the pain I was feeling had pierced through to my soul. All I wanted was to get a degree, and at that moment it felt as if all of it was being taken away from me. The cruelest part was that I had been allowed to sample what it was like, the hours of studying, attending classes, interacting with other students, and hanging out. I had experienced a wonderful first year, and had completed the first semester with a 3.9 and the second semester with a 4.0. One thing was certain. If given the opportunity, I could make it. My mother was the force behind me achieving my goals. Not a positive force, but a force nonetheless."

Gwen attempted to interrupt, "'Trice, you don't have to continue."

Patrice replied with a slow nod, "Anyway, he took me to his apartment, which was close by. I never thought to ask until I got inside if he was married. He explained that he had a live-in girlfriend, but that she had moved out a month before. She had wanted to get married, and he wasn't ready, so they parted as friends. He offered me some tea and warned that he would put a little brandy in it so I could relax. That really didn't bother me, because I had drunk a little at parties and was just very cautious about doing it excessively. I had too many relatives who were alcoholics and thought it was a hereditary disease like diabetes or heart disease."

Taking a long sip of water, Patrice dabbed at the corner of her eye with a fingertip. "We talked and he told me that he would loan me the money and I could pay it back after I finished school. I wasn't too comfortable with it, but he even mentioned that we could have a document drawn up; that way I wouldn't feel like he was just giving me a handout or that he wanted something in return. From that evening on we became friends and we spent a lot of time together. Then one day after class, I went to his office like I normally did and he confessed that he was falling in love with me. He said that he wanted to take care of me, and I wouldn't have to worry about my tuition, books, school supplies, clothes, or anything else I needed."

"What did you say? I mean, how did you respond." Gwen wondered about her own response if she had been in a similar situation.

"I didn't know what to say," Patrice admitted wearily. "He sealed it all by giving me the keys to his apartment and telling me that I was free to come and go as I wanted. As wrong as it probably was, I saw this as my opportunity to complete my educational goals. I didn't love him, but I cared about him, and at that moment I felt that was enough."

Gwen blinked back her own tears and Patrice continued. "Sure enough, by the time you returned for the fall semester, my entire bill was paid and I had all the books I needed, a new fall wardrobe, and money in my pocket. And all he wanted was a little time. Once he discovered that he was my first lover, I believe that just sweetened the pot. It was easy to spend time with him because I often studied in the evening anyway; I just did it at his place instead of the library. He would always bring me back to campus at a decent hour. You assumed that I was studying in the library, so all was well. It didn't really affect my college life because I was all talk and no action. Flirting, laughing, and joking was about all I did with the boys anyway."

"Yeah, I remember the countless verbal beat-downs I got whenever you were a no-show," Gwen reflected, recalling almost every incident.

"That continued until my senior year, and then he decided that instead of me paying him back, I would just marry him. Somewhere between that first year and the month before graduation, he had convinced himself that I was in love with him. Sure, I had said some things in bed that could have been taken as one being madly in love, but all that was just pillow talk. I was young and naive and didn't know the difference. When I told him that I couldn't marry him because I loved him in a different kind of way, he exploded."

Gwen's facial expression changed. She touched Patrice's hand again, and it felt icy cold. She began to massage it in hopes that the warmth would return.

"The week after graduation, I called his office and was informed that he had resigned. I immediately went to the apartment. When my key didn't fit, I went to the office downstairs and they told me he had moved out. For another week, I waited to hear from him and he never called. I had his mother's number in my address book; he had given it to me in case of an emergency. I called her and she told me he killed himself a couple of days before I called." Patrice began to cry, not thinking about what the people at the nearby tables might think. Gwen moved her chair beside her and held her tight.

"He had shot himself in the head. Gwen, I felt responsible."

"Oh my God, 'Trice." Gwen had not been prepared for the blow those words delivered.

"That day before I hung up, his mother shared with me that he told her all about me. He told her that I was much younger, and that despite his not wanting to, he had fallen madly in love with me. He said that I had declined his offer of marriage and he just needed to stay with family until he decided what his next move would be or until he could summon up enough pride to call me and ask again."

Patrice was hiccupping through the pain. "When I told her how sorry I was, I expected her to be mad at me. I remembered him telling me that she was a religious person, but still I didn't know what to expect. All she said was that it wasn't my fault. That her son had a lot of past hurts and he just couldn't take another one.

"What I realized most after that day was that a part of me really had been in love with him, I just didn't know it. He was a good person, and if it wasn't for him, I don't know if I would have made it through those years. He kept me from having to go back home, and for that I will always be grateful."

"Regardless of all that, him taking his life wasn't your fault," Gwen stated flatly.

"Well, that day, I vowed that no matter what, I wouldn't love another man. And to keep from loving, I decided that I just wouldn't care. And until last night, I was never in danger of that." She looked up at Gwen. Her mascara now running and her eyes overflowing with emotion, she spoke again. "So now you see that as nice as Bryan seems, he could never be for me."

Gwen continued to hold Patrice and had started rocking her without realizing it. "I'm so sorry. I had no idea. I wish you had told me this. I understand so much more now, but don't you ever keep something like that to yourself ever again. We are too close for that."

Gwen got up and pulled her bag off the arm of the chair. She got her wallet, pulled out a twenty, and placed it on top of the check. She turned and helped Patrice up and walked toward the exit.

Once they were outside, the warm air touched Gwen's

cheek. It stung a little. Patrice seemed totally drained, and Gwen had just experienced another roller-coaster emotional ride. If she had to learn just one more secret, she didn't know how she would live through it. An old saying echoed in her head: "What don't kill you will make you strong." She was a little tired of that and would try to erase that folk saying out of her head.

Gwen walked Patrice to her SUV and asked if she would be all right.

Patrice smiled. "I'll be just fine. Actually, finally letting you in on all that feels like a weight was lifted off my shoulders. Gwen, this time was supposed to be for you to deal with all that's going on in your life, not to listen to the dark secrets from my past." Patrice reached into her bag and pulled out her cosmetic case, removing her MAC. She lightly touched it over her face and then proceeded to apply a coat of lipstick.

"Somehow, I think I'm being made stronger by all of this. Obviously the plan is for me to take my eyes off my own pain and feel someone else's. Doesn't make sense, but somehow I think that's what's happening."

Patrice glanced at Gwen and her right eyebrow went up. "What in the world? Gwen, your whole cheek is covered with hives. I'm so sorry. If it weren't for me venting, you wouldn't have broken out again. Please call the doctor and see if he can see you about this. You can't go on this way."

"Don't sweat it. It happens so often, I don't even let it bother me. I'll just take one of the pills I have and they will go away. Hey, don't you have a meeting?" Gwen purposely changed the subject.

"Yeah, I do. But please call someone, and I'll be by as soon as I get off work." She turned, pushed the keyless entry button on her remote, and climbed in.

Gwen walked over to the car, clicked the alarm, and unlocked the door. Turning on the ignition and the air, she reached in her bag for her cellular phone. She had to agree with Patrice. It was time to call someone. She had already decided that, but that someone would be a psychiatrist. She believed that somehow the hives were connected to something that was much deeper than what any dermatologist could find. Remembering the name of the one Kyra had suggested, she dialed 411 and asked to be connected.

CHAPTER 13

Patrice rushed in the door just as the phone stopped ringing. Whoever it was would leave a message or call back. She stood in the middle of the foyer, put her bags down, and flipped through the mail while kicking off her shoes. In lieu of the hectic day she'd had, she was much more relaxed now. After her meeting had ended, she stopped by the school, picked up Gina, and they spent a couple of blissful hours at Macy's. They concluded their impromptu spree at the nail salon.

Depositing her bounty on the bed, she couldn't believe that her boss had rescheduled the merger meeting for the day after tomorrow. She would have to rush through packing and read the final reports on the plane. It was in times like these that being a businesswoman wasn't worth the many sacrifices. Well, there wasn't anything she could change about it now. To be completely honest with herself, she liked the power.

Right now, though, she would call Gwen and they would spend an evening at Club Andre's. Smiling to herself devilishly, she decided her second call would be to Andre and Marcus to let them know that she and Gwen would be joining them at the club. More importantly, it would give Marcus a little preparation time to put another plan in motion for Ms. Gwen.

Dressed to the nines, they pulled away from Patrice's condo.

"I'm glad you decided that it was time for you to share all that bottled-up stuff with me today. I feel bad because somehow I should have picked up on something. There should have been some sign and I missed it." Gwen exhaled softly as she pulled down the sun visor and opened the lighted mirror, grabbing a bottle of rewetting drops from her bag. She dropped a few drops in her right eye, and then her left. Taking out a tissue, she dabbed around her eyes making sure the light makeup she applied wasn't smeared.

Patrice sighed. "Please. You have no reason to feel bad. I covered everything up so well I think I probably could have won best actress award or something. I never wanted you to see the pain or know that I was going through all that drama. I always noticed that you carried everyone else's weight. I never wanted to burden you with mine. It was just important to me for us to share things and lean on each other."

Gwen was quiet for a moment. That's why their friendship was so special; both of them keenly recognized the uniqueness and rarity of what they shared. "And that is why I love you so much. You have always been so unselfish when it comes to our friendship. But still I wish you had talked to me. I feel as if there was a whole part of your life that I knew nothing about, and wasn't really a part of." Gwen was attempting to sound as though it didn't bother her that much, when in fact it hurt her terribly.

"I'm sorry, Gwen. I was handling it the best way I knew how." Patrice downshifted and sped off onto the merging ramp. "I know you would have helped me get through it; and believe it or not, even though you didn't know it, you did. Now listen to me very closely. I need you to let it go. I have.

As far as I'm concerned, Aunt Virgie is my mother. I take care of her and do everything in my power to make sure she is comfortable. That's my way of thanking her for all she did for me. As for Brenda Henderson, when she calls to ask for something, I provide. I guess it's because I want her to know that I can afford it, and despite the spell she cast on my life, I'm living large. Aunt Virgie even tells me how often she hears her bragging about how well I'm doing. Every time I land in the paper here, she bends over backward trying to get a copy of it so she can show all her crazy-ass relatives and friends. As for Hansel and Gretel . . ." Patrice laughed at the nicknames that she used to refer to her brother and sister. "They call occasionally. Of course not to give me some love, but to complain about home and Mom and then to ask me for money or help with some new plan they have for making a fortune. A lot of what they feel for me is sibling rivalry, but if anyone should be bitter about the early years, it should be me. Even though I should just go off on them, sometimes I actually send whatever it is they need. At other times I just say I'll get back to them and never do. Sooner or later, they get tired of leaving messages on my answering machine or talking to my secretary. Some of their emergencies amount to the pain and suffering of a paper cut. Once I learned to determine the difference, it was easy for me to deal with them."

"I can't believe that your mom would honestly think that you've forgotten all that she did. Not to mention your spoiled brother and sister thinking that you should take care of them. Especially Shelby, since she thinks that she is the only person who has ever had two kids. And your mom hasn't helped. She brought Shelby up to believe that she is God's gift and that everyone else should cater to her. That is so old. I love you, but I could never get into Shelby. Do you know what I mean?"

"Yeah. I know exactly what you mean. I love Shelby, but I don't like her. I wonder sometimes if we have the same daddy. As far as Shelby's children go, they aren't just your everyday Baby Gap–wearing kids, but Grandma's perfect angels. Grandma's precious joys." Patrice was mimicking her mother's voice. "I can bet you if I had at least one, they wouldn't get half the love and attention she showers them with. But you know what, Gwen? It's all good. And like I said, I want you to let it all go because I have." She turned and smiled weakly as they pulled in front of the club and waited for valet parking.

"Girl, how do you do it? Go through all that stuff and still care about them? Talk about divorcing a family!" Gwen rolled her eyes back in her head, knowing that if things didn't improve she would be going through a similar scenario with her own mother. After all the years of having her mother there and knowing that she was always in her corner, she had to prepare herself in the event that it ended up just that way.

"Why do you think I never miss church on Sunday or any program that I have an opportunity to attend? Or why I pay my tithes and help out in the church in any way I can?" Patrice put the car in park and looked at her. "Gwen, it takes the Lord to get you through some difficult things. I have a long way to go in following the right track, and God knows that my spiritual life needs a lot of attention. But I do know a little something about ordering my life."

Gwen couldn't believe it was Patrice talking, because for a moment she sounded just like Tiffany used to. "I hear you."

Patrice realized that her attempt to talk about spiritual things went over Gwen's head. A tall, young gentleman opened the driver's-side door, handing Patrice a ticket. He smiled widely and assisted her in getting out of the car. "All right, girlfriend, let's go see who wants to get lucky."

"See, I knew you couldn't last an hour. You have barely gotten out of the car and you're already talking about scouting."

"I did say that I had a long way to go." She walked around to where Gwen was standing and pulled her along beside her.

Music was pumping and everyone was bouncing along with the beat, eager to get inside. Noticing that some of the crowd were a lot younger than their usual thirty-and-up group, she turned to Patrice. "I didn't know that Andre's catered to a mixed age group."

"You must have forgotten my telling you, then. The lower level caters to the thirty-and-under crowd and the high-rise area is for us old folk. You know we got to have our oldie and goodie music and the occasional electric slide, while the youngsters groove to my boy Nellie and my shero Lil Kim. Me, I would prefer going downstairs hanging with some fellas that got the kind of energy this body requires."

"Girl, stop your tripping. You know as well as I do that those young studs would put a hurtin' on your butt. You may be good, but these guys do it a little differently than what we're used to." Noticing Patrice's baffled expression, she added, "Should I be speaking for myself?"

"Definitely. 'Cause I, for one, like to venture into new territory every chance I get. I feel it's my duty to check out the new breed. Just call it community service."

Vince McGuire walked up behind Patrice and spoke in her ear loud enough for Gwen to hear. "Talking stuff as usual, huh, Patrice? Girl, when you going to allow a real man to squash all that mouth and give you the experience of a lifetime?"

Gwen hadn't seen or talked to Vince since the day of Tiffany's funeral. Nothing about Vince had changed since she had met him as a high school junior at Huguenot High School. He was an exact duplicate of his older brother, Marcus, except his eyes were a piercing light brown and hid behind the curliest eyelashes she had ever seen on a guy.

Vince, who majored in business and earned an MBA in marketing, promised Andre that whenever Andre was ready to open the club, he would be right there at his side making things happen. True to his word, his winning personality was just the added touch they needed on the front line. Women fell all over him. His promises of a shared drink and a couple of dances were just enough to get them to pay the cover charge and walk through the doors of Andre's to wait for Vince to sweep them off their feet. He continued his day job at a reputable downtown insurance firm, but if business increased as they projected it would, he would resign and become a partner in expanding the club and offer his expertise as a consultant for small struggling insurance firms.

Patrice turned around and pulled on his tie until he was right in her face. She spoke seductively. "Vince, if you can direct me to a real man who can handle all of this"—she used her other hand in an up-and-down gesture—"then I would be more than glad to speak only when spoken to."

"You guys together are still such a trip." Gwen moved closer toward them and kissed Vince on the cheek.

"What's up, Gwen? I thought I was going to have to make a trip across town just to see you. Of course, everyone else has already spent a little time with you. Mom even came by the house and told me all about dinner and how she enjoyed your visit. And Marcus . . . Well, let's just say we've been staying under the same roof since he came to town to help Andre out with the club, so I've been the roomie sounding board. There is no peace once that boy gets started talking about you."

"We all know what you mean. But you know the sayings, 'Birds of a feather flock together,' and, 'The apple doesn't fall far from the tree.' And since you two fell from the same tree, you could be stepping on your own toes. I'm sure he has to listen to you talk about whatever woman you bedded the night before." Patrice folded her arms over her breasts with a satisfied look on her face.

"Gwen, come on and let me get you and your guest in."

Patrice said, "Oh, so I'm just Gwen's guest now, huh? A few minutes ago you were all up on me and now I've been reduced to a mere guest of someone you know. Boy, you're still a trip."

Vince laughed and walked past the crowd of people with Patrice and Gwen on his heels. He spoke to the guys working security at the door and the young lady with shoulder-length black hair and heavy makeup who was collecting money. Once he maneuvered past the congested doorway and reached the entrance door, he stood to the side so that Patrice and Gwen could walk in front of him.

The music was louder now. There were paintings on both sides of the walls in the large foyer area that opened up to an etched-glass elevator lit up with multicolored lights all around it. Straight ahead was a bar centered in the middle of the floor. Small tables and chairs were surrounded on both sides with mirrored walls. The ebony marble floor sparkled like new money. The ceiling was all glass too; everything on this floor glistened. A polished-looking bartender dressed in a black high-collar shirt and black pants leaned across the counter chatting with a couple of guys. The shelves behind him were stocked with every type of liquor imaginable. Obviously, this main level was for those who just wanted to sit back, relax, and have a drink. Looking to her left, Gwen noticed a spiral staircase that led to the high-level area. To her right was a staircase that gave the illusion of a pitch-black hole. From the distance, she could see dim lights along the sides of the wall that shed enough light to reach the lower level safely. Vince was explaining that there were no restrictions on the lower or the upper level; it just depended on the kind of party you wanted to indulge in. A person had to be twenty-one to get in the front door, but once inside, a person was free to indulge in whatever fantasy he or she had that particular evening.

Walking to the bar, he turned and handed them each a glass of Cristal.

Patrice lifted her glass and tilted the heavy crystal from side to side slightly. "Bubbly. Vince, you shouldn't have."

"I didn't. Just following the boss's orders. I was told to treat you two like royalty when you came in."

"How did he know?" Gwen stopped and just looked at Patrice. "You're pitiful. You just had to pick up the phone and tell them we were coming by tonight. So much for surprising Andre."

"I just called to ask Andre about the dress code. That was innocent. My God, you would think I committed a crime." Patrice fought the urge to smirk.

Gwen wouldn't dignify her second setup with any further questioning. She just looked at her coolly. "Sad. Your loyalties are just so mixed up."

Vince continued to walk and Patrice fell in step behind him, suddenly interested in the tour he was giving. He walked them through the dining area, which was also on the main level. Gwen was very impressed. The dining room was in unison with the rest of the main-level décor, and nothing short of elegant. Andre definitely had a class act going on here. Artwork was placed selectively on various walls; once she was close enough, she could see why it all seemed so familiar. Andre's cousin Chanel had done all the pieces. Patrice once had Chanel personalize a piece as a Christmas gift for Gwen, which Gwen had placed above her fireplace.

After following Vince through the kitchen and sampling some of the beer-battered shrimp and fried vegetables that were just coming up, Gwen smiled an approving smile. She was really enjoying the tour and could hardly contain the pride she felt. She was so proud of Andre for making his dream a reality.

Ever since their freshman year, he'd always talked about opening up his own club. He took a job selling real estate until he could save up enough money to have the caliber of club he wanted and not just a hole-in-the-wall establishment. Finally, her boy had made it, with Vince at his side and Marcus back in town to handle some of the details. Together, they pulled in many favors from people all over, just to make sure that all the grand-opening activities were as classy as the club itself.

Marcus had made it and was doing big things in the entertainment industry, but he hadn't neglected any of his friends. Everyone tasted the sweet nectar of his success along the way, right along with him. Gwen was probably the only one who never accepted invitations to events or award ceremonies when yet another group felt his contributions should be highlighted and another award placed on his mantel. He had even taken everyone on a Bahamian cruise a couple of years ago. Patrice shopped for weeks and was preparing like crazy to go; she kept pressuring Gwen to accept, but she continued to turn Marcus down.

The day before they were to sail, Patrice became surprisingly sick, and had to call to cancel and apologize to Marcus. The next day Gwen came home in a foul mood realizing that all of her friends were sailing away with Marcus and she was being left behind because she couldn't face him. She hadn't even bothered to park her car in the garage; she just pulled up in the driveway and jumped out. Swinging the front door open, she turned the alarm off and started to undress before she even hit the bedroom. Reaching down to take off her pumps, she noticed a pair of shoes near her bedroom door. She didn't remember leaving shoes there. Pushing the door open a little farther, she noticed Patrice lying across her bed, sound asleep.

Breaking Gwen out of that memory, Vince spoke. "Okay, girls. That really ends the tour except for the dance areas, and I believe Andre wants to do those honors. So with my work done as Club Andre's official tour guide, I will deposit you to the office and get back to the front door." He walked toward a glass wall and reached for what obviously was a hidden door. Pushing it open, he kissed Gwen on the cheek, playfully tapped Patrice on the butt, turned, and walked away.

They stepped down into the thickness of the rich, brown carpet on the floor. Andre was seated behind a huge mahogany desk, kicked back in a tan leather executive chair, and talking on the phone. Marcus stood gazing at two monitors positioned in two large mahogany stands. Both men were dressed in black outfits that were almost identical to the outfit that Vince wore. Obviously, black was Club Andre's signature color. Gwen's eyes were fixed on Marcus, who was unaware that they had walked in. He was deep into monitoring the flow of customers in both the lower- and upper-level sections of the club.

Andre looked at Gwen and Patrice and started grinning from ear to ear. He was a big guy, standing six four, and was just as attractive as Vince and Marcus were, but in a rugged kind of way. "Look, guy, let me holler at you a little later on. I'm definitely interested in getting some prime-cut meat at the prices you're mentioning. Yeah, well, you just make sure inflation don't hit before I call your cheatin' ass back in the morning. Peace." Removing his feet from the top of the desk, Andre pushed his chair back so he could stand up. "Well, Marcus, man, check this shit out. Our girls finally decided to grace us with their presence. We've only been open for—what? three, four days and this is their first visit. If they didn't look so good, I'd throw their trifling asses out." He chuckled and pulled both of them to him in a bear hug.

"Boy, you're lucky I'm up in here at all. I've got a flight at six o'clock in the morning, and I haven't had the best day. But I told Gwen that if we didn't come soon you would never forgive us." Patrice turned to get an acknowledgment from Gwen, but noticed that Gwen's eyes were locked on Marcus. His eyes were taking in the sight of her as if he hadn't seen her since forever.

"Marcus. Damn, man, could you stop salivating long enough to jump in this conversation? Your ass is pitiful. I wish Gwen would blow on your shit, sit on it, or something so you can stop acting like a strung-out virgin who ain't never had none."

"Oh, I'm sorry, Andre." Marcus closed the gap between himself and Patrice and kissed her on the cheek. Then he turned his attention to Gwen again, who was standing before him and wore a red halter minidress. Her legs were shaped perfectly and she wore a pair of black ankle-wrap sandals. He noticed that her hair was still slightly damp and the minimum amount of makeup she wore was all she really needed. Her beauty radiated; he could look at her forever. "Gwen, you look beautiful tonight. Please tell me you bought that dress just for me."

"I'm sorry, Marcus, I didn't. But if it would make you feel better, you crossed my mind when I was slipping into it." Gwen smiled seductively.

"That's all I needed to hear. I would ask if I could have the luxury of taking it off this evening, but since we're in the company of others, I'll just hold that thought."

Before Gwen could answer, Patrice giggled. "Don't mind Andre and me. Just pretend we aren't here."

"Let's not." Gwen turned and looked up at Andre. "Andre, the club is very polished-looking, and the décor is awesome. Boy, when you were dreaming back then I never knew it was in full color. But now, looking around at the fruits of your labor, I can see all that sketching, numbers crunching, and planning really paid off. I'm so proud of you, big brother." Gwen reached up and kissed him lightly on the lips. This gesture didn't seem awkward or uncomfortable since all of them were like brothers and sisters; a smack on the lips was not uncustomary for them.

"Hold up now. What do I get? I put a lot of energy and guidance into this project. Not to mention holding my boy's hand through all of this." Marcus reached over and pulled Gwen into his arms. He kissed her on the nose and allowed his lips to travel the short length down to her lips. A warm sensation rippled through Gwen's body, causing her to look away from him and into the eyes of Andre and Patrice, who stood by, looking dumbfounded.

Gwen struggled to gain composure and tried to dismiss the familiar stirring in the pit of her stomach. Lowering her head, she attempted to clear her throat. "Can we please see the rest of the club, Andre?" Her voice cracked and went up two octaves. Once everyone in the room heard it go up and down as if she was auditioning for the opera, they all exploded in a fit of laughter.

Marcus smiled at her, showing all of his pearly whites. "Baby, I didn't know I still had that kind of effect on you. Imagine if I had given you a little tongue."

"Stop harassing my sidekick, Marcus. And, Andre, I know you're not even busting on Gwen. You know you're just a big teddy bear and can hardly stand a firm hot body rubbing against your chest." Patrice came over and stood by Gwen in support, even though she hadn't quite recovered from the laughing episode.

Marcus and Gwen both looked at them with a surprised expression. "Do either one of you want to tell us what we missed? And, Patrice, girl, how do you know what bothers Andre?" Gwen was interrogating them and trying hard to sound serious.

Marcus couldn't resist adding, "And when did Andre become a teddy bear? 'Cause when I think of teddy bears, I think of something all warm and cuddly."

"Can't two people share a moment without you two wanting everybody else to be as hopelessly in love as you two are? After all these years, you two still can't get the shit right." Andre opened the door and continued to fuss on his way through the bar area. Patrice followed, agreeing with him all the way. Marcus and Gwen just walked out behind them with wide grins on their faces.

"Well, Marcus. I think we hit a nerve." Gwen smiled.

"Yeah, I think so too. I believe these two have some secrets that they haven't shared with either of us. Riding Andre for the next couple of days will be oh so sweet."

By the time they caught up with Andre and Patrice, they were standing by the entrance of the club and watching a crowd of customers come in. Marcus positioned himself beside Andre and was talking to one of the security people at the door.

Patrice stepped around both of them and sat at the end of table that displayed the hours of the bar, dining room, and both club levels. At the far end of the table was a small table-top easel displaying the dinner specials for the evening. "Girl, this place is jam-packed with folk. It looks like both levels are hopping and I for one can't wait to get my party on." Patrice was snapping her fingers and bouncing her head to the mixture of beats that came together from the two floors.

"I hear you. But it seems that the guys are being held up. Do you think they would mind if we went on upstairs?" Before Gwen could finish her statement, her mouth fell open and she couldn't continue. Scott was coming through the double glass doors while removing a navy blue do-rag. Gwen blinked once to make sure that it wasn't just someone who resembled him. He was dressed in a loose pair of jeans and a navy blue jersey-knit Sean John shirt. Clipped to his side were a pager and cell phone. He was in the company of three other young guys in similar attire, and they were in deep conversation as they took the steps that led downstairs.

Gwen turned to Patrice. "I think that was Scott from next door. He looked just like one of the guys in one of those BET videos." She was stumbling, trying to find some words that fit what she had just witnessed. "I mean, he looks so different from the other night. The outfit, the headgear."

Patrice touched her arm. "The word you're looking for, Gwen, sweetheart, is thug. Boyfriend definitely had the thug motif thang going on. Which isn't a bad look, mind you. Everyone should experience a little thug action."

"What?" Gwen looked at her with her mouth partially opened.

"I bet you didn't find that appealing in the least bit. Girl, you have got to stop being so uptight. You are going to miss out on a lot in life if you continue to try to rationalize and make everything fit in a neat damn box all the time." She looked at Gwen, annoyed.

"I wasn't trying to rationalize anything. I just said he looked different, that's all." Gwen attempted to try to sound convincing, when in fact the sight of Scott and his friends was sending a message that she wasn't sure about.

"So, of course, you no longer find him attractive?" Patrice lifted her right hand and held her nails to the light as if she was expecting to see something different now than she had when she left the nail salon after work.

"I never said I was attracted to him. I just enjoyed his company the other night. Besides, I thought he was a little young, and this only proves it."

Before Gwen could continue, Marcus and Andre walked over to where they were waiting. "Girls, are you ready to see the dance areas? We can check out the young action first and then go upstairs to see if you two still got it." Marcus started walking before either of them could reply.

The lower level was spacious with the DJ's quarters in the far left corner behind tri-color glass. Tables were positioned along the walls, and the center of the floor was packed with hardly enough room to move.

Gwen scanned the room quickly, trying to catch a glimpse of Scott before they went back upstairs. After her eyes adjusted more, she saw him in the middle of the floor dancing with a petite high-yellow female with a head full of weave, wearing a tight black spandex dress with her back out. The dress was all the way up her butt, and Gwen could tell by the twists and turns she made that undergarments were not a part of her attire for the evening. One of the guys who came in with Scott was sandwiched between two girls. The girls were obviously friends of the hot number that was pressed up on Scott. They each wore outfits similar to Scott's mate's and obviously had joined her in going downtown to the Korean

Shop to get the same type of hair, Jacked-Up 2-B. All of them seemed to be having a good time. At that particular moment, Gwen felt a lot older than her thirty-five years and the rap music of Snoop and Pharrell, and the girls sporting the too-tight, too-short outfits that left nothing to the imagination weren't helping matters.

As she walked up the steps behind Marcus, she turned one last time and looked in the direction where Scott was dancing. The music changed and his eyes caught hers for a moment. She smiled slightly and tried to register the look that was on his face. Before she knew it, Marcus was tugging on her arm. She continued behind him and listened as the tempo changed and the DJ announced the next song was for lovers. She wondered if Scott engaged in a slow dance that was meant for two people in love, and at the same time chastised herself for even caring.

"Penny for your thoughts?" Marcus reached over and ran his long slender finger over her temple.

"I'm not ready to share my thoughts, but I am ready to dance." She stood up, took his hand, and led him to the dance floor.

They danced through five songs right along with Patrice and Andre. Finally they all retreated to their seats. Gwen's dress was sticking to her butt. She couldn't believe she had danced that hard and long.

It was a little after midnight. Gwen had long since passed her two-drink minimum, and just finished her fifth glass. She was on the dance floor when Patrice came over and told her she was leaving and that she would talk to her later. Marcus agreed to take Gwen home. Gwen knew she had drunk too much, because she didn't bother to put up a fight. In fact, she was feeling the full effects of a buzz. Gwen's champagne was replaced with ginger ale when she started grinding Marcus on the dance floor. Although he was enjoying the extra attention, he knew that it was not her.

When they called for the last dance, which of course was

a slow one, they walked out on the dance floor hand in hand. Gwen looked up at him as she slipped her arms around his neck snuggly. Luther Vandross's "If Only for One Night" started to play. They had spent so many evenings cuddled up listening to the king of love ballads, songster Luther. The first concert she ever went to was with Marcus, and Luther was performing. His music was always special, because it reminded her of them together. As Marcus whispered in her ear, she started smiling and imagining him doing the things that he was now teasing her with through his whispered words. Looking around Marcus' shoulder, she noticed that Scott was standing by the elevator. She'd started seeing two of everything a long time ago, but she was sure that at least one of the Scotts by the elevator was looking straight at her. As she lifted her head up a little, she looked in that direction and wondered if either of the Scotts she saw felt the way that she did as she watched him dancing with the young lady downstairs. Why it bothered her, she couldn't really explain. It just did and the alcohol she drank hadn't cushioned the strange feeling she felt.

The car came to a stop. Gwen tried to open her eyes, only to feel pain pulsating under them. She should have known better than to drink more than her limit. Gwen could remember the last time she felt like this, and had vowed at that time never to feel like it again. Yet here she was, feeling as if her head was going to explode.

"Come on, baby girl. I don't know why I let you drink like you're grown. You and I both know you can't drink more than a glass of orange soda without getting light-headed. You can't even hang with a glass of Pepsi or Coke. The last time I counted, you had downed seven glasses of champagne."

"Seven. I thought I stopped at five. I must have lost count somewhere between the cha-cha slide and one of our slow dances." Gwen reached over and rubbed her fingernail over his muscled upper arm.

"Let's get inside." Marcus opened and closed the driver's-side door and then walked around to let her out. Since it took her more than a second or two to talk her legs into swinging around, he looked down at her and laughed. "Girl, you are messed up. Let me just carry you in."

Gwen didn't even say no. Marcus picked her up and lifted her into his arms in one smooth motion. She placed her head on his shoulder and closed her eyes as his scent enveloped her into another plateau. She raised her head long enough to hand him the keys from her satin evening bag and returned its throbbing form back to the safety of his shoulder while mumbling the alarm code. Marcus turned off the alarm but never stopped to deposit her on the floor or the sofa as she assumed he would. Instead he turned on the dimmer switch leading up the staircase and took the steps with ease as if the weight of her was no more than a newborn infant's.

Pushing the master bedroom door open, he walked in without turning on a light and placed her on the oversize bed. Gwen wanted to move her head and sit up and try to remove her clothes and search for something to wear to bed, but she couldn't move. The few words that she heard come out of her mouth were incoherent.

She could feel Marcus removing her shoes and he turned her over a little so he could unzip her dress. She tried to obey, but halfway over she felt like she was going to be sick. She struggled to turn back over. He sat down beside her and said he would try to do it without her having to move so much. When he finally got the dress unzipped and off, she lay there with only a red thong on. The dress she wore didn't require a bra, so she had opted to go without one. Even though she couldn't open her eyes because of the nausea and the intoxicated feeling, her mind alerted her to the fact that she was just lying there with nothing on except a skimpy pair of underwear. When she opened her eyes a little, Marcus was looking down at her. His eyes softened and his lips were partially opened. Neither of them said anything. Marcus, because he was rendered speechless, and Gwen, because speaking was just not something that she could muster at that particular time.

"Baby, you look so good. I can't believe it, but your body hasn't changed in all these years. I can't tell you how many times I would close my eyes at night and see your delicate body beside me. You always looked so fragile and beautiful, and touching you was like someone giving me permission to touch the most exquisite and beautiful flower in a garden. I have never stopped loving you, girl. You've got to know that. I've never looked at anyone the way I look at you. If I could just turn back the hands of time, things would be so different. You would be in my life, and every night I would just enjoy holding you in my arms and telling you how much you mean to me."

Without thinking, she lifted her arms up, beckoning him to come to her. Slowly he closed the gap between them and kissed her, softly at first and then with a force. Gwen pulled him closer as if she wanted their bodies to join together as one. As if by instinct, he cupped her breast with one of his hands and rubbed it back and forth slowly. The kiss deepened even more. She could hear Marcus moaning and felt him squirming on the bed beside her. She wanted him so badly, and even though she was feeling the champagne, what she was feeling even more was a longing inside her being that wanted this moment to happen more than anything else in the world.

Marcus stopped kissing her and she again opened her eyes a little and rubbed her fingers through his wavy hair. "Gwen, baby, I want to make love to you so much. I want to enter you and feel the love that I know you still have for me wrap around every part of me. But . . ." He sighed. "When I make love to you, real love, I want it to be something that you are fully aware of. I want you to be able to look in my eyes and know that the love I'm giving you comes from deep inside me, and that it's not just me satisfying some fantasy that I have of you, or finally doing what I've wanted to do for so long. I want it to be me making mad, passionate love to you because I love you. Nothing has ever been more important to me than loving you. I want to erase the biggest mistake I've ever made by hurting you, and if I make love to you now, I will feel like I'm taking advantage of you."

Gwen wanted to tell him that she wasn't as drunk as he thought she was. That she was fully aware of everything, and that the intoxication she felt when they first came through the bedroom door disappeared the minute he started caressing her body. Gwen wanted to tell him that she wanted him as much as he wanted her and that she would always love him. But all she could do was look at him through slightly hazy eyes. She reached again and rubbed her index finger over his lips. He opened his mouth and sucked on it before withdrawing it with his own hand and kissing it gently.

Marcus stood, walked over to the armoire, and pulled open a drawer. When he turned around, he was holding a turquoise nightshirt. His voice was barely a whisper as he said that he would help her into the nightshirt and sleep on the sofa downstairs. She guessed he didn't trust himself to sleep across the hall.

After helping her on with the nightshirt, Marcus went into the bathroom and returned with a couple of aspirins and a cup of water. After she took the aspirin and drank from the cup of water, she rested her head on the pillow. The nausea was threatening to return, and she thought that if she closed her eyes it would go away. Gwen felt the sheet being pulled up over her. As if time had indeed stood still and nothing changed between the two lovers, she mumbled, "I love you."

He turned around to see if she was talking in her sleep or if she was suddenly wide awake. Turning on the small lamp that was situated on the nightstand, he kneeled beside the bed and looked into her face with so much love and admiration. Even though she could hardly keep her eyes open, she saw everything that she had wondered about for such a long time. It was all so visible at that very second. She knew without a shadow of doubt that Marcus still loved her, and in his eyes she saw a thousand apologies.

"Gwen, I love you too."

Her droopy eyes followed his walking form until he turned off the light at the door and disappeared into the hallway. Unable to ignore her body's need for rest, she reached over and grabbed the large down pillow that was neatly placed beside the one that she was resting her head on. Finally, allowing sleep to take over, she hoped that her dream would pick up where Marcus left off, and that for the first time in almost thirteen years, their bodies would intertwine. She would finally give him what both of them desired more than anything, for him to be inside her.

CHAPTER 14

Sanding out the last section of the faded, dull, and withered oak color that was visible on the large china cabinet, Thomas James wiped at the sweat that created a clammy wetness at his temples. He'd been in his workshop since 7:00 a.m. and peering down at his watch, he sighed when he noticed that it was now almost noon. He murmured to himself, "Where in the world did the morning go?" Reaching up, he removed the goggles that were fitted tightly on his face and stretched to relieve the sore muscles at the back of his neck. He had been working on this cabinet for more than a couple of weeks and couldn't wait to surprise his wife with the finished product.

The china cabinet had belonged to his grandmother, and when he and his two brothers went to clean out the old family house before its new owners would take over, he couldn't help but feel a twinge of guilt for agreeing to leave most of the things intact. His brothers had talked him into selling the place and because of all the emotional turmoil that he had been dealing with, he reluctantly agreed in hopes that they would allow him some peace. He knew that their desire to sell was more out of greed than anything else; but they tried to convince him that they didn't have time for the upkeep of the place, and since the last tenants had asked repeatedly if they could buy the home, he saw no reason to continue to say no. The two-story wood frame house had been in his family for as long as he could remember.

Prior to his living in it as a teenager, his grandparents had lived there until their deaths. He recalled how big it always looked when he spent countless summers there when school let out. It was always full of laughter and wonderful aromas. His grandmother was a chubby little lady who was as jolly as they came. No matter when anyone came to her, she always had a smile on her face and something sweet in the kitchen.

The last day he and his brother Pete were moving the last of the things that the new tenants didn't want to keep, he stood in the kitchen and stared at the china cabinet. He remembered his grandfather bringing it home one hot summer day from some white folks' house where his grandfather used to do odd jobs. His grandmother's face had lit up; you would have thought that his grandfather had gone out and spent a fortune for it. A day or so later, she polished it and shined it up, and displayed her best china in it. Not all of it matched because they didn't have much, but she was proud nonetheless and would make sure that everyone who visited her home saw that beautiful cabinet.

When he explained to the new owners that the cabinet was a very sentimental piece to him and that he would be willing to pay whatever they requested since the house deal was already negotiated and in the final stage of being closed, the young couple were moved by his story. They begged him to take it and not to insult them by wanting to pay for it. The wife had been raised by her grandparents, and she could understand how he felt. She couldn't imagine parting with anything that was so special.

That day he brought the cabinet home and placed it in the workshop. He shivered now as he took another glance at it, glad that it was now in his home. It may not have been in the residence where it had become a fixture all those years ago, but it was in the home of someone who cherished it as much as the lady who cried soft tears of joy the day she laid eyes on it. He rubbed his hand across his balding head and hoped that this family heirloom would bring his wife as much joy as it had his grandmother.

Hearing the noise of a vehicle coming into the driveway, he turned and noticed a green Ford pickup truck circling around the house and pulling into the rear driveway. He walked closer and noticed that the driver was Claude Foreman. Claude had retired some time ago and was now working with Cornerstone Memorials right next to Mines Funeral Home.

"Good afternoon, Thomas. How's it going? I declare, you are the busiest man in town. You're always out here in this shed or somewhere in the community lending a helping hand to somebody." He smiled and patted Thomas's shoulder.

"You know what they say about the hands of an idle man. So, I do my best to make sure mine don't stay idle long. What brings you by?" He motioned toward the enclosed patio and walked behind Claude until they were out of the heat.

"Well, Claire called yesterday and asked if I could come by and take some measurements in her new garden. So, since I had to come out to see Old Man Neal down the street here, I thought I would kill two birds with one stone."

Thomas tried not to look surprised. "What are you taking measurements for, Claude? Claire been in and out so much for the last couple of days, she didn't say you'd be comin' by." He hoped that he didn't sound as put out as he actually was by all this.

"Oh, she wants to put a pictorial monument to Tiffany in the center of her garden. I believe she said that she would also have a wooden bench placed near it so that you all could sit out there from time to time."

Thomas couldn't believe his ears. Claude's visit caught him off guard, but he was now speechless. What he heard about was not something he would consider a pictorial monument, but more of a shrine that everyone would have to see as they came around to the back of the house. He didn't even want to think of what such a visible memorial to Tiffany would do to his grandsons Baron and Darion.

As if he could read his mind Claude spoke up. "You know, Thomas, a lot of people are doing it nowadays. Not so many of our folk, but a lot of white people are doing it as a way to always remember their loved ones and have some type of reprieve whenever they like."

"Claude, I understand what you're saying and all. But this ain't a good idea for us, not right now anyways. This is somethin' that Claire may think she wants, but she ain't accepted Tiffany's death and how the rest of us would feel about this picture thing."

Not wanting to give up on it, Claude spoke again, this time more assertively. "I can take the measurements—that way if you decide that you want to go ahead with it, you can just give me a call."

"Claude, I know you're a businessman and all and you want to make a sale, but believe me, today ain't no good day to talk about it. Matter of fact, I don't reckon any day being a good time to talk about making my backyard some type of graveyard. Now, I need to go and find my wife. You can let yourself out." Visibly upset, Thomas marched through the patio and swung open the door that opened into the kitchen.

He called Claire's name a couple of times as he entered the kitchen and proceeded on into the dining room and then the den. When she didn't respond, he knew exactly where she was. Taking a deep breath, he walked up the steps and stopped in front of the room two doors down from the bedroom he shared with his wife.

He tapped on the door lightly a couple of times. "Claire,

you in there?" He really didn't need to ask; she had spent almost all of her time in this room since Tiffany's death.

Claire jumped up from the bed, quickly walked to the closet, placed the book she had been holding under a bunch of blankets, and quietly closed the closet door. "Yeah, Thomas, I'm here. I was just about to go downstairs and fix you a sandwich," she was explaining as she opened the door.

He could tell that she had been crying. Her eyes were red and slightly swollen, and the smile she tried to attempt was only half there. "Whatcha doing in here?"

"I was just putting up some things that needed to be put away." She avoided eye contact and started to go downstairs.

Thomas followed her down the steps. "Claude Foreman was just here." He waited for a reply, but didn't get one. She picked up a basket of dirty laundry in the hallway and hastily moved toward the utility room as he spoke again. "What is this about some kind of picture memorial that you want in the garden?" He used every fiber in his being to keep from exploding. Although that was what he felt like doing, he knew that in her condition it would only upset her more.

"I thought that it would be nice to have a pictorial memorial placed in the center of the new garden. It's the perfect location for it. You would be able to stand in Tiffany's bedroom and look out at it." She started the washer and added a cup of Tide liquid laundry detergent and a little Clorox bleach. Never taking the time to look up at him, she concentrated on the items she was placing into the tub.

"And what did you think something like that would do to the rest of us? I mean, did you even stop to think about Baron and Darion?" Thomas moved closer to her and continued. "And sweetheart, having to look at it every day yourself just won't help you get past Tiffany's death. No matter what you do, she ain't coming back."

"Don't you think I know that!" She picked up the laundry basket and threw it in the corner. It tumbled against the wall and landed upside down on the floor. "I think about nothing else night and day except that I will never see my baby again. And here you are, telling me I can't put whatever I want in my garden."

"Claire, I'm not saying that, and you know it. All I'm saying is, it would be hard for all of us to look at it every day without breakin' down. Poor Gwen is out of town now trying to get her life back together without the sleepless nights, the hurt, and those terrible hives."

"At least she's alive." She looked coldly at her husband. She wished that she could take back the words, before they were completely out. But she wasn't sure she regretted saying them. It wasn't that she didn't care for her oldest child; it was just that Tiffany was her baby, and Gwen had been the one to convince everyone that taking Tiffany off the life support would allow her life to take whatever course God desired for her. She didn't see how this could have been God's desire. Tiffany's body was tired, and they hadn't given her a chance to build up her strength and fight back. That day, she lost her baby, and she just didn't see how she could forget how the decision was made and how she was forced to go along with it.

The comment his wife had made took the last bite of composure he had. "How in the hell can you say that, Claire? Yes, Gwen is livin', and that is something that you should be happy about. We lost one child, and God knows we can't stand to lose another. I know you're upset, and I know that you're hurtin', but you are not the only one who lost a child. Not just us, but Gwen and T.J. lost their baby sister, and all you want to do is sit around all day and have a pity party. You change things around upstairs to suit the one person who can't see or enjoy it. Did you stop to remember that the room you are fixin' up didn't belong to Tiffany only? No, of course you didn't, because you're so busy tryin' to punish Gwen for saying somethin' that neither of us had the willpower to say. She loved Tiffany. They were as close as two sisters could be. I don't understand you right now, and I'm not sure I want to." Thomas turned briskly and walked away, never looking back to see what state he was leaving his wife in. All he knew was that he needed to leave the house before he said something more that he would end up regretting.

Claire stood at the kitchen window and watched as he climbed into his pickup truck and sped around the house and down the driveway. She wanted to run out and stop him, to say something that would make up for the comment she had made.

But she had made the only comment that she thought would let him see just how much losing her baby had damaged her. Why couldn't he see things her way, and why couldn't anyone other than her see that Gwen could have kept her mouth shut that day and allowed Tiffany the time she needed to regain her strength and fight? Tears started to fall as she began to wash a dish that was on the counter near the sink.

She walked slowly to the nearby breakfast table and sat down in her usual chair, reaching in the pocket of her apron and removing an old photo with curled-up edges. She looked intently at it as though it was speaking to her. Slowly she lifted it to her heart and held it tightly. After a couple of minutes, she looked at the photo again and smiled at the faces of her daughters. Gwen and Tiffany stood under a pear tree in her sister's backyard.

Claire remembered the day that the photo was taken. They had spent the night with her sister while she spent the night at the hospital with T.J., who had had his tonsils removed. That day, she dropped off T.J. with Thomas and went straight over to pick the girls up. When she arrived, they were in the backyard picking pears that their Aunt Georgia was going to preserve. When she got out of the car, she watched from the distance as they laughed and played while picking pears up off the ground. She couldn't resist taking a photo of them. Now she looked at the two innocent children in the photo yet again. As many times as she looked at the picture lately, this was the first time she noticed how Gwen stood beside Tiffany and held on to her as if she was going to run away. Gwen had always taken such good care of Tiffany, and that was the way she always wanted it to be.

Claire began to feel worse about the comment she had made. She wished that she could take it back somehow; and yet the one thing that still remained crystal clear was that her baby had died a horrible death. After looking through all of Tiffany's things, she had still found no final letter to her, and she didn't understand why.

So forgiving Gwen in her mind was not an option that she was going to exercise. Talking to the silence in the room, Claire spoke. "I can't let anyone tell me how long to grieve. Gwen will be fine, but my Tiffany's gone."

CHAPTER 15

Gwen turned over and attempted to pull the crumpled sheet with her. When the sheet didn't budge, she tried to force her eyes open instead. The sun was shining brightly through the bedroom blinds as she tried to figure out what time it could be. Even though the clock was positioned on the nightstand, it would take entirely too much effort to make the little hand and the big hand make sense in her hazy mind. Drinking was not for her; she could kick herself for having had more than her usual two drinks. On top of that, she had had the nerve to gulp down the champagne like she was drinking Kool-Aid.

Turning all the way over onto her back, Gwen rubbed her burning eyes and realized that she had fallen asleep with her contacts in her eyes. She started to remember the scenes from the club. Then, all of a sudden, she remembered Marcus helping her into bed. She sat up slowly and closed her eyes as the entire evening flashed before her. Gwen's emotions were mixed. On the one hand, the evening could have ended differently and he could be in the bed next to her now, resting after making love for hours. A part of her had wanted that to happen, but another part was pleased Marcus had decided not to take advantage of her in such a weak state.

Gwen recalled him saying, after turning off the lights, that he would sleep downstairs. Willing herself to a full upright position, she swung her legs over to the edge of the bed. "Never again. I feel awful." Gwen was talking out loud as if she was convincing someone other than herself to keep her away from the devil's firewater. Standing up, she went into the bathroom and started the shower while she brushed her teeth twice and took several swishes of mouthwash. She dropped a couple of drops of foam facial wash on her washcloth and cleaned all the residue of the makeup she had worn last night. She removed her contacts and deposited them in some solution, and dropped the nightshirt on the floor. Stepping into the shower, she allowed the hot water to attack her body. Lathering a couple of times, she rinsed off, quickly washed her hair, and turned off the water. Toweling off, she walked back into the bedroom and reached across the end of the bed for her robe. After moisturizing, oiling and lotioning down, she added a little leave-in conditioner to her short hair and went in search of Marcus. When she got downstairs, she noticed that everything was in its place and the sofa had not been pulled out. The pillows did look a little off-centered, and there was a note on the coffee table.

> *Gwen, I'm sorry I couldn't stay around to fix you breakfast, but Andre had to go out of town and I needed to be at the club to receive a shipment for him. I'll call you a little later. Thanks for letting me tuck you in.*
>
> *Love, Marcus*
>
> *P.S. I know you feel like crap; make sure you eat something. It will make you feel better.*

Gwen was a little disappointed that he was already gone, but it was probably better that he was. Her defenses were still down and there was no telling what might have happened. After all, she had gone downstairs looking for him, freshly showered with only a robe on. Looking down at the note in her hand and at the thin fabric of her robe, she thought, *What was I thinking?*

Before she gave way to the disappointment that was threatening to pitch a tent over her day, she forced herself into the kitchen to fix something to eat. What she really wanted was to go back upstairs and throw herself in the bed, but that really wouldn't make her feel better, and she would more than likely end up there for the remainder of the day.

After gathering all the ingredients she needed for her breakfast, she quickly went about the task of preparing a Belgian waffle with fresh strawberry topping, turkey bacon, and completed it all with a glass of freshly squeezed orange juice. Resting her head against the headrest of the chair, she inhaled deeply, realizing that she'd just wolfed down the entire contents of her breakfast. She was draining the last drop of juice from the glass when the phone rang. Jumping up, she reached for the cordless, hoping that it was Marcus. In a cheery voice that she wasn't feeling, she spoke clearly into the phone. "Hello."

"Yes, good morning. I'm trying to reach Ms. Gwendolyn James."

"This is she." Gwen glanced out the window with a puzzled look on her face. She had no idea who the person was on the other end of the phone. Who else knew she was staying in Kyra's home? And who, for that matter, knew she was in Richmond?

"Ms. James. This is Dr. Ryan. You called my office yesterday afternoon. I'm sorry I wasn't available to talk with you, but I was out of town attending a seminar. Kyra did mention to me before she left town that you may be calling to set up an appointment."

Gwen was embarrassed that she had had to contact someone in this lady's capacity at all. "I see. Well, I was calling to see if I could do just that, set up an appointment. It's been a while since I've lived in this area. Kyra recommended you and seemed sure that you may be able to help me." The thought of her sanity resting in someone else's hands bothered her, but she just couldn't go on the way she had been. As much as she wanted to hang up and tell Dr. Ryan that she was sorry to have bothered her, she knew that she had to follow through with it and see her at least once.

"I understand. Well, Ms. James, I am pretty booked, but I can see you next week." She was clicking keys, obviously checking her availability electronically.

"That long?" Now that she'd made the first step, Gwen couldn't believe she would have to wait. She sat down on the stool next to the breakfast nook.

"Just a second. Let me check to see if I have any cancellations. Maybe I can fit you in."

After a few minutes she spoke, informing Gwen that she noticed a cancellation that her secretary had recorded in her daily planner. "Can you be here around one p.m.?"

"Of course. That won't be a problem."

"Do you know where my office is located?"

"I believe so. Kyra wrote the directions down for me. I'm familiar with that area of town, so I should have no problem."

"Fine, then. I will see you at one o'clock." The phone disconnected. Gwen immediately got up and started cleaning the kitchen so that she could go upstairs and get ready for her appointment. She was planning on allowing at least half an hour more than it would take her to get across town to Dr. Ryan's office, just in case the lunch traffic was a little thick.

Not sure what the rest of her afternoon would involve, she decided to take a couple of aspirins and hope that at the very least the appointment would bring her a little insight into what she was feeling. Ideally, it would bring her a whole lot of comfort. If she were lucky enough to get one out of the two, she wouldn't be disappointed. Swallowing her pride

and finally doing what everyone thought she should have
done a long time ago would be well worth it.

  Gwen walked into Suite 202 a couple of minutes before
her appointment time. Behind the simple oak desk sat an
older lady dressed in a colorful smock. Gwen introduced
herself and informed her that she had a one o'clock appointment. The receptionist offered Gwen a cup of coffee, which
she declined.

  Retreating to the reception area, Gwen sat down in the
empty room and looked through the magazines that rested
on the oak table. The room was decorated with the same
simplicity as the receptionist area. Sounds of classical music
could be heard in the background. For her it was a little unnerving, but Gwen guessed that for some, classical music
could be very soothing. Her big question was, who selected
the music that most medical offices played, anyway? You
would think that they would want patients to feel relaxed and
at ease and not overdosed with music that was only meant to
be played at funeral parlors.

  Nervously, she placed the old copy of *Ebony* back on the
table and began glancing around the room. She watched as
the lady behind the desk looked at the computer screen,
cursing loudly enough for Gwen to hear. Every time she hit
a key and waited for something to happen, she swore. The
computer obviously was not a piece of equipment that she
used to make her work go smoothly. Gwen couldn't help but
smile; the lady reminded her of Patrice's Aunt Virgie when
she tried to learn the basics on the computer that Patrice
sent. Patrice wanted her to learn how to surf the Internet, and
especially how to receive and send e-mails. Gwen agreed to
help, but after spending almost a week at it, she knew that
teaching the more seasoned folk was not her cup of tea.

  The door situated behind the receptionist's desk squeaked
open and a small gentleman walked out. A tall, mocha-

complexioned lady dressed in a white linen suit, who appeared to be around Gwen's age, walked out behind him. Her small-rimmed glasses sat on top of her head, and she had a beautiful smile that seemed comforting and reassuring when she spoke to the man. He smiled back at her and said a few last words, and was on his way to the elevator.

The woman spoke softly to the lady who sat behind the desk and who was visibly disturbed. Reaching over the older lady's shoulder, she assured her that she was doing fine. Hitting a few keys on the computer keyboard, she explained a couple of things, while at the same time removing the hex that was on the machine that kept it from obeying the commands of the older lady. After handling the situation, she turned her focus to the sitting area. Walking the short distance around the desk and across the aisle, she came over and extended her hand. "Good afternoon. You must be Gwendolyn James."

Gwen managed to speak in the affirmative. "Yes, I am."

"Its nice to meet you. I'm Samatha Ryan." Her small hand wrapped around Gwen's warmly. She continued to speak. "And this is my mother, Mary Ellen Smith. My secretary is out sick this week, and Mom here agreed to handle the front end of things for me. Had I known that she was going to beat up the office equipment, I would have hired a temp." She started laughing.

"Talk about me all you want, but this thing is a waste of money if it don't do what you want it to do." Her mother continued striking the keys like it was a piano in need of tuning.

"Come on in, Ms. James. Let's leave Mother to her work." Amused at the way mother and daughter were kidding around, Gwen smiled and walked into the office behind her.

Once inside the office, Gwen looked around for a couch. However, she noticed that unlike the shrinks' offices on television, this office was bright and airy. There were two large, upholstered high-back chairs with oversize armrests that were positioned on both sides of a small oak table. The table held an antique brass lamp that gave off a soft glow against the cream-colored walls. The actual lighting in the room was minimal, and Gwen noticed that the curtains were drawn with only a hint of sunlight trying to spill through the slight crack that existed. The oak desk matched the rest of the décor, which consisted of two wall bookcases and a credenza that held a seventeen-inch monitor. The smell of aromatherapy candles settled in Gwen's nostrils. The lavender and vanilla fragrances were very inviting; she immediately wanted to sit down, cross her legs, relax, and enjoy the mixture of scents for a while—which, she thought, was Dr. Ryan's ultimate goal in combining the two scents.

Turning around in the middle of the floor, Dr. Ryan said, "Please, Ms. James, have a seat. Can I get you anything? A soft drink, coffee, or water?" She walked over to the window closest to her desk and opened the draperies.

Gwen replied, "No, thanks. I'm fine."

Dr. Ryan pointed to one of the chairs located beside the table. She took the seat next to it and shifted a little as if trying to locate the ideal comfy spot in the chair. "Kyra and I have been friends for a while. We met a few years ago at a fund-raiser and hit it off immediately. Both of us have very busy schedules, but whenever we can squeeze in a couple of hours of free time we get together for dinner or drinks." She reached for the bottle of Dasani on the table and poured a little in the cup next to it. " Since I have heard so much about you, I feel like I know you."

"I don't know if that's good or bad." Gwen attempted a weak smile.

"Of course, it's good. Kyra thinks very highly of you. She called before she left town and told me that she would be leaving my number with you just in case you decided to talk to someone." She spoke professionally and confidently, but the relaxed and warm look never left her face. "Now, she only mentioned that you were having some problems coping with your sister's death, and that it might help for you to open up a little. So, with that said, I'm going to let you fill me in a little more."

Gwen glanced nervously around the room and crossed her legs at the ankle. "Well, Dr. Ryan, this is all new to me. I've never had to talk to a psychiatrist before, and I don't know exactly where to start."

"First of all, don't be caught up in what I do for a living. Just talk to me. I'm not in this position to judge you or to tell you what you should and should not be feeling. My job is just to help you make sense of your feelings. I realize that this first visit will be a little awkward and might make you feel somewhat uneasy, but trust me, it will get easier as we go along. Just start anywhere you like, and I'll jump in when I need you to elaborate on something."

"Do you mind if I start by walking around a little? I'm more than nervous, and if I sat here facing you like this, I'll probably never be able to say more than my own name."

"No, I don't mind at all. Do whatever makes you feel comfortable." Dr. Ryan removed the glasses from her head, set them on the table next to her, and settled back to listen to the problems that lay at the core of Gwen's being. In part, these were Gwen's constant hives and the sleepless nights that had seemed to be caused by Tiffany's death. But Gwen would learn that what she felt went a lot deeper than Tiffany's death.

Gwen stood looking out the window at the parking lot. She had been talking for almost the entire session. She felt as if she would shut down at some points, but she managed to lift herself out of the emotional pit that threatened to consume her being. At one point, she started crying, but she never stopped talking. Dr. Ryan handed her a cup of water and a couple of tissues. Dr. Ryan's voice in the distance reassured Gwen that she understood and that she could stop anytime. Eventually, though, Dr. Ryan's voice became just a noise in the distance. She wasn't sure when it happened, but after a while, it wasn't Dr. Ryan she was opening up to anymore but a part of herself that desperately needed to understand and be released from this trauma.

Now she turned and seated herself in the chair beside Dr. Ryan, trembling at the rawness that she felt after sharing such intimate parts of herself.

"Gwen, I want you to understand that what you are feeling and what you are going through are not something that is foreign to me or to anyone else who has ever lost someone close to them. I believe strongly that the hives are connected to the psychological part of you. They are your body's way of saying, *Hey, I'm dealing with some messed-up stuff, and I can't take it.* People handle things differently, and this is how you're dealing with your sister's death. But that is not the only thing that you are dealing with."

Looking at her, puzzled and a little dazed, Gwen lifted an eyebrow as if questioning her comment. "What do you mean?"

"In short, I believe that you are suffering two losses: the loss of your sister and the loss of your mother. You have some hostile emotions about how your mother has turned her back on you and how she blames you for what happened. Because she is your mother and you were raised from a child to love and obey her, you are not releasing what you feel, you're holding it all in. I won't get into the details about all that. Gwen, what is important here is that you're suffering, and if you continue this way, what you are suppressing psychologically will begin to manifest itself in a physical illness, something much more severe than the hives, and I can imagine that the hives alone have been pretty bad. This is my professional opinion. But the good news is, I believe that I can help you. And if you're willing to see me a couple of times a week, I can help you get past this stage and get on with your life the way it's meant to be. How does that sound?"

Gwen still wasn't sure that this was the best option, but

she was tired of the emotional turmoil. Defeated and drained, she spoke. "Anything is better than where I am with all this. How long do you think it will take? I'm going to be in the city a while, but I didn't plan on seeing a shr . . . I mean, someone like yourself the entire time I'm here."

Dr. Ryan smiled. "I know. You don't want to spend your time off with a shrink. I don't mind you using that term. But what is important is that I help you. Call me whatever you like." Standing up, she picked up her glasses from the table, walked behind her desk, and took a seat. "I can't really say how long it will take. It really depends on you and how well the sessions go. Your unlocking the door to all that you're feeling is going to be the key. I would like to go ahead and schedule you for next Monday. This time is fine with me if it suits you."

"That's fine. I'm pretty flexible." Standing up, Gwen walked over to the front of Dr. Ryan's desk and extended her hand. "Thanks so much."

"Before you go. I don't believe in writing prescriptions that much. But since I believe that the hives are linked to your emotional distress, I'm going to write you a prescription for a low-dose antidepressant. Take it whenever you feel an outbreak of hives, and it should relax you a little and get rid of them a little more quickly. What is basically happening is, your body is going into overdrive emotionally, causing the hives to appear. The ingredients of these pills are just a way of assisting your system to calm down. As it does, the hives will disappear. Try them and let me know if they help at all. Now, I'll see you next week. If you need me before then, just call."

Gwen removed her sunglasses and looked at her reflection in the rearview mirror. She focused on the small lumps still visible under her eyes and along her jawbone and frowned. Reaching in her bag again, she removed the prescription and looked at it. She wasn't a big fan of medicine, and the thought of taking an antidepressant didn't sit well with her. The pills that her allergist had given her had done little more than make her light-headed and drowsy. Placing the prescription back in her bag, she sighed. Leaning her head forward against the steering wheel, she spoke to the dead silence in the car. "What should I do?" She closed her eyes and waited for the tears that stung her eyelids to come and wet the heat that she felt on her cheeks. After a few minutes, she noticed that the tears weren't coming, which was surprising, especially since tears had been as much a part of her daily ritual as combing her hair. What she felt in their place was something she had wished for and hadn't been fortunate enough to have—hope.

Today was the first step toward that, and it didn't feel half bad. Putting her sunglasses back on, she put the car into drive and mentally gauged her location and the distance to the nearest pharmacy.

CHAPTER 16

Taking a leisurely drive around the south side of the city, Gwen was surprised when she glanced at the digital clock on the dashboard and saw it read 7:05. She'd left Dr. Ryan's office over five hours ago. Three of those hours had been spent walking through the mall while she waited for the prescription that she'd dropped off at Walgreens. Being an impulsive buyer, she ended up picking up a pair of shoes and a couple of outfits, and stopped off at the MAC counter in Macy's, picked out a new lip color, and replenished her supply of foundation. She concluded her spontaneous shopping trip with a double-dipped cone of Dutch chocolate ice cream from Baskin-Robbins. But now two more hours had gone by and here she was back at home.

The phone was ringing off the hook as Gwen threw everything on the counter and grabbed it, panting pathetically. Clearly, her next span of time needed to be spent in a gym working her cardio system. She answered in a raspy voice, "Hello."

"Gwen, did I catch you at a bad time?" Kyra asked.

"Hey, girl. No, I was just walking in the door and had to rush to get the phone. I was going to call you, Kyra."

"Right. I'm sure you've been much too busy to even think about me. I've been busy settling in myself, but I wanted to call and make sure you were making out all right."

"Yes, I have, and you know that you didn't have to go out of your way making sure everything was at my fingertips." Gwen walked into the living room and sat down in the wing chair facing the fireplace. "You know that everything was so well stocked, I haven't even had to go to the grocery store yet. Kyra, you didn't have to do all of that. I was happy enough just to have a place to stay while I'm here."

"You know I wasn't just going to leave without making sure I stocked everything for you. Did you find everything else you needed? I left so many notes here and there, and by the time I got here I wondered if I left something out."

"No, you didn't. I can't believe how detailed you are. After about the tenth note, I remembered that you live by an organized code that most people would think is a little much. But you know I appreciate everything, don't you?"

"Yes, I do. And you know that I go overboard like that because I love you and I want to make sure that you have everything you need while you're relaxing. Speaking of relaxing, where is Patrice?"

"Oh, she had to go out of town for a meeting, but she'll be back by Friday or Saturday. I had to convince her that I would be all right here alone. I think the both of you have forgotten that I used to live here. I was the third musketeer."

"You're right. But you know I'm just a phone call away, and I'll just leave it at that." There was a little pause before either of them spoke. "Look, I've got to run, but please tell Patrice to slow her fast ass down, cancel some of her evening freak dates, and spend that time with you."

In the background, Gwen could hear someone announcing that dinner was being served.

"Girl, excuse the noise. I'm at an opening dinner ceremony for the program that I'm in. They are probably serving something that I either won't like or can't have. I've been trying to lose this extra cargo around the butt area and it has been an uphill journey."

They both knew that although Kyra wasn't pleased with her plus-size figure, she was truly a beautiful person, inside and out. "Girl, go ahead and enjoy the dinner. I'll call you soon. Love ya, bye," Gwen said.

Just as Gwen hung up the phone, there was a tap on the patio door. Without looking, she knew it was Scott. She wasn't sure how she could mask her disturbance at having seen him at the club in thug attire and hanging with that weave-wearing hoochie. She reminded herself on the short walk to the door that it wasn't her concern, and that she wouldn't bring it up.

"Hi, Scott. What's up?" Gwen stepped away from the door after opening it and gave him enough room to walk in.

"Oh, nothing. I just came over to check on you and to see if you were busy. I don't have any plans for the evening, and thought you might want to join me for dinner." He stood there dressed in a pair of khaki slacks and a chocolate-brown, cotton short-sleeve shirt. The person who stood before her was far from a thug; it was hard to imagine this outfit being in the same closet with the one he had sported the night before.

Her eyes were frozen in a deep concentrated stare. Gwen felt a stirring inside that was vaguely familiar. She fought mentally to combat the stirring, knowing too well that it was not a common occurrence.

"Gwen, did you hear me?" Scott questioned.

"I'm sorry, Scott. My mind was somewhere else. Where were you planning to go for dinner?"

"I wasn't sure. I thought I would check out this new place off West Broad."

"Look, I've been out all day, and I'm a little exhausted. I spent last evening with my friends. Since we don't get together much and we were celebrating, I had a little too much to drink. I've spent most of the day paying for it." Gwen searched his face and waited to see if he was going to mention seeing her at the club.

"Yeah. I was at the club myself. I didn't get close enough to say anything to you. I was a little surprised to see you there."

"Likewise." She couldn't say anything else and was hoping that her expression didn't show what she felt. "I was there with Patrice. Andre, the owner of the club, is a good friend of ours."

"Oh, that's right. Kyra did mention an Andre in your group, but I never got a chance to meet him over there. I didn't know he was the owner of Club Andre's. I was at the club the first night it opened and had such a good time, I thought that I would check it out again. I'm glad I did, it was off the chain. I mean hopping. He's got a good thing going on down there, and the location is perfect. Things have been dead in that area of town for a while, but Club Andre's will more than likely be the beginning of a new birth for that area. There are a few clubs in that area, but none that cater to us."

"Well, I'll be sure to let him know that you are planning on being one of his loyal customers." There was still no mention of the company he was keeping last night, so she continued. "I don't want to alter your plans but how about ordering something from the Italian restaurant up the street? Kyra left me a detailed list of places to eat and, of course, a list of who delivers."

"That sounds good. The food there isn't half bad. I'll accept your offer to eat in this time, but the next time I want to take you out and you decline, I'm going to get offended and think that you don't want to be seen with me outside the security of your temporary home."

God, that was the truth. "Please don't take it personal. I'm just not up for an evening out again." Smiling, she touched his arm in an apologetic manner. The minute Gwen touched his arm, a warm sensation came over her. All she could do was look away. He didn't say anything, but Gwen believed that he felt the same sensation because his words trailed off and became just muffled sounds.

"Excuse me, Scott. What were you saying?" Gwen attempted to act as though she was undisturbed by the strong current of electricity that just rippled through her body like a tidal wave.

"Nothing. Everything is cool." They both smiled at one another and went to the kitchen in search of the menu.

They enjoyed Italian cuisine and allowed an easy conversation to flow between them. Gwen listened attentively to what Scott had to say and, much like the first night, she relaxed, breathing a comforting and carefree sigh. Gwen wasn't sure what vibe Scott was sending but she was sensing that he was attracted to her, and what unnerved her even more was the curiosity she felt whenever she was in his presence.

Scott volunteered to help Gwen tidy up the kitchen and return everything to its perfect order. He picked up the dishtowel and wrapped it around his hand nervously. "Gwen, do you mind if I ask you a question?"

"If I say no, you'll probably figure out a way to ask me anyway. So shoot." She continued to wipe off the kitchen counter.

"What's the story between you and the guy you dated in college?" He wanted to know the answer to the question. Somehow he had to find out if the two really were history, or if there was a chance that she would allow history to repeat itself.

Gwen turned around slowly, reacting as if she had been knocked off her feet. It took a minute for the question to fully register, and when it did she had to take a deep breath. "Whatever happened to safe questions like what's your favorite color, your favorite food, your zodiac sign? Instead of those questions, you take a plunge head-first all up in my personal business."

"Sorry. I didn't mean to be so forward, but like I've said, Kyra has told me some things about the past and I was curi-

ous, I guess. But if you'd rather not answer, hey, I understand." He tried not to sound serious about his reply, but in
fact, her answering the question was important to him. He
knew that she had no notion how important.

She turned, leaning her back against the kitchen counter,
raised her hand up to her waist a bit, and twisted the ruby
birthstone ring that was placed on her right hand. "The mystery guy of whom you speak is known as Marcus. Mr. Marcus McGuire. And yes, we were what one would consider an
item back in the day. He was the one man I would have attempted to move heaven and earth for. The problem was that
he knew it. I guess you could say he played my feelings and
me. I thought we had the makings of a great relationship. We
were friends first and we both had a thirst for life and pur-
sued our degrees with determination and drive. I mean, we
had everything, and I do mean everything, in perspective."
Gwen frowned a little as she continued. "We had fun, don't
get me wrong, lots of it, but we always knew when to get serious about our schoolwork. I guess because we always vowed
that our future mattered, because my future was his future,
and vice versa." Gwen's eyes narrowed on the emerald-green
diamond shapes on the tile floor. "Anyway, I guess we weren't
meant to be, because I caught him in bed with one of his fraternity sweethearts."

"Dag. That's deep. But you were both very young. Did
you ever consider forgiving him? I'm not making an excuse
for what happened, but it was one incident, and from what
you're telling me, you two had a good thing going."

"You know, Scott, you're not telling me anything that our
friends didn't tell me back then, and still continue to tell me
to this day. But there is one important fact that I can't seem
to overlook or forgive."

Scott moved toward her impulsively, not wanting to miss
her next comment. "What was that? It couldn't possibly be
that bad."

"For the life of me, I can't get over catching the man I

loved, more than anything, with his head between the legs of another woman. If you figure out a way that I can somehow forget that and forgive something that disgusting, let me know. Because I, for one, ain't feeling that kind of forgiveness."

Shocked, Scott couldn't find any words to say, and could only reach out and caress the hands that she was wringing in her attempt to compose herself. "What can I say, Gwen? I mean, some men don't realize a good thing, and I'm sure that Marcus has regretted it more than one day. I was once told that one man's mistake is another man's good fortune." He wanted to say more and tell her everything that he was feeling. But fear of rejection and wanting first to maintain a friendship halted him in his tracks.

Gwen decided to let all that go and changed the subject. "Scott, do you play backgammon? I was thinking that if you didn't have anything to do, you could play a couple of games with me. I'm so wired from the overdose of food, I won't be able to get to sleep for a while."

"Yes, I play. But I was thinking that we could go for a drive. I know you didn't want to go to dinner, but it's a nice night out and it would be a waste not to enjoy it. Come on, I won't keep you out long. I promise."

"I don't know, Scott. I was out until the wee hours of the morning, and I've been running around all day." Gwen was making every attempt to discourage him.

"I won't take no for an answer. I'm not going to let you be a prisoner here. And besides, Kyra wouldn't want you to spend so much time stuck in this house."

"All right, Scott. Just let me go and get my purse and keys." Gwen went up the steps into the bedroom and reasoned with herself that it would probably be okay to take a drive with him.

Before she went back downstairs, she ran a comb through her hair. Cupping her hand over her mouth, she decided that she probably needed to brush her teeth and gargle a little too.

Walking into the bathroom, she took a couple of minutes to take care of her dental hygiene needs; before she realized what she was doing, she applied a little light makeup to her face and a fresh coat of lipstick. Taking in her reflection, she asked herself, "What in the world are you doing, Gwendolyn James?" She couldn't believe she was doing any of this. Who cared what her mouth tasted like, and who would get close enough to find out? Turning around, she flipped the light off and went back downstairs.

"I'm ready to roll, Scott." Gwen walked into the living room and quickly scanned the room in search of Scott.

Walking up behind her, Scott leaned his head over her shoulder. He was so close she could feel his breath on her neck. "Hmmm. You smell good. Did you freshen up just for me?"

"No, I did not." Gwen tried to control her emotions, but the truth was that the nearness of him had thrown her off balance.

"I'm sorry. I was just waiting patiently for you to come down. I didn't think you would be that long; it's obvious you did a little extra while you were up there."

"Look, Scott. Why would I do anything extra than my normal routine to hang out with you? Now, if you have an older brother you want to hook me up with, I'm game. But I feel completely safe with you and in no danger of a head-over-heels romance."

"Ouch. That hurts. I don't have any siblings, but I would warn you that looks, my sweet Gwen, can be very deceiving." He was more than a little hurt by her comment, but knew that he needed to play it off. There would be a time when he would reveal what he was feeling for her, and he was hoping that time wouldn't be far away. Gwen would see him for who he really was, a man who was very capable of knowing how to love a woman.

Just as he was getting ready to open the door, his cellular phone chimed a tone that sounded like a nursery rhyme. Retrieving it from his pocket, he spoke into the compact electronic gadget. "Scott." Gwen stood nearby, watching him and trying to eavesdrop on the part of the conversation that she could hear. "What, no one else can do it? Yeah, well, I know that. I'll be there in a little bit." Scott looked down at the vinyl runner that covered the carpeted entryway. Flipping the phone closed, he glanced at Gwen out of the corner of his eye. "You know I have to go, don't you?"

"Yeah. I gathered that much. It's okay, though. I'll just spend the rest of the evening reading a good book."

"Oh well, let me go so you can get started. I wouldn't want to detain you from your hot evening. I'll come by tomorrow, if that suits you." Scott attempted to camouflage his disappointment.

"Sure." Gwen couldn't understand why she was reacting so coldly. They were just hanging out together and she was totally cool with that.

"Good night." He turned, opened the door, and walked out.

Gwen went into the kitchen, opened the refrigerator, and glared at the wine bottle on the shelf. She reasoned that since she would be starting to take the prescription pills tomorrow, she could indulge in one glass of wine tonight. Deciding against it, she sucked her teeth, closed the refrigerator door, and turned off all the lights downstairs.

Walking up the steps in the dark, she smiled, knowing that her latest book selection was waiting to capture her attention from the first page till her eyes couldn't stay open. Why couldn't she have someone ready to cater to her physical needs, instead of her having to cuddle up with fictional characters whose romance was as close as she could come to the real thing? She thought about her social life. To be completely honest, she hadn't been happy or content in any of the short relationships she had been in since Marcus. Now she couldn't even spend more than a couple of hours with Scott. Gwen swore under her breath. She couldn't see herself being involved with Scott, but his company was something that she was getting used to.

Who knows? Maybe there was some truth to what her Aunt Rose had told her about scorned lovers burying the underwear of the one they wanted to always remain loyal to them. Gwen was told that once it was done, the person would never be happy with anyone else. They would stray, and sometimes stay away for years, but eventually they would end up back with the scorned lover.

Recalling the story that she had dismissed as a lot of superstitious nuisance, Gwen spoke out loud. "Marcus, am I under your spell?"

CHAPTER 17

The days passed quickly. Gwen couldn't believe that it had been a week since Patrice left. What was supposed to be a two-day trip turned into a week, and she was missing her terribly. Earlier in the day when she had received a call from Patrice, she tried to catch her up on everything that had been going on since Monday. She finally gave up when Patrice's biggest concern was whether or not she had gotten any.

Gwen chastised Patrice for her overactive sexual imagination. "I know that you didn't step out of your ongoing meeting to call and see if I had tripped the light fantastic."

Patrice snickered. "If you're telling me that you ended the drought and actually let something other than your bath pouf touch the promised land, I'll put you on hold, go back down the hall, and end the meeting. Gwen, if you gave up the drawers, I'm on the next plane home, 'cause I need to get a play-by-play face-to-face."

"Oh, you're too funny. If I did, and I'm not admitting anything one way or the other, I wouldn't give you the pleasure of harping on it for the next decade."

"Girlfriend, if you did, I would definitely know. That prissy little walk would be a thing of the past. Your stance would be more like James Arness from the television show *Gunsmoke,* or the notorious John Wayne." Patrice's high-pitched laughter filled the phone line as she pictured Gwen standing bowlegged.

"That's enough. Was there a real reason for your call?" Gwen tried not to burst out laughing. but she had to admit that Patrice's comments were funny.

While Gwen waited for Patrice to answer, she reminisced about the summer after she'd finished college. She had been back home for all of two months, and Patrice had come to spend the weekend with her. That was the summer when, along with losing her mind over Marcus, she also lost her virginity. It was funny what loneliness and a little too much free time could do. But she never regretted her relationship with Ric Davis, or the fact that he was the one she decided to share the most intimate part of herself with.

Ric was everything any woman would want in a man. He was, of course, fine as he could be, a good listener, and above all, he was so committed and provided the security blanket that she needed. Even though everything with them happened so fast, losing him after having given up something that she considered sacred was never a concern. She trusted him wholeheartedly and believed that he would never hurt her. That was no easy task after what she had been through. The one thing she'd admitted to herself early on was that Ric was nothing like Marcus.

She remembered the first evening they spent together. He told her how he had sacrificed his college education to look after his father and mother. His father had suffered an accident at the beginning of his senior year, which rendered him disabled. Ric had been a star basketball player at one of Gwen's rival schools in the county. Everyone knew that he would be slated for a scholarship with no problem. But instead of continuing to earn the accolades of every high school coach in the area, the entire hometown, and going on to play for some big-name college and possibly the pros, he sat out his senior year and worked part-time to help make ends meet.

His story touched her heart. She admired his stability and assertive attitude. Even though he only attended the local community college, he mapped out his life to the letter. His five-year plan made her indecisiveness seem even more immature. After six months, he wanted to take their relationship to another level. But no matter how hard she tried, she could not shed the feelings she had for Marcus. As much as she wanted to be with Ric, she knew that she could never love him the way that he deserved to be loved. He was, of course, disappointed and hurt, but they managed to stay friends. The last she heard, he was married with a daughter who looked just like him and was without a doubt the apple of his eye. Funny how life goes on for some; for her, it just stood still somehow, like a train always in motion but with no true destination. For Gwen, happiness was always just slightly out of reach.

Snapping out of her daydream, she listened as Patrice continued. "Yeah. But now that I've spent the last ten minutes entertaining myself with your situation, you may not even consider my request."

"What is it? Not that I even want to know what it is you could possibly want me to do for you."

"Chill. It's pretty innocent, actually." Patrice did her best plea for getting Gwen to take over her session with the girls. After Gwen accepted, Patrice went on to tell her what she planned and that everything was already in motion since she knew Gwen wouldn't turn her down. Before she could get yelled at, she thanked her and said that she would see her tomorrow morning when she picked her up from the airport.

Patrice and the girls looked forward to their sessions. It allowed the girls to relax and express themselves without fear of being told they were too loud or their opinions were too out of the box. The fact of the matter was that they were teenagers and their actions were typical of the average inner-city girl. Patrice had taken the responsibility of addressing their concerns and talking to them about everything that was important to them. No subject was a hot topic or one that she didn't deal with. For most of them, she was the only older person who was willing to listen and help them make sense of an otherwise complicated existence. While she never encouraged them to have sex or indulge in activities that would lead to sex, she did talk about protecting themselves and how to avoid making decisions that could affect them negatively.

Gwen thought about Patrice's involvement with the girls, and hoped that she would be a good substitute for her best friend. She wasn't the world's best authority on the topics that she was sure the girls would want to know about, but for friendship's sake, she would do her best.

Sitting quietly on the floor pillow in the living room deliberating on her visit with Dr. Ryan and the activities of the past week, she had to admit that she was feeling a lot better emotionally. Even though today's session had only been an hour, she was already beginning to feel comfortable talking to her. Feelings of peace were going to her brain and overpowering the dismal feelings of uncertainty. She was even beginning to believe what Dr. Ryan told her, that if she would release some of the anxiety and concentrate on healing herself, the sessions would work and she could return to a normal life. What Dr. Ryan didn't know was that Gwen couldn't remember when she had ever had a normal life.

Picking up the remote, Gwen turned off the television. It was on merely out of habit and not because she was interested in a particular show. She went into the kitchen and grabbed the ingredients she would need to make one of her baked homemade wonders. She was soon humming and busying herself with the exact amounts, stirring them together in hopes that the girls would enjoy the time and effort that went into baking the homemade cake. Putting the cake in the oven, she picked up the phone to place the carryout order that she would need for the session with the girls. Just as she was finished relaying the list to the caterer Patrice used monthly, the phone beeped. Clicking over, she answered, "Hello."

"Hey, big sis. You too busy to call me these days?" T.J. said.

"No. I've been calling both you and Dad. Every time I call, you have either just left home or haven't gotten to Mom and Dad's yet."

"I know. I've been getting your messages. I just couldn't resist giving you a hard time."

"That's just like you. Anyway, I did speak to Baron a couple of nights ago and he told me about all the changes that Mom is making." Not sure if she even felt like talking about any of it, she hesitated and then continued. "He mentioned that the bedroom upstairs looks just like Tiffany's room that was in Atlanta. And that Dad was upset because Mom wants a garden just for Tiffany's memorial."

"The boys must have overheard me and Kim talking. I was going to tell you about all this myself a little later, but since my son beat me to the punch, I'll tell you what's been going on." T.J. wasn't thrilled with the task set before him. He realized that all of what he had to say was going to be quite a mouthful and a little too much drama for Gwen to deal with. However, since she obviously wanted to know, he couldn't willingly keep it all from her.

"Gwen, Mom is tripping, and it's gotten to the point that she isn't even listening to Dad. He's trying his best not to explode because he knows that she is grieving, but he's frustrated. She acts as if she is the only one that is hurt and angry."

Gwen posed a troubling question. "Have you tried to talk to her? I know she can be as stubborn as hell sometimes, but there has to be someone who can reason with her."

"Well, that person isn't me. Been there, tried that. She told me to mind my business and that she could do anything

she wants to any room in the house. And that if she wanted
to add a garden to keep Tiffany's memory alive she would do
that too. She acts as if she is upset that we all aren't feeling
the same way that she is. I know that I lost my sister, but I
want to go on with my life and not dwell on it day after day.
And that's what Mom wants to do. If you're in the room with
her longer than five minutes, the conversation shifts to
something about Tiffany. It's gotten so bad we don't even
allow the boys to go over there that often. She was over there
telling them that Tiffany isn't resting and that she was taken
away before her time. That's just a little too much for them to
absorb."

Gwen leaned forward and squeezed her eyes shut. "Well,
I don't know what to say. You know she isn't going to be re-
sponsive to anything I have to say. And after she hung up on
me, I don't care to make another call or travel the distance
back home to comfort her. Forgive me if I sound cold."

"I understand. You have a right to feel that way. Don't let
any of this stress you any more than it already has. Dad will
work it out and I'll be here to help him. So, how was your
appointment today? Kim told me that you two talked about
the first session and that you had another one this afternoon."

"It went pretty well. It helps that Dr. Ryan is so easy to
talk to. Somehow I feel like I've known her for a long time.
I know that's strange, but there's just something about her."
Thinking about what she was sharing with T.J., she continued. "But most of all, I think that she can help me."

"That's all that matters. I miss you, but I know you're in
the best place right now. You need a break away from this
drama. But remind me to be mad as hell at you later for leaving me here alone to deal with this mess."

"Okay. You know I love you, not only for shouldering my
part, but because you're the best brother a sister could have."
Gwen could feel herself getting a little emotional. What her
mother was doing bothered her, but she felt a little relief

knowing that her dad and brother were upset about it too. For her, though, the hurt was a bit deeper, because her mother's actions were directed at her. It was pretty clear to Gwen that the whole ordeal was being done to make her feel that there was no place for her.

"So, how's Marcus?"

"Who?"

"Don't play me cheap. Kim tells me everything once her head hits the pillow. In that territory she becomes all mine. My loving is like an intoxicating force; girlfriend tells any- and everything."

"Darn. She got it bad. The last thing I told her was not to tell you under any circumstances."

"Well, now you know. So answer my question."

"Marcus and I have been spending a little time together. And I've enjoyed doing just that. I'm not ready to call it anything other than two friends hanging out. In fact, I'm pretty comfortable with the time we are sharing. Who knows? I might actually think about a real date sometime in the future."

"Boy, did he make a mistake by pissing you off! I'm not taking up for him or anything like that, but an inmate on death row would have a better chance of getting a pardon from the governor than Marcus would of your forgiving and forgetting what happened more than ten years ago."

"Well, I can't help that." Gwen frowned at the mention of how long it had been since she and Marcus separated.

"Well, sweetness. I've got to go and take the boys to the barbershop. I'll call you later. If you need me, you know where I am. Love ya."

"Love you, too." Gwen held the phone and listened to the hum of the dial tone. Placing the cordless phone back on the holder to charge up, she went into the kitchen to wait for the last few minutes of baking time so she could remove the cake from the oven.

She didn't want to say anything to T.J. or Patrice because

they would blow things out of proportion, but she'd spent a few evenings and almost every morning with Scott. They dined together and spent time just hanging out. Yesterday they even drove up to Skyline Drive to enjoy the scenery and walk around the campus of the University of Virginia. They stopped in one of the little pubs for a couple of Long Island iced teas and nachos. When the waiter asked Scott for his ID, she was reminded again that he was much younger than she was.

She had to confess, though, that his conversation and the attention that he showered on her made her forget about the age thing. He was the perfect gentleman, and his ability to listen more than talk was one that most men his senior could use a lesson in. Nothing about anything they did was ever rushed; he always acted as if what he was doing at that particular moment was more important than anything else. That day had been so much fun. When she returned home that evening, she could hardly believe that they had been together since eight o'clock that morning; it was almost midnight. As soon as they stepped into the house and were ready to relax a little, his pager went off. The sound of it not only let him know that someone wanted to reach him, but it let her know that as much as she enjoyed his company and was learning so much about him, there was still so much she didn't know. Gwen wasn't sure if his mysterious actions should be ignored for the sake of having someone to hang out with, someone who was not a romantic threat; however, she honestly enjoyed his company. Deep down though, a part of her was stirred by Scott's presence. The truth of the matter was, it felt so good she didn't want their time together to end.

Gwen navigated for what seemed like forever, not sure exactly where the youth center was located. She failed to get the directions from Patrice, assuming that it couldn't be that difficult to find. She was fairly familiar with that section of town; it was just that she didn't expect one of the neighboring streets to have turned into a one-way. After going around and around in a circle, she finally gave up and asked for directions from a kindly old gentleman who was out walking a snow-white toy poodle. He gladly pointed her in the right direction. Realizing that she was simply going the wrong way each of the three times she attempted to get to the Brook Avenue Youth Center, she felt a little perturbed when she pulled up in front of the center, which now stuck out like a sore thumb.

Just as she went around to the back door on the passenger side to remove the food and drinks she'd picked up, she couldn't help but notice a white S500 Mercedes Benz coming to a stop across the street, almost causing a major collision. A van almost ran into the back of the vehicle because it hadn't pulled over properly or signaled that it was stopping. Focusing on the car, she tried to see what was going on behind the heavily tinted windows when suddenly the back door opened and Gina jumped out. The person in the backseat put the window down and yelled after her. "Gina, girl, your ass better be ready when I come back through here in two hours."

She never turned around to acknowledge that she heard the person, but seemed visibly upset when she walked past Gwen.

"Hey, you. You want to help me get this food and stuff in?" Gwen tried to act as if she hadn't witnessed firsthand the loud comment.

"I'm sorry, Ms. Gwen. I didn't see you there. Ms. Patrice called me at home earlier today to tell me that you were going to be taking over the session for her tonight."

"Don't sound so excited about it. I promise I won't be a complete bore, despite what Patrice probably told you."

"Oh, I don't think that you will be. I was just thinking about some other things. Let's go get this stuff inside. The girls are always starved." Gina started removing bags, trying to cover up the shakiness she was feeling. Quincy, her boy-

friend, had been screaming at her from the time he'd picked
her up from school. He'd wanted her to pick up a package
from across town because one of the girls he usually used
was sick. Gina had told him she wasn't comfortable with
doing it, and he'd started tripping on how much he did for
her and how she didn't love him. She loved him, but he was
changing more and more each day.

Gwen wanted to ask her what was going on and why she
was so upset. Instead, she walked behind Gina and into the
recreation room where some tables were already set up and
most of the girls were waiting.

"Hey, hoochies. This is Ms. Gwen. You all remember her.
She was at the game a couple of weeks ago with Ms. Patrice."
Some nodded that they remembered. "She'll be conducting
our speak-out session tonight. Ms. Patrice told me to tell you
all to be nice, and don't give Ms. Gwen a hard way to go by
asking a million questions. If any of you decide to pick
tonight to be a wiseass, you will have to answer to me."

"I don't think that will be necessary," Gwen said. "I trust
that everyone will be on their best behavior. Right, girls?"
They all responded slowly. "Now, with that out of the way,
Gina, tell me, what is the usual procedure for the evening?
Do you all eat while you talk or what?"

"Well, Ms. Gwen, we just grab some food and a drink, sit
down on the floor, and talk while we eat."

"All right, then, let's get started. Oh, by the way . . . I
know that Patrice is not much of a cook. She had included an
apple pie from Reggie's Restaurant, but I opted to make a
homemade apple spice cake instead."

Everyone clapped and yelled. One of the girls spoke up.
"God, Ms. Gwen, we love Coach Patrice and all, but can you
join us every speak-out session so we can get some real
food?" The other girls laughed and agreed.

Once the food was served, the conversation started. Surprisingly, Gwen had done very little in the way of replying
and explaining. The group of girls knew everything, and she

did mean everything. The one thing that bothered her was that they didn't really know enough about life and love to be entertaining the sexual issues that they brought up. At one point when she was trying to explain why it was best to wait to get involved in a sexual relationship, she wanted to tell them about her sister.

Although Tiffany was much older than they all were, she had trusted someone like many of them were doing, and that trust had ended up costing her her life. Telling them to wait because it was the best thing to do just wasn't hitting home for them. They were so young and so impressionable. The one common thread that linked these girls together was that they all wanted a good life and a ticket out of the projects. None of them wanted to turn out like their mothers, aunts, and sisters; yet she wondered now, as she looked around the room, how many of them would be able to dodge the system that was not set up to assist them in becoming all that they could be. Being with them struck a chord. She just wanted to help them in some way, but her life was already full, with a lot of other things she had to do. Yet she knew that they were placed in her life at this particular time for a reason. Folding the last table and helping Gina put it up against the wall, she mumbled, "Why me?"

Gina looked up through eyes that seemed much older than her sixteen years, and asked, "Did you say something?"

"Not really. I was just thinking out loud." The rest of the girls hugged Gwen, said good night, and all just walked out in time to catch the transit bus at the corner that would take them to their destinations. Gina was the only one who didn't have to catch the bus. She told the other girls to go ahead, that her man would be coming to pick her up. "Gina, can I ask you a question?"

"Sure. Shoot." She pushed her braids out of her face and walked closer to where Gwen stood.

"Are you sexually active? I mean, you don't have to an-swer that if you don't want. I was just wondering, because you were able to answer many of the questions that the girls had about sex."

"I don't mind answering, Ms. Gwen. I've been having sex since I was thirteen years old. I mean with Quincy, that's my boyfriend. We've been together since then. Off and on because sometimes he just be acting like a fool wanting to be with other girls and stuff. But he always comes back. Quincy is my man and he takes care of me. Makes sure that I have things and money in my pocket to get my hair and nails done. Stuff like that."

"I see." Gwen proceeded with the rest of her questions with caution. She didn't want to upset Gina and cause her to storm out of the one place that obviously was safe for her. "Was that Quincy in the backseat of the car that dropped you off?" Gina nodded. "I couldn't help but notice how he yelled at you when we were coming in here tonight. Does he do that all the time?"

She turned away quickly before Gwen could look into her eyes. "Gosh, no. He was just in a hurry tonight. He had to make some runs and he wanted me to go, but I told him that I had to help you out as a favor to Ms. Patrice. He understood. He just be tripping sometimes."

"Well, I do appreciate you being here to help me out." Gwen checked to make sure everything was returned to its original order. Satisfied that everything was in place, she put an arm around Gina and turned off the light. The muggy night air hit her across the face. She laughed at Gina dancing to some beat she heard coming from a passing car.

"Gina, if I tried that dance, you would be coming to visit me at the hospital. This body cannot do anything close to that."

"Sure you can. You and Ms. Patrice are still young, and so pretty. You two don't look like you even out of college. Both of y'all did the education thang, and now you're living the 'phat' life."

"We haven't done anything that you can't do. I want you to remember that." Gwen looked at her seriously. She wanted to continue, but the car that Gina had gotten out of earlier pulled to the curb and the driver was blowing like it was recess.

"Gina, girl, come on. I gave you extra time and you still out here yapping like we don't have stuff to do."

She turned with a look of panic on her face. "I'll see you next time, Ms. Gwen. And tell Ms. Patrice that I took real good care of you tonight."

Not sure why, Gwen quickly asked, "Gina, can you come over here quickly and give me a hug?"

"What?" She turned and looked at her, puzzled.

"You know . . . a hug. Two people get close together and embrace."

"Yeah. I know what a hug is, I just wasn't sure I heard you correctly." She walked over quickly, reached up, and hugged Gwen tightly. Pulling away, she smiled and said, "My mommy doesn't even give me hugs anymore. Thanks." The horn blew again. She ran to the curb and jumped into the backseat beside the guy who had to be Quincy.

Gwen knew that he was dealing in some negative foul stuff, because brother didn't even have to drive himself around.

CHAPTER 18

Gwen drove aimlessly after pulling away from the Youth Center. She wasn't quite ready to go home and face an evening of boredom. The only exciting thing planned was conditioning her hair. Since she wasn't striving to be another Paul Mitchell, making an event out of grooming her hair was not exactly her idea of an interesting evening.

Coming across the Power Heights Bridge, she merged off the first exit she got to and headed back toward the center of town. Changing the radio station to something a little more upbeat, she paused when she heard the loud thunderous sound of Nelly coming through the surround-sound speakers. The bass of the music was so loud that if Gwen closed her eyes, she would think that Nelly and the St. Lunatics were in the car performing just for her. Bouncing her head to the music, she cracked the window and took a couple of whiffs of air into her lungs. It wasn't the best smell in the world. The aroma of the nearby cigarette plant was pungent and consumed most of her nasal senses. Still, there was something about it, coupled with the lights and sounds, that always made her feel at home. Even though it held some memories that weren't so pleasant, she actually still loved the area.

Gwen continued to bounce to the sounds as she slowly blended with the late evening traffic. Gosh, Scott was having an effect on her. She had listened to that kind of music so much during the past couple of weeks when she was around him that she didn't think the music was half bad. In fact, she was beginning to acquire a taste for it. Jazz and smooth R&B were still her first and second loves, respectively, but hip-hop was really growing on her.

Absently, she reached into her overloaded glove compartment for the CD Scott gave her to check out. One of his friends from the old neighborhood was about to blow up and take her sound nationally. He raved about how talented the sista had always been and how proud everyone was that she achieved her lifelong dream, and that stardom loomed within a reachable distance just ready for her to grasp hold.

After manuvering and switching buttons, she inserted Antoinique's CD. Suddenly a sultry, spellbinding sound filled the car and Gwen understood immediately why Scott boasted. Antoinique's voice was mesmerizing and Gwen could hardly encapsulate a summation that would adequately describe this gifted songstress.

Gwen slipped deeper into the butter-soft leather seat, adjusted the volume, and smiled, thinking that she would have yet another reason to thank Scott. Antoinique's music would no doubt be demanding regular CD rotation on groovy evenings.

Thoroughly enjoying the ride, Gwen found her thoughts switching to Gina. She didn't understand why she had asked her for a hug; it just seemed at the moment that she was looking at a scared little girl who was fighting to be a woman, even at the risk of living a life that was anything but typical for a young girl her age. Gwen knew that underneath that tough exterior, the makeup, the latest clothes, and the mature attitude was someone who just wanted to be loved. She suspected that Gina was getting it from Quincy, and in return she was doing any- and everything he wanted her to do.

Gwen wondered if Patrice's efforts and the time she was giving the girls were making a difference in their lives. She assumed that she was making some type of headway because they always showed up and had the utmost respect for Patrice. Still, Gwen couldn't believe how draining the experience of talking with them and trying to instill a sense of worth into them had been. So many of them seemed to want to give up on life already, without even trying to succeed. The conversations and the many questions echoed in her mind again and she chuckled to herself. These girls, especially Gina, probably knew more about sex than she did now. The only advice that she could give these girls at this point, based on her own experiences, would be to jump on the first express anything and head straight to the nearest convent.

Before she knew it, she had made a beeline straight toward Broad Street and turned toward VCU. The campus was situated in the middle of the city and wasn't separated from the neighboring streets. Some buildings were clustered together and others were nestled in between other city buildings and areas of interest. There were a lot of buildings and structures that she didn't recognize, but many that she remembered. She played the mental game of recalling some event or occasion that had happened in one place or another, and was amazed at how much she still recalled as if it all happened yesterday.

Pulling her car in front of Payne's Ice Cream Shop, Gwen smiled as she leaned over, glancing out the window at the near, faded sign that marked the popular shop that boasted of being the best ice cream spot around. For Gwen, though, its very structure located along Grace Street marked a location that locked in an eidetic memory that would be etched in her heart and mind forever. Thoughts of Marcus immediately surfaced and an unwelcoming sensation ran through the length of her body. Closing her eyes tight, she fought to remain untouched by the intoxicating memory. *Not today,* Gwen thought while reaching to turn off the ignition. She got out of the car, hit the power lock device, and circled the car to stand on the sidewalk.

A group of young girls passed her, laughing, giggling, and acting as if there was no other place on earth that they would rather be. Their young faces showed so much. A hint of eagerness, naiveté, and vulnerability. It was like looking in a mirror; instead of their faces, she saw herself and her friends when they had walked these very grounds. Gwen wondered if the young ladies were as sure of their direction and what they wanted out of life as she had been. Boy, were they in for a rude awakening! Their desires and the people that were so neatly intertwined in their lives now would change a thousand times. She wished she could call them over and share that with them, but what would be the use? Life lessons were always better learned than to have someone tell you about them in hopes of detouring you from your journey.

Walking into the ice cream shop, Gwen stood in line and peered at the large overhead menu board displaying various ice cream flavors and delectable mix-ins. The smell of the homemade waffle cones floated through the air and made Gwen's impromptu stop worthwhile.

The red-headed guy behind the counter finally nodded at Gwen. "What can I get for you?"

Gwen glanced over the flavors one more time and smiled at the thought of so many choices. "Yes, I'll have a double dip of butter pecan in a waffle cone and could I get a spoon and extra napkins?" She couldn't believe that despite all her choices, she was sticking with something as simple as butter pecan. But why change and sample something that wouldn't be as tasty as her regular and tried and true choice. As she reached into her pocket to retrieve the money, a strong voice spoke up behind her. "Can I have what the lady is having?"

She couldn't believe someone was rude enough to yell out their order instead of waiting their turn. Gwen spun around to look at the menace and was shocked as she came face-to-face with Marcus. "What in the world are you doing here?"

Laughing at Gwen's reaction, Marcus replied, "I could ask you the same thing."

"Well, I was driving through the area and suddenly had an urge for ice cream. This used to be the best place back in the day."

"Still is in my book." Marcus reached around Gwen, laid a $20 bill on the counter and retrieved their waffle cones.

"I could have paid for mine." Gwen took the ice cream from his extended hand.

"I know, but let me treat you." Marcus watched as Gwen licked the ice cream slowly. He doubted if it was meant to be seductive, but he couldn't take his eyes off the work her tongue was doing. Marcus shifted his vision away from her lips. "Hey it's a nice evening, would you like to take a walk?"

"With you?" Gwen questioned.

"Yes. I just thought it would give a chance to chat a little and just enjoy our old stomping ground."

"Well, I may regret it, but I guess I'll join you. Did Andre give you the night off?" Gwen was hoping that he would suddenly remember that he was needed elsewhere.

"No, but suddenly I have a whole new agenda."

"Is that so?" She looked at him mischievously.

"Yeah. So let's walk." Marcus reached out and took her hand without giving her a chance to reject his offer.

"I can't believe how much this place has changed, but in some ways a lot of it has remained the same." Gwen looked around as they passed the library and the building that housed the Business Department.

"Yeah, I agree. Every time I come home to visit, I always try to come by the yard. I am amazed at how many new buildings are coming up and what other renovations are being made. But the place does look good. Damn, I wish we had half the stuff they have here now."

"I don't know about that. You and your gang managed to utilize everything that was at your disposal—and then some."

"I won't dignify your comment with a reply." They walked in silence for a few minutes before Marcus spoke again. "Gwen, do you remember the first night I kissed you?"

"Vaguely." Gwen was lying through her teeth. She remembered every detail about that night as if it had happened yesterday. "We were walking someplace and we had ice cream. Was that the night?"

"Yes, it was." Marcus looked disappointed that she didn't remember the evening in more detail. "I can't believe that you don't remember it. You were studying, and I came by the room and asked you to go to the grocery store with me. Of course, I didn't have to go; it was just my way of getting you to walk with me. The truth was, I had been trying for three months to build up the courage to tell you that I liked you. I couldn't tell the boys because they would think I was crazy for not being able to just step up to you. After all, I was the one that was always so together, and the one that they modeled themselves after. So who did I go to for advice? Mom. And she told me to just ask you to go for a walk or drive with me and just let things happen."

Gwen couldn't believe what he was saying. She recalled getting back to her room that night and calling Mama Bea. She allowed her to go on and on when all the time she knew that Marcus was the guy Gwen had fallen for. Obviously, Mama Bea knew more about the two of them than she thought. "Really?" That was the only thing Gwen could say.

"I regretted waiting that long to tell you about my feelings. I always felt that so much time was wasted."

"I don't think so. I got a chance to be your friend. Don't get me wrong. The early part of our relationship was great, but I always felt that it worked out the way it did because it was based on a friendship first. To be honest, that's probably the only reason I'm even able to talk to you now. The Gwen that was in a relationship with you can't stand to even look at you, but the friend Gwen remembers all that we were, the laughs, the tears, all the sharing. She still cares deeply about you."

"I'm glad that you're still my friend. I appreciate that. Don't get me wrong, but I miss the woman who loved me probably more than I ever thought I could be loved. She was my everything, and I was too young and crazy to hold on to her."

"Marcus, I thought we were just going to walk and not get into any of this. That was a long time ago, and nothing we can say or do now will change what happened."

"Maybe not. But you need to know how sorry I am, and that I have lived all these years thinking about it and wishing that there was something I could do to mend your heart. To somehow erase the pain that I caused you."

They stopped in front of the Tucker Bed-and-Breakfast Inn and sat down on the bench. "You know, I have never even had a relationship with anyone for any longer than a year. I believe a year was the longest. I put everything into my business and establishing the career that I always wanted. I did that a lot sooner than I thought I would be able to, and I thought it would make me happy." Marcus laughed to himself. "Having money and success really isn't anything if you don't have anyone to share them with. Billy Dee Williams in *Mahogony* was right about that." Marcus turned to face Gwen, who was looking everywhere else but directly at him. "Look at me for a minute?"

Here we go, Gwen thought. *If I look at him, then he will see a hint of vulnerability and dive right in after the prize.*

"Please, Gwen? It won't kill you to look at me for a moment."

Gwen fought the sensible part of herself and lifted her

eyes to meet his. "I'm looking at you. What is it that you so desperately need to say?"

"Gwen, I love you and I've never stopped loving you. I allowed myself to be weak that night all those years ago. I didn't intend on sleeping with Janice, but when it started happening, I couldn't stop. The part of me that waited so long to sleep with you won over. It wasn't about love or anything else. It was about taking care of a physical need."

"You know what, Marcus? I could forgive you for that happening. I know that I wasn't putting out, and that I was holding on to my virginity because I wanted the first time for us to be special. I never doubted back then that you would be my first. I always knew that it would be you. What hurt the most was that your head was between her legs. How in the hell can you even explain that? If it wasn't about love, then why do something like that?" Gwen finished her words and turned away again.

Marcus swallowed hard, realizing that explaining what happened all those years ago was as hard now as it was then. "It was a mistake, Gwen."

Gwen frowned. "Do you realize how all that sounds?"

"Honestly. I'm not lying to you. She told my fraternity brothers that I had completed the final step of my probation period, and that was all they needed to allow me to go over. At that time, she only said that I owed her and I didn't care, I was joining the best fraternity on campus. Janice was taking a class that winter too, and I had seen her at the library earlier that day. The next thing I knew, she was knocking on the door wanting to use the phone. She came out to the apartments to visit one of her friends who wasn't home, and her car wouldn't start. I went down and checked it, but you know how limited my car maintenance skills are. After I couldn't get it started, she came back upstairs to call her dad. While she waited, I went into the bathroom to wash my hands. When I went back out into the living room, I didn't see her. I searched the kitchen and then finally the bedroom, and there she was on my bed fully undressed."

"Marcus, please. I don't want to hear any of this."

"No, Gwen, you need to listen." Marcus took her hand, held it tightly, and continued. "We had been talking for a year, and that whole time I hadn't been with anyone else. When I told her to get dressed and get out, she threatened to lie and tell you about what she had been sleeping with me off and on the whole time that we were together. And I was silly enough to think that you would believe her. I couldn't risk losing you, and I didn't know if our relationship was strong enough to stand that kind of test. So, I did it and it cost me my life."

"What do you mean your life?" Gwen asked with hostility in her voice.

"Back then, you were my life and I didn't know it. And now I'm sure that you were then and still are, because I haven't been able to live a day without thinking about how much I hurt you that night. I don't know if you believe me, and I don't have anything to gain by telling you anything other than the truth now. That's what happened. I've waited all this time to have a chance to tell you, and I'm glad that I have." The silence that lay between them was deadly. All these years, and she never knew why it happened. Now that she did, she wasn't sure it made a difference. Hurt was hurt; the reason behind that hurt was irrelevant.

"I don't know what you want me to say, Marcus. That the pain isn't as bad now that I know why you did it. I wish it were that easy. I've lived all these years, the same way you have, without being able to fully love someone because a big part of my heart still belonged to you. Most of all, not being able to trust anyone because you took that away too. I loved you so much, all I wanted that night was to show you how much by finally making love to you. Instead, I stood there watching you make love to someone else." Gwen tried to hide her tears.

"I'm so sorry, Gwen. God, if I could take it all back, I would. Can't you understand I've lived a life of hell since that happened? God knows Mama reminds me every chance she gets. But please, give me a chance to prove how sorry I am. Let me ask you something. If you say yes to this, then I will walk away and forget any chance of us ever being together." Again he reached for her hand and held it tight. Gwen turned around and looked into his brown eyes that almost seemed to swallow her up. No words escaped his mouth, but she was reading so much in his eyes. "Have you ever stopped loving me?"

"What?" Gwen tried to pull away her hands, which were covered with light beads of perspiration. When he didn't release her hands, she turned away and watched an elderly couple cross the street hand in hand. She wondered silently if the elderly lady ever had to overcome such a traumatic hurt in their early relationship. Her steps were a lot slower than his, and seemed at times to almost cause her to tilt over. Yet he never stopped holding her hand tight as she maneuvered across the street and made it safely to the other side. It was so obvious that she trusted him, and he, in return, was patient, smiling at her as if he just discovered how beautiful she was.

"No, don't do that. Don't look away, and don't remove your hands from mine. Have you stopped loving me?"

Gwen saw the same eyes that she had seen the evening that he first kissed her. She saw the eyes as he sat in her living room that night trying to apologize, when she knew that the words that needed to be said back then were words that he had still not learned. Only maturity and time could mend the kind of hurt that had taken place then. Nothing he could have said would have made a difference; and yet tonight as she sat on the bench under the lamplights, forgiveness seemed within reach. She had not been able to love anyone else, and she knew that Marcus was a bigger part of her life than she wanted to admit. All of a sudden, it seemed that loving him the way she had years ago might actually be possible. Trusting him was something altogether different, but she knew one thing, and that was that she still loved him. "No. I haven't stopped loving you."

Those words to Marcus were like the words to an unfinished song. They were served up with a completeness that made his heart seem to fill up. Knowing that she still loved him gave him a new hope; and as long as there was hope, then he couldn't give up. Not sure how to proceed, he only squeezed her hand and smiled. "Come on and let's continue our walk."

She had walked the same tree-lined streets, with their weathered brick sidewalks, countless times when she was in school and needed a break away from the books and the hectic existence. Tonight, as she strolled along with older, more seasoned eyes, she was aware of every crack in the sidewalk and the battered signs detailing the streets, and was amazed that she now could identify almost all the trees that they passed. Because this neighborhood was occupied by mostly students, faculty, and other professionals, the traffic on the streets was minimal. Instead, bicycles and walkers passed on both sides of the streets, heading to unknown places. The houses that were nestled together had been standing for more decades than she could even imagine. Most of them had been restored and renovated and now served as homes for many and businesses for others. All of them were historical houses and held a hint of nostalgia. Just observing them made you feel like you had flipped through the magazine pages of some of the finest historical homes in the country. The city had a lot of nice neighborhoods, but this area, in her opinion, was the most tasteful and refined.

They walked in no certain direction for what seemed like hours, talking about old times and all the crazy things that they had done back then. Before they knew it, they had walked all the way to Boulevard Avenue. Just when they decided to turn around and walk back to campus, the sky opened and released a downpour of rain. Marcus took Gwen by the hand, and they ran back in the direction they had come from. Instead of heading back toward the campus, Marcus pulled Gwen down Bell Street, stopped about two blocks down, and headed up the steps of a town house. Reaching quickly for the keys, he opened the door. As soon as Marcus got the heavy mahogany door open, they slipped into the foyer drenched from head to toe. The rain came falling down with no early warning signs. There had not even been a cloud in the sky all day.

"Slip out of those shoes and come in. I'll go get something for you to change into." Before she could object, Marcus was up the steps and out of sight. Walking around the corner, she smiled at the highly polished maple hardwood floors and the black leather sofa, matching love seat, armchair, and ottoman that sat on top of it. Glass-accented tables were placed in front and on the sides of the pieces. The high cathedral ceilings gave the room an airy and classy appeal; so did the large windows covered with contemporary-style draperies that hung on heavy black cast-iron rods. A couple of large paintings hung on the wall, arranged far enough apart to create two dramatic focal points. Several pewter sconces and candles were placed around both paintings and on the two walls separating the entryway. A gold-framed photograph of Marcus, Vince, and their mother sat on top of the fireplace mantel.

While Gwen was admiring her surroundings, Marcus came back into the room. "Here, take these clothes and go in the bathroom down the hall and change out of that wet stuff. I don't want you to catch a cold. I'm going to turn off the air. Vince has it freezing in here all the time."

Gwen was going to object, but she was soaked, and changing into something dry wasn't a bad idea. "I'll be right back."

By the time she came back into the living room dressed

in an oversize Spike Lee T-shirt and quarter socks, Marcus was sitting on a cotton throw in front of the fireplace. The only lighting radiated from the few candles that were lit and strategically placed around the room. The bright embers of the fireplace created shadows that played softly against the beige walls. Getting closer, she could see that Marcus only had on a pair of lounging pants and a smile.

"Don't you think it's a little warm for a fire?" Feeling awkward standing there dressed only in the T-shirt and socks, Gwen crossed her arms over her chest.

"Oh, it's only for the ambiance; the gas burner behind it isn't lit. Come on over here and have a seat."

"Do you think you can throw my clothes in the dryer so that we can head back to campus as soon as the rain stops?"

"Sure. No problem." Marcus popped up, passing Gwen on the way to the laundry room. She closed her eyes and inhaled the lingering scent of him. It had to be a sin to smell that good. When they were in school and living on their very limited budget, he would splurge on cologne and then come to them for partying money. His mother provided the necessities, but wouldn't give him a dime extra for the extracurricular stuff. Closing her eyes even tighter, she immediately recognized the fragrance. It was the same smell that had enveloped her that night at Humphrey's, and now it played in the fragments of her mind, confiscating her entire being.

She walked unsteadily to the throw and sat in front of the fireplace. Rubbing her fingers through her damp hair, she rotated her neck and tried to relax. It was a difficult task because she was as naked under the thin cotton material as she had been the day she came into the world. She had never been one to feel totally comfortable in the nude either, alone or in the company of someone else. Not wearing panties under certain garments was one thing, but being totally nude was something else altogether. It was probably one more of those hang-ups that she needed to address with Dr. Ryan. God, would the list never end?

At that moment, she realized that she had sent Marcus to put her soaking wet garments in the dryer. He probably took great pleasure in handling her lace thong, and that was more than likely the reason why he hadn't gotten back from the task that should have taken him only a couple of minutes at the most.

Just as she was getting ready to go search for him, he came bouncing into the room, still smiling. "Would you like something to drink?" He pointed to the bottle that was chilling in the ice bucket.

"No, thanks. I've been taking a prescription medication, and I'm not supposed to mix it with alcohol."

"I'm a step ahead of you. It's only sparkling grape juice. The last time you drank, you got a bit thrown off. I want to make sure your mind stays completely clear this evening." Pouring the juice into long-stemmed crystal flutes, he passed the first one to her and returned the juice to the chilled ice bucket, sat beside her, and took a sip. He tried to slow his rapidly beating heart by breathing in and out a couple of times; but when he glanced down at Gwen's legs that were crossed at the ankles, it took everything he had, and then some, to fight the urge to reach out and touch the soft-looking cocoa-brown skin.

"Would you like something to eat, or would you like to watch television or listen to some music?" He spilled it all out without his usual calm, slow demeanor.

Grinning at his nervousness, Gwen answered, "No, I'm not hungry, and I don't want to listen to any music." She knew that adding music to the mood he was already setting wasn't wise. "I would like to watch a little television, though."

Clicking on the big-screen Toshiba, Marcus turned the volume up a little and surfed until Jacque Reid's face filled the screen. They watched the remainder of the news show in silence while sipping their grape juice. The steady drops of rain tapped methodically on the roof and made the atmosphere of fireplace, candles, and make-believe wine even more romantic.

When the show went off, *Midnight Love* claimed its regular time slot. The first video was an old one: Freddy Jackson's *You Are My Lady*. The minute the music started, they were thrown back in time, both nodding their remembrance of the song and the video. They began to sing what words they knew, cracking up because Marcus was good at a lot of things but singing was not one of them.

Gwen, however, had been singing since she could talk, and was blessed with an angelic voice. She and Tiffany were often called upon during many church programs to sing a duet, which they carried out willingly, rendering the church into a "praise the Lord" state. Their grandmother used to say, "If my grandbabies couldn't lead a person to Christ with their singing, that person had no intention of coming to Him at all."

Gwen began to relax even more. Noticing this, Marcus placed his hand on her knee and she didn't have the strength to resist, nor did she really want to. Her body was telling her to let go and release the past, but her mind was trying hard to reason with her. She attempted to remain anchored in reality—but the more she thought about her surroundings and being with the man she still loved, the more she couldn't help but want the evening to end with her calling out his name. She wanted the morning to commence with her waking up in his strong arms.

A couple of videos later, Luther Vandross was serenading them, and they were slow-dancing to the music. Marcus smoothed her baby-fine temple hair away from her forehead and planted light delicate kisses all over it. When she didn't object, he continued down her face and slowed as he tongued her dimple with enough force to cause her to move her lips to his suddenly. They stood transfixed, completely consumed with the task of kissing one another. When they finally broke away to breathe, Gwen noticed that the room suddenly appeared so small. She was only aware of the little space that separated them. All she wanted was to get so close that their bodies would merge together and become one.

Marcus rubbed her shoulders and continued to rotate slow circles on the back of her neck. Gwen could only look up at him, not daring to speak or blink for fear that the trance would be broken and good sense would win over, halting what was happening between them. She stood on tiptoes and gave him greater access to her mouth. He claimed her lips and allowed his tongue to sample every inch of the deep inferno. When she heard a slight moan she tried to move, but some force beyond her control closed her arms tightly around his neck. The passion that was brewing stirred all of him, and he was losing control.

Marcus took one of Gwen's hands and slowly guided it to the front of his lounging pants until he firmly placed it on his hardened member. Not wanting to pull away too quickly and appear like the same inexperienced girl who didn't know the first thing about how to please a man, she swallowed hard and boldly dipped her hand inside his pants. She started to masterfully rub the throbbing shaft, all the while looking him in the eye, biting her bottom lip a little. The combination of the attention she was giving his risen anatomy and watching her nervously bite her lip was bringing him close to the edge. He couldn't let that happen. He had waited a lifetime for this very moment, and now that it was almost happening he wouldn't rush it.

"We better stop before I won't be able to. You're making me feel so good, and I'm about ready to explode. Unless you don't want us to stop."

Gwen was too far ahead of herself to say no. She couldn't think of any reason to say no. It felt so good, and she had to admit that she didn't want to stop. "No, Marcus, I don't want to stop."

"Baby, am I hearing you right? You don't want to stop?"

Marcus was breathing harder and his palms were moist as he rubbed the sides of her face.

Gwen looked up at him, totally mesmerized by the moment. "I don't want to stop and I don't think you want to either."

"Come on upstairs. I want this to be special. Something that neither one of us will ever forget." Marcus blew out the candles, picked Gwen up, and started for the steps. Gwen held on tight and laid her head on his chest. She closed her eyes and prayed that this was the right time for them. That all of her hesitations would be replaced with a certainty that she belonged with Marcus, and that no one else could fill the void because this moment in time was predestined.

Before she could adjust her eyes to the darkness of the room, Marcus placed her on the oversize four-poster bed. Leaning over her, he kissed her nose and whispered, "Gwen, baby, tell me that you're sure about this. I mean, I want this to happen more than anything in the world, but I don't want you to have any doubts."

"Marcus, I've never been more sure of anything." Before the last word hit the stillness of the bedroom, Marcus was out of his pants and had settled beside her on the bed and begun yanking the shirt over her head. Gwen lifted her hips to allow it to rise up so he could slide it off. While he busied himself with that, she was busy kicking off the socks that seemed to be held on with ten-pound weights.

With his breathing harder than ever, his voice became raspy. "I can't believe how beautiful you are. Nothing has changed, except maybe you're more beautiful now than you were back then, if that's possible." Tracing a line down the middle of her stomach down to the triangle between her legs, he continued. "You are so perfect."

Embarrassed by the comment, she could only look away. He leaned over to the foot of the bed, lifted the lightweight throw over her, and nestled beside her again. "Is that better?"

He remembered that she never felt comfortable with his looking at her nude body. He never understood why, but he hoped that after tonight, when he made love to her over and over again, not leaving any part of her untouched, she would have no more doubts about how much he loved her and her body.

"Much." Gwen knew she was being silly.

Reaching under it, he found the soft mound between her legs and started a torturous rotation within its folds. Just as she was about to squirm and let out a sound that was unfamiliar to her, he covered her mouth with a deep, sensual kiss.

Gwen was about to lose it when he moved his head down between her breasts and started to lick and suck on both of them, creating a rhythm that matched the one going on farther down. She tried to hold on, although she could feel the impeding tide threatening to overtake her. Not knowing what to expect next, Gwen hoped he wouldn't go down on her. That would remind her of what had happened before.

As if he were reading her mind, he spoke. "Not now, but later."

Gwen responded by kissing him deeply and squeezing his nipple with her thumb and pointer finger. Gwen turned slightly and slid down him and kissed his rock-solid inner thighs. The combination of all of it caused Marcus to sigh his approval and attempt to speak without the reinforcement of sound. Her hand found his manhood again and she started moving it around and up and down. He gasped, "Baaaby, stop. I need to be inside you. Please let me make love to you."

Giving in, she kissed him sofly and positioned her body next to his. She could hear him ripping something open.

Marcus tried to steady his hand enough to prepare himself for the pleasure that was only seconds away. He begged his hand to stop shaking and his pulse to slow down. He didn't want it to be over before it started. He was going to have to find control from somewhere within.

Taking a deep breath, he whispered, against the hollow curve of her neck, that he loved her and slowly pushed into the sweet tunnel of love that had awaited him all these years. He listened as she gulped in a large breath of air and exhaled slowly. Waiting until she gave him some physical sign to go on, he felt her finally squeezing him tightly, and he started moving slowly inside her. Nothing had ever felt as good as this. He wished that he could freeze time and stay inside Gwen forever. He looked deep into her eyes, and was astonished to see that she was looking at him through enduring eyes that threatened to close with each movement he made. He couldn't hold back a tear that was cradled in the corner of his eye. He wanted to reach up and smooth it away, but he didn't want to release the hold he had on her.

Gwen couldn't believe that she had denied herself this pleasure for so long. It was not until this very moment that she was aware that she had only been played with in her past sexual escapades. That no one had ever truly made love to her. Gwen's body was transformed into another state. It was there that she felt her heart swell to the point of bursting open. Just when she thought she couldn't take any more and her throat became dry from gasping and calling out his name, she felt a wet drop on her face. She thought at first that it came from the sweat that accumulated on his brow, but when he turned slightly she could see that he was crying softly.

Gwen was so overwhelmed, she couldn't bring herself to interrupt the moment or to question exactly what he felt. Deep inside, she knew that they both felt the same way. Marcus appeared to Gwen at that moment to be all the man she had ever wanted. She knew he shed those tears for her and for the pain he had caused. For the first time since that horrible night, she knew that he was sorry.

They changed positions several times and repeated acts one and two over and over again. Each subsequent act was created with more vigor and intensity, dripping with the essence of passion. Finally, when neither one could summon the energy to continue, when they realized that it was not a dream and that there would be other times, they held each other tight and mumbled about wasted time, a love that had lasted, and never letting go.

CHAPTER 19

Startled at her surroundings, Gwen lifted her head quickly. When she saw the back of Marcus' wavy head beside her, a flood of memories from the evening and early morning came back to her. Wanting to make sure that what she remembered had actually happened, she lifted the sheet, peeped under it, and saw the backside of his naked body.

It had only been one night, and already she felt like an addict. She reached over and started to rub his chest. Marcus smiled and cleared his throat. "Hey, you. Why you up messing with me? Or is it that you want more?"

"You looked so cute sleeping, I just couldn't resist waking you up." Turning his body all the way over, she looked at the alarm clock on the nightstand and panicked. "Marcus, please tell me that you still set your clock fast so that you can get a head start on things."

"Yeah, I do. But not this one."

"So it really is eight o'clock." She rubbed her hand over her head, which she knew had to be a mess.

"Yeah, baby. Why? You got someplace to go this early?" Marcus was completely puzzled.

"I got to pick Patrice up from the airport in forty-five minutes. If I call her cell phone and leave a message for her to catch a cab, I'm only asking for trouble. You know that she will put two and two together and come up with us."

"And what is so terrible about that?" Propping the side of his head up on his hand, he scrutinized her as she went on and on. "Gwen, you're not sorry that you did this, are you?"

"No, I'm not sorry. I still love you. I never stopped loving you." She smiled down at him. She didn't want to tell him that in addition to the good feeling it was mixed with something that she couldn't put her finger on.

"I know you said a lot of things last night other than, *Marcus, baby, oh, Marcus, please, baby. Oh, stop. No, I mean don't stop. Love me, Big Daddy."* He was on his back laughing uncontrollably.

"Stop lying. You know I didn't say all of that. I can't believe that you would tease me to build up your pitiful ego." Gwen couldn't help but laugh. She had, in fact, said everything except the Big Daddy part, and the only reason she hadn't was that she didn't think of it at the time.

"Come on now and help me get myself together so that I can get to the airport. I know I can't make it in exactly forty-five minutes, but I know that she won't leave without hearing from me." Her shyness now a thing of the past, Gwen slid to the side of the bed and stood up, grabbing the T-shirt.

Marcus smiled, noticing that she had a new boldness about her, not to mention that she was still on a high. As he had held her in his arms and she'd drifted off to sleep just hours before, he couldn't help but wonder if she would wake up and tell him that it was all a terrible mistake. That she was sorry she let things go that far and she still couldn't put the past behind them. Now he lay there watching her run around the room like a chicken with her head cut off.

"Marcus, how am I going to get to my car?" She hopelessly plopped back down on the bed.

"Sweetheart, please relax. I heard Vince come in earlier, so I'll take his car and drive you back to campus and you can head to the airport to get 'Trice. When he wakes up, I'll get him to drop me off to pick up my car. I would walk, but you decided to prove some point and had me participate in some things that I have never even tried before."

"Stop the innocent act, why don'tcha? I was only a follower. You did all the leading. Now get up and go get my clothes. No, wait. What are you going to tell Vince? Do you think he heard us?"

"Gwen. Stop and breathe. Why are you so uptight? We are all grown, remember? Vince knows that I love you, and he assumed that you still loved me. Case closed." Marcus stood up, his manhood standing straight out in front of him.

Gwen tried to turn away, but gave up the task and just stared at him with an appealing grin, no longer thinking or worrying about what anyone said. She was proud to claim this prize as hers, and didn't care who knew it.

Pulling on a pair of shorts, Marcus spoke again. "Go ahead and hit the shower." He pointed her toward his private bathroom. "You should be able to find everything you need, including an extra toothbrush in the cabinet. I'm going to go get your clothes."

He disappeared from the bedroom and came back in before she opened the bathroom door, "I'm sorry, though, babe, the way you were calling out my name, I know that Vince heard you."

"You!" Gwen screamed at him and threw a nearby pillow at the door as he dodged it and closed the door behind him.

Gwen drove like a madwoman, making most of the journey on the interstate in an effort to avoid the morning rush-hour traffic. When she walked through the revolving door of Richmond International Airport, her watch showed that it was 9:05. She grimaced, a little upset that she was breaking her habit of always being on time. She also knew that Patrice would have a field day with her tardiness and spend the entire drive trying to find out why.

Walking toward the monitor that displayed arrival and departure times for all of the flights, she noticed that Patrice's flight was right on time. Gwen assumed that she was already in the baggage claim area getting her luggage, or in that vicinity. A crowd of people stood around trying to identify their belongings on the carousel that rotated tons of Samsonite, American Tourister, and other designer luggage. She couldn't help but notice Patrice standing with her back to her leaning her cellular phone against her shoulder so that her hands were free to grab her tote bag. Her hair was pulled up into a jenny ponytail, and she was dressed in a lime-green floral minidress and flat black slings.

Gwen tapped her on the shoulder. Patrice turned, ready to go off on whoever it was who decided to be forward enough to interrupt her. "Girl, I was about ready to curse someone's butt out. I was just calling the house for you. I thought maybe something had happened because you are always on time."

"Well, I'm here now. I had to stop and get gas, and I ran into traffic." Gwen pulled the handle out on Patrice's Gucci Pullman so that she could roll it behind her. She didn't even look up, knowing that her eyes wouldn't support the story she was telling.

"Oh, I see. Well, tell me why it is that your clothes are wrinkled as hell, your hair is doing its own thing today, and you look like you just got out of bed. By your hyper actions, it wasn't alone."

"I don't know what you're talking about. I told you that I got stuck in traffic. I didn't realize you wanted me to don formal attire just to pick you up from the airport. Jeez." Gwen hoped that pretending to be disturbed by the questioning would be enough for Patrice to change the subject.

"All right. Don't get touchy. But as always, I want to look

out for you. Believe it or not, I only have your best interest at heart, which is why I need to give you a little something."

Thinking that Patrice had brought her something back from her business trip, Gwen pulled the luggage over and stopped in front of the phone booths. "You know you didn't have to bring me anything."

Patrice rummaged through her Gucci bag with determination. "Oh, here it is. I'm giving you this because I love you." She handed Gwen a bottle of Nivea lotion.

"What is this?"

"Girl, I appreciate you rushing, really I do. Think of this like you would your American Express card and don't leave home without it. Your ashy-ass elbows and ankles are in serious need of some attention. Damn, don't Marcus have some lotion or something over there?" She chuckled and started walking away.

"I wasn't with . . ." Gwen decided to give up the charade. She looked at Patrice like a little girl having with her hand caught in the cookie jar before supper. "How did you know?"

"When I called you before I left the hotel and couldn't get you, I got a little suspicious. Then when the airplane landed and I tried you again at the house and on your cellular, I got worried. The very first person I called was Marcus. At first he would only say that he saw you last night and he was sure that you were all right. Of course, you know the brotha can't stand pressure and breaks up like a bad phone connection. After a little trickery, he was confessing your night of passion and that it was his fault that you were running late. You would think that since I'm your girl and all that you would have come in here ready to spill your guts. But oh no, you decide to come in here jacked up and be all closemouthed."

"Dag, 'Trice. I was going to tell you. It wasn't like it was my first time or anything like that."

"One question before we get in the car." They stood side by side as they placed Patrice's bags in the trunk.

"What?"

"How was it?"

"I can't believe you're asking me that." Gwen tried to act upset, then burst out laughing. "Girl, do you remember how Whitney shed that one tear in *Waiting to Exhale*?"

Patrice widened her eyes and bopped her head to acknowledge her remembrance of it.

"Well, I'll just say that Marcus shed the tear but I was too busy trying to peel myself off the ceiling."

"Come on, cowgirl, and let me buy you some breakfast; I'm sure your butt is starved. And, Gwen, don't even think about leaving anything out." Patrice grabbed the keys and directed Gwen to get in on the passenger side. She opened the door, got in behind the wheel, and revved up the engine. Rolling the window down, she handed the parking attendant a five-dollar bill. As he turned to get change, Patrice pulled her shades down on her nose a little and checked out his backside. He was an attractive guy, and she wouldn't mind giving him a little play. Before she could cover up her lustful look, he turned around with a wide smile. "Here's your change and a little something extra."

Patrice glanced down at what he had handed her and noticed that she not only got back three dollars in change, but a number scribbled on a piece of paper.

"Thanks so much." She lifted the paper up and licked her lips. "I may actually use this."

Gwen was sitting in the passenger seat with her arms folded across her breasts, ready to scold Patrice. "Do you ever stop?"

"Not hardly." She pulled into the right lane and headed for the Aunt Sarah's Restaurant that was located not far from the airport.

"Yeah, baby, I miss you too. I'll just be glad when you're ready to let everyone in on our secret. Not being able to share my happiness with my boys is killing me." Andre reached for the gold-monogrammed letter opener and rubbed his finger over the pointed end. He'd been dating his mystery woman for the past six months and was more than ready to announce it to the world. She, on the other hand, wanted to hold off until the time was right. Andre felt there was no time like the present, and he had been preaching that repeatedly for the past couple of weeks. He decided to limit his preaching because he was obviously speaking to a deaf audience.

"Well, if that's the way you want it, I have no choice but to understand. Just know that it drives me crazy every time I have to jump on a plane and pretend I have business out of town just so I can see you."

Marcus came through the door singing a chorus of "I've Got Sunshine." He picked up the copy of *USA Today* off the glass coffee table and fell onto the tan leather sofa, grinning like he just got the secret recipe for Bush's Baked Beans from Duke.

Andre turned around in his executive swivel chair and faced the wall. "Baby girl, you go on back to prepare for your midday gig, and I'll call you tonight." Smiling at what he was hearing, he mumbled, barely audible to Marcus' nearby ears, "No doubt. You know I can't wait."

Spinning around, Andre inhaled deeply and observed Marcus for a minute as he tried to act as if the news he was reading about was of major importance to him. "What's up, black man? Why you come up in here after the disappearing act you did last night singing about some sunshine?" Andre placed the letter opener in the gold pencil holder that was on the left corner of his desk and stood up and stretched. He examined his crotch to make sure that his recent conversation hadn't left him with a visible sign of yearning.

"I could be asking you about the end of your conversation that was all muffled and hush-hush." Marcus continued to flip through the pages of the sports section. He was checking out Tiger Woods, who was so popular these days, one would think that he had been in the golf circuit for a lot longer.

"You could, but I probably wouldn't give you any details. When the time is right, you will be the first one I share it with."

"That hot, or that special?" Marcus finally closed the paper and placed it back on the coffee table.

"Man, she is both. I can't believe every area of my life is falling into place. I mean, I never thought that things would come together like they have. I'm one blessed brotha, that's for sure. Enough of that. I know you're not even tryin' to front me like this. What the hell is up with you and the relaxed, goofy look on your face? If I didn't know better, I would think you spent the night with Gwen bustin' a nut."

Andre rustled through some papers on the edge of his desk. Not looking up right away, he waited for Marcus to give him a negative reply. When no reply came, he dropped the papers. "Wait one damn minute. Something just ain't right here. You didn't show up at the club last night. You didn't even bother to call. You didn't answer the phone at home or your cell phone. You didn't respond to my page or Vince's."

Marcus' only response was a wide grin. He rubbed a finger under his nose, leaned over on the sofa, and put his hand on his crotch. "What do want to know? I was at home, but I wasn't alone. Gwen and I spent some much-needed quality time together."

Andre walked across the room, closing the gap between them in a couple of long strides. He sat down on the edge of the leather recliner next to the sofa. "Talk to me, big daddy."

"Boy, your ass is wild. What can I say? I've waited all these years to apologize to Gwen, and she finally listened to me. You can't believe how relieved I was to get all that out in the open so we can move on. Man, she listened with an open mind and heart, and, Andre, man, she is willing to put it all behind us."

"Word! I can't believe that she is willing to let that go. I mean, I'm glad she is because it has been an obstacle that has existed much longer than it needed to. I still get pissed every time I think about you jeopardizing your relationship with Gwen with that trick Janice when you knew good and damn well what she was about."

"Don't go there, Andre. You more than anyone else knew it was a mistake. The worst mistake I have ever made in my life. If I could have taken it back and not hurt Gwen, I would have. She means the world to me. Nothing and no one will ever change that."

"I know, Marcus, you're preaching to the choir. I love both of you, but I just want you to proceed with caution. She has been through so much, and it's going to take a lot for her to trust you again. I'm not saying it can't happen, but it won't happen overnight."

Marcus stood up and walked over to the black compact refrigerator in the corner under the shelf that held the mini-bar. He pulled out a couple of Snapple iced teas. He handed one to Andre and returned to his seat. Marcus shook the bottle upside down a couple of times, opened it, and took a long swig. "You ain't said nothing that I haven't thought about all morning." He paused as if trying to find the right words. "But when we made love last night, everything felt so right. It was as if time stood still and nothing about what we shared changed. She still loves me, Dre, and I'm not making any mistakes this time. I won't give up or stop loving her until I make her my wife. I know that's your baby sister and all that, but trust me, I got her this time and I'm not ever letting her go."

"Well, if you feel like that, then what can I say? Go for it. As always, I gotcha back, and I'll start rehearsing my best man toast. Besides, you two have taken entirely too long to get together. I just can't believe you got the drawers. No wonder you're acting all goofy and shit."

"Well, waiting a decade for one woman to give herself to

you could cause any man to act a little out of character. Just when I thought I couldn't love Gwen any more, she takes me to another level." Marcus turned away from Andre when he felt a little too emotional. He couldn't believe that he had actually cried last night. He had just been so overwhelmed with love. Although he'd wanted to speak and tell her what he was feeling, he couldn't say a word or stop the tears that fell. They created a window that displayed the depth of love he felt in his heart. "I love her, man. She's my world."

"For the first time in my life, I can say that I know what you mean." Andre stood up and walked out of the office, realizing that his normal tough guy exterior was shedding. He couldn't advise Marcus without displaying the same emotional overflow that he'd just witnessed.

Marcus pondered Andre's words and knew that as much as he wanted to believe that Gwen could forgive and forget what had happened, he would have to do everything he could to help her do just that. He had to gain her trust. He knew it would be a difficult task, but it was one that he was up for. He would never hurt her again; that he could promise her, and he would swear it on his father's grave.

He jumped up from the soft coolness of the sofa and walked over to the desk. Marcus fumbled through the top left drawer, pulling out the Yellow Pages. He flipped to the "Florist" heading and ran his fingers down the column until he saw the name Floral Thoughts. It was the florist that his mother used all the time. He quickly dialed and after a couple of rings someone answered. "Floral Thoughts. May I help you?"

"Sure. I would like to speak to Betty, please." Marcus took a seat behind the desk and waited.

"Floral Thoughts. This is Betty."

"Betty. This is Marcus McGuire. Yeah, Bea McGuire's oldest boy. I've been fine, how about yourself? That's great. Listen, I need to send some roses to a special lady." Marcus ordered two dozen long-stemmed yellow roses arranged in a crystal vase with lots of baby's breath and Hershey's Kisses.

He told her what to put on the card and gave her his platinum VISA card number and the delivery address. As a last-minute gesture, he ordered a dozen red roses and sent them to his mother.

"And what would you like that card to say?" Betty questioned.

"Thanks for reminding me to cherish the gift of real love." He smiled, thanked Betty, and hung up the phone.

Marcus joined his mother for dinner prior to his trip to campus the night before. She cooked enough for an entire family as usual and he feasted on fried trout, potato and cheese casserole, fresh tomatoes, and spoon bread. The sweet aroma of the freshly baked rice pudding was the perfect ending to a wonderful meal.

They talked about everything that had been happening in both their worlds. He even discussed the progress of his tentative plan to relocate back to his hometown. He'd talked with several of his board members and senior staffpersons about making Richmond his base office, and they all saw no potential problem with moving from the West Coast to the East Coast. He hadn't talked to anyone else about it yet, not even Vince or Andre, but there was no way he could keep it from his mom. She was both shocked and thrilled. They even spent a couple of days scouting around for the ideal office location.

Mama Bea had always been a constant shoulder of support for him. Although she had been hesitant for him to have been so far away from home, often so busy that he hardly had any free time to himself, she always made her presence felt by countless phone calls, letters, and cards. Being so far away from his family hadn't been easy, and it took a lot of commitment and focusing on the larger piece of the pie. But he had paid his dues, and was now comfortable enough financially that he could work from whatever location he chose.

He thought about the remainder of their conversation.

She told him that if he really wanted to win Gwen's heart again, he would have to do everything within his power to build her trust in him. She loved Gwen like a daughter; while she wanted nothing more than to see the two of them back together, she wanted Gwen to be free to love him without any reservations. Mama Bea was wise beyond her years, but she was always careful to make sure her children followed their own hearts and did what was right for them, without them doing what they assumed she wanted them to do.

"Marcus, what you need to do is court her and make her feel like no one and nothing else matters except her and the happiness that you want her to know. That child done had enough hurt to last a lifetime, and she is overdue for a bundle of happiness."

"Mama, you know I love Gwen more than anything in this world, and I want to spend the rest of my life proving that I do. If she will accept me and all the love I have to give, then I know we can make it work."

Mama Bea looked at him with tenderness, pride, and love beaming from her weathered eyes. The same eyes that had watched him grow from a boy to a careless and reckless young man. Now those eyes locked on her son, who had become so caring and responsible, and who, although he never came right out and said the words, was ready to start a family of his own. Her oldest child had arrived grandly into manhood, and she couldn't be more proud. "I guess I need to give you something. I've been keeping it much too long, and you just might be needing it soon."

Marcus sat in his mother's comfortable side chair that had seen better days, and yet she refused to replace it or move it from the spot across from the twenty-seven-inch floor-model television. He sat with a confused look on his face. "There she goes; Lord only knows what she's back there looking for," he whispered to himself and turned the channel from *Judge Judy* to ESPN. If she were in one of the bedrooms searching, she could come back with just about anything.

She had been gone for more than ten minutes and Marcus had started to get up and go see if she needed any help when he heard her footsteps shifting slowly down the hall. When she came into view, he noticed a small box in her hand. She walked past him and took a seat on the sofa.

"Marcus, you asked me to hold this for you a long time ago." She began to remove something from the outer box. "So much has happened since that day, and so many things have gone wrong, but I held on to it." She finally removed a tiny blue velvet box.

A flood of memories came over Marcus. He had forgotten all about asking her to hold it until the New Year's Eve before graduation, but he did remember the day that he'd picked it out.

He had spent all day at the mall searching every jewelry store for that one special engagement ring. He couldn't find anything that he liked in his price range. Instead of heading back to campus, he went home disappointed and planted himself in front of the television. Mama Bea had come home from work feeling exhausted and worn out. All ready to change into her housedress and relax, she noticed the look on his face and dared to ask what was wrong. He told her that he wanted to ask Gwen to marry him after graduation, but he couldn't afford a ring. Instead of relaxing, she picked up the phone and made a call. After talking in the kitchen a couple of minutes, she came back in, grabbed his arm, and drove across town to a small jewelry store that he hadn't even known existed.

A portly, old, balding man greeted them, hugging and kissing Marcus' mother's cheek. She introduced Sam Baker to Marcus. Without wasting time, Mr. Baker told Marcus to look in the nearby case and see if he liked anything. He only needed to glance once. Sitting up on a separate display was a perfect marquise-cut diamond in a channel setting. There was no need to look at anything else. He knew that if he could afford it, this would be the ring he would give Gwen. He twirled around to the man. Before he could say anything, Mr. Baker responded, "I know exactly which one you have your eye on. I removed it from another case a couple of minutes before you got here and put it on a separate individual display." He walked behind the case, unlocked it, and removed the ring from the display. "Here. Take a closer look." He handed it to Marcus.

"What do you think, Mama?" He held it out and marveled over the way it glittered and caught the rays of light, sparkling as he turned it from side to side.

"I think it's perfect." She smiled, not being able to recall a time when she had seen him so excited about anything. Mama Bea silently wished that her Zach was there to see his son. Marcus was not only ready to tackle the world, but he was ready to make a commitment to Gwen, and she knew that in time she would have a daughter. One day, she prayed, she would have little ones walking around the house that she could spoil to no end. She was so proud of all of his accomplishments and would continue to be there for him every step of the way.

"Man, this must be a carat, easy. I can't afford anything close to this." He sighed as he looked down at the ring.

"No, baby, you sure can't afford that ring alone, but you can if I help you." She walked closer and removed the ring from his finger that was stiff from holding it in a tight grip.

"Mama, you know I can't let you do that. You have enough bills already. I can just pick out something a lot cheaper, and later on I can give Gwen a ring just like this one."

"Look, Marcus, I'm happy that you've found someone like Gwen, and I pray that the two of you will be together for as long as the two of you have breath in your bodies and share the kind of love that your father and I shared. And besides, I've already set my sights on spoiling them grandbabies that I know you two are going to give me. I have made up my mind, and if this is the ring you like, then this is the one that we are going to get."

She handed the ring to Mr. Baker. "Sam, we're going to take this ring."

After finding out that the ring was Gwen's size and would probably only need a slight adjustment, Mr. Baker wrapped it and they were on their way.

Now years later, Marcus held it in his hand again, and was as excited as he had been that day. They had planned to exchange gifts on New Year's Eve that year. After the incident that Gwen had walked in on, though, he wasn't able to make the commitment. But he was ready to make it now.

He grimaced at the thought of the incident that had changed everything and struggled to focus on the now. "You're right, Mama, I will be needing this." As always, his mother knew what was best for him. From all the times that his stubborn streak and strong will had butted heads with her commands, she knew exactly when to let silence reign. This was one of those times.

Coming out of the daydream, Marcus picked up the phone again and dialed slowly. "Hey, baby. How are you feeling?"

Gwen had been asleep for the past couple of hours, and his voice on the line was the only reason that she was struggling to a fully awake state. She lazily replied, "Fine. I was just relaxing a little."

"Are you tired or something?"

"What do you think? I have muscles that ache in places I didn't know I had them. I feel like I went ten rounds with Laila Ali." Gwen rolled over on her back and rubbed the inside of her thighs.

"Well, then, I guess I didn't dream it. We made beautiful, passionate love to one another." He leaned back in the chair. "Gwen, you know that we're going to get it right this time." He wanted to take back the words that just escaped his lips, knowing that not getting it right the last time was his fault. Marcus stuttered, "I mean, I want it to—"

"Marcus, stop. I know what you mean. And in case my response didn't come across loud and clear last night and all of the other times this morning, I'm ready for us."

Almost simultaneously they both closed their eyes as if listening for their special angel to play a tune on the harp just for them and bring them that much closer together. Finally, Marcus spoke in a husky whisper. "Me too, baby. Me too."

CHAPTER 20

Patrice pushed away from Jason's death grip. She thought for a moment how ironic it was that his name was Jason, because tonight he was no doubt planning to kill her kitty. Normally, she wouldn't have a problem with his expertise, but tonight she just wasn't feeling him. She indulged in hot steamy foreplay for nearly an hour, but the more he caressed her body, the more she felt like upchucking the lobster and steak that he'd treated her to at the Hard Shell before they reached her place.

Patrice had thrown herself into her business meetings while she was in New York, and unlike her past business trips, her schedule hadn't included any activities that would cause her pulse to race and the thick hairy mound between her legs to leap in total satisfaction. Of course she had a few Big Apple connections, but she hadn't bothered to have either of them on standby in case she needed a little maintenance.

She'd been back in town over a week when she thought about making an appointment with her gyn, because she woke up one morning and realized that she hadn't been sexually active in almost four weeks. Not even a good, torturous session of juicy mouth to lips. Not one person had entered her haven since Bryan, and she still felt shivers every time she thought about that night.

Patrice had done her best to avoid running into him after their escapade, and was successful the first couple of days. But on the third day, she came back from lunch a few minutes late because her pedicure appointment took a little longer than usual.

On a cloud from the pampering she had received, Patrice was finishing off the last bite of the hot dog she'd picked up from the street vendor at the corner, when she walked onto the elevator and bumped right into Bryan. When the door closed with only the two of them on, he spoke softly. "Ms. Henderson, it's good to see you again. I presume that you received the assorted bouquet of roses I sent you yesterday? I thought it would be the perfect welcome back from your business trip."

Trying to sound unappreciative, she responded coldly, "Yes, I did. Thanks. But how did you know . . . Never mind." She balled the napkin up in her hand.

The elevator stopped on her floor, but before she could put one foot in front of the other and get off, he suddenly pushed the button to close the doors and hit the button for the basement.

"What's up with you? You know I'm not supposed to know you."

He invaded her space in one quick step and was tracing a circular motion around her right nipple. She could feel it threatening to peep through the silk material of her blouse.

"That's not what I want. In fact I want to get to know you better."

She tried to look serious and discard the weakness that she felt from his toying with her nipple. But when she looked at his sexy body, she could hardly stand still. Even dressed in simple black slacks and a white rib-knit cotton shirt, he was absolutely sexy as hell. "That's not possible."

The elevator stopped again, and before he could get any more ideas she quickly hit the button for the fifteenth floor.

He chuckled. "You can't possibly be afraid of me after all the things we did together not so long ago."

"Me. Afraid? Don't get things twisted. I fear very little, and you, Mr. Chambers, are not someone I fear. Sorry."

"Good. I've got two tickets for the gospel play tonight. Would you care to join me?" His eyes were focused on hers and she couldn't even blink.

"Let's see. The play isn't being performed in your home or mine. That would mean we would be out among people, and I don't know you, remember? So, no, thanks."

Not wanting to let him down completely in case she decided she wanted another sample of the goods, she leaned into him and traced his lips with her finger. He parted them a little, circled his moist mouth around her finger, and sucked it softly. Wanting to get in on the game, she moved her other hand to his crotch and squeezed slightly. "Now, if you're down for another one-on-one, and I'm not talking basketball, call my office. Otherwise, we are just two souls that pass in the Donovan Building."

When the elevator opened this time, she dashed through the doors and didn't stop until she was safely behind her desk. She opened her legs and felt the wetness between her inner thighs. Patrice reached for a tissue off her credenza as she thought, *Of all the days not to wear undies.*

Now, she was in the middle of her bed trying to get it on with Jason, who had satisfied her cravings on so many other occasions. Her body was set and ready to groove to her mental rendition of Teddy P. but all she was hearing was the big band sound, and it just wasn't what her body flowed to.

"Stop, Jason. This isn't working tonight." She sat up and wished that she smoked; maybe that would relax her enough to finish what they'd started.

"What do you mean stop?" His breathing was heavy.

"Girl, I ain't been with your fine ass in a couple of months, and I got a lot of loving for you." He grinned.

"I'm just not feeling it. Look, I've had PMS for several days without the final showdown and I'm feeling lousy. Maybe I just need to drink something hot and get some rest."

"I was hoping to help you relax. But I got to respect your vibe. Listen, why don't I stay a while and snuggle up with you? If you change your mind, I'll be more than ready to continue." He pulled her into a bear hug and kissed the top of her moist head.

"Not tonight. I'll call you when I feel better. I promise." Patrice turned to him and tried to look sincere, when in all honesty she didn't have a clue when she was going to call him again. Moving off her water bed, she grabbed the purple silk short robe and wrapped it tightly around her naked body. She reached down on the bed and returned the condom that was still in its bright red package to the candy dish on her nightstand. Most people filled their candy dishes with candy, but she filled hers with her favorite assortment of condoms. It included a wide array in various colors and flavors. Whatever the pleasure, she was sure to have something accommodating. It was all about addiction; and her addictions were always long, hard, and ready.

Patrice opened her bedroom door and turned the ceiling light up. "I'm going into the kitchen. You can let yourself out." She heard him swear, but before he could object or express his displeasure at being dismissed, she was out of the room.

She decided to have a glass of ice-cold lemonade. It wasn't PMS she was experiencing, but just a case of not wanting to get laid by Jason. She was tempted to call Gwen, but this was Gwen's first official unsupervised date with Marcus, and she definitely didn't want to interrupt them. She was pleased as punch that they were getting back together and that Gwen had finally let go of her treasure. If nothing else, she knew for sure that it would mellow her out. Patrice jumped as Jason slammed the front door behind him. She didn't mean to lead him on tonight but she just wasn't feeling him.

Patrice stretched out full-length on the sofa and looked at the ceiling. She wasn't accustomed to boredom, never being still long enough for it to settle in on her. Sickness was the only thing that limited her, and that wasn't often because she was as healthy as a thoroughbred horse, including her teeth. In certain cultures, she was sure she would be considered a good catch since many of the men were only concerned about a woman's healthy body and teeth. She reached for her briefcase and opened it. Flipping through some papers, she came across a business directory. There in the first column were the name, address, and telephone number of the one man she avoided like the plague, and yet craved desperately.

She couldn't understand why he chose to list not only his business number but his home number as well. She had been in the business a while and created a nice portfolio, but she never gave out her personal number. Her long list of clients didn't seem to be bothered by her conducting business only within business hours.

Not wanting to take the coward's option and dial, listen, and hang up, Patrice pumped herself up and told herself all the reasons why calling him was a good idea. Finally she searched for her black cordless phone. After three rings, she was ready to hang up. She felt like a fool; in the haste of things, she hadn't even noticed that it was 11:30 p.m.

A deep baritone voice answered, "Hello."

"Bryan, did I wake you?" She held her breath and closed her eyes. Maybe if she focused on her G-spot mentally, his voice alone would be enough to cause her to erupt and she could go to bed, having been spent.

"No, I was just reading. And what can I do for you, Ms. Henderson?"

"So you have caller ID, huh?"

"Actually I do, but not in this room. I'd be able to recognize your voice if it was mixed in a group of a thousand women. Some things make a lasting impression; your voice and some other things about you are among them."

The pitch of his voice was so smooth and even, she could fall asleep just listening to him talk. Patrice wondered why she erased that sound after their night together. Then again, she knew exactly why, and that brought her to the reason for her call. "Look." She inhaled deeply and placed her French-manicured nail between her two front teeth.

"I'm bored as hell, and I must admit I don't allow boredom to keep me company much." She closed her eyes again and thought about his features that she could only describe as close to perfect. Not perfect, because perfection would bring her defeat, and then she would have to relinquish her hard-core, straight-up enjoy, and step style. Thinking about the image that she worked so hard to achieve, she said, "Look. It's prime-time booty hour, and I was wondering if you'd like to come out and play."

"I'd love to, but wouldn't you prefer to come here? That way I wouldn't know that you live at 2820 Treetop Terrace Lane." He remained cool when she knew he must have felt pretty good about the little investigating he'd done.

"Actually, I'd like you to come over here to my playground. I'll see you in half an hour. And, Bryan, no need to bring anything, I've got a few toys I'm sure you will enjoy right here." Patrice hung up, eager to satisfy her sexual hunger. "Let's go get cleaned up, Kitty."

CHAPTER 21

"Gwen, despite what you may be feeling and how much further you think you need to go, you have made significant progress." Dr. Ryan reached to turn off the recorder and uncrossed her legs. Gwen learned that this was an unspoken signal that her session was ending.

"I do feel a lot better, actually. I owe you a lot. I don't know if I could have dealt with all of this alone. I feel like everything is in the open and uncovered now—yet I believed even after the first few sessions that exposing my life would make me feel like a complete failure. Like someone that just wasn't able to deal with life alone. But surprisingly, I feel like it was the best decision I could have made. I thought that dealing with Tiffany's death was the only thing that was holding me in bondage, but now I know that while it was a major issue for me, it wasn't the only issue." Gwen removed her left leg that was tucked comfortably under her and slipped her foot back into her black leather mule.

"Well, as I told you, releasing things, especially things that have caused you to withdraw, is no easy task. You felt that your job as a sister and as a daughter to your mother was to always take care of Tiffany, no matter what. When Tiffany didn't tell you she had AIDS and died before you could discuss it with her, you felt responsible. Like you could have stopped her from dying somehow.

"You must know, Gwen, that there was nothing that you could have done to change the way things happened. Your mother thinks that you took her daughter away by voicing your opinion to remove her from the life support system. What you did was the most unselfish thing any one of you could have done. You saw her pain and her suffering, and you had the courage to say that she wasn't really alive, but living only through artificial measures.

"Then, and even now, your mother probably doesn't agree with you speaking out, but one day she will see that you were only doing what she didn't have the courage or the will to do." Dr. Ryan turned a little in her chair and leaned toward Gwen as she spoke the next words. "I believe that she is upset the most because you were stronger than she was. That you were able to step away from the entire trauma and the pain that you felt deep down, and acknowledge that Tiffany couldn't go on in the state she was in. All of that was absorbing your very soul, but you were still able to say hey, this is enough."

Gwen leaned farther back in her seat before replying. "Yeah. I guess you're right."

"When you think about it, she was a mother who was blessed with three wonderful children, the one who spent so many years tending to the needs and concerns of those three people and who believed that she knew each of you better than anyone else. She didn't respond to Tiffany's silent cries, but you did, and that is what is destroying your mom. Not what you did, but what she couldn't see. Your mother is the one who should have recognized what she had allowed to blind her."

"I don't know, Dr. Ryan. My mom will never, ever forgive me, or accept what she thinks I did. And I don't know if I can forgive the way she has turned her back on me." Gwen rubbed her forehead and rocked her head in her unsteady hands. Suddenly it seemed as if someone ignited a furnace. The office that she had walked into an hour before now seemed to be located in the pit of hell itself. The weather was cool for the middle of August, and she had driven over to her appointment dressed in a fuchsia fitted tee and a black skort. She had rolled the front windows down and opened the sun-roof, enjoying the slight breeze and basking in the warmth of the sun. But now she felt like she was suddenly burning to a crisp.

"I know it's going to be difficult, but in order to completely heal, you have got to release any angry or negative feelings that you're having. It will only get in the way of all the progress you're making." Dr. Ryan paused, not sure how to approach her next statement in a manner that would be received by Gwen as a necessary part of the treatment process. The last thing she wanted was for Gwen to be thrown further into a state of repression. "In order to free yourself and move on, you have to openly deal with every obstacle that can be viewed as having a negative impact on you. Now, from everything that we have discussed, I think there are some issues at the core of this that need to come out, and your mother holds the key to unlocking them. That means that you will have to talk to your mother, tell her how you feel, and listen in hopes that she will open up totally."

Gwen jumped up. "What? I can't believe that you think talking to her is going to help me in any way. I mean, isn't she the reason why I'm in counseling? Sure, Tiffany's death has thrown me into mental anguish at its worst, but if I could have talked with my mom and made her understand that I did what I did because it was what Tiffany wanted, I probably wouldn't be here. If she'd let me in instead of shutting me out like some stray animal, then I would only be dealing with Tiffany's dying and not with the guilt of passing along her wishes. My mother was holding on like she was the only damn one who wore her knees out praying and expecting a miracle."

Dr. Ryan knew the anger that Gwen was releasing was necessary and that she had pushed an emotional button that controlled a lot of pent-up hostility over all that had happened between Gwen and her mother. She knew it was a good time to end their meeting and allow Gwen to pull herself together emotionally.

"We've covered enough today. Why don't you go home and get a little rest? Better yet, spend some time with the rekindled love of your life."

Sounding a little worn and feeling absolutely drained, Gwen spoke softly. "I think that's a very good idea." She hadn't meant to yell at Dr. Ryan, but she couldn't fathom seeking answers to her many questions from her mother, of all people. Gwen knew that if she were about three shades lighter, she would be all red and flushed, but her skin tone hid well what she was feeling. If her emotions could mask the anxiety as well, then she wouldn't be walking out of Dr. Ryan's office fearing what she knew would come. What she knew had to come: a confrontation with Claire James.

Gwen stopped by to have a quick conversation with Patrice before she went out on a date with Bryan. She couldn't believe Patrice finally decided to be seen out in public with this guy after doing little more than the occasional toss in the hay, but he finally wore her down. Patrice swore this was the first and only time she would do it, but Gwen also noticed how excited she was about the whole ordeal.

She wanted to tell Patrice about her session with Dr. Ryan and the ludicrous thing she wanted her to do. Talking to Claire James was out of the question, and she wouldn't do it unless Jesus himself came down from up high in all his glory and majesty and escorted her there. At least, that is what she told herself all afternoon, but somewhere between helping Patrice dress for the evening, and convincing her to wear a strapless bra under the silky fabric of the after-five red Gucci chain-back halter dress rather than have her nipples respond to a cool breeze, she was having second and third thoughts.

"It's not a date, and I really don't care if he notices that my nipples are hard. If I'm lucky, he'll forget this whole opera thing and we'll head straight to his place and he can give me what I really want."

Gwen fought hard to listen and be attentive to what Patrice was saying, but her mind was fixed on her plight.

"Girl, why can't you just relax and enjoy a nice evening that doesn't necessarily have to include sex? That can happen, you know." Gwen stood looking at her reflection and before she knew it she had blurted out all that was discussed in her session earlier.

Without looking directly at Gwen, Patrice spoke evenly. "You know, Dr. Ryan is right. You need to talk to Mama James." Gwen turned around and reached for her purse. Patrice twirled her around. "Wait a minute and listen to me. I know the way she is treating you is messed up, but if it's going to help you get past some of this, then I think you should face the music and get it over with. I mean, there is too much going right in your life for you to couple it all with the negative. If you want, I'll go with you. You know that. But, Baby Boo, you've got to do this."

Gwen looked down at the black satin comforter and wished that she could just escape with only the positive things in tow. "I hear you. Look, I've got to meet Marcus at Andre's. I'll call you tomorrow. Don't forget that I'm picking you up in the morning to meet him for this secretive meeting that he's planning."

"Did he ever tell you what the surprise is? I mean, in between rounds." She laughed, trying to sidetrack the issue.

"Nope. Not even a clue. Have a good time and be good, please?"

Patrice continued to apply her lipstick and peeped over her shoulder. "I'm always good."

"You are such a ho. But I love you."

"Love you back."

Gwen sashayed through the doors of Andre's private dining room, realizing that she was more than fifteen minutes late. She had become less and less predictable these days, and couldn't remember the last time she actually arrived any place on time. Along with so many other changes she was making in her life, being more relaxed and spontaneous was right there at the top.

Marcus looked up in time to see Gwen walking through the door. She was even more beautiful than she had been when he left her bed that morning. He hadn't bothered to wake her up, but just stood over her for a while watching her chest rise and fall in the idle, exhausted state of sleep. Her left arm was thrown across the pillow that he'd slept on, and she looked so at peace. He knew that she was beginning to feel comfortable with him and was letting her defenses down a little. With each day after that revelation, he vowed to the powers that be that he would never, ever disappoint her or take for granted the love he lived without for so long.

"What's up, Lil' Sis? Girl, you look too dangerous in that dress." Andre couldn't have been more happy for his best friends, who, after much too long, were finally a couple again.

Before Gwen could respond, Marcus took in the sight of her with piercing eyes and added, "I loved what you had on this morning when I got out of bed. But this dress is working overtime. I almost pinched myself when you walked through the door to make sure I was not in the midst of a dream. Sweetheart, I am one lucky man." He took her hand in his and slowly brought it to his lips and kissed it lightly. Yielding further to the yearning deep within, he pulled her to him and kissed both cheeks and then parted her lips with his tongue to explore the inside of her mouth in a slow, sensual kiss.

Gwen opened her eyes, a little dazed from the depth of the kiss. "Are you trying to let me know just how much you missed me today, Mr. McGuire?"

"If you care to skip dinner and the rest of the evening I have planned, I can show you just how much." Marcus smiled, hoping she would agree to exchange dinner and dancing for the early show.

"Not a chance. I'm starved. In fact, I haven't had anything since early this morning." She rubbed her stomach to drive her point home.

"Well, you two spend more time dining here in the private dining room than my paying patrons."

"You know we're good for it. And besides, when I told you I was taking Gwen someplace different tonight, you almost lost it. You swear nobody can cook a meal like your head chef Levi. So, bring on the grub, my baby's hungry and don't try to cut no corners." Marcus took Gwen by the hand and led her to the candlelit table that was arranged for two. Everything was accented in gold, including the stem glassware. He pulled out Gwen's chair, and after she was seated he sat across from her, still laughing at Andre's speechless expression.

"Gwen, enjoy your dinner and I'll see you before you leave tonight. Marcus, man, remember what payback is."

Gwen and Marcus talked throughout their meal and enjoyed every morsel. Gwen couldn't believe that she had managed to eat every portion of food that was placed before her. She savored the flavor of the roast duck and orange sauce and licked her lips when she placed the last fork of black forest mousse pie into her mouth.

"What's on your mind? You look like you're a thousand

miles away, and that's a little too far away to make me feel comfortable."

"Nothing, really. I was just thinking about something that Dr. Ryan suggested today." Gwen tossed her napkin on the table.

"And what was that?" Marcus moved his chair over next to hers and wrapped his arm around her. He knew that whatever it was, it had her a little despondent.

Gwen took a deep breath and blew it out while she played with the rim of her wineglass. "She thinks that I need to talk to my mom. She believes that I need to discuss how I feel with her and to see if she is willing to open up to me." Marcus tightened his arm around her and didn't speak right away. "Say something. What do you think I should do? I went over to see Patrice before I came here tonight. She had no problem telling me that I need to talk to Mom and get on with my life. Please tell me that you don't agree with them? You, of all people, should be on my side." She spent a lot of evenings bending Marcus' ear and allowing some of the torturous pain to subside in the warmth of his embrace. Marcus had not been the only one willing to listen. When Gwen wasn't with him or Patrice, Scott had become her faithful hanging-out partner. She dismissed the attraction she witnessed in his eyes and told herself that their time together was harmless. Truth be told, Gwen could have easily been just as attracted to him. That is, if it wasn't for Marcus and their flame being fanned by history and by their friends. And of course, there was the small tidbit that Scott was younger than any man she had ever dated.

"Gwen, baby, there is no side to this. The only side is getting you through all of this, and yeah, for you to get on with your life, our life together. I know from what you've told me that it isn't going to be easy, but in the end I do believe it will be worth it."

Shifting in her seat a little, she turned to him. "You're

right, I guess. I mean, she will either talk to me or she'll continue to shut me out, but right now I'm going crazy trying to answer all these questions I have in my mind. I don't want to go, Marcus. I wish I didn't have to. I'm so happy with this part of my life." Gwen pointed to him and then to herself. "The us in my life is the only thing I feel is progressing. I know we aren't where we need to be, but I know we are working on it. I guess I'm just scared. What if she doesn't say anything more than what she says to me on the phone? How will I accept that?"

"If that's all she says, then you will tell her how sorry you are that she can't release her own hurt and anguish, but that you will go on. And if that happens, then somehow, Gwen, with all of our help you will survive this. But you got to face this, baby. You can't hide behind Tiffany's death and pretend that the truth, or whatever you could learn that would make it easier to endure, doesn't exist. You've got a lot of strength, much more than you know. Look at me."

Marcus touched the side of her left cheek lightly and traced the outline of her face, between her eyes, her nose, and her lips, as if he were memorizing each delicate detail and embedding the image in his soul. "Whatever you find out or don't find out, I'm going to be there, holding you up and reminding you that you are loved and that things are going to work out. When I think about all the time I wasted and all the things I should have done and didn't, I want to kick myself. But right now, right here, that's what we have, and I'm going to love you with all that I have for as long as you'll let me."

Gwen tried to push the lump down in her throat by swallowing hard. "Thanks for your offer. I know there is no way around it, so I guess I'll just have to go."

"You know that I leave for California tomorrow afternoon for a couple of days to tie up a few things, but the minute I get back in town, we'll jump in the car and ride down there. You can always change your mind and go to California with me. That way we can fly from there. I can't believe that you didn't want to join me in the first place."

"It's not that. I just want you to concentrate on your business so you can come back a whole lot quicker. If I join you, you won't get any work done. I'll take the next trip. I promise."

"Well, if you promise, then I'll see if I can condense a three-day trip into a two-day trip. The idea of leaving you even for a couple of days just isn't sitting well with me." Marcus tried to cover up his disappointment. He knew that it was probably crazy, but he was afraid that if he left Gwen behind so soon after they'd finally gotten things back on track, he would return and she would decide that she'd made a mistake. He would just go to California, take care of a few pressing details, and head back. He estimated that it would only take a day and a half if he worked liked a madman. And that was exactly what he planned to do. Relocating his headquarters to Richmond was important, but Gwen was also a part of his life equation and he wouldn't be content having a thriving business and not have the woman of his dreams to share it all with.

Pulling himself away from his private thoughts, he snuggled closer to her and inhaled the wonderful scent of her perfume that combined with her natural fragrance and created a seductive aroma that was so sweet and exotic, it sent his senses into a state of overdrive.

"Come on, I want to take you upstairs. Vince finally talked Andre into having salsa dancing every Tuesday night." Marcus got up and took her by the hand, heading out of the dining room and toward the upper-level dancing area.

"Marcus, sweetheart. News flash for ya. I've never salsa danced in my life." Gwen stopped walking and looked at him for another suggestion.

"Yeah, baby, but your body is made for salsa dancing. All

the stuff that you need to groove to the taste of salsa is packed into that tight, compact body of yours. Just follow my lead and trust me on this."

Gwen followed him hesitantly. It wasn't the salsa dancing that worried her. She was sure that she could catch on to that. It was the uneasy feeling she got at the mention of her trusting him. What was it that was lurking around in the recesses of her mind? Before she could give it any more thought, the loud thumping of salsa music enveloped them and she and Marcus blended into the crowd of dancers.

Marcus couldn't believe how quickly she caught on. Before long she was twisting, shaking, and working her body along with the rhythm and it seemed that all male eyes were on her assets. He envisioned this being her dance but he wasn't prepared for everyone else noticing how easily she flowed to the music with her eyes closed as if she was in a trance. The dress she wore was clinging to every curve and exposing her smooth, well-defined thighs while her breasts seemed to swell with every movement.

Gwen was beginning to enjoy the music and felt her anxieties melt away and a welcomed relaxation take over her being. She wasn't Latino, but for tonight she would allow the music to overtake her. She would flow with it and dance the dance of love.

CHAPTER 22

"I can't believe we are up so early, and that Vince and Andre are actually going to leave their den this time of the morning to come over here. You know those boys live like vampires. Sunlight will probably reduce Vince to the immortal blood-sucking animal he is," Patrice said.

"Leave Vince alone," Gwen responded. "You've been cranky ever since I picked you up. What happened? Didn't you have a good time with Bryan? And before you decide to lie to me, remember that I know you like a book." Gwen spoke briefly to the doorman of the building, who was standing post and apparently waiting to be relieved of his midnight-to-7:00 a.m. shift. He was standing erect with a large white and red lunchbox dangling from his fingertips, wearing puffy circles under his eyes like a businessman wears his cuff links. He was desperately in need of several hours of uninterrupted sleep. Marcus had asked everyone to meet him here at 7:00 a.m. since he moved his flight up to 9:00 a.m. He also made everyone promise to be on time so that he wouldn't miss his flight.

"No, the opposite actually. I had a nice time. The opera wasn't even that bad, and Bryan was a perfect gentleman. Of course, I thought of nothing else the whole evening except getting him back to my place and helping him out of that stuffy tuxedo. Instead of coming inside and completing the evening in style, he walked me to the door and said that he had a headache and was going home to take a couple of aspirins. Girl, I was too through."

Gwen burst out laughing. "Maybe he did have a headache. But what I really think is that he likes you and he doesn't want to be your sex toy."

"Well, that's the only thing I want from him. I don't do nice guys. You know that. Now come on. This is the suite." Patrice checked out the light oak door and the number 2107 that was etched on it. "I hope this doesn't take long; I plan on going back home to relax since I don't have to be in the office until this afternoon."

Gwen couldn't believe the foul mood Patrice was in. She had never seen her react like this over any man she bedded. Suddenly it came to her loud and clear. Patrice must really like this one because no one ever touched her emotionally. Gwen decided that she would let it all go until later and then she would get all in Patrice's business since she always made it a habit of doing the same thing to her.

"Oh, finally." Marcus was standing by a large window with a stunning pictorial view of the downtown businesses. Mama Bea planted herself on a comfortable oversize blue sofa. Vince and Andre were seated on either side of her, trying to get comfortable enough to fall back asleep. She didn't look uncomfortable, but as if it was the most natural place for the two overgrown boys to be. "I can't believe that Vince and Andre beat the two of you here."

"Well, we're here now, so let's get this meeting of the minds, both large and small, started." Patrice flopped down in a large, matching chair that was positioned in a corner beside a large potted plant.

Gwen walked over to Marcus and stood on tiptoes to kiss

him warmly on the lips. "Good morning again, lover. Don't mind 'Trice. She's been like that ever since I picked her up."

"I'm sorry that I had to get all of you together so early in the morning, but I will be leaving town a little earlier than I planned originally so that I can return swiftly." He turned and reached for Gwen's hand. "As you all know, my headquarters has been located on the West Coast since I started McGuire Productions and I have done well enough to have offices in both Atlanta and New York. I've poured every fiber of my being into making a lucrative business. I have made a lot of sacrifices and I've spent a lot of time away from all of you. Mama always kept me grounded and reminded me daily, even while I was there, that home is where you have people who love you, not for what you are accomplishing, but for who you are." Marcus turned slightly and winked his eye at Mama Bea, who responded with a smile.

"I never considered California my home. My only focus back then was getting far enough away from the mistake I made and one day waking up and not having it haunt me. That never happened. I had to live with it. While I did, I grew up and became the man I needed to be, the man I knew my father always wanted me to be."

Marcus' voice faded a little, and Vince and Andre were now wide-awake, realizing that Marcus was getting a little sentimental.

"It wasn't until Gwen decided to allow me to make up for some of the time I lost that I actually began putting my plan in motion. I don't want to put any pressure on you, Gwen, but I am hoping that the decision I have made will let you know how serious I am about us being together. As of yesterday, I leased this entire building and will be relocating the headquarters of McGuire Productions to Richmond." Marcus tightened the grip on Gwen's hand. "Sweetheart, when the time is right and when you trust me with your whole heart, I would like to ask you to marry me."

Although his speech had been for everyone, the last few words were meant just for her. Gwen couldn't help but stand there, wide-mouthed and stunned. Before she could say anything, everyone in the room was up, surrounding them and expressing how happy they were, not only because he was coming back home, but because he was offering Gwen the rest of his life.

They all planned to continue the celebration when Marcus came back from finalizing things in California. Everyone cleared out, knowing that the two wanted to be alone.

Gwen stood smiling and hadn't said much since the announcement. She was looming someplace between elation and ambiguity. She stood in the very same position Marcus had when Gwen entered the office suite earlier, looking out over the city. The hustle of the people below was mute to her ears, but she could feel their urgency to get to their destination and go about the affairs of their daily lives. It was funny how situations that seem so bleak could change in a fraction of a moment in time, and people would either adjust, cope, or move on. What was life anyway if it wasn't about change? For once, maybe she would know certainty; she would live without holding her breath and crossing her fingers. Maybe it was time for her to live again.

"Hey now, what's up with you? Don't think that I didn't notice how silent you got after I made my announcement. I was expecting you to send up a couple of happy balloons." Marcus sat on the windowsill in front of her, placed the palms of his hands on her hips, and pulled her into him.

"I'm happy for you. Really I am." Gwen attempted a half smile that didn't alert her dimples to deepen as they usually did when she was feeling a real smile.

"Why don't I believe you? Come on now; if something is wrong or if I said something, you've got to talk to me. That was our arrangement, remember?"

"Yeah. I guess I'm just a little scared. Sure, it all sounds great, but is there some kind of guarantee I can get that something messed up won't happen, or that someone I love won't be taken away from me the minute I start singing the happy, happy, joy, joy song?"

Marcus loosened his hold on her so that he could look into her eyes. "Gwen, baby, there are no guarantees, and I can't say that nothing bad won't ever happen to you again. But what I can promise you is that I will never, ever . . ." Gwen turned her head away from him and gazed at the empty wall. "No, look at me. I won't ever hurt you again. I'm not going anywhere this time. If we end, it will be because that is what you want—and even then I will still be around, waiting for you to come back. Gwen, my word is my bond. I gotcha on this. Baby Boo, I love you, girl. Trust me."

Gwen wanted to believe every word that Marcus uttered. Her heart needed a balm, and the best balm she could think of was Marcus McGuire. He was her world and had been a part of her for as long as she could remember. She would have to rid herself of all insecurities and move on. He deserved that at least. "I love you too. I want to trust you . . . I need . . ." Before she could finish her sentence, Marcus was pulling her Just Do It Nike T-shirt over her head. She stood before him braless; her nipples glistened from her early shower and Victoria's Secret shimmering body gel and lotion. Before she could object, he was tonguing her nipples, softly urging her to moan and sway her body closer to his.

"Marcus, don't you have a plane to catch?" Gwen was fighting the wonderful feeling that was consuming her upper body. She was getting light-headed and her legs were trembling.

"Actually, not until noon. I told everybody that my flight was leaving at nine o'clock so that we could spend a couple of hours christening our new suite. As long as you have your way with me and drop me off at the airport by ten forty-five, we're good." He spoke long enough to get those important points across before he licked and teased her belly button, slipping her sweats down to her ankles. "Gwen, baby . . . damn, where are your panties?"

Gwen chuckled. "Don't need any. Didn't you ever hear that less is more? It's not like it's cold outside, and even if it was, I'm here with you and I believe that you know exactly how to warm me up." Gwen had a new boldness about herself and was beginning to do things that were totally out of character for her.

"In fact, I do. Don't move." Marcus moved slowly to the floor to remove her sneakers and help her out of her sweatpants. When he finished the task, he kissed the insides of her calves and worked his way up to the insides of her thighs. He continued the torturous action until he felt her right leg wobble against his shoulder. He parted her legs, placed his fingers inside her, and moved them slightly in a circular motion. She was already wet, and he coaxed his body to hold on tight for just a little longer. This morning, he wanted her to feel pleasure beyond anything she had ever known. He wanted to hear her echo his name throughout the walls of his new office. He wanted her to beg him to soothe her and anchor his heart to her soul, allowing it to rest in the place where it always belonged. Pulling her hand to him, he kissed it softly and held it before he continued. Marcus looked up at her. Gwen finally opened her eyes when she felt his warm glance. She smiled nervously when she realized that it was a different kind of look. He was seeking her permission to continue, and she knew this time wouldn't be like the times before. This time he would take her to another place. Some place that was created just for the two of them and for the love they shared. All that it was, and all that it would be.

"Baby, I've got to do this. I want to love you in every way possible. I need you to know that I love you, and that this time it means everything to me." Before she could inhale or nod her head in an understanding gesture, Marcus placed his tongue between her lips and she stumbled backward. He held her tightly and allowed her to relax her back against the windowsill. He parted her legs a little more, plunging his tongue deep inside her and drowning in the sweet taste of her. He wasn't sure if it was his sounds filling the room or hers. He was on a whole different plateau, and was doing everything he knew to do to take her with him. When he felt her grip his head and tighten her legs around his neck, he slowed to a rhythm and methodically continued. Suddenly he felt her body clench and she was yelling out his name. In the flood of her words, he listened as she told him how much she loved him, would always love him, and that it felt so good.

Before she could fully recover, he picked her up and carried her over to the large light oak desk and laid her still-moist body on it. Marcus undressed without interrupting the intense look they shared. He was afraid that she would have been embarrassed by what he had done, or even angered by it, but what he saw was love and a yearning that he desperately needed to fill.

He leaned over, kissed her softly, and laid his head on her chest. She rubbed her fingers through his hair and caressed his back. Finally, he lifted her body and pulled her to the edge of the desk, wrapping both legs around his arms. He entered her and answered all of her questions, quieting her spirit with all the reassurance he could offer. Gwen's nails dug lightly into his back. He wrenched from the sensation that was immediately drowned in the intense throbbing orgasm that swept over him. He realized instantly that their bodies were in complete unison as he felt Gwen release and call out his name again. Breathing heavily, he managed to speak. "Trust me, baby. I just need you to trust me."

Gwen shared a quick shower with Marcus. They managed to leave the suite before ending up in each other's arms with little chance of getting to the airport on time.

*　*　*

Two hours later, Gwen felt like an idiot. She couldn't believe that she stood in front of the departure gate crying like she would never see Marcus again. Forty-eight hours from then, he would be back in her arms and they would be on their way to her parents' home to deal with what was inevitable. Still, she knew that she would miss him. The hardest part was watching the intense look on his face and noticing that in the depth of his beautiful brown eyes that always mesmerized her, there was a hint of uncertainty and woefulness. She spent the last few minutes before his flight reassuring him that she would be right there waiting for him when he returned, and that what they'd managed to recapture after all those years would remain intact.

Gwen was a little exhausted from getting up so early that morning after only a couple of hours of sleep. Since it was still morning and she had no place to be, and since Patrice would be going into the office that afternoon, she all but confirmed her appointment with her pillow, and the comfortable bed that waited for her like an old lover. She hadn't spent any nights alone at Kyra's house in weeks. The conclusion of her evenings almost always found her in Marcus' arms. They had certainly made up for lost time. She really didn't mind, though; waking up with him right next to her was like the finale to a long, long, tireless race. A race that she ran sometimes knowingly and sometimes unaware, yet the prize she hoped to gain was always slightly out of reach. That is, until now.

Stumbling out of the car, she got out and stretched. Making love in the windowsill and again on the desk was something straight out of one of the BET Arabesque made-for-television movies. She just never imagined that she could play one of the leading roles. Gwen could only shake her head at what she had allowed Marcus to do. And more surprisingly, she shook her head at how open she was to his advances. Patrice would definitely be proud of her, but this morning would be something she would keep to herself, at least for a while.

Shifting slowly along the cement walkway with keys dangling in her hand, she looked up and noticed that Scott was still at home. A twinge of guilt surfaced. She hadn't spent that much time with him in over two weeks. She had gotten used to the early morning jogs they shared, mid-day chats or early evening drives. Whenever she was home alone Scott made it a point to occupy those spare moments He'd left several notes on the door saying that he missed her company. Just last week, he'd left a cute little white teddy bear on the patio chair with a note attached to the red ribbon around its neck. She couldn't help but smile when she read it. *I was wondering if you've seen my friend. We used to kick it together, and I guess I'm missing her.* When she'd placed it between the pillows on the bed, she had every intention of inviting him over or taking a little time to hang out with him. But Marcus called with tickets to a WNBA play-off game at the Coliseum.

In the flurry of the days that followed, Gwen forgot about the bear and her intention of checking in on Scott. She hadn't neglected to tell him that she was back with Marcus and that things were good. Gwen told him all about what happened between them all those years ago, and he listened attentively. His first comment when she disclosed the whole sordid ordeal was that she deserved to be treated with much respect and real love. Scott reassured her that what it boiled down to was having a man who truly understood a woman's worth. Talking about what happened that night at Marcus' apartment hadn't been easy, but Scott made her feel at ease and like he really needed to know about that part of her past.

Time had a way of standing still. It really didn't seem like she had been back with Marcus that long. She lost track of time and everything and everyone else outside of their cozy intimate relationship. Of course, she made time for Patrice because she was in their clique and a part of the gang. They spent as much time together as she had with Marcus. She and Patrice spent countless hours together, shopping, talking endlessly, and just enjoying each others' presence. She let them all in, and they were overindulging her in attention. The only time she was alone was during her sessions with Dr. Ryan, and although they all pleaded to go with her, she wasn't ready for that to happen.

The one thing that she realized when she passed the front doorstep, walked through the hedges, and headed over to Scott's house was that she missed him. His conversation, laughter, and fun-loving ways had been a godsend when she needed noise and a presence to remind her that she was not alone in the unfamiliar surroundings that would be her home for a while. He had been what she needed, and she was so appreciative to have him next door watching over her.

She couldn't believe how easily she could relate to him; it was like having a new best friend who just happened to be a sexy-as-hell tight-bodied man. He had even taken her to a shopping mall while they were in Charlottesville. The first store they entered had the widest variety of shoes she had ever seen. She spent three hours trying on different styles and brands. He finally succumbed to her shopaholic tendency and helped her pick out two pairs of sandals in hopes that she would call it a day. They concluded their shopping with a trip into the jewelry store. While Gwen stood over the glass case preoccupied with picking out a new ankle bracelet, he doubled back into the shoe store and purchased the pair of blue and white Nikes that she liked but swore she didn't need.

They had spent so much time at the corner Blockbuster's that the store clerks knew them by name and would shake their heads as they watched them fuss over whose turn it was to choose the movies. One clerk went so far as to tell them that they should go ahead and get married because they made the perfect couple. Gwen was going to correct the lady and say that they were just friends, but Scott quickly smiled and pulled her close to him. He became her hanging-out partner, and she knew that she owed him an apology for neglecting him. Now that she was standing in front of his door about to ring the bell, the words "no time like the present" came to mind.

Gwen rocked back and forth on the heels of her shoes until Scott answered the urgent doorbell ring. She pushed it three or four times causing the chime to announce her need to speak to the owner of the premises posthaste.

"Hey, you. I can't believe that you've ventured into my humble abode." Scott stood in the opened door with a burgundy towel wrapped around his waist and another slung over his left shoulder. He looked even more attractive than she remembered, and the towel beckoned her eyes. She strained extra hard, hoping she would develop X-ray vision if only for that moment.

Swallowing hard, Gwen forced her eyes to stroll back up to his face. She couldn't believe she was standing in this young man's doorway observing him like he was a tasty entrée at a smorgasbord. "Hey, yourself. I'm sorry I interrupted your shower. I just wanted to come over and chill out with you for a little while. That is, if you're not too busy or if you don't have other plans."

"Well, actually, I was going out for a bit." He kept his hand on the doorknob as if he was ready to close it and return to his task of getting ready.

She tried hard not to look disappointed. After all, why should he adjust his schedule to accommodate her after she had been MIA for several days? Gwen hadn't exactly been the ideal friend of late. She was all ready to turn around and head back across the yard, a little hurt.

Without a warning or an alert, his face softened. "But since I've been trying to get with you forever and a day, I better jump on the chance to spend a little time with you. God knows when it might happen again."

Gwen waited for a laugh after his comment, but there was none.

"Come on in and have a seat while I go throw something on."

Gwen stepped down into the living room and kicked off her shoes before lounging on the cocoa-colored oversize sectional. She twisted her butt into the softness of the suede microfiber texture. It felt so good, and she tried hard to find just the right, sweet spot so she could relax her body and unwind.

Scott's house was tastefully decorated. While it wasn't crowded with lots of furniture, what it did consist of was spaced out and accented perfectly with classy and upscale pieces. She was sure that his mother had spent a great deal of time going from one furniture store to another to achieve just the right look and have it complement the interior design of the house with its wood trim and tasteful shades of paint on the textured walls. She fixed her eyes on the large audio system. As if on cue, music flowed out of the ceiling speakers. Its softness was a welcome sound since some of the music that he played contained too much bass and could hardly be considered tasteful by some standards. She always had to remind herself that it was music nonetheless. Some of the same loud, bass-heavy, difficult-to-understand lyrical tunes had been added to her car stereo CD collection since she had been kicking it with Scott. Gwen admitted that it had grown on her and now she enjoyed every thump of it.

"Do you like that?" Scott came into the room, dressed in a simple white T-shirt and black shorts, and paused on the step before proceeding. "If not, I'll change it."

Gwen's body started to relax, and she could feel the tightness in her shoulder muscles loosen up a little. Scott was standing close enough for her to catch a whiff of his usual cologne and feel his strong presence. "It's very nice. Who is it?"

"It's Heather Headley. I thought that you would like the sound." He walked around and sat on top of the etched-glass coffee table, stretching out his legs and crossing them at the ankles. "So, what's good? I've been seeing you come and go, but you haven't taken the time to slow up long enough to include me in a small portion of your agenda."

"I know that. I've been thinking about you, though. In fact, I was on my way over here the other night after you left the teddy bear on the lawn chair. That was really sweet." Gwen playfully swatted at his leg.

"Well, I wanted you to know that you were on my mind. Seriously, though, what's been having you on the down low like this?" Scott waited for a reply but knew the answer already.

"I'll tell you all, but on one condition." Gwen leaned forward.

"What's that? You want me to agree to wait another month to see you?" Scott didn't mean for his question to sound so callous, but his words had already crossed his lips. Still, the look she gave him seemed as though someone had taken the air out of her balloon in midair.

"Look, I'm sorry. Obviously I'm keeping you from something or someone and I'm not being fair by monopolizing your time." Gwen stood up and reached for her shoes. "Just give me a call or come over when you have some free time, and I'll make sure that I'm available." She turned and attempted to muster a weak smile.

"No, come on. Wait. Let's just start this conversation all over again. Better yet, why don't I go pick up a pizza and a couple of videos, and we can spend some time just relaxing? That way I can fill you in on what's new and I'll allow you to bore me. Deal?" Scott extended his hand for her to shake.

"All right. But since I'm the one making the truce, I'll go get the pizza and stop by Blockbuster and pick up a couple of movies. Do you mind meeting me next door in about an hour and a half?"

"No problem. I'm going to make a few calls and I'll see you then." Scott tried to look like it was no big deal when in fact he'd waited weeks just to be in the same room with Gwen.

Scott had become consumed with deliberating about a private practice offer. The whole package was so attractive that the only thing his college chum didn't do was wrap it all up neatly with a big red bow. Even after he'd talked with his mother, and she advised him to go ahead, the thought of turning the offer down lurked around in his head. She had lightly kissed his forehead, told him that it was the opportunity of a lifetime, and that it really wasn't that far away. However, his motive to stay had more to do with the feelings that he had not expressed to Gwen than his needing to watch over his mother. And now as he looked at her, he found it hard to be disappointed over her lack of time for him; he would just make the best of what time she offered.

Funny, but as he wandered around the kitchen trying to decide how he was going to tell Gwen how he felt about her, it was as if his mind and his emotions were on two different wavelengths. His heart was telling him that sharing his feelings with her was the right thing to do, and his mind was telling him to wait. The certitude he'd always known when charting out the course of his life suddenly hit a boulder, yet he felt that somehow opening up was the only logical answer.

He went into the kitchen and picked up the phone. "Hi, Donna. This is Dr. Elliott. I'm going to be tied up for a while this afternoon, and probably part of the evening. Could you please ask Dr. Carter to cover my afternoon rounds for me? Yeah, tell him that I will cover both our rounds in the morning. Thanks a lot, I appreciate it." He hung up the phone. The new receptionist for the west wing of the Children's Hospital was a little more than friendly with him. She had gone so far as to leave her phone number on his car. And when he didn't respond, she made sure that she was assigned to work every shift that he did, just so she could expose every known body part to him and try to engage him in thoughtless conversation.

She wasn't a bad-looking girl, but the pile-high weave,

light brown contact lenses, and two-inch neon nails were just not what he was looking for in a woman. It was perfect for the hoochie club scene, but he wanted a woman who was versatile. One he could take to hospital functions and family gatherings, someone who could hang out and feel comfortable on both levels of Andre's, the mellow jazz side of things, and of course, the hip-hop, bump-and-grind side. He wanted someone who looked good on his arm dressed to the nines, demanding the attention of everyone in the room by her mere presence, and just as good in one of his large UVA T-shirts watching hours of television (not excluding sporting events). Scott needed a lady who would act the fool with him and then finally roll into his bed on cue, ready to make his body holla. A lady who could unleash the inner man and explore all the possibilities of the true art of making love. He glanced out the window and watched Gwen back out of the driveway. Scott mumbled to himself, "Yeah, someone just like you, Gwendolyn James."

Gwen's trip to Blockbuster and the pizza joint at the corner only took an hour. She managed to shower again and change into a long purple caftan, and was back downstairs opening a liter of Sprite when Scott came in. She was feeling so relaxed and comfortable, more comfortable than she had been in a couple of weeks. She wondered why, and quickly dismissed it as having been busy and constantly on the go.

Scott let his disappointment at being put on the back burner subside and eased into their usual routine. As she laughed and joked, he focused on every word and played along, enjoying every moment.

"I can't believe that you didn't bring back anything action-packed and hard-core," Scott complained as he picked a pepperoni off his slice of pizza and popped it into his mouth.

"Stop tripping. You've been sitting here misty-eyed and heaving right along with me."

They watched the ending of *Love and Basketball* in silence. She kicked her feet up on the sofa pillow and rotated her ankle. "Gosh, what a difference a full stomach and a good teary movie can make. I feel more relaxed than I did when the movie started."

"What else did you pick up?" Scott reached over and pulled the other tape closer for inspection. "Gwen, baby, *Shrek*?

"Don't laugh. I wanted to end with something light tonight. But if you're going to bust me up, we can see what's on the television." Gwen was trying to look serious, but the truth was she was hoping to end the videos early and talk to him about her and Marcus.

"No, by all means, if you want to get your *Shrek* on, don't let me stop you. I'll put it in and then we can sort of talk and watch at the same time. Cool?"

"That sounds good to me. I guess we really need to catch up. I haven't had a chance to just chill with you in a while, and I miss your butt."

"My butt?" Scott turned and gave Gwen a half smile.

"I missed you. Come over here, silly, and sit." She lifted her knees to her body and patted the cushion beside her.

Scott sat down, reached for her feet, and placed them in his lap. Without even looking at her, he began to massage her feet with trained hands, working every bone in them. He knew exactly which ones to touch that would relieve the tension that consumed her upper body. Gwen had been taking the pills that Dr. Ryan prescribed, and remarkably they seemed to be working. The hives, while they had not fully gone away, weren't as constant. Now she was closing her eyes, enjoying the moment.

"Gwen, what's up with you and Marcus?" The question was out and Scott rested his head back into the cushion of the sofa while seconds ticked by without a response. "If it's none of my business just say so and I'll squash on it."

Gwen swallowed hard. She planned to tell Scott, but now that he opened the conversation up to that subject, she wasn't sure how to explain it to him. She didn't want him to think she was a fool to go back into a relationship with someone who had hurt her so badly. And how could she explain that she loved Marcus so much, she was willing to take a chance, setting a part of herself aside just in case the worst did happen again?

"Well, we've been seeing each other again. I know it sounds crazy, but I've never stopped loving him despite all the stuff that happened back then. Everyone is so happy for us, and I've decided to just go with it and take it slow."

He stopped rubbing her feet and looked at her with eyes that were so different from all the other times. She wasn't sure she recognized what his eyes were silently saying. "You say that everyone is happy. What about you, Gwen? Are you happy?"

"Yeah. I guess I am. Marcus is a wonderful person, and he has changed a lot. We were both so young then. Maybe I was wrong for expecting so much from him when both of us had a lot of growing up to do."

"Hurt is hurt. And being young or lacking maturity doesn't excuse taking the heart of someone who trusts you and nonchalantly toying with it. Loving someone means loving them unconditionally, encouraging them to seek their dreams, believing in them, and never allowing doubt to cloud the vision of happiness that you share. It's loving them more than you love yourself, and trusting that they will hold your heart as the most treasured jewel that you can give, as if it's the most precious gift in this world. Believing that each day the sun will rise and you will love them more than you did the day before, watching the sun set, knowing that tomorrow you will love them even more."

By the time he finished speaking, he was holding her hand tightly in his, secretly praying for her to listen to the words and know that they were coming from his heart. Exactly when he had fallen in love with Gwen wasn't important, nor was the fact of the short length of time that he had actually known her. What did matter at this precise moment was that this was the woman he wanted in his life, and he was going to let her know that.

"That was so sweet, Scott. The lady who ends up with you will be one lucky person. I almost envy her." She tried to chuckle and realized that the heat in the room was coming from the chemistry between them. "If you weren't my little brother and I wasn't back with Marcus . . ."

Before she could finish, Scott lifted her up in one swift movement and placed her light body on his lap, never taking his eyes off her. He slowly moved his head toward hers until she could feel his warm breath on her face. It was happening so slowly, she knew that she could stop him, and yet she waited, watching his slow movement through dazed eyes that couldn't blink. Finally, his lips touched hers. Slowly he parted her lips and lightly explored the inside with his probing tongue.

Gwen's heart was beating wildly inside her chest as she tried to make sense of what was happening, but she could only yield to what was making her feel so good. She had been kissed before, and she knew that she had loved Marcus almost all of her life, but this kiss was registering off the Richter scale. As much as she wanted him to stop, she wanted him to continue.

Scott pulled away and cleared his throat. "That wasn't a kiss from a little brother, but from a man. A man who thinks that you are special and that you deserve to be loved with a truthful, honest, open, and caring love. Gwen, I care about you and I'm not going to hide it anymore. Now, how you perceive me may hinder that, and your being back with Marcus probably gives me no chance in hell of being with you. But I'm putting it all out here in the open, and I'm not apologizing for this kiss or for what I feel. The one thing it is, Gwen, is real."

Gwen removed her arms that had snuggled around Scott's neck, stood up, and walked over to the fireplace with her back turned. She played with the base of the pewter candlestick holder. The heaviness she felt in her heart right now was something she couldn't label. "Scott, you are something else. But you have to know that we could never be. You have been here for me since day one, and have become my little brother. I just couldn't entertain the idea of you being anything other than that. There is so much that we don't know about each other, you're so much younger than me, and of course I can't deny that I am with Marcus." She turned to face him. She saw so much hurt in his eyes that she wished she could take back the words she had just uttered and return them to the place they came from.

"One day, Gwen, you will learn that age isn't a factor, and that everything is not always as it appears." Scott lifted his body up from the sofa and headed toward the patio. "Just be careful with your heart this time. Thanks for the pizza and the movie."

Before she could say anything else, he was out the door. She walked to the door and her eyes followed him. This time there was no skip walk, but slow deliberate steps carrying him closer to his back door. Scott appeared like a man who walked the earth long enough to be sure of his destination and purpose not only in this one isolated journey, but throughout his entire existence. She was sure that there was something different about him. Gwen stood with the door ajar and inhaled the fragrance of him that lingered in the air long after he was out of sight, wondering if she had been wearing blinders.

CHAPTER 23

Gwen woke to the shrill sound of the doorbell. Her body was damp with perspiration even though the room was cool and dark. Her sleep had been restless and despite her effort to fall into a stage of snooze just beyond REM sleep, she had been unable to. She talked to Marcus for more than an hour after she went upstairs to read a while before she retired. He wanted to hear her voice and let her know that his trip would take a little longer than planned because his vice president for marketing had decided to resign without notice. After assuring him that she would be fine and that he should take all the time he needed to handle his affairs, his smooth voice came through the line and serenaded her, making her feel like he was just across town and not more than two thousand miles away.

The doorbell rang again. The person on the other side of the door was impatient, and clearly didn't understand that waking someone was not the brightest of ideas. Especially if that person had had no more than a couple of hours of sleep. Pulling the short kimono robe tighter around her body, Gwen swore as her toe hit the bottom banister. *This better be good.* Leaning the side of her head against the door, she yelled out, "Who is it?"

"Girl, open this door!" Patrice yelled back, sounding more aggravated than Gwen was to have been disturbed.

Fumbling with the dead bolt, Gwen opened the door wide enough for Patrice to get in and peeped out against the bright rays of the sun with one eye open. "Okay. Where is the fire? And since it's not here, why do I have to be informed about it?"

"I just need to vent. I didn't want to wake you so early, but since I was going to anyway, I went all the way over the bridge to get fresh honey-glazed doughnuts from your favorite spot. My drama probably seems like minor stuff compared to real problems, but you know me. If it isn't something I can readily control and fix, it nags the hell out of me."

"If I didn't love you so much and if you weren't standing there with a peace offering, I would knock your butt out. Come on in and tell Auntie Gwen what's ailing you."

"Funny. I'm not Baron or Darion, so stop with the auntie stuff. What I need is a shoulder and quick."

A little baffled about Patrice's actions, Gwen slowly walked into the kitchen behind her and listened while she went on and on about people leaving her emotions out of situations and allowing her to remain the way she had always been. The way she wanted to be. Patrice busied herself with pulling two juice glasses out of the cabinet and turned to the refrigerator to get the orange juice. "What, no orange juice?"

"Before you lose your mind and pull a .357 magnum out of your purse just because I'm out of juice, calm down. I bought some oranges and I've been making my juice fresh. Give me a minute and I'll get you something to wet your whistle and calm your nerves."

Once Gwen had enough juice for a couple of glasses, she carefully poured the freshly squeezed orange juice in a carafe. The coolness of the tile against her bare feet reminded her that she'd turned the air up to almost freezing earlier when she couldn't sleep.

With Patrice needing her right now, sleep would be eluding her for a while longer. She moved toward the breakfast nook and sat on the stool across from Patrice. "'Trice, are you all right? You can sometimes be obnoxious, but it usually only lasts a couple of hours. This has been going on a couple of days. What is so earth-shattering that you had to wake me up and bring me doughnuts? I mean, don't get me wrong, I appreciate the food offering, but you're scaring me."

Gwen took a sip of her juice and savored a bite of the light, airy sugary treat. She, Patrice, and Kyra had inhaled so many dozens of Tasty Bakery doughnuts during their college years, she was sure that their frequent patronage helped fund one of the Smith girls' braces.

"I was with Jason again last night." Patrice rubbed the back of her neck trying to ease the tension that was threatening to attack at any moment.

"And . . . that's a pretty normal evening for you, isn't it?" Gwen continued to chow down on the doughnut, leaving a residue of glaze on her upper lip.

"Yeah, but by the time we left Andre's and got to his place, I froze again. The more he tried to turn me on, the colder I became. Finally, I came up with another excuse and hauled my ass out of there, went home, and climbed into the bed." Patrice's voice was breaking up with sobering emotion. She bowed her head as if she were praying for her sexual prowess to return.

Gwen examined her for a moment and chose her next words carefully. She didn't want to upset Patrice or suggest anything that she herself wasn't ready to face. "Is it just Jason that you're experiencing this . . . lack of desire with?"

"Jason is the only person since Bryan. Wait a minute; my not being able to get my freak on has nothing to do with him.

It's probably some medical reason why I'm not my normal self." Patrice picked up the phone and dialed frantically.

Gwen watched as Patrice went through the motions of contacting her gynecologist and scheduling an appointment. After assuring the receptionist that it was something that couldn't wait until her yearly exam that was only a couple of weeks away, she hung up the phone with a satisfied look.

Overhearing the whole thing, Gwen spoke matter-of-factly. "What if they tell you that everything is fine physically?"

"Then I'll just carry my happy butt over to Dr. Ryan's, stretch out on the sofa, and tell her how much I love sex, that I'm happiest when I'm getting some, and that I will pay any amount of money for her to fix whatever the hell is going on with me psychologically. 'Cause I just got to have my stuff on a regular basis." Patrice was adamant about her plan.

"Why can't you admit that you are slightly attracted to Bryan and maybe, just maybe, you want to be with him physically and no one else right now?" Gwen pushed her stool back a little, expecting Patrice to yell so loud that her ears would ring.

"I will not admit anything when it comes to Bryan. He may have everything going for him, and yes, he is the closest thing to Adonis that I've ever seen, and heaven knows he knows how to please, but I'm not interested in anything serious, and I'm not changing my MO now. Case closed.

"Now, do you want to tell me why there are two glasses and two plates on the coffee table in the living room? I could have sworn that Marcus hopped a plane to the West Coast yesterday." Patrice was happy to change the subject and was now challenging Gwen with a smug look on her face.

In all the years that Patrice had been dating, no one ever before threatened to tear down the thick wall that surrounded her heart. The one time she'd loved, she realized it much too late, and although she went on, she never forgot what happened. She had it all: a career, close friends she loved, and the girls she mentored. All of those things had become an integral part of who Patrice Henderson was. A love interest just wasn't in the plan.

"Oh, those." Gwen mused to herself, *I can't believe I went up to bed without cleaning this stuff up.* She walked toward the living room and started picking up the remnants of last evening. She moved around hastily, trying to remove all the visible signs of Scott's presence, which screamed out at her then and now, much like a neon sign that could be seen for miles.

"Yeah, those. Who came over? Let's see. Andre and Vince were at the club. Mama Bea went to visit her cousin for a week. Who does that leave?"

"Scott and I had some pizza and watched a couple of videos. It was a fun afternoon. I hadn't taken the time to go over and thank him for the teddy bear that he left for me. So when I came in yesterday afternoon, I went straight over there." She tried to talk quickly so that Patrice couldn't interrupt. "Since we both had a little time, I invited him over. No big deal. It's not like the first time we hung out."

"I don't doubt that. Does he have any playmates that can help me out of my slump?" Patrice giggled as she helped Gwen tidy up the room.

"Isn't that what got you in the slump in the first place? Not knowing when to say when? Besides, if he does, I'm sure they are as young as he is."

"And that's a problem for who? I told you before not to judge a book by its cover. He is a cutie pie and he obviously likes you. So I give him a few cool points for having good taste."

"Thank you, I guess." Gwen lifted her eyebrow, not sure if that was a compliment. "Well, I would argue the point, but after his confession last night I can't even fake playing dumb."

"Whoa. Stop what you're saying. What confession? And

when were you going to tell me?" Patrice stopped fluffing the square pillow that matched the love seat and sat down on the edge of it.

"I didn't have time. You came in here acting like a black Scarlett O'Hara and you ask me why I didn't interrupt the theatrics? You know that when you start, there is no interrupting you." Gwen sprayed lemon Pledge on the cherry-finished coffee table and wiped it off with the dustcloth.

"I know I'm having a moment, but it's just a moment. The doctor will check me out, prescribe something, and I'll be back on top in no time." Patrice winked her eye mischievously. "But right now, sit down and tell me about the confession."

Gwen sat on the ottoman and ran her fingers through her hair, making a mental note to call and make an appointment for a trim. "I felt a little hesitant, but I told Scott that Marcus and I were back together. I could tell he wasn't delighted. I didn't want to defend my choice or be judged for allowing history to repeat itself. Anyway, he ended up telling me about the kind of man I deserved, and the more qualities he mentioned, the more emotion I saw in his eyes. His eyes darkened, and his usual light, jovial attitude was replaced with a seriousness I hadn't really seen in him before. He revealed that he cared about me and could be all of those things to me." Gwen sighed deeply before she finished. "Then Scott kissed me."

"Tongue and all?" Patrice opened her mouth and mimicked placing her tongue into the mouth of an invisible person.

"He didn't leave nothing out, and the boy has mad skills. To think he put all that in a kiss. Imagine . . ."

"I am imagining. I can't say I'm totally surprised, because I saw it coming. I knew that he had a thing for you. How did you handle it, and what are you going to do?"

"Nothing. It's probably just a crush, and if that's what it is, it will go away. I told him that we can only be friends and that I'm in love with Marcus. Besides, 'Trice, he's much too young. Even if things hadn't rekindled between Marcus and me, I couldn't go there." Gwen leaned forward, placing her elbows on her knees. "I won't lie, though. When I saw the disappointment on his face, I felt like the biggest heel. What scares me even more than his confession is that when we kissed, the earth moved. Later, when I watched him walk across the yard, I felt like I was seeing him through different eyes." A moan escaped Gwen's lips. "Does that sound crazy?"

"Not at all. The way things have been going lately, nothing's crazy. Look. My appointment isn't until three thirty. Let's get out of here and do something other than dwell on the issues. Since you're pulling younger men these days, let me add a few more outfits to your wardrobe."

"I'm down for the shopping, but I'm picking out my own stuff." Gwen laughed. "Before we hit the mall, I need to stop by Marcus' office and meet with the decorator. It shouldn't take long."

"Sounds good to me. I'll help you."

"Thanks, but no thanks. Tiger and leopard prints are not exactly the look I'm going for. The offices will actually be used for something other than work done in the horizontal position."

"Don't knock it till you've tried it." Patrice bubbled over, knowing that Gwen couldn't stand illicit anything.

"Been there, done that." Before Patrice could utter a sound, Gwen was on her way upstairs to get dressed. She knew that she had gotten the best of Patrice and that she would be bum-rushing her with more questions. She had to admit that victory in the arena of living out sexual fantasies was exhilarating.

The next week was so jam-packed, with such a long to-do list, that Gwen hadn't had time to breathe. Marcus again postponed his return date and was in touch with her almost every hour, trying to assist her with the planned opening of the new headquarters. She was interviewing potential office staff, meeting with the decorator, assisting the other offices with transitional plans, and exercising every PR muscle to the point of overexertion. She had to confess, if only to herself, that she was enjoying every busy second of it.

What made it even more rewarding was that she was doing it all for Marcus. Knowing how important it was to him and helping him build a credible extension of his already glowing well-known Fortune 500 conglomerate was all the inspiration she needed. She was good at what she did, and she would make sure that his new headquarters had her signature style all over it.

Now, finishing up a session, Gwen rested her head against the chair in Dr. Ryan's office. Dr. Ryan had walked out only moments before to make a house visit and told her she could take a few minutes to get herself together before she left.

Today's session had been an extremely difficult one, and she used more than her usual share of tissues. Gwen had accomplished so much, and felt a lot better about everything. Still, as she made more progress, she was brought to tears more and more and couldn't seem to control them.

Every session for the past month had ended the same way: she had to confront her mother. It was the hurdle she had to jump before she could cross the finish line. She rubbed her numb fingertips over her right arm.

Gwen pulled her cell phone out and searched through her programmed numbers. Biting on her fingernail nervously, she listened as the phone rang for the fifth time.

"Hello."

Thank God. "Daddy. Hi. It's me, Gwen." She smiled at the husky sound of her father's voice. Sure, it sounded a little rough, but it did nothing to cover up the demeanor of the caring, sensitive man that it belonged to.

"Hi, baby. How've you been? I must've talked you up. Your name just came out of my mouth. I just walked in the door with your two nephews. They both have colds so I picked them up from school."

"Are they okay? Maybe Kim should take them to the pediatrician," Gwen replied, full of concern.

"They're going to be just fine. I'm gonna fix 'em up with some honeyed tea and lemon and just a touch of some old Jack Daniel's. A toddy will cut that cold right out of them. Then I'll rub them down with some mentholated salve and toss them under the blanket. Remember when I used to do that for you?" Her father's hands were large, callused, and hard to the touch from working through all kinds of weather and different conditions, but they could still manage to soothe a forehead warm with fever or rub a stomachache away. He was always the one who made her feel better instantly.

"I sure do. My cold would be gone by the next morning. Of course I didn't smell that great, but I sure did feel better. How's everything?" She didn't want to come right out and mention her mother, but she was concerned about how things were.

"If you mean your mama, she's the same. Still upset 'cause I won't agree to that crazy graveyard garden idea. It's gonna be all right, though. Don't you worry yourself none 'bout it. Stress is no good for you."

"I'm fine, Daddy. Look, Dr. Ryan thinks it's time that I come back home and talk to Mama. I don't want to, but I can't get better unless I talk with her and try to deal with some of what happened."

"Do you think you're ready to do that? I think it's a good idea after a while, but I don't want you rushin' into it."

"I'm not rushing. She believes I'm ready to deal with it all, and as much as I don't want to admit it, I think I'm ready to."

"Well, not talkin' 'bout it won't make it go away. When

are you comin'?" His southern drawl blared loudly through the phone.

"As soon as Marcus gets back. He's finishing up some things in California."

"How are things between you two lovebirds? T.J. told me that you two were talkin' again. Make sure he knows that if he messes up this time, I'm gonna bless his hide and it won't be pleasant."

"I will, Daddy. Listen, I'm going to go now, but I'll call you the minute Marcus gets back in town. Kiss the boys for me. I love you."

"I love you back, baby. You take care of yourself." Gwen held on to the warmth her dad's words gave her as the phone went dead. She sat for another moment, thinking more about her decision to face whatever truth she might learn. Whatever the outcome, she knew she would have her friends to lean on, and more importantly, a better understanding of the whole situation.

Walking into the house, Gwen was out of her shoes and halfway out of her shirt when she noticed the light blinking, alerting her that she had several messages. She pushed the button methodically and poured a glass of water to drink while she listened. The first was from Marcus, letting her know that he loved her and would call later. Gwen smiled and felt a warm sensation below her belly button. The next message was from Kyra and the last message was from Patrice, asking Gwen to meet her at the center. She was giving Gina a surprise birthday party. Her voice sounded a lot calmer since she had gotten all the test results back and was given a clean bill of health. After a couple of nights, one of those with Kyra on the speakerphone, Patrice accepted that nothing was wrong with her physically. Still, she wasn't quite ready to accept that Bryan was the largest factor in the "can't have sex" equation, but she was more willing to admit that she was changing, and there was no zest in the old way she did things. Since then, she had been going out with Bryan. Of course, she made it clear that it was on her own terms; he was all for that if it was the only way he could continue to see her. With Patrice's sexual saga at bay, things were starting to look up.

CHAPTER 24

A little after the dinner hour, Patrice admired the neighborhood where the center was located. This section of town was unaffected by overcrowded low-income apartments and was still considered the prime real estate area for up-and-coming Afro-Americans. There were a few signs that advertised a Neighborhood Watch troop that patrolled the area, making sure nothing foul entered or violated their territory. She noticed several teenagers huddled together on the steps of the school across the street from the center, listening to outrageously loud music. A few others walked along the sidewalks with no intention of heading toward their residences. It was their time for a little socializing, and it didn't appear that anyone was headed to their residence until it was dark enough for the streetlights to come on.

Just as she was ready to park her car, a young guy who didn't look much older than fifteen or sixteen stepped right in front of her, not bothering to speed up or to even acknowledge that he'd stepped in front of a slow-moving vehicle. His jeans were almost to his knees, and he was wearing a pair of unlaced hiking boots. His scrawny chest was covered only in a plain, oversize white T-shirt that was partially tucked into his jeans. His head was wrapped with a black do-rag. Had it not been for his arrogant and obnoxious attitude, he would have been almost cute.

She looked around as she finally pulled into a parking space and got out of the car. Checking the doors to make sure they were all locked, she clicked on the alarm and glanced around to see if the young guy was still in the proximity, but he had moved across the street and was talking to the guys in front of the school. If she had decided to drive the Escalade, there was no way he would have been bold enough to step in front of her. She dismissed his ignorance and started to unload the trunk of the car. She smiled to herself as her focus returned to Gina and the excitement of planning the party for her.

An hour later, Gina looked around as she got out of the Range Rover. Quincy hardly waited until her feet were on the pavement before he sped off. They had been arguing all afternoon at his brother's house. Quincy had picked her up right after school and fussed at her from the time he pulled up in front of the school until seconds ago when she closed the car door and blocked out the hatred he was displaying.

Tears burned at Gina's eyes. Her emotions ranged from hurt to disgust to anger. She couldn't believe that he accused her of sleeping with one of his boys. She would never give him or anyone else any time. Quincy would kill her and she knew it. Furthermore, the whole gang had a code; they didn't do the same girl at the same time. If one of them grew tired of the handholding situation and decided to move on to the next girl, then it was an open game.

For as long as she could remember, she had been Quincy's and he treated her special. No one even looked at her out of the corner of their eye or made advances toward her. He wouldn't allow them to ever disrespect him or his property; and she, from the first pair of Nikes that he bought her, had become his property. She was his exclusively from the time that he took her virginity until now. He was everything to her; even when he yelled, screamed, and did things she would rather he didn't, she loved him.

Gina knew that she was pretty and that her body was the envy of every girl in her school and on her corner. But hearing it from him was something she lived for. Now he was accusing her of sleeping around.

Going directly into the restroom, she looked at her reflection in the mirror. She had been crying so long her eyes were puffy and red. She pulled her Guess backpack off and searched for her eyeliner and lip gloss. She hiccupped through another crying spree and flipped open her Motorola phone to call Quincy. After a few rings, it forwarded to his mailbox and she mumbled, "Q, I'm sorry. Whatever I did I can fix it. Just don't leave me. Please, I love you and I need you. Please, Q."

Gina fought to compose herself, repaired her face, and attempted to bring it and her heart back to life. She didn't know if it was possible, especially if Quincy was serious about breaking up with her. She pulled out her orange Steve Madden sunglasses and slipped them on, hoping to hide the grief her face showed much too clearly. They were a perfect match for her tight, orange Baby Phat baseball-style crewneck short-sleeved tee that was secured firmly at the waist inside her low-riding black stretch jeans.

Anxious to get the weekly get-together over with, Gina put on her happy face and headed toward the conference room. Noticing that the room was dark, she was ready to turn around and check at the desk to see if Ms. Patrice and the girls were upstairs. Instead, she pushed the door open a little and peeped in.

"Surprise!" The lights popped on and everyone was yelling. Her homegirl, Sonya, came out of the corner and embraced her. "My girl's here. Now, y'all, we can get this party started right."

The DJ started the music without skipping a beat or waiting for another invitation to begin. Keith Murray thumped through the speakers and all the girls were on the floor.

Gina was trying her best to muster a smile. She couldn't believe they had planned all of this without letting it slip out. Before she could pull them out of the small crowd, Patrice and Gwen walked up to her. "How does it feel to be the leader of a troop that didn't let this top secret out of the bag?" Patrice beamed.

"I can't believe the hos, I mean my girls. I've been with them almost every afternoon for the past couple of weeks, and they didn't say nothing." Gina crossed her arms across her chest and pouted.

"They were sworn to secrecy. So try not to be upset and don't bully them. Just enjoy yourself." Patrice hugged Gina.

Gwen opened her arms. Gina swung her braids out of her face and embraced Gwen, kissing her on the cheek. "I appreciate you coming by to holla at me."

"It's no problem at all. Go ahead and have fun."

Gwen pulled a chair out from under the long table. The table was covered with every kind of party food you could name. Realizing that she was hungry, Gwen grabbed a toothpick and stuck it into a sausage and cheese ball. She sat there for a few minutes, munching away and watching the action.

Patrice was busy walking around chatting with the girls and a few of the other mentors. By the time she got around to Gwen's side of the room, she was bubbling over like a proud parent hosting her daughter's sweet sixteen party.

"I see you're having fun," Gwen taunted.

"Actually, I am. Gina was so surprised and she's never had a party before."

"Really. How'd you find that out?" Gwen leaned forward in her chair and placed her chin in her hand.

"Her mom told me, right after she commented that she couldn't be here because it was bingo night. She had the nerve to tell me that she doesn't miss bingo night for nobody. I was about ready to pull her through the phone. Talk about a trifling woman. Parenting isn't for everyone, that's for damn sure." Patrice grabbed a fork and started to fix herself a plate.

"That's where you come in. Gina has established a special bond with you; anyone can see that. I mean, she is a walking, talking Patrice doll. Sure, there are a few things about her that are still a little rough, but I believe that she will be one of few who will survive her situation."

Patrice looked across the room. Suddenly, a look of panic covered her face. Her mouth opened but she couldn't say a word.

"What's wrong, 'Trice?" Gwen's eyes followed where Patrice stared without blinking.

Gina was doubled over and screaming out in pain. Before Gwen could push back the chair and stand up, Patrice was pulling Gina into her arms and trying to get her to stop screaming long enough to find out what was wrong.

"I'm hurting, Ms. Patrice. My stomach feels like it's about to explode." Gina fell to her knees and held her stomach tight.

"Someone, please call 911 and have them send an ambulance over here, quick. Hang on, baby, I'm going to get you to the hospital."

Patrice paced back and forth inside the emergency waiting room. The ambulance had taken Gina a couple of blocks away to the Memorial Hospital. Now the waiting was driving Patrice crazy. She looked down at her wrist and noticed, for the first time, there were scratches all over both of them. Gina must have scratched her when she was clutching on to her, trying to ease the pain and discomfort that writhed through her midsection. In addition to worrying herself silly for the past three hours, Patrice had left a message with Gina's sister to get in touch with their mother. She hadn't arrived yet.

"Please sit down over here beside me, 'Trice. They aren't going to come out any quicker if you continue to pace back and forth." Gwen rubbed Patrice's arm warmly, trying to reason with her best friend. She didn't think Patrice could have worried any more if this child had been conceived by her and handed to her wrapped in a soft blanket right after birth.

"They've been in there so damn long. What in the hell could be going on back there? I can't stand it. I'm going back up to the desk and ask them if they can get their lazy asses up and go back there and see what is taking so long."

Just then, a middle-aged white female came through the doors, flipping through a chart and asking who was with Gina Webster. Before she could come to a complete stop, Patrice was standing so close the doctor took a couple of steps back.

"I am. I'm Patrice Henderson, Gina's mentor. She was under my supervision when she got sick. How is she? What's wrong with her?"

"Calm down, Ms. Henderson. Is Gina's mother here yet? The nurse told me that she has been called." The doctor spoke calmly.

"No, she hasn't gotten here yet. But please, could you just tell me what is going on with Gina? I've been out here for the past three hours, and while I'm not her mother, at this particular time I'm the closest thing she has to one. Gina's mother signed a consent form allowing me to handle emergencies in her absence."

"Okay, Ms. Henderson. Please follow me." She walked toward a quiet corner away from the noisy area of the waiting room.

Gwen walked with them, even though no one had invited her.

When the doctor looked at Gwen, Patrice spoke up. "She's my best friend and has been helping me out with the girls. Whatever you tell me can be said in front of her."

"Well, Ms. Henderson. Gina has a severe pelvic inflammatory disease that she apparently got from an untreated case of chlamydia."

Patrice's hand went immediately to her chest. "What? Are you sure?"

"Yes, we've spent the last three hours running some tests. How long she went untreated, I'm not sure at this point. My guess, though, is that it's been at least six months, maybe longer. Her reproductive system is severely inflamed, and some of the cell lining along her uterus and her fallopian tubes has been affected. She probably only had a little pain here or there, but nothing to cause her real alarm. With someone so young and sexually immature, the few minor warning signs more than likely went unnoticed, and she didn't know that she had chlamydia."

"Is she going to be all right?" Patrice had so many other questions, but this seemed like the most important.

"We've started her on an intravenous antibiotic and a little something for the pain. She is resting now. I'm going to keep her here for a couple of days. You can see her as soon as they take her up to a room." The doctor closed the chart, tucked it under her arm, and removed her glasses from the tip of her nose.

"Well, I'll go call her house again and see if anyone has located her mother. Thanks again, Dr.—" She glanced at the doctor's name badge.

"Robertson. Kaye Robertson. One more thing, Ms. Henderson, there's a chance that this disease may leave Gina sterile. But I won't know for sure until I do some other tests tomorrow." She watched Patrice's eyes widen and placed her hand on her shoulder. "I will take excellent care of her and try to do all I can to prevent that. You obviously think a lot of her and your name is the only one that she has been calling out." Her eyes softened as she continued to speak. "She is much too young to be going through something like this. Listen, I will tell the nurse to come and get you when they have Gina settled into a room."

Gwen closed the small space between them and wrapped her arms around Patrice. "She'll be just fine. Dr. Robertson is going to take good care of her."

"Thanks for being here with me. I know how hard it must be to have to subject yourself to this setting. I know that damn Quincy gave it to her. I can't believe she's so young and dealing with something so complicated that she probably doesn't even understand."

Suddenly, there was a loud disturbance at the front desk. When they turned around, Patrice immediately recognized the face that belonged to the person causing the commotion. She had only seen Gina's mother once, but she couldn't mistake her or the loud blustering voice that now pervaded the small, overcrowded emergency room.

"Ms. Webster. Hi, I'm Patrice. We met at Gina's school several months ago." She knew that extending her hand was the polite thing to do, but she didn't feel that Gina's late and obviously intoxicated mother deserved such a gesture.

"Where is she with her fat ass? What has she gotten herself into now? She pregnant?" she blurted out and released a spray of saliva with each word.

"No, she isn't. She has a pelvic inflammatory disease that came from a sexually transmitted disease."

"A what?" She was rocking back and forth, and by the overwhelming smell of alcohol on her breath, both Patrice and Gwen knew that bingo wasn't the only thing that she had been doing.

"Her pelvis got infected from a venereal disease that wasn't treated. You know, VD." Patrice broke it down to the simplest terms, about to lose her temper.

"I knew something like this was going to happen. Up and down the streets all times of the night with that drug-dealing boyfriend. Where she at? I'm taking her ass home and beat the hell out of her."

"You're not going to do that." Before she could catch herself, Patrice stepped up to Gina's mother, who stood there

drunk and dressed like the street-walking trash that Patrice
knew she was. What the hell did she expect from Gina?
Children do what they see. Gina's only fault was trusting a
guy whom she'd assumed loved her and did more for her
than her mother or father, whoever he was.

Gwen pulled Patrice away. "No, don't even go there with
her." Gwen spoke up, hoping to give Patrice a moment to
calm down. "Ms. Webster, you can't take her home because
they are going to keep her here for a couple of days."

"What? I don't have no insurance and no way to pay no
damn hospital bill. She's going to have to come home and
I'll take her to the health department tomorrow."

Patrice stared at her angrily. "I'll pay her hospital bill,
don't worry about that. Right now she needs the kind of care
that she can only get at a hospital. Do you want to come and
sit with us until we can go up to see her?"

"I can't stay. My friend's waiting for me outside. I
thought we was just going to pick her up and take her home.
Look, I'm going home. Tell Gina to call the house when she
ready to get out of here." She swung her tangled blond
braids over her shoulder and stumbled toward the exit doors.

"I can't believe that. I'm calling Social Services first thing
in the morning. Right now I'm going to sign the responsible
party forms, and then I'm going to stay here until Gina can
walk out of here with me."

Before Gwen could say a word, Patrice walked purpose-
fully toward the desk. After speaking briefly to the receptionist, she was directed to a partition to the left.

Gwen sat in silence, listening to the rain hit the roof. She
spent the night at the hospital in a reclining chair beside
Patrice, who refused to leave the room for little more than a
restroom break or to stretch her legs. Every time a nurse
came in to check Gina's vital signs, Patrice was at her bedside just in case she woke up. The medication that they had

given her was pretty strong, and she had done nothing more than toss and turn.

Now, after carrying Patrice a fresh change of clothes and a couple of other necessities, and stopping by the shopping mall to get Gina a couple of gowns, a robe, slippers, and other toiletries, Gwen was trying to unwind. She knew she needed to go upstairs, shower, and try to get a little sleep before going back to the hospital, but first she would just close her eyes a moment and quiet things in her head.

Everything happened so quickly yesterday; as much as she wanted to isolate Gina's situation to her alone, it reminded her of how one wrong choice can change any person's life. A life that deserved to be lived fully, without being hindered and reduced to a small semblance of just existing. No one would ever know the whys, and she knew that it wasn't her place to ask. Yet she wished that the sky would open up and disclose an answer that she could live with and one that would allow her to go on without the weight of it all on her shoulders.

Standing to her feet, Gwen walked over to the French door, hoping to catch a glimpse of a break in the clouds that would indicate that the rain would be stopping soon. What she saw instead caused her to flinch from the emotional blow to her stomach. Scott was coming out of his house with several suitcases and bags. She stood there staring in a trance while Scott was busy loading suitcases, tote bags, and other things into his SUV. He was at the task for more than a half hour while she stood there watching the entire thing. At first she thought he was just taking a short trip, but somewhere in the midst of being completely caught up in his movements, something deep inside told her that this was more than just a trip.

She wished she could run over there, tell him that she needed his friendship, that she had become used to his protective and caring ways. Ever since she moved in, he had become a constant in her life. Sure, she enjoyed his company, and at some moments she felt more than a big sister emotion for him. But he had to know that the idea of being with her was ludicrous. She just couldn't bring herself to date him or to allow things to get out of hand.

Gwen shifted her weight to the other foot and leaned closer to the glass door as she watched Scott close the hatch, walk around, open the door, and climb into the driver's seat. He never even glanced toward the house that he knew she was in. Never even took the time to say good-bye. Stretching her neck a little, she watched as he drove around the circular driveway and finally out of sight.

He was gone. Gwen couldn't will her legs to move or her eyes to take in something other than Scott's house. Just knowing that he was there and that he was always watching out for her was so comforting. It didn't matter that she hadn't really been there long; time has a way of making mere hours, days, weeks, and months seem like a lifetime. Who would keep a vigil over her now? Who would she laugh with, joke with, and spend hours in front of the television with? Gwen came up with no answers to her own questions. As hard as it was to admit, Scott was the only person she wanted to do those things with. The thought of Marcus, Patrice, or Andre replacing him didn't even cross her mind.

She continued to stand there and tried to answer her silent questions, to no avail. What did ring louder than a church bell on Sunday morning was that she was standing there already missing Scott. If Marcus was her heart's desire, why did she watch Scott drive away and feel as if she'd just lost a big part of herself?

CHAPTER 25

The roaring of the car's engine and the rotation of the tires against the recently repaved roads that covered the miles along the interstate did nothing to soothe Gwen's nervous stomach. In fact, she cringed hopelessly as she looked out the passenger window, viewing the mile markers that indicated she was getting closer to their destination. She thought she had mentally prepared herself during the two days since Marcus had returned from California, but now she was a complete wreck.

She was in the middle of packing an overnight bag when Patrice called earlier that morning. Ms. Webster had finally agreed to let Gina stay with Patrice while she recuperated. Before she was released, Dr. Robertson had performed an exploratory laparoscopic procedure to examine the internal damage to her reproductive system. They were all relieved when she informed them that the damage was repairable and that with further treatment she would have no difficulty conceiving.

The battle, though, was only half won. Gina's self-esteem would have to undergo a healing process as well. She was certain that she needed Quincy in her life and was willing to forgive what happened. Patrice had already started rebuilding what was torn down and wouldn't stop until she had Gina believing that she was worthy of so much more than what Quincy was providing. She had every prayer warrior at Gilead Full Gospel praying for Gina. The physical recovery report was proof enough that prayer really does change things. Gina's report would no doubt be a part of Patrice's next Sunday service testimony, and Gwen was quite sure that it would conjure up a harmonious amen from the congregation.

Gwen had to marvel at the good news and for a fleeting moment she believed that everything, including this trip home, would commence a newness that she would embrace with open arms and welcome like an old friend who had been gone much too long. She closed her eyes and suddenly felt the strongest urge to pray. Although she hadn't felt an urge like this one in a long time, she decided to yield to it. She knew deep down that prayer does change things, and right now, she needed a change. She needed the good Lord to step in and work a miracle on her behalf.

"Gwen, sweetheart, we're almost at your parents' house." Marcus reached over and rubbed his hand over her thigh. He had noticed when she closed her eyes an hour or so ago, and her breathing changed a bit, that she had fallen asleep.

He had lain awake last night unable to summon sleep and watched Gwen toss and turn. He was worried about her and prayed her trip would not be in vain. Around three in the morning, Gwen restlessly gave up trying to sleep and they ended up propped up in bed, talking about the office and all the events that would follow in the next month.

"Oh. I can't believe I fell asleep on you. I'm sorry." Gwen blinked her eyes a couple of times and reached for her bag. After removing a comb and fixing her hair, she looked a little better.

"It's no problem. I had the radio and you snoring to keep me company." He snickered, knowing she couldn't stand anyone telling her that she snored.

"I do not snore. I can't even believe you would sit there and tell a lie like that. You really need to stop. What time is it?"

"One o'clock."

"We have a little time. Pull over and let me drive. I know that I need to talk to my mom, but I want to take you someplace first."

The smell of salt water teased Marcus's nostrils. The weather was perfect, and the blue sky spread over them was nothing short of tranquil. The seagulls circled overhead and there were several boats in the distance floating farther out into the ocean. "Gwen, this is nice. This resort area is beautiful."

"Well, I never really visit Ocean City that much anymore. I grew up close by, and spent almost every other Sunday here during the summer months. You can only eat so much caramel popcorn, cotton candy, and candy apples. And you know I'm not much on amusement rides. But this is the best time of the year to enjoy just the beauty of it all. Without the crowds and noise."

They got out of the car and headed for the boardwalk. Marcus and Gwen strolled along hand in hand. After taking in the broadwalk sight, Marcus wanted to take a walk along the water's edge. "Come on, baby. I can't believe you've never walked along the ocean without shoes."

The cool sand slipped between Gwen's toes as she held her shoes in her hand. Marcus snuggled in beside her and wrapped his free arm around her back. They walked in silence, enjoying the sounds of the ocean and the warmth of being close to one another. Gwen wasn't aware of Marcus' exact thoughts, nor was he aware of hers, but neither one of them wanted to interrupt the emotions that drifted through their minds and bodies and their overwhelming need to have it last after they walked away from this perfect place.

More than she would have liked, she thought of Scott and wondered why he had to complicate things by expressing feelings that were better left alone. She hadn't been able to shake their conversation that night, or the kiss, or his walking away. Gwen had finally told Patrice that she liked Scott a lot more than she wanted to acknowledge. She couldn't understand why she felt so lost without Scott. The realization of that scared Gwen and she wondered if something was somehow out of sync. What she did know was that there was an ache deep inside that Marcus' return hadn't been able to soothe. Fighting to regain her thoughts in her present company, she leaned her head on Marcus' shoulder.

Gwen was so calm and at peace when they walked back to the car and headed toward her reason for coming all this way. "Well, I guess truth awaits, huh?" She gave Marcus a sideward glance.

"Yeah, it does. But, as I've told you before, you're not facing any of this alone. I'm here, and you've got to know that this is for the best. Not knowing is hurting you more than finding out and dealing with it. So, sweethcart, it's all going to work out. Trust me."

His words were a source of comfort and she knew that he was right.

They drove the distance to the James residence in silence. Marcus wanted to keep things light, but he also knew that she had a lot running through her mind.

Before she knew it, they were pulling into the driveway of the house that held the memories of all of her yesteryears. Coming around the driveway, she saw T.J. in the distance coming out of the workshop.

"Hi, girl. What's up?" T.J. swung the car door open and had pulled her out of the car and into his big muscular arms in about three seconds.

"Did you miss me?" Gwen was smiling and enjoying every moment of the attention that he was giving her.

"Just a little." He let her feet hit the ground and walked around to Marcus. "What's up, brother? It's been a while. How you living?"

"It's good, man. How 'bout yourself?"

"I'm hanging in there. Taking care of the family and doing the nine-to-five thing. It's not as exciting as having a hand in the music industry, but it pays the bills." The two of them embraced. She had never noticed it before, but they were the same height and build. T.J. was handsome; she'd heard people say it all the time, but standing next to the man she would vote Mr. *GQ*, he seemed even more so.

Before she could say anything, her dad came out of his workshop in the backyard. "Daddy! God, did I miss you!"

"Come here and let me look atcha." He reached in the pocket of his denim shirt, pulled out his glasses, and placed them snugly on his face. Her father looked a little weathered to Gwen. His eyes were hazed with gray; all the years of sharing wisdom and carrying the load were visible in his dark brown eyes. "You've lost a little weight. Don't tell me you've been eating, 'cause I know better."

"I've only lost a few pounds. And it didn't really hurt me. If it will make you feel better, I will have a large meal with you today before I leave." She couldn't believe that her dad could tell that she had lost a few pounds. No one else had noticed; she herself couldn't tell by looking in the mirror. It was only after she had stepped on the scale a couple of days ago and noticed that it read 120 instead of 130 that she realized it herself.

"That sounds good. In fact, I've been in the garden pickin' some fresh vegetables for you to take back. It should be enough to tide you over till you're ready to come back home."

Home. What a mouthful. Gwen wasn't sure that this was home anymore. Richmond wasn't exactly what she referred to as home either, but she was almost sure that it was the closest place to it these days. The outcome of today's visit would answer that question. Something unknown was already orchestrating the results and preparing her for the outcome.

Her eyes were drawn to a spot under the willow tree that

had newly planted flowers and a small marble stone bench to the left of it. She recognized the gardenias, red and yellow tulips, and red roses, but she couldn't identify the other flowers. She did know, however, that this was where her mother had planned to place the memorial for Tiffany.

It was the same tree that they had sat under so many afternoons while waiting for their dad's old blue pickup to pull into the yard. Gwen would watch Tiffany jump up and rush over as he opened the loud, squeaky door, smiling as he picked Tiffany up with one arm and wrapped the other around Gwen's shoulder. He would kiss them both on the cheek, rubbing the rough texture of unshaven beard against their smooth, baby-soft skin. Then he would slip them a lollipop that he knew they shouldn't have until after dinner. It was their routine.

"Where's Mom?" Gwen had asked the question before she even wanted to. She had hoped that her mother would have come outside and greeted them before now, but that was expecting a little too much and she knew that.

"Inside. I believe she's canning some pears. Go on inside, she probably didn't hear the car pull up." He tried to soften the ignorance his wife displayed. The window over the kitchen sink had a bird's-eye view of the backyard and the driveway. Everyone who pulled into the yard was easily seen from that window. It was also the window that his wife looked out of almost every other minute. There was no way she couldn't have known that Gwen was there.

"Gwen. While you're visiting with Mom, I'm going to take Marcus with me to pick up the boys. They should be finishing up soccer practice by now."

Marcus didn't step toward her, but he did embrace her with his eyes. "I'll be back in a little while."

Gwen glanced at her father, who nodded and walked back toward his workshop. Turning toward the back door, Gwen walked like a person on death row going toward the electric chair.

Her mother sat at the kitchen table looking toward the small color television that sat on the edge of the counter. She was busy placing preserves in Mason jars and didn't bother to look up when Gwen closed the door behind her.

She took a deep breath, although she couldn't feel it reaching her lungs. "Hi, Mom." Gwen sat down in the chair across from her mother.

"Hi, Gwendolyn. Thomas didn't tell me you were coming. Did you call and let him know that you were dropping by?" She never got up to hug her or even cast a shadow of a smile her way.

"I spoke with Dad last night. He probably just wanted it to be a surprise. How've you been?" She knew how her mother had been, but for lack of better conversation, she just went with it. Gwen couldn't believe that her mother didn't use her nickname. Claire herself had been the first one to use the abbreviated name when Gwen was only a few days old. In fact, she told everyone what her name would be and what she was planning on calling her from the minute she had known she was pregnant. Gwendolyn was reserved only for reprimanding purposes. She knew that it was her mother's way of letting her know that all was not forgiven.

"How was your trip? It's a pleasant day outside. Perfect for traveling. Sister Connie told me they were doing some work to the interstate highway. Is it finished yet?"

Gwen couldn't believe that her mother was sitting here talking to her like she was a stranger. This whole conversation was going to be difficult, and it was obvious that her mother didn't plan on making it any easier.

"Actually, they are still working on it." Gwen got up from the table, opened the refrigerator, and pulled out a bottle of water. What she needed was something that came off the top shelf at the liquor store, but at least this would be cold and help to wet her palate enough to talk. "Mom, I need to talk to you. Could you please stop canning long enough to talk to me?"

"What do you want to talk about? I can't imagine that you

would have anything to say that would demand my undivided attention." She pushed the Mason jars from in front of her and wiped her hands on the front of the red-and-white-checkered apron.

"We haven't talked since . . ." Gwen paused. "Since Tiffany died." She hadn't wanted to say that word today. Gwen hadn't used it since it happened. Somehow it just made it all too real. Saying that she was gone, no longer with her, in a better place; all those things were much easier to endure. But "died" was just that. "Died."

"I wasn't aware that you had anything to say. The last thing I recall you saying was more than enough." Claire never turned around. She looked straight ahead as if Gwen were only a figment of her imagination.

"Look. I'm not going to let you do this to me. I'm not going to apologize for saying what everyone else was afraid to say. What I said was what I knew Tiffany wanted me to say. She is gone. I know that. There isn't a day that goes by that I'm not reminded of the fact that I have to live life without her. You can't make me feel any worse than I already do. I blame myself because I should have known she was sick. That is the guilt I feel, but you want to blame me for stopping the breathing machine. If Tiffany were going to live, she would have lived without it. She would not have wanted to be kept alive that way." Gwen placed the bottle on the counter and walked around to the side of the table so that she could see her mother's face.

"I'm sorry that you think I spoke out without any regard for Tiffany's life. Her life meant everything to me. Everything. If it would mean that you could have your baby back, I would give my life." Gwen couldn't hold back the tears any longer. Her heart ached, and she desperately needed to release all that had been dead inside her.

"A part of me wants to be upset with you for what you're doing out in the yard, to the room that Tiffany and I shared, and to our family."

Her mother finally spoke. "How can everyone be so ready to forget? What I'm doing, I'm doing to keep her memory alive. To remind all of you that she existed and I'm not ever going to forget her."

"What about what you're doing to us? Me and you, Mom. I want to be upset with you, but I can't because I love you. I pray that one day you will understand that what I did was the most unselfish act I will ever do in my life. That day I said good-bye to my best friend, and I let her go because she asked me to."

"She only needed more time to get well. That's all. More time. Why did she have to die? Why did my baby have to die that horrible, ugly death?" She blinked back hot tears.

"Don't you think I've asked myself those very same questions? There are so many questions that I have, so much that I need to know. Mom, you know that my answers are in the journal that Tiffany kept, and yet you won't let me find peace in knowing what happened and why she didn't tell me."

"There was no journal. There are no answers for you. So if that's what you came here today to find, you can get right back in the car and return to Richmond." Claire James knew she had said a mouthful and that her words would wound Gwen further, but she was hurting and her wound would never heal. "Now, if you don't mind, I'm going to continue canning my preserves. I have a church meeting later and I don't want to be late."

Gwen felt like someone had knocked the wind out of her. Her stomach was turning over and over and her heart was aching. She stood for a minute longer waiting for her mother to say something, to reach out and touch her and let her know that everything between them was just fine. She needed to know that her mother still loved her and that they would deal with Tiffany's death together.

As Gwen stood there unable to breath, no words flowed from her mother's lips. The only sound in the room came from the ticking of the *God Bless This Home* clock that hung on the wall over the kitchen table. All the years of knowing and receiving the nurturing touch of her mother were forever tarnished. It would take more than what wasn't accomplished today to set things right in Gwen's heart and mind. The very thing she prayed for didn't happen, and if there was a master plan in place, it wasn't in plain view, and since it wasn't, Gwen felt dispirited.

Gwen struggled to speak. Her next words were hardly a whisper. "Mama, I'm going to try to move on, and one day I'll understand all the whys. I'll never stop missing Tiffany and I'll never stop loving you." She didn't wait any longer for a reply. Everything in the James family home was familiar and it would always be a part of her. But she knew now that everything familiar wasn't always home.

She walked in a daze with tears burning her eyes and a heart heavy with the burden of the conversation. When she reached the door of the workshop it opened. Her dad watched her cross the yard and was waiting to comfort her. "Come on in, baby."

Gwen looked at him as if she expected him to remove the hurt and pain and make things better, the way he always did. He didn't want to disappoint her, but he wasn't sure if he had any answers that would ease the pain. He pulled her into his arms and allowed her to cry. When the trembling in her body subsided a little, he moved over to the wooden bench that he'd built along the wall.

"I'm sorry that she didn't tell you anything or even acknowledge that you are hurting too. I can't say that I'm completely shocked. I was praying that she would reach out to you, just 'cause you need her and 'cause she is your mother. There are some things that only a mother can fix, and this is one of them. I wasn't sure I was ever gonna tell you this, but since Claire won't ease your burden, maybe it will help to understand what she thinks she's hiding and why all of this ain't just about losing Tiffany."

Gwen looked at her father cautiously. She wasn't sure she

could stand to hear anything earth-shattering and the look on his face let her know that what he had to say was exactly that. "Daddy, I don't know if I'm up for this. Maybe we can save it for next time."

"No, Gwen. There have been enough next times. Just sit here beside me and listen to what I'm gonna say." He reached for her hand and wrapped it with his large one. "From the day that Tiffany was born, your mother was always so protective of her. Tiffany was a little frillier than you, and of course she was the baby so everyone thought that it was normal for your mama to feel that way. You were always instructed by your mama to look out for her and to handle her like fine glass. It wasn't long before you took the big sister role and did just that and then some. Pretty soon you was like a little mother hen and wouldn't let nothing or no one come close to Tiffany. Your mother was proud of the way you cared for Tiffany, and after a while Tiffany didn't want you out of her sight. I loved you girls with all my heart. The both of you and your brother were the reason I worked so hard. I wanted to give you all a good life, didn't want you to come up not having. Did the same with your mom."

Gwen trembled a little. She looked directly at her father, and his vision was fixed straight ahead of him on some unseen object that was draining the energy and the color right out of his body.

"Your grandma lost your grandpa early in their marriage and she had to provide for the six of them alone. She could get away with murder, your mother could. When everyone else was in the fields working hard, she would fake some sickness and go home while the others continued to sweat till the sun went down. I knew that she would need a lot of love and attention. The first new dress your mother ever wore, I gave to her on our wedding day. She was the prettiest and the sweetest girl and I knew I would spend my life tryin' to make her happy. I gave her everything I knew to give her. Fancy dresses, a nice house, a decent car—but she was always just a little unhappy or it seemed that I just didn't give her enough. Some evenings I would come in after working hard all day and she would find things to argue about, but you know your daddy. I would never fuss and I still don't. I guess most men would consider me henpecked and I reckon I am, but I love Claire with all I have in me."

Gwen smiled; she knew that everything her father said was true. And she never doubted that he loved her mother. It wasn't only most men who saw him as henpecked; she herself wondered why he always gave in to her mother, never stood up for himself. But she knew that it had nothing to do with not being a proud, strong, black man, but everything to do with love.

"Well, anyway, when she got pregnant with Tiffany she was a little upset. I believe she thought we would just have you and T.J. and I assured her that we had more than enough love and room in the house for one more. She changed some, and at first I didn't know the reason for the changes and I just continued to do nice things for her and help out around the house more, just to make her happy. That really never worked. She grew more and more bitter as her stomach did big. Then a month before your sister was born, someone in the neighborhood confronted me. And it wasn't long after that that I came home early one day and your mother wasn't here. I waited and after a while someone let her out at the end of the driveway. I never said a word and I never treated her any differently.

"You know that your mother had some trouble bringing Tiffany into the world and Tiffany had some problems afterward and she needed blood. Well, your mother was still out of it, and after her blood didn't match, I went right away to the hospital and gave them some of mine. The doctor had to tell me that mine wasn't a match either. Boy, I was blown clean away. I remember jumpin' in my old truck and just riding. I couldn't believe that neither one of us matched our child's blood type. They didn't have all the modern stuff that they have today, but it didn't take a rocket scientist to figure out that I didn't father Tiffany."

Gwen's face was lifeless. She tried to pull away and not listen to any more of this nonsense. Not only had her mother refused to talk to her, her dad had lost his mind. "What are you talking about, Dad? That is just insane."

"No, Gwen, it's not. Now you listen so that I can finish while I can still go on." He moved slightly and stared back across the room. "Before I knew it, I ended up across town at his house. I called him outside and told him what I figured out. Then I told him to get to the hospital, give some blood, and after that if I caught him around my wife and daughter I would kill him with my bare hands. He did as I told him to. I never asked the hospital anything. All I know is, Tiffany got better and so did your mom, and I carried them home. I never asked her about what happened then because I really didn't want to know. I never asked why. I loved your mother then and I love her just as much now. And as far as I'm concerned Tiffany was as much mine as you and T.J., and I spent every day treating her that way. To my knowledge, your mother doesn't know that I know. If she does, she never mentioned a word of it." His voice was harsh now from all the talking, and the light in his eyes that had grown dim was coming back a little.

"So you see, sweetheart. Your mom wasn't only protecting Tiffany; she was protecting her secret. What no one saw, her heart and mind knew, and she has had to live with that all these years. I forgave her 'cause you can't legislate love. And as much as I wanted her to always love me, for some reason for a while she didn't. If she does now, I pray so, but I can't be sure. And she loves you, but she has gotten so caught up in what she hid that she has forgotten you're not the big girl she raised so quickly to watch over her secret, but her daughter who needed her just as much as her baby had. Come over here with me."

He walked with a slight limp from sitting too long. Working so hard throughout his life to provide for his family, he was a fit man but had developed high blood pressure and arthritis in both knees and shoulders. He opened the door to a closet that was filled with every tool you could name and reached behind some cans of spray paint and pulled out a book. "Here, I hope this answers the rest of your questions."

Gwen noticed the front and right away she knew that it was Tiffany's journal. "Dad, how did you find this?"

"Your mom was spending almost every night in your room reading somethin'. I decided to snoop around, figuring it had to be the journal you'd been asking her for. She put it in the top of the closet and I took it down. I figured that if your mom wouldn't give you no answers, then maybe Tiffany left a few for you." He attempted a weak smile. "You just go find you a quiet place and put your mind at ease." He walked back to the front of the workshop and out the door.

Gwen wondered if he had read the journal himself. What was most important right then was reading it herself. She glanced around and like a lightbulb going off in a dark room, she thought of just the place. Walking out the back door of the workshop, she moved toward the other willow tree that was situated a short distance behind the workshop and out of plain view of the house. She sat down under it and leaned her back against the trunk of the tree.

Gwen folded her leg under her slightly and opened the book. She read every page and every single entry. Her heart ached at all that she was learning. She didn't think about wiping the tears that fell on the pages and caused some of the ink to run, because she knew that once she was finished, the book would be closed forever and placed in a safe place with the rest of her memories of Tiffany. The last page was addressed to Gwen and she took a couple of deep breaths before she continued.

I know what you're thinking—why didn't I tell you that I was diagnosed with AIDS? Why would I endure this disease for so long and keep it and the damage it is doing to my body away from you? I tried so many times to tell you. I made trips home, I called so many late nights and early mornings and could only muster the words "I love you." But that you knew. So why didn't I tell you? Because for once in our relationship I wanted to protect you. You spent your entire childhood and most of your adulthood taking care of and protecting me, and just once I wanted to do the same for you. I knew that you would want to fix this, and as much as I wanted you to, I knew that you couldn't. You could not make this go away or change what would happen to me.

I knew from the first day that the doctor told me the results of the test that I would never be able to live my life out the way I planned. You know how I always like to plan things out and make sure that my life is following the course I set forth when I was barely big enough to spell "life." I thought of all the things that we wouldn't do, and your kids that I wouldn't get a chance to spoil, and I felt cheated. I did the pity party and I asked God why so many times and yet I knew that none of my questions would change anything. So, I stopped asking and I just started thanking Him for each day I opened my eyes and could have a normal day of just moving around with no pain in my body. I asked Him to restore my health and I prayed until my earthly tongue ceased and my spiritual tongue took over, and one day a strong calmness came over me and I stopped praying for a restoration of my health but for His will to be done. Since that day, I've just lived each day and at the end of it I give Him the glory. I don't really want to go into the who and the how because it wouldn't accomplish a thing. But since we are cut from the same cloth, I will give you the short version so that you won't ask yourself that question for the rest of your life.

Gwenee, I kept the most precious gift I had been saving for the right moment and the right guy, and when he came along my soul danced and came alive with a love I never knew before. I loved him with all that was in me and then some. Was he my soul mate? Oh, Gwen, he was the very extension of me and I of him. When we decided that we wanted to spend the rest of our lives with one another, we weakened and explored and followed the heat of our passion, and boy, did the earth move! He had only been in one serious relationship before giving God his life. We never touched each other in that way again, but we made love so many times in our minds and you know what? It was just as good as the physical time.

Ours was short-lived. A few months later I took him to the emergency room for what we thought was a chest cold. This visit was repeated a couple of other times with the same symptoms. We learned that he was HIV positive and our worlds came to a crushing halt. I was tested immediately after that and learned that I was negative. He was so relieved and God, so was I. But it didn't erase the truth that he was positive. He asked me to walk away from him, from what we shared, and I just couldn't. I wanted to be there for him and to take care of him. He loved me so much that he didn't want me to go through the agony of watching him slip away. One afternoon when I was leaving work, I decided to go by his house before heading home. I used my key to let myself in because I figured that he was resting. Everything was in its place, but when I got upstairs the closet and all his drawers were left open and all his clothing was gone. On the bed was a note addressed to me. He left me, not because he wanted to, he said, but because he had to. I looked everywhere I knew to look, called everyone we knew, and no one knew where he had gone. Eventually I stopped looking, but my heart never stopped loving. Two years later during a routine yearly exam, I was informed, after doing the blood work required for HIV testing, that I was positive. And I have been living with full-bloom AIDS for six months now. I loved and although I wished so many times that I had fallen in love with someone who was completely healthy, that wasn't in the plan for me. I never brought him home with me or told anyone about him because he was much older, and I just couldn't stand for anyone to not agree with my choice and tell me that he wasn't the right one for me when in my heart and soul I knew that he was.

I never wanted to leave you and yet I know, as certain as sand falls through an hourglass, that my time is short. You have always been my strong tower, the yin to my yang, and I love you, big sister. So if I have to go, and I can't see how I can escape my course, please know that I am always with you and that you have to go on and make me proud like you always have.

I'm telling you all this because I promised you a long time ago that I would never not tell you things. I know that since Marcus you have kept your heart locked away, not allowing hurt to reside there again. And after what I experienced, I can't say that I blame you. But you have to love again. I have many regrets, but I have never regretted loving him. It has been the one thing that has kept my insides alive, even when the outside of me started to wither away.

Remember one thing—true love is found when you look for it with your heart and not with your eyes. Dad and T.J., like you, will be just fine . . . but Mama will need time. Make her see that if I could ever speak from eternity, it would stem from your heart and come through your mouth. If my time has come, I want you to stop grieving for me and go on and live . . . don't

*worry about me because wherever you go, whatever
you do, I am with you. Haven't I always been?*

Gwen had to laugh after reading the last words. Suddenly
she felt her heart lightening and a tremendous weight being
lifted off her shoulders. Tiffany hadn't left her out. All she
did and didn't say, she did to protect her because she didn't
want her to feel helpless in the face of something she couldn't
change or control. She quickly read the letter again, and this
time her breathing was more relaxed and normal. Gwen
spoke to the emptiness around her. "All this time I thought
you left without telling me your thoughts."

Suddenly, she envisioned the likeness of a childhood
Tiffany sitting beside her with a lopsided grin on her chubby
face. When she reached out it was an adult Tiffany who
touched her hand. "I would never not tell you my thoughts. I
love you. Now you go ahead and live." Just as suddenly as
the child Tiffany appeared, the adult Tiffany was gone. Gwen
shook her head several times, trying to release herself from
what had to be a daydream. She was sure that she would
need additional therapy sessions after this. Tiffany coming
to her in a dream was one thing, but she was sitting under the
willow tree wide-awake and yet she felt her presence as
keenly as before.

Gwen glanced up toward the sky and the heavens, imagining her Tiffany adorned in regal angelic attire and talking
spiritual talk with the others assembled together. A strong
breeze blew through the tree, shaking the brittle branches of
the old willow tree, and the journal she was holding tightly
fell out of her hand. Without giving the sudden stirring a
thought, Gwen reached down to pick it up. Something made
of gold fell to the ground. Glancing down at it, she noticed
that it was some type of jewelry. Picking it up slowly to get a
closer look, she recognized it as the gold necklace that Tiffany
had worn all the time. At the end of the eighteen-inch chain was

a charm. A small heart, a cross, and an anchor were nestled together to create the charm that symbolized faith, hope, and love. With shaky fingers she placed it around her neck and allowed it to fall in the hollow spot between her collarbones. She hadn't seen the necklace when she flipped through the journal the first or second time. She wasn't sure if she should dismiss it and assume that it had been there all the time. Whether it was or wasn't, she didn't even want to question, she just knew that it was meant for her and she would wear it as Tiffany had, believing that the greatest of the three virtues was love.

The left side of her face was warm from the rays of the sun that was now getting ready to set and retire behind the horizon and await the commencement of another day. One that was new and would bring with it greater expectations than the days before. Wiping the remnants of the tears that she had shed minutes ago, she was amazed that there were no hives on her cheek. After further inspection of both arms and her chest, she noticed the areas were completely clear and free of the bumps that had become a daily nuisance.

Walking around to the front of the workshop, she saw that T.J. and Marcus were back and were in deep conversation with her dad, whose head was under the hood of his old pickup.

T.J. inspected her first. "Are you all right?" He put a hand on both sides of her elbows and observed her carefully.

"Yeah. I'm going to be just fine." Gwen tilted her head and looked at Marcus and smiled a knowing smile, letting him know that she was okay. She knew that life as she knew it had forever changed, but she was optimistic about the future and was willing to take it all in stride and just live.

She hugged her dad tightly and whispered in his ear softly, "I love you so much. It took a lot for you to tell me all you did, and I want you to know that I appreciate you opening up and letting me in."

"I love you too, Gwen. You remember all your dad told you, now."

"I will, Daddy." Gwen closed her eyes and enjoyed the warmth of his touch and the rhythm that only he could create in the small of her back. "I will."

Turning back to T.J., Gwen began to speak. "T.J., tell the boys and Kim I'll see them in a couple of weeks when I move the rest of my things. I decided a little while ago to move back to Richmond and get on with the rest of my life." She glanced at her father, who stood by speechless but didn't seem to be shocked. "And if you and Kim would accept, I want to offer you my house. I know you've been saving for a bigger house for a while and I won't be coming back to stay. I could never understand why I bought such a big house in the beginning." She paused. "Listen, you don't have to answer now. Just talk it over with Kim and let me know. If she agrees, I'll have the papers drawn up and we can seal the deal with a kiss."

"Word. Girl, that would make the load a whole lot easier. Your house is perfect and the location is ideal. I'll talk to Kim but I know the answer is already yes." He was beaming all over. He didn't want to think of Gwen being more than a short drive away, but he knew that there was too much water under the bridge.

Marcus hadn't said a word but was relieved that she had come to terms with all that had happened since Tiffany's death. He was surprised about her moving back to Richmond and had already thought of proposing during the Christmas holiday, if he could wait that long.

"Now, Mr. McGuire. I believe that there is a busy city with bright lights waiting for us. Come on, sweetheart, it's time to go." Marcus said his good-byes and fell in step beside her.

Gwen noticed her mother standing at the kitchen window peeping out around the curtain. She looked over her shoulder several times and walked slowly to the car, hoping that she would run out to stop her. She didn't.

CHAPTER 26

Gwen was about to fall over and couldn't believe that she talked herself into doing that extra mile. She was more health-conscious these days and had worked hard on changing her diet and incorporating an exercise program. It had been a month since she started her new lease on life and she was determined to stick it out.

Finally, the top of the house came into view and she got another boost of energy and pushed on. Slowing down and toweling her face off, she noticed a car in front of Scott's house. When she got closer, one of Scott's friends was waving at her. She decided to walk over and ask about Scott before she lost her nerve.

"Hi. I'm Gwen." She extended her hand after wiping it off.

"I know who you are. I'm Kip, one of Scott's homeboys." He pulled the mail out of the mailbox and glanced through it before sliding it into a plastic bag.

"How is Scott doing?" She bit her lip and added, "I didn't get a chance to get a number or an address before he left." It wasn't all a lie. She just didn't bother to tell him that Scott hadn't offered one.

"He's fine and things are going good with the partnership. He does miss home, though."

"Oh, that's great. I'm glad to hear that things are working out well for him. He and I spent a lot of time hanging out and I miss my buddy." She looked away and hoped that he didn't see that she was fishing for information.

"Gwen, do you have any idea how much Scott thinks of you? He was hooked from day one, and would talk about nothing but you and how he was planning on telling you how he felt. He would get so upset whenever the hospital beeped him while he was spending time with you."

"Wait a minute. What do you mean the hospital beeping him?" She looked at Kip, astonished.

"Gwen, what do you think Scott does for a living?" Kip sat on the edge of his car with a wide grin across his face.

"I don't know. I never asked. I just assumed." She was stumbling over her words and couldn't believe that all her training in communication was of no use at that moment.

"Seriously, what do you think? I mean, he lives in this big house, drives a nice ride, wears nice clothes, hangs out with his boys on a regular basis, and we spend time hanging out over here like we're at the Marriott. He's strapped with a cell phone and beeper everywhere he goes. And both were going off repeatedly whenever the two of you were together."

"All right, Kip. I thought that he could be doing a little bit of trafficking." She was embarrassed. Obviously what she had thought from day one was wrong.

"I thought so and so did Scott. He didn't bother to correct you or set your mind at ease because he wanted you to get to know and like him for who he was and not what he did. After your first day here he called Kyra and told her not to tell you about his occupation or anything else about him."

Gwen looked even more confused. "So what does he do, if you don't mind me asking?" It was enough to be embarrassed, but he was obviously having a good time taunting her and she didn't like it at all.

"Scott is a pediatrician and before he left town he was on staff at the Children's Hospital. His father worked hard all his life and wanted Scott to do more than work as a janitor like he did. He saved every penny and sent him to school, and the year Scott started medical school his Dad had a massive heart attack and died. But what was surprising was that he left Scott enough money to pay for school and buy this house." He spread his hands out, displaying the house that he was just as proud of. "His mother lived here a while, and then she moved in with Scott's aunt, who has been sick for a while."

"I can't believe that he didn't tell me. We spent enough time together and I told him things about myself, and yet he couldn't at least tell me that he wasn't dealing drugs."

"That was your assumption, honey. Why should he have to defend an assumption? He stills hangs out as you've seen and he has gotten us to all think seriously about our lives. All of us have real jobs, but we just keep it real and we don't try to shy away from what we really are. Wearing the attire that some would think of as thuggish doesn't stop us from walking up into those jobs we have in professional gear. But after hours, we get down like this and it's all good." He pointed to his Timberland boots and velour Gucci sweat suit.

"I never judged Scott. I just wanted to get to know him better." Gwen was all ready to go to her house, get out of her damp running clothes, shower, and overcome the stupidity she felt at drawing the wrong conclusion.

"I'm sorry. I guess I'm just a little bitter that you dismissed my boy the way you did. He says that you're hooked on the past and trying to change history." Kip spoke confidently. "It comes a time you have to let things go. History does not always repeat itself in the way we want it to. That's why they call it history and memories are called memories."

Gwen felt like a fool. "I don't know what to say. I like Scott and I told him that we just couldn't be anything more than friends. I made a choice for history's sake, and regardless of what happens, it was my choice." She was already having second thoughts about her decision to stay with Marcus. After she had dealt with her mom and learned that Tiffany not only answered her whys, but encouraged her to move on, she didn't want to hang on to anything or anyone that would hold her hostage to past hurts and pains. As much as she didn't want to admit it, her relationship with Marcus still held the remnants of their painful past.

"Well, shorty, I respect that. Scott really cares about you and I can see why now. You're bright, beautiful, and you've got it going on. If this guy from your past makes you happy, that's all Scott really wants. I'll tell him that you asked about him." Kip stood up and started to walk around the car.

"Kip, can I ask you something else?"

"Sure, shorty. Anything."

"How old is Scott?" Gwen gave him a wary look, not sure if he were going to give her the same song and dance she had been getting for the past half-hour.

He started laughing. "Yeah, he told me about the age thing too. He would kill me if I told you, but hell, you two probably won't see each other again, so I'll tell you. Scott is thirty-two years old. I know he looks young as hell. I've been telling the brother that if he found the fountain of youth, he should tell somebody.

"He is the oldest in our trio and he sort of adopted us as brothers since he didn't have any.' Kip rubbed his neatly trimmed goatee. "Now that you know you wouldn't have been committing jail bait, can I go back across town and jump in my professional attire and go visit a couple of the stores I manage?"

Gwen lifted her eyebrows.

"Girl, stop your stuff. I told you we all got jobs. But I guess in your circle they are called careers." He burst out laughing again and jumped in his pearl-white Lincoln LX, equipped with a sunroof and chrome rims.

* * *

Gwen walked through the office suites and double-checked to make sure that all the furniture had been delivered and positioned. She had spent the last couple of months finalizing every detail, and now everything was sparkling and was the epitome of professional personification.

In a week, McGuire Productions would be in full effect in its new headquarters. After taking the time to visit the other two locations and the old headquarters that was located in L.A., Gwen was pleased with all that she had done with the new place. While the others were all tasteful and conducive for the industry, this look was totally fresh and had an appeal that was both contemporary and hip. Not only was she the responsible party behind the face-lift project, she had set the publicity wheels in motion and everyone on both coasts and internationally was aware that a relocation of McGuire Productions had occurred. There were people standing in line ready to jump the rails and be a part of what McGuire Productions would offer.

Somewhere between her visit home and jumping head-first into Marcus' affairs, she was pretty content with herself. Her last visit to Dr. Ryan was more of a farewell party than a final session. They decided to meet at a small Italian restaurant across the street from Dr. Ryan's office. The two talked and laughed and for the first time since they had been meeting, Dr. Ryan didn't check her watch. The hives were a thing of the past and she definitely didn't miss their unannounced intrusion in her life. Gwen promised to keep her number nearby and that if she needed to talk, day or night, she would call.

Dr. Ryan was relieved. Gwen's was a success story, and to have a patient so stressed out and distraught and assist her in releasing all the negative influences and the hurt that bonds to the heart like a necessary organ was worth all the long hours she'd put in. Adding another friend to the fold wasn't a bad outcome either.

Life was good again, but there was one thing that Gwen

still had to do and she was waiting in the lobby of McGuire Productions for Patrice to get there. Just as she was about to ring her on the cell, because she was more than an hour late, she noticed Patrice strolling through the automatic doors.

Gwen took one look at her and thought that she was up to her usual noonday tricks. "I'm not even going to ask."

Patrice looked at her mischievously. "What? For once, Gwen, I'm innocent. I was just coming from Gina's school. I had a meeting with the guidance counselor."

A look of concern registered on Gwen's face. "Is everything okay? I thought she was adjusting fine to her new living situation."

"Oh, she is. And not only is she adjusting, but her mother called last night to tell me that she appreciates my helping out. Her calling me was enough to floor me, but then to have her say she appreciated me helping out was the clincher."

"Well, maybe she does appreciate you. You're providing a positive atmosphere for Gina, and right now after all that has happened, she needs that. Even a coldhearted, uncaring mother can't argue with that."

"You are only partly correct, my best friend. It has more to do with the social worker than anything else. But whatever the reason, I'm glad Gina is benefiting. That is all I care about. Bump the rest of it and her mother."

"So how has your love life been going?" Gwen tried to look serious but knew that she wasn't going to be able to pull it off. The moment Patrice lifted her sunglasses and gave her the crazy eye, she was ready to explode in a fit of laughter.

"If you must know, I do me Monday through Thursday and by Friday I'm too exhausted to even think about repeating any of what I did. But I know that you didn't call me over here just to get my freak schedule. What's up, buttercup?"

"I talked this over with my dad, T.J., Mama Bea, and Marcus."

"This must be serious if you went through all those channels. What the heck is up? Walk and talk. I'm hungry, and

since it doesn't look like lunch was part of your planned-out
agenda, I'm going outside to the vendor stand and get an
Italian sausage."

Realizing that she hadn't eaten a thing since she'd had an
early breakfast with Marcus, Gwen cheerfully went along
with Patrice. "I've been thinking a lot about the brush that
Gina had with the pelvic inflammatory disease and all the
questions that the girls asked in the group afterward. At one
time I never thought that I would be willing to discuss
Tiffany dying from AIDS." Patrice was about ready to interrupt.

"No, let me finish. I know how important those girls are
to you. The first time you asked, I couldn't see past my hurt
and what it would feel like to open up that part of myself or
to even share her story, but now I've healed some and it
would be selfish of me not to share what could make a difference in at least one of their lives. So I will speak to the
group during the Awareness Program."

"Oh, Gwen. I don't know what to say. I was trying my
best to respect your wishes. Tell me what got to you. My
begging or my using Marcus as a pawn in the chess game of
life?" Patrice turned to order two Italian sausages with green
peppers and onions and two Cokes.

"Neither. The next time you decide to send Marcus on a
mission, make sure you equip him with anti-Gwen ammuni-
tion. That boy is putty in my hands. He mentioned it somewhere between going to bed and getting out of bed, and if
you asked him, he wouldn't be able to tell you what I said."
Gwen was feeling pretty cocky. She hadn't been at the game
long, but she was very proud that she had mastered the sport
and was enjoying every moment of it.

"Girl, I am scared of you. I know you had it in you. It just
took being around me to bring it out." Patrice licked her finger and took a big bite of her sausage.

"Please. Let's just go to your office and you can give me a
few details about the program and I can be on my way. You

are still meeting us later to celebrate Andre and Tori's engagement?"

Patrice smiled. "Wouldn't miss it. I still can't believe they are engaged. I hope it's not contagious.

"You are in no danger of catching it. Unless . . ." Gwen chuckled.

Patrice rolled her eyes and changed the subject. "You know tonight is salsa night and right after the celebration I'm hitting the floor to get my twirl on."

CHAPTER 27

Gwen's eyes were wide with nervous energy as she watched Patrice on the stage of the large auditorium. The room was full to capacity and although she glanced out a few times, many of the faces were unrecognizable; however, Marcus, Andre, Tori, Vince, Mama Bea, Thomas, T.J., Kim, and Bryan were sitting in the front row. The dance troop had just finished performing and the crowd was still buzzing about their great performance and the dance rendition of Yolanda Adams's "Open Up My Heart."

Now she stood transfixed, wishing that she had delayed this moment a little longer. Gwen knew what she wanted to say and whom she was saying it to, but now she wondered if she could go through with it. Telling the story, Tiffany's story, wouldn't bring her back—that she knew, but it could make the difference in someone else's life. If that were even a small possibility, then she had to stand before them, reach deep, and talk to them.

She watched as Patrice's lips moved and she strained to hear what she was saying, and although the room had quieted down, she couldn't make out a word. The dull ache in her heart and the nervous energy that rested in the pit of her stomach were drowning out everything. Patrice backed away from the microphone and started clapping, waiting for Gwen to come forward.

When she walked the deafening distance to the podium she felt like she had just run a mile at top speed with the wind in her face and an angry force behind her back. Out of breath and trembling, she looked at Patrice as if she were begging for a lifeline. Patrice's response was a simple smile and a whisper. "You can do this. Just focus on Gina and the girls and talk to them."

Stepping up to the podium, Gwen smiled at her family and friends and lingered on Marcus' smiling face. Her glance fell on Gina's face next and the girls sitting beside her, and she had to tell them the torturous truth that had once threatened to consume her entire being and now was a memory that, although still hurtful, had to be shared. After this day, she would return it to its Pandora's box and pray that it did some good and reached at least one.

"Good evening. My name is Gwendolyn James and I'm pleased to be here this evening. To be completely honest, at one point I was ready to walk out of this place without sharing with you all a very important story. But when I looked into the faces of Gina, Tabitha, Kennedy, and the others, I felt obligated to talk about a personal experience that changed my life." Gwen went on and before she knew it, something took over and enabled her to share Tiffany's story and to emphasize the importance of safe sex and making the right choices.

All eyes were fixed on her and the room was so quiet, hearing a pin drop would be a major understatement. Watching the faces of the girls was more than enough to encourage her to continue. They were wide-eyed and openmouthed and not one of them spoke the entire time Gwen was speaking. In their youthful minds, none of them considered the consequences of having sex only once and being condemned to living life with a deadly disease lurking over your head, not knowing when it would demand that you give up the fight and die. She told them how important it was to trust someone and how real love is anchored in that type of trust. While they all assumed that it couldn't happen to any of them or to anyone they knew, they watched in complete awe as the lady who had become a vital party in their mentoring sessions told them how it happened to someone she loved. She had even gone as far as to have several photographs of Tiffany arranged through PowerPoint to drive home the point that you can't tell by the way someone looks what kind of job they have or what income level they fit in. Gwen's emotional conclusion was a driving force, and Patrice, who stood behind the curtain with tears streaming down her face, was sure that it would ring in the ears of not only the young, but every person in the room long after this program ended.

Gwen stepped away from the podium and was unaffected by the clapping and numerous people standing up. She walked behind the curtain and fell into the arms of Patrice. It was over. She had told what needed to be told and now she was able to continue on with her life. Her body was shaking and her makeup was smeared, but she was free, and tonight that was what mattered most.

One of the other mentors ended the program and bade everyone a good night and cautioned that they drive safely.

Patrice spoke solemnly. "Gwen, that was awesome. I know it took a lot but I am so proud of you. I believe that you got the point across and there probably isn't a girl in this place who would indulge in unsafe sex for a while."

"Let's hope for a long, long time. Come on, I'm sure everyone is waiting for us to come out, and I believe that Tori is going to corner us and ask us to be in her and Andre's wedding."

"Girl, I still can't believe that they've been seeing each other unbeknownst to any of us. Love is definitely in the air. I just pray that Bryan doesn't think that since we've been seeing each other on the regular, I'm planning on changing my routine."

"'Trice, there is hope for you yet."

"Gwen, don't wish that on me. One little step is all I can manage. Don't expect miracles."

Marcus was beaming and couldn't help but meet her halfway down the aisle. "Baby, I am so proud of you. What you did up there took a lot of courage and heart. You are finally able to walk into your tomorrow with only the memories."

Gwen attempted to speak. Marcus lifted a finger and gently pressed it against her lips. "You have got to let me do this."

Gwen looked at him totally perplexed. "What are you talking about? We are standing in the midst of a crowd." She knew that she needed to talk to Marcus about their relationship. Truthfully, she just wasn't sure if the timing was right.

"Sweetheart, just let me finish, because if I don't, I won't ever be able to tell you this." Marcus's jaw was set and a look of seriousness covered his face and created a crease in his brow.

At that moment, Patrice was approaching but noticed the seriousness between them and walked away toward a couple of parents who stood enjoying the refreshments.

Marcus continued, "You stood up there and confronted the pain and the suffering that had burdened you for so long now, and that is such an accomplishment. For the first time since I've known you, I really heard you. Not that I hadn't been listening to you before, but this was different. When you hurt, you hurt deeply, and as much as it hurt you to lose Tiffany, what I did to you back then hurt just as much. Not the same kind of hurt, but hurt nonetheless. I never wanted to think that, and God knows you've said it repeatedly, yet you are willing to trust me again despite all the hurt. Not because of what you feel deep down, but because you have such a big heart and you don't want to hurt me now.

"I can't allow you to free yourself tonight, and hold on and deal with the pain that I've caused, that you may never be totally free from. I wish that the pain that you endured at my stupidity eased when the pain of losing Tiffany eased, but I really don't think it did." Marcus' eyes began to water. "I love you so much and I know that letting you go is the right thing. You deserve that. I've held your heart for much too long and I've never been worthy of it or you. The funny thing is that now that I've grown up and can appreciate both, it's too late."

Gwen couldn't speak, but the lonely tears that nestled at the corner of her eyes were saying what she felt. He was saying the words that she wanted to say, but it didn't make her feel any better.

"Don't cry, because these people will be exposed to this grown-ass man crying like a little boy who just dropped his ice cream cone." They both tried to laugh.

"You know what, though? I saw someone here who watched you in complete awe tonight. In fact, what I witnessed shocked me."

Gwen hiccupped. "And what was that?"

"I saw him looking at you the same way that I do. It was easy to recognize because it mirrored what I've felt for all these years." He turned toward the door and she followed with her eyes and noticed Scott standing in the doorway.

"Gwen, I think young blood over there has something to say to you." He looked down at her, struggling to do for her what she had done for him so many years ago. When he was much too young and wild to commit to a serious relationship, she had let him go and gave him room to grow. Most of his life had been filled with so many life-altering situations, he had lost count, but right or wrong, he had lived through them. Yet Gwen had spent her life loving him, even after setting him free, so much so, that she never had a chance to really live. Now it was his turn to do the freeing.

Gwen looked at him awkwardly. "What! I just can't leave you."

"Yes, you can. Now go ahead before I make you spend the rest of your life with me. Sweetheart, you gave me the first thirteen. The next thirteen are on me." Marcus was trying to smile, but inside, his heart was breaking piece by piece.

Gwen stood up on tiptoes and kissed him like she had never done before. When she opened her eyes and turned around, she noticed that Scott was turning and walking away.

Smiling at Marcus one last time, she pivoted around on her heel and ran to the exit door and tried to catch up with Scott.

"Hey, Scott. Wait a minute."

"Hi, Gwen. You were great back there. I believe that you made a real impact." He stuffed his hands in the pockets of his jeans. His attire was a little more seasoned and she couldn't help but notice. "I just wanted to come by and check you out. Kip talked with Kyra and she told him that you were speaking tonight. I hope you didn't mind him telling me."

"Is that the only reason you came by?" Gwen tried to hide her disappointment.

Scott's eyes settled on the perfect angle of her face. "No. But don't you have some unfinished business back inside?"

"Actually, Scott, not anymore. I could use a ride, though. You think you can handle that?"

"That, Gwen, and then some."

EPILOGUE

Gwen stood staring out the balcony door of the bedroom. The city was waking up and beckoned the start of a new day. It was as if the sun was putting on a special performance as it ushered in Sunday morning. At a distance she could see the sun rising up over the new housing development being constructed around the corner. A chill crept up her spine as she marveled at the view from the bedroom of her new home, reminding her that so much had changed.

All that happened and all the things that held her hostage had released their hold on her. So much had happened in the six months since she'd spoken at the Awareness Program. Patrice was more in love with Bryan than she would admit and was actually committed to the relationship. Tori and Andre were planning a June wedding, Marcus had settled into his new headquarters, and Gwen was managing the newly established Richmond office of Westcott and Windsor. Not wanting to lose one of his top executives, Mr. Windsor finalized acquisition of a failing firm and believed that this new location would enhance their already thriving communication industry. Then there was Scott. He returned to Richmond and was going into practice with another of his medical school chums and had spent the last couple of months sweeping Gwen off her feet.

Gwen mused, for today would be the culmination of another new beginning. Gwen would surprise Patrice and make the eleven o'clock morning service at Gilead Full Gospel Baptist. It was time for her to renew her spiritual relationship and acknowledge that all things are truly possible.

Glancing over her shoulder at the bed that held the sleeping body of the very person who held her heartstrings, she wanted to kick herself for being so narrow-minded. Scott had become a major part of her life, and as much as she hadn't seen it in the beginning, deep down she'd always felt it. Yes, it frightened her a little, but she'd also felt that she could relax in knowing that they possessed the ingredients that true love is made of.

She started to reflect over the past year and how much she had grown. Finally, she had accepted that her mother was bitter and angry, she simply prayed for a time when they could be mother and daughter again. She had wonderful memories of Tiffany and Marcus acknowledged that in truly loving someone you have to set them free. She would always adore him but she had to admit that overcoming the hurdles in her life was a sweet victory.

She whispered. "Gwendolyn James, life has come full circle."

She had discovered love in her own backyard and she was letting go of the past, unlocking the chamber of her being, and would love without the fear of being hurt. And if hurt came again, she wouldn't let it steal all that she was. But with Scott she hoped that she would never have that to worry about.

The sun was continuing its ascent into the day and she knew it would be beaming over the city before long. Gwen marveled at the reality that she was more than halfway there; heck, this was her tomorrow, and she was going to bask in the glow of it.

Just then Scott turned over with half-opened eyes. He slowly stumbled over and stood behind Gwen so close that he circled his forearm tightly around her waist and spoke into her hair. "Hey, what's wrong? It's still early. You should be lying in my arms."

Noticing the longing in his last statement, Gwen paused with renewed excitement and whispered thanks to her angel. She couldn't believe that she had fallen asleep in his arms last night and they managed to hold each other and not seal the physical bond between them. Despite the physical attraction and beauty of falling more in love every day, they had held to their decision to wait. It wasn't that she didn't desire this man, because she did with her whole being. Gwen wanted the timing to be right, with a ring in place and a commitment that hinged upon a lifetime of mutual love. Her heart swelled when she thought of all that her future could be with Scott by her side. Knowing that Scott agreed and felt she was worth the wait made everything complete.

Turning slowly into his rock-solid body, she wrapped her arms around his neck and looked lovingly into his half-awakened eyes. "I was just thinking."

"I hope you don't have any regrets. Gwen, I really love you and I want us to work. If you will give me a chance, I know that I can make you happy."

"Scott, I can't tell you the exact moment that it happened, but I've loved you for a while. And trusting anyone after all the hurt is going to take some time. You know that past hurts don't just go away that easily. They leave a residue." Gwen leaned her head back to capture the adoration in his eyes and smiled knowingly.

"But I'm going to try, and I have a feeling that trusting you, Dr. Elliott, isn't going to be that hard. I just want to take it real slow."

"I can do slow. That will give me that much more time to show you just how much I love you. Now come lie in my arms—it's not morning yet."

Reaching out to Scott and her future, she took his hand and cuddled it against her heart. Slightly biting her bottom lip, which was more habit now than nervousness, she smiled. "Tomorrow is finally here."

Dear Reader,

Life affords us a measure of many things. For me, it has included the love of family and friends, an abundance of faith to persevere through the storms, and enough hope to believe that there will be many bright tomorrows. All of these are grounded deeply in a strong sense of spirituality and recognition from whom all blessings flow. So it is only fitting to first thank my Lord and Savior for instilling this gift and allowing me to share it. I'm blessed; in fact I'm better than blessed and so very thankful.

To my anchors: George, my husband—"Silk," all that creates my unique being is embraced by the love of an SBM. Loving you daily is a treasure. Chanel, I still marvel in watching the woman you are becoming, and I continue to be proud of who you are, even though you think you are still finding yourself. You're going to be so surprised that what you seek has always been there and it shines with a wonderful splendor. What a jewel you are, just waiting to be discovered. Gee, still my sensitive, caring, cool, forever loving son. You are ready for the world and the best definitely is yet to come. Never forget who you really are and trust that it will always be enough to propel you into what was created uniquely for you and your talent.

A big hug and kiss to my parents, Alfred and Helen Anderson, for showing me the way and loving me enough to find it for myself. My blood crew, Alfred Jr., Shirley, Kenny, and Leslie—for all the love, support and belief you give, my heart opens up and returns each in abundance. To my nieces and my nephews, each of you makes my life complete and I love you with my entire being and then some. You are all special. For all the love and support I receive from my extended family and friends—you'll know that I know and that's all that matters.

There can be no success without someone spiritually watching over me. Where would I be without my pastor, Dr. Michael T. Scott, and leading lady Tamara Scott? I can't imagine and I thank God I don't have to. Tracy Price-Thompson, you are a talented sistah who continues to shine with every release. Thanks for always sharing your expertise and for being my friend.

The best for last . . . Mr. Roy Glenn, the "thinker" behind Urban Soul, I'm glad you're extending the torch and believe I have a measure of talent to carry it. Thanks to everyone at Urban that breathed literary life into this book and those that will follow.

Finally, finally, finally, to everyone that will travel through the pages of this novel, and for those who are taking a second spin through the Urban Soul label, thanks for taking the journey.

Bc 4-cvcr Blcsscd,
Rená